S0-BBB-014

ISBN-13: 978-1-335-58285-0

9 781335 582850

50725

EAN

LAKESIDE MYSTERY

CAROL ERICSON

Denver flicked a finger at the window that looked out over the beach.

"Is someone giving you a heads-up about this case? How do you know it's not the killer of that girl in the trunk? How do you know he's not just toying with you? Hoping for some publicity?"

The skin around Ashlynn's luscious mouth turned white. Her blue eyes watered, and she dabbed her nose with a napkin.

"Who said anyone is contacting me about the case? I literally stumbled over a car in Lake Kawayu and then came out to Venice for a walk. Someone decided to conk me on the head and mug me."

He narrowed his eyes. "That's the way you want to play it? Clicks or whatever you're after are more important than finding the killer of this girl?"

She swirled her drink. "I don't have anything to give you, Detective—no evidence, no clues. I can't solve this case for you."

"You got that right." He smacked his hand on the table, rattling the glasses. "So don't even try."

LAKESIDE MYSTERY

CAROL ERICSON

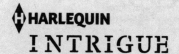
HARLEQUIN
INTRIGUE

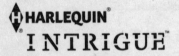

HARLEQUIN®
INTRIGUE™

Recycling programs
for this product may
not exist in your area.

ISBN-13: 978-1-335-58285-0

Lakeside Mystery

Copyright © 2022 by Carol Ericson

For questions and comments about the quality of this book,
please contact us at CustomerService@Harlequin.com.

Harlequin Enterprises ULC
22 Adelaide St. West, 41st Floor
Toronto, Ontario M5H 4E3, Canada
www.Harlequin.com

Printed in U.S.A.

Carol Ericson is a bestselling, award-winning author of more than forty books. She has an eerie fascination for true crime stories, a love of film noir and a weakness for reality TV, all of which fuel her imagination to create her own tales of murder, mayhem and mystery. To find out more about Carol and her current projects, please visit her website at www.carolericson.com, "where romance flirts with danger."

Books by Carol Ericson

Harlequin Intrigue

The Lost Girls

Canyon Crime Scene
Lakeside Mystery

A Kyra and Jake Investigation

The Setup
The Decoy
The Bait
The Trap

Holding the Line

Evasive Action
Chain of Custody
Unraveling Jane Doe
Buried Secrets

Visit the Author Profile page at Harlequin.com.

CAST OF CHARACTERS

Denver Holt—This LAPD detective will do almost anything to get on the homicide squad, even if it means cooperating with a meddling blogger with questionable motives.

Ashlynn Hughes—She took over her murdered brother's true crime blog and now has the opportunity of a lifetime to prove herself her brother's equal...if it weren't for the sexy detective cramping her style.

Tiana Fields—A political volunteer, she winds up dead in the trunk of a car, and her murder sends shock waves through the LA mayoral race.

Angel—An anonymous tipster to Ashlynn's blog, he claims to know Tiana's secrets...secrets that just might get him killed.

Veronica Escalante—This savvy politician is challenging the mayor and will do anything to replace him.

Kent Meadows—Veronica's wealthy husband is happy to fund his wife's campaign, as long as she doesn't snoop into his extracurricular activities.

Mayor Wexler—The mayor of LA is up for reelection, and the last thing he needs is a whiff of scandal and a blogger with inside information.

Chapter One

A shiver snaked through Ashlynn's body, even though the sun streamed through the branches of the trees, creating a dappled pattern on the ground. She hugged herself, clutching her pepper spray in one hand against her upper arm. Her brother, Sean, had agreed to meet someone near a lake…and it hadn't ended well for him.

Of course, she wasn't exactly meeting someone, and Sean had traipsed out in the dead of night. Unlike her foolish brother, she'd ventured out in the middle of the day with hikers panting along the trail and mountain bikers kicking up dirt as they trundled up the hill. Her nose tingled with tears and she wiped her sleeve across it. Nobody could tell Sean anything.

He had been a successful true crime blogger because he'd embraced danger, taken those necessary risks. She'd have to remold herself in his image if she hoped to keep his blog going strong. She didn't want *LA Confidential* to die with her brother.

She puffed out her cheeks and trudged onward. She'd venture as far as the lake, have a look around, maybe take a few pictures, and wait for the next message—if there was a next message. If her anonymous contact didn't send her another communication after the first one about a submerged car in Lake Kawayu, she'd look for another story to feature on the blog.

Stopping under a tree, she tapped her phone to bring up the trail map and had to lunge out of the way of oncoming runners. She called into their dust. "Where's the turnoff for the lake?"

One of them yelled something unintelligible but pointed to his right. Another several yards and Ashlynn spotted the weathered sign pointing toward Lake Kawayu. How could a car possibly make its way down a trail like this to plunge into a lake?

She veered to the right between two oaks, their leaves dripping water from the rain the day before.

Ashlynn shuffled downhill through the debris of leaves, twigs and pebbles that littered the trail. Any minute she expected to see the lake through the branches of the trees, but spring had done its job and the forest bloomed and flourished around her so that she could barely see beyond the next bend.

When the foliage thinned, and a couple toting a fiberglass canoe squeezed past her, she knew she was close.

She rounded the next corner and caught her breath as a dark blue ripple appeared below. She had to scrabble down a small incline to reach the shore of the lake, and she placed her hands on her hips and took a deep breath of the pine and earthy muddy scent that assailed her.

She scanned the perimeter of the body of water, her gaze lingering on the north shore where a dirt parking lot boasted several cars belonging to people who knew they didn't need to hike a mile and a half to reach the lake. She also realized that if a car were going to plunge into the water, that parking lot had to be its origination point.

Shading her eyes, she judged the distance to the parking lot to be another half mile. She glanced at the sturdy sneakers on her feet and pulled a bottle of water from her small daypack. She took a long gulp of water and watched the couple launch their canoe into the lake with a splash. She'd come prepared—and she needed a new story for the blog.

Her shoes crunched the coarse sand lakeside as she started walking the semicircle to the parking lot. She didn't know why her anonymous tipster had contacted her—probably because *LA Confidential* still sported the sheen of her brother's success—but she didn't want to dismiss it. Sean had told her some of his best stories started as anonymous bits of information.

If this were just a submerged car, she'd blow it off, but the tipster had claimed there was a dead body in the car. The least she could do was check it out. It's not like she had a lot on her plate. She'd quit her job at the magazine when Sean was…killed. She couldn't go back to it now, and she didn't want to. Sean had died just when his blog had hit peak popularity, and she felt an obligation to carry on with it. She'd had a modicum of success with her first story—an exposé of Reed Dufrain, addiction recovery guru turned drug dealer—but she couldn't rest on her laurels.

A few families frolicked in the water, and Ashlynn shivered. Must be out-of-towners, because it was definitely too cold for thin-blooded Angelenos to take a dip. Summer was still a season away, and the sun starting to make its appearance every day lacked the wattage of an August or September in LA.

Still, Ashlynn had a one-piece on under her clothes and a towel rolled up in her pack. How else could she spot a submerged car? Maybe one of these swimmers would discover it first and save her the trouble of a chilly dip.

When she reached the parking lot, she downed more water from her bottle. She nodded at a group stoking the flames in a hibachi, paper plates of bratwurst and burgers standing by. She was pretty sure the city didn't allow an open fire like that in Angeles Crest, but she wasn't here to be Smokey the Bear's helper.

She wandered to the edge of the dirt lot, facing the water. No barrier or lip separated the lot from the lakeshore, and plenty of tire tracks indicated that people drove right up to the water's edge. Into the water?

She scuffed through the sand and rocks up to the dark, oily water lapping the banks. No swimmers had ventured into the lake from the parking area. They most likely preferred the cleaner-looking water down from the trees, but that probably explained why nobody had found the car yet.

Sighing, Ashlynn swung the pack off her back and dropped it in the dirt. She fished out her towel, shook it and set it next to her daypack. Then she toed off her shoes and wriggled free of her clothes, quickly, kicking both onto the towel.

She waded into the water, her arms folded over her chest, goose bumps crawling across her bare flesh. When the water reached her hips, she pushed off the rocky bottom with her feet and paddled into the murky lake. The parking lot wasn't that wide and a car launched from the banks couldn't go that far. She did a breaststroke in a line horizontal to the shore, kicking her legs in a wide circle and peering into the water. She moved a little farther into the water and repeated her course back the other way.

A few people from the barbecuing bunch in the parking lot stood at its edge, staring at her. She supposed she must look a little crazy to people watching, but as she took another stroke, she muttered, "I'll never see them again."

The lake had gotten deep fast, and her toes no longer even skimmed the bottom. A whole car could definitely be submerged under the water and nobody would notice it from the shore.

As she circled into another wide turn, her fluttering feet made contact with something hard and smooth…and big. Holding her breath, she ducked beneath the water and opened her eyes. She flipped and swam downward for a few feet. Her hands met solid metal before she saw its glint.

Her lungs bursting, she propelled herself to the surface and gasped in a long breath. She'd found the car. Was there a body inside?

DETECTIVE DENVER HOLT stared over his clenched hands on the steering wheel at a knot of people gathered at the edge of the murky lake. The hoist to lift the car from the cloudy depths was already in place, and he could imagine the divers below hooking up the winches. His captain had sent him on another thrilling adventure to assist the traffic division with an accident or possible stolen while his name languished on the list for Robbery-Homicide.

He smacked the steering wheel with the heels of his hands. He'd sworn to protect and serve— even victims of auto theft. He exited his sedan and strode toward the commotion, his wing tips crunching the sand and gravel on the shore of the lake.

"Detective Holt." Flashing his badge at the uniform, he asked, "Have the divers indicated yet if there's anyone in the car?"

"Officer Brooks." Brooks tapped his nametag and shrugged. "If they found anything, they haven't told me about it. I'm here for crowd control."

Denver scanned the smattering of people and smirked. Some crowd. "Who discovered the car?"

Brooks jerked his thumb over his shoulder. "The woman with the towel and the wet hair— Ashlynn Hughes."

Denver lifted his sunglasses and squinted at a redhead wearing jeans, a wet T-shirt sticking to her body. She'd draped a striped towel over her shoulders.

He snorted. "What did she do, jump off her canoe to get a closer look?"

"She wasn't in a canoe. She saw it while she was swimming." The cop rolled his eyes and held up one hand. "I know, I know. Don't ask me."

"How close are they to hauling it out?" Denver dropped his sunglasses back over his eyes and fished his notebook from his jacket pocket.

"They've been at it for a while. Should be anytime now."

"Thanks, man." Denver picked his way across the rocky shoreline to the woman fluffing the towel through her red locks that glinted with fire every time they caught the sun.

"Ms. Hughes?" He thrust out his hand. Even in bare feet, this tall drink of water almost stood nose to nose with him. "I'm Detective Denver Holt. I understand you're the one who spotted the car and called 9-1-1."

She grasped his hand with a firm slightly damp grip. "I am. I mean it's weird, right? A car in the lake? I wasn't just going to swim on by without telling someone."

His pulse jumped and his gaze behind his dark lenses sharpened. That was a lot of words for a simple yes. "Weird. Definitely weird. Could be an accident, stolen car, insurance fraud. Thanks for calling it in, Ms. Hughes."

Her shoulders beneath the towel slumped as she nodded. "Yeah, I thought so. You can call me Ashlynn."

"Okay... Ashlynn." He flipped open his notebook. "What were you doing in the lake?"

Her blue eyes widened. "What?"

"The lake." He leveled a finger at the body of water. "What were you doing?"

"Swimming." She plucked her soggy T-shirt from her chest, revealing the outline of a one-piece suit beneath. "I went for a swim."

Denver tipped his head back to take in the sky with a few clouds scudding across the sun and hunched into his suit jacket against the sudden breeze. "Not exactly swimming weather."

She flapped her hand toward a few kids paddling and splashing in the water beyond the parking lot. "Tell *them* that. Some of us aren't as...sensitive as you are, Detective."

He cracked a smile. He should've expected feisty with that hair. "So, you decided to drive down to Lake Kawayu and head straight from the parking lot to the water for a swim, and while paddling through the...crystal-clear water you notice a car below you?"

She jutted out one slim hip and wedged a fist on the curve. "Don't put words in my mouth,

Detective Holt. I hiked down the trail to get here and jumped in the lake to cool off. While I was swimming, I went vertical to make sure I wasn't going too far out, and my feet skimmed a slab of metal—not what you'd expect to find in a lake."

"Not what I'd expect." He tapped his pen against the notebook. "You ducked down to see what you could see?"

"Yes, and even though the water was cloudy, it was evident that I was floating above a car. I swam back to the shore and called 9-1-1."

"Did you see anything inside the car?" He glanced over his shoulder at the beeping sound from the tow truck. They'd find out soon enough anyway.

She clasped her hands in front of her, knotting her fingers, her sassy demeanor fading as fast as the sun overhead. "I—I didn't get a good look. I didn't want to dive down any deeper, and it was dark and murky."

"Good decision. Did anyone else go into the water after you to take a look?" He made a half-turn to watch the progress of the car as the roof broke the surface of the lake and the water sluiced over the metal.

"I didn't tell anyone what I'd found. I called 9-1-1 and waited for the police. These other people started gathering when the cop car showed up, and then the officer wouldn't let anyone in the water after that." She bit her bottom lip as the dark sedan cleared the water and swung from the pulleys like a bloated fish on the line.

Denver shaded his eyes against the sun glinting off the lake. "Doesn't look like it's been sitting there too long."

She shivered and rubbed her arms. "No, it doesn't."

"Thanks for the information, Ms. Hughes." He stuffed his notebook into his pocket. As he turned, she covered her mouth with both hands.

He stopped. "You don't recognize the car, do you?"

"No, no, of course not."

He strode toward the tow truck, grabbing his cell phone from his pocket. He took several pictures of the car as it dangled above the lake.

He stood back as the winch settled the vehicle on the shore with a groan, water pouring from its orifices. He borrowed a flashlight from Brooks and crept toward the waterlogged car, which was still hissing and weeping. He leaned toward the windows and aimed the beam of light inside. It illuminated the empty front seat He shifted the focus to the back seat and saw nothing.

He let out a breath and called to one of the divers emerging from the lake, removing his mask. "Anything or…anyone around the car down there?"

"Nope, but the doors were closed and no broken windows, as you can see, so it doesn't look like anyone escaped from the vehicle, either."

"But the water pressure could've closed an open door, right?"

"Could happen."

"Key fob's in the cup holder." Denver pulled on a pair of gloves and tugged on the door handle. The door opened with a whooshing sound. More water gushed from the car, soaking his shoes. He leaned inside and snatched the key fob from the cup holder.

He almost bumped into Ashlynn Hughes as he backed out of the vehicle. She'd followed him beyond the yellow tape.

"Nothing in the car?" Her breathless voice matched her wide eyes and wayward hair.

It was like the shock of finding a submerged car was just hitting her.

"Nothing." He cupped her elbow. "You can move back, Ms. Hughes."

She shuffled back a few steps as he raised his phone to take pictures of the California license plate and the interior. He'd call it in. They still might be able to read the vehicle registration if it hadn't gotten too soggy. The car looked new. Maybe someone had stolen it or abandoned it for insurance fraud. Different scenarios popped into his head as he took pictures. They'd have to get into that trunk, too.

"Are you going to check the trunk?"

The redhead was still hovering, and he swung around, phone in hand. "You really need to step away, Ms. Hughes."

"Ashlynn, and don't you usually open the trunk?" Her shirt had dried, but her teeth chattered, and she pulled the towel tighter around her body.

Officer Brooks huddled close to the rear of the car with a crowbar in his hand. "Do you want me to do the honors?"

"The key fob was in the cup holder." Denver dangled it from his finger. His thumb trembled slightly as he smoothed it across the trunk button on the fob. Then he stabbed it.

The lock clicked and one of the divers, who was standing behind Brooks, let out a sigh. Denver held his breath as he nudged up the trunk with two gloved fingers.

The lid swung high, and Denver's heart slammed against his chest. Looked like he'd got his homicide, after all.

Chapter Two

Ashlynn gagged and stumbled backward, covering her nose and mouth with one hand to ward off the smell emanating from the trunk—part rotting meat, part swamp creature.

Detective Holt turned on her and shouted in her face. "I told you to get back."

And I told you to check the trunk.

She clamped her lips shut and gritted her teeth, which helped keep the nausea at bay, anyway. She ducked under the yellow tape and pressed a fist against her stomach.

Her anonymous tipster had been right. How much of her story should she reveal to Holt, now speaking into his phone?

"Homicide, it's Holt. I went to investigate a car submerged in Lake Kawayu and found a body in the trunk."

Ashlynn narrowed her eyes. The hot detective didn't even work in homicide. As Holt continued to yammer on about license plates and registration, Ashlynn scanned the crowd that had grown bigger when the tow truck hauled the car to the surface.

Had one of those spectators already known there'd be a car in the lake? Had he or she already known about the body? Was someone watching her? Now that the tipster had proved to be accurate, Ashlynn needed to contact him or her—ask for more.

Sean would know what to do at this point. She'd look through his old exchanges with other informants to see how he'd handled it. This could be her chance to revive *LA Confidential* to its former glory under her brother.

She glanced at the pale flesh in the trunk of the car and her stomach turned. Sean had started the blog to get justice for victims after someone had murdered his friend AJ, and the case had gone cold. She couldn't lose sight of that mission. Sean would want her to get justice for that woman in the car.

And her brother didn't always play by the rules.

She squared her shoulders as Detective Holt marched toward her, his suit jacket flapping in the breeze, revealing a broad chest and flat belly beneath his dress shirt. He stopped on the other side of the tape from her, and she could see herself reflected in his dark glasses.

"Why were you so anxious for me to open the trunk? What were you really doing out here... Ashlynn?"

He'd finally used her first name, and it sounded like a sneer on his lips. She cleared her throat. "I wasn't anxious. I figured you'd be opening the trunk anyway. Right?"

His face reddened. "Of course. I don't need you to tell me how to do my job, but I still don't understand why you were swimming in Lake Kawayu, a body of water more suited to boaters and kids splashing on the shore than serious swimmers."

"Serious? Who said I was a serious swimmer? I hiked almost two miles and fancied a dip in the water to cool off." She clamped her teeth together to stop the tremble rolling through her body. "It's not against the law to swim in this lake. Then my foot hit the submerged car, and I called the police. Why am I in the wrong here? You should be thanking me."

Detective Holt opened his mouth and then snapped it shut with the arrival of a dark sedan, similar to the one the tow truck had just hauled from the lake. Holt held up his index finger instead and said, "Don't go anywhere."

She had no intention of leaving. As he strode toward a tall woman getting out of the car, Ashlynn aimed her phone at the people clustered beyond the yellow tape and started taking pictures. Her tipster could be one of them.

Thirty minutes later, after consulting with the woman from the unmarked police sedan and bagging items from the car, Holt returned to her with a decided spring to his step. How anyone could be in a chipper mood after hovering around that trunk was beyond her, but cops had a different sensibility from civilians. Sean had always had a love-hate relationship with them.

Detective Holt stuffed a hand in his pocket and pulled out a business card. "Here's my card. Don't hesitate to call me if you remember anything else about the discovery of the car…or why you were swimming in a dirty lake on a day that reached sixty-six degrees tops."

Snatching the card from his fingers, she said, "I gave you all I got, Detective. D-did you identify the victim yet?"

"No." He tipped his sunglasses down to the end of his nose and tagged her with a stare over the top of his lenses. "Fingerprints were hard to get, license plates came back to a different vehicle, so we know they were swapped out, no registration in the glove compartment, and a filed-down VIN."

Her mind got stuck on the image of the victim's fingertips, and she shook her head as if to clear it. He'd surprised her with the details he'd provided—and seemed to surprise himself, as well.

His jaw hardened and he shoved his glasses back into place. "I may be calling you to follow up."

I should be so lucky. She watched his broad shoulders encased by his suit jacket as he returned to the car. While they had been speaking, a coroner's van had shown up at the scene and a few officers had tented the car with a pop-up, blocking the view of the onlookers.

She didn't want to watch the guys in biohazard suits load that body in a bag, anyway. She crouched to pick up her daypack and slung it over one shoulder. Her T-shirt had mostly dried, but the seat of her jeans was still damp. She twisted her hair into a bun and started the trek back down the trail.

Her contact had proved to be accurate about the car and the body. What else did her anonymous source know…and how?

DENVER SPENT ANOTHER HOUR at the crime scene before packing it in and heading back to the Northeast Division. His anger and disgust at discovering that poor woman in the truck of the car tempered his satisfaction with his temporary assignment to Robbery-Homicide to work this case. He'd been on loan to Homicide as a floater before, and had been itching for another opportunity. Too bad the death of that woman had landed him his chance.

On the other hand, he'd do his damnedest to find out who'd killed her and deliver justice to her family. Justice the Portland PD had failed to deliver to his own family when his father was murdered.

Someone had gone to a lot of trouble to disguise the car—swapped out the plates, removed the registration, and filed down the VIN. But all those efforts would prove to be fruitless, as most car manufacturers placed the VIN in a couple of places—some not readily apparent. LAPD's auto theft should be able to figure it out soon enough.

When he got back to the station, he checked in with Captain Fields and then got down to business. Identifying the victim took precedence over everything else right now. He pulled up the database for missing persons in Los Angeles County and narrowed the search based on gender, age and race. Date range would be tricky, as the medical examiner at the scene couldn't pin down anything specific due to the condition of the corpse in the water that had flooded the trunk.

As Denver clicked through the photos and details of the missing women, a hand clamped on his shoulder and he jumped.

Detective Billy Crouch nodded toward the computer. "Heard you're working the case of the woman found in the trunk at Lake Kawayu. What race is she?"

"I'm helping out. It's Detective Marino's case." Denver flicked his fingers at the waifish blond, one of the missing women, peering at them from the monitor. "Caucasian."

Crouch snorted. "If Marino caught the case, that means you'll have a lot of work to do. Anything yet?"

"Not yet and no viable prints from the victim."

"Let me know if you need any help navigating that database… I'm an expert." Crouch twisted his mouth into a grimace before heading out the door.

Crouch obsessively homed in on any case involving a dead woman, as his own sister had been missing for years. If the woman in the trunk had been African American, Crouch would've demanded to see her, no doubt.

Denver could understand that kind of fixation. His father's murder had galvanized his own determination to work Homicide. He didn't need a therapist to figure that one out.

After more than an hour staring at the computer monitor, his eyes began to glaze over. The missing woman on his screen had been gone for three years already. He massaged his temples. How did the families cope with that?

His phone rang and he grabbed it, grateful for the interruption. "Holt."

"Detective Holt, this is Dr. Saleh with the ME Coroner's department. We haven't done an autopsy yet on the victim in the lake, but we do have a preliminary cause of death."

"Go ahead." Denver brought up the file on his computer that contained the details from the case.

"Gunshot wound to the head."

The breath Denver had been holding escaped in a noisy rush. "So, not drowning."

"I did say *preliminary*. Of course, seeing the wound leads us to believe death by firearm, but we can't yet rule out the possibility that someone shot her first, shut her in the trunk and let her drown."

Denver's gut lurched. "All right. Thanks for the call, Dr. Saleh. You'll let me or Detective Marino know when you have the full autopsy?"

The doctor clicked his tongue. "Yes, I just tried calling Detective Marino, but he didn't pick up, and your name was second on the list."

"I'll be sure to let him know. Thanks, again."

When he ended the call with the ME, Denver drummed his fingers on the edge of the keyboard. Crouch had been right about Marino. He had a reputation for laziness, and Denver planned to take advantage of that fact. If he could solve this case without much input from Marino, he might be on the fast track to Robbery-Homicide.

As he thumbed through his notebook to make sure he'd transferred all his information from its pages to his file online, he stopped at Ashlynn Hughes's name. What had she really been doing in that lake? No sensible adult would be swimming laps in Lake Kawayu.

Maybe she'd witnessed the car going into the lake…or something worse, and hadn't wanted to get too involved. But finding the car itself had put her smack in the middle of the investigation. He'd give her a call, have her come into the station. Sitting in an interrogation room seemed to prompt people's memories.

He reached for the phone and stopped when he heard a wail from down the hall. That didn't sound good. He jumped to his feet and followed the sound of the commotion—jagged crying and soothing voices—right into the Robbery-Homicide division.

Clinging to the doorjamb, his gaze swept the room, landing on Crouch sitting on the edge of his desk in front of a red-faced woman flailing her arms in the air.

In contrast to Crouch's low voice, which Denver couldn't hear, the woman cried out, "I know it's her. She's been missing for three days. I've checked everywhere."

Denver's pulse picked up speed and he took a few steps into the room, raising his eyebrows at Crouch.

"Here's the detective working the case, Mrs. Edmunds." Crouch cupped his hand and gestured him forward. "I'll let you talk to him."

Denver squared his shoulders. Nobody liked this part of Homicide. On his way to Billy and the woman, he pulled out a chair next to an empty desk. "Mrs. Edmunds, I'm Detective Holt. Why don't you take a seat, and we can talk?"

He did have photos of the dead girl in the trunk, but he'd never show those to a mother—whether the picture was of her daughter or not.

Mopping her face with a handful of tissues he was sure she'd gotten from Billy, Mrs. Edmunds walked toward him with a jerky gait. When she sat, he wiped his own hands on the thighs of his slacks. If he could be half as good as Billy at this, he'd ace this encounter.

"Start at the beginning, Mrs. Edmunds. What's your daughter's name?"

"Tiana Fuller. H-her father and I are divorced, and I remarried."

"You say she's been missing for three days? Did you report her disappearance before this?"

He hadn't seen a Tiana Fuller or Edmunds in the database this afternoon.

"I'm reporting it now." Her gazed shifted to Billy, now logging off his computer, his head cocked, listening to their conversation. "My husband and I were out of town. We drove down to San Diego to visit his aunt, who'd had a fall. Tiana is twenty-one. S-she lives in Long Beach, near campus. She's just home for spring break and to housesit for us, so we left her on her own. We didn't realize she was missing until we came home this afternoon and couldn't reach her. I thought at first she might've gone back to her place in Long Beach."

"Were you in touch with her while you were in San Diego?"

"We exchanged a few texts the first day. She didn't answer later texts, but Tiana's been living on her own for two years at school. We didn't want to…hover." She dropped her head and balled the wad of tissues in her fist. "We should've. We should've come home sooner."

"And you're here now because you heard about the woman found at Lake Kawayu?"

She nodded without lifting her head.

"What makes you think this is Tiana? Did she frequent that area?"

Her head shot up and she pinned him with her

wild, red-rimmed eyes. "I just know it. I have a feeling."

Denver massaged his stiff neck. Any parent of a missing child would feel the same after learning of the discovery of a dead woman. "Do you have a picture of Tiana, Mrs. Edmunds?"

Sniffling, she dug into her purse, eager to be doing something at last. With a trembling hand, she held out a picture of a young woman with light brown hair and a turned-up nose.

Denver swallowed. The woman in the trunk had brownish-blond hair and a slender build like Tiana's—but so did a lot of young women. He took the photo from her and studied the face, keeping his own impassive as Mrs. Edmund's gaze probed him.

She croaked. "Is it her? Is she the girl in the trunk?"

"I can't say right now, Mrs. Edmunds. Do you have any idea what she was wearing when she last went out? What car she'd be driving?"

"Her car's at home." She shredded the tissues. "I don't understand why you can't tell me if she's the one in that trunk."

His gaze darted to Billy, who was taking his sweet time logging off and packing up his stuff.

Billy cleared his throat. "We can't make a positive ID based on just a picture, Mrs. Edmunds. Leave the photo of your daughter with Detective

Holt. The next step is to provide us with your daughter's DNA—hair from her brush, toothbrush—something like that."

She bit her bottom lip. "You can't show me pictures of the dead girl? I'd know Tiana anywhere."

"That's not advisable at this time, Mrs. Edmonds." Denver shifted forward to meet her gaze. She had to know what he meant. "As Detective Crouch said, we want to wait for a positive ID through DNA first."

"Okay." She slumped in her chair.

She obviously hadn't been looking forward to the task of collecting her daughter's DNA. What made her think she could look at a picture of a dead body that had been submerged in water?

Once Denver got more information from her and gave her his card, he walked her to the exit and then jogged upstairs to talk to Billy.

Denver leaned against a desk and crossed his arms. "Thanks for rescuing me."

"You would've figured it out." Billy hitched his bag over his shoulder. "Who found the car, anyway? Doesn't seem like a boater would run into it or hit it with an oar. You can't see anything in that lake from the air."

"It was a swimmer. She went vertical, and her foot brushed the top of the car."

Billy's jaw dropped. "A swimmer in *that* lake?

I mean, I know little kids like to splash around the shore, but swim?"

"That was my reaction. I was just going to call the witness to invite her in tomorrow and grill her a little more. She seemed…vague."

"Same age as the victim?"

"Older, but not by much. Different last name, of course, so no link there. Hughes. Ashlynn Hughes is her name."

Billy whistled through his teeth. "Oh, boy."

"What?" Denver pushed off the desk, his heart pounding. "Do you know her?"

"Not personally, but I know who she is, and I knew who her brother was."

"What?" Denver shook his head, pain lancing the back of his neck. "Her brother? What are you talking about?"

"You know the true crime blog, *LA Confidential*? Her brother, Sean Hughes, wrote that blog until he was murdered, and his sister's picked up where he left off."

Denver clenched his jaw. Know it? He not only knew about *LA Confidential*, that blog and Sean Hughes had made his life a living hell.

Chapter Three

Ashlynn wedged her feet against the edge of the coffee table and flipped open the computer in her lap. Holding her breath, she navigated to the private message area connected to the blog. If readers didn't want to post something publicly to the comments section, they could message her directly. That's how her anonymous tipster had sent her the first message about a car in Lake Kawayu—with a body in the trunk.

She scanned the direct messages, skimming over the ones asking her to take on a case, tearing up over the ones with condolences on Sean's death, and deleting the marriage pitches and indecent proposals. Had Sean gotten those?

She slumped against the couch and took a sip of green tea, lolling the mellow flavor on her tongue. Nothing new from her source. He or she must've seen the discovery of the car and the body in the lake. It had been all over the news. Detective Denver Holt's face had been all over the news. A girl could get lost in those chocolate-brown eyes.

She took a quick gulp of tea that went down the wrong way, and she hacked and wiped her eyes. That's what she got for straying from her purpose.

Neither Holt nor the news reports had mentioned her name, so maybe her tipster didn't realize she'd been the one to report the car. She scooped in a breath and poised her hand over the keyboard. She'd have to remedy that and keep those tips coming. The more firsthand knowledge she had of the case, the more she could engage her readers—and take them with her on to her next adventure.

At the time of Sean's death, he'd been working on morphing his blog into a podcast. She'd been helping him with the project, never imagining she'd have to go it alone.

She flexed her fingers and typed in a response to the initial message, thanking her source for the tip and letting him—her?—know that she'd been responsible for finding the car and reporting it.

She hit the return key with a flourish and watched the blank space below her message. Sighing, she wrapped her hands around her mug. Sean had been so much better at this than she was proving to be. Sean had been so much better at most things.

She slid her laptop onto the couch and took her cup to the kitchen. As she rinsed it under the faucet, her cell phone buzzed. She hightailed it back to the living room and swooped down on the phone as it vibrated on the coffee table.

She screwed up one side of her face. She usually didn't answer calls from unknown numbers, but she was operating in a different world now. She answered, willing the trepidation from her voice. "Hello?"

The man on the other end dispensed with the niceties. "You are a liar and a fraud. What do you think you're playing at?"

Ashlynn pressed a palm against her skittering heart. "What? Who is this?"

"You know damned well this is Detective Holt, and I know who you are. *LA Confidential.*" He spat out the words so forcefully, she twitched.

The edges of the phone dug into her hand as she gripped it. She'd been expecting this. Sooner or later, Holt would've become aware that she was featuring this case on the blog. She'd just hoped it would've been later.

"I didn't lie." Not really. She sank to the couch, her knees hitting the coffee table. "I was swimming in the lake and I discovered the car."

He gave her something like a growl over the phone. "That's a lie. You pretended like you were there by chance when you went in that water specifically to look for that car."

She needed Sean's bravado about now. "It doesn't matter why I was in the water, does it? I found the car and did the right thing."

"Who told you about the car? How'd you know it was there? Why didn't you call the cops when you got the tip?"

"Well, I'm just not going to answer those questions. This was confidential, anonymous, information."

"You're not a psychiatrist or an attorney." The sneer in his voice slid through the phone and slithered under her skin.

"I'm a journalist." She enunciated each syllable.

"Is that what you call it? Encouraging online sleuths to launch their own investigations. Hampering the police. Smearing people's names." He stopped the tirade and took a big breath.

She could picture his dark, narrowed eyes, flushed cheeks, thin line of his lips. She shivered, glad they were on the phone and not across from each other.

"Whatever your opinion of journalists, we need to protect our sources." She sawed at her bottom lip with her teeth. "Besides, I couldn't tell you, anyway. The tip was anonymous. I don't know who this person is."

"You got the tip on your computer?"

"I'm not answering that."

"We can trace activity on your computer."

She muttered a curse. It hadn't taken him long to trick her. "You could trace it if you had my computer. You don't."

He lowered his voice and almost purred in her ear. "Don't you want justice for this young woman?"

She blinked. He didn't fight fair. "O-of course, I do. Look, I don't have any information that's going to help you find her killer..."

He heard the pause. "Yet. Is that what you mean? You don't have anything yet, but you hope to solve this case—you and your wannabe detective minions. Butt out, Hughes."

He elongated the *S* at the end of her name, sounding like a snake.

"You do your job, Detective Holt, and I'll do mine. Maybe the twain will meet at some point, and we can help each other."

"Don't count on it."

He ended the call before she could form a retort. Instead, she said it to the empty room. "Whew, someone woke up on the wrong side of the cage."

She'd known Detective Holt wouldn't be

thrilled that she planned to feature this case on *LA Confidential*, but she hadn't expected him to get so mad about it.

From what she understood about him, he didn't typically work Robbery-Homicide. If he were on loan for this case, an arrest would make him look good—better than he already did. Maybe she could help him. Maybe they could help each other. She'd have to get past that wall first.

Ashlynn tucked a leg beneath her and dragged the computer into her lap. She entered his name in a search engine and her eyes popped at the number of entries. This had to be him. Who named their kid Denver?

She clicked on a promising link and read the article with a sick feeling in her belly. Denver's father had been murdered in Oregon years ago. They'd never found his father's killer.

She clicked on a more recent link and smacked her hand to her forehead. *LA Confidential*, her brother, had done an investigation into the murder of Denver's father and had insinuated that his mother was the killer.

"Oh, Sean." She covered her face with her hands. Denver Holt didn't just hate blogs—he hated *her* blog and her dead brother. Could she blame him?

She accessed Sean's archives for the blog.

Why had her brother even dug into the Holt family tragedy in Portland? *LA Confidential* usually stayed true to its name and focused on crimes in Los Angeles. It's not like this city had a shortage.

As she scrolled through the archives, her computer dinged, indicating a new private message on the blog. She navigated to the in-box and her hand trembled just a little when she clicked on the message.

She read it aloud. "'Knew I could count on you. Have more but don't want to be traced through these messages. Meet me tonight.'"

The blood pounded in her temples. This is exactly how Sean had lost his life. He'd gone to meet a source…and wound up dead.

She massaged the back of her neck. That was different. Sean had made contact with a serial killer. He was acting as the conduit between a murderer and the cops who were trying to stop him. This was a concerned citizen, afraid to go to the police, trying to get justice for a murder victim. Wasn't it?

Sean's voice echoed in her head, warning her that she'd never succeed if she weren't willing to take risks. Her parents' voices chimed in, predicting she'd never continue the blog's popularity without Sean.

She pushed her hair from her face and asked

for a name. A message popped up immediately: Angel.

Did her silent partner mean to put her at ease with that? Angel could be a man or a woman, or could stand for guardian angel. Ashlynn asked for the meeting details, already more than half sure she'd be going through with this.

Angel suggested Venice, the slice of Washington Boulevard near the pier, loaded with bars and restaurants. She'd walk along the sidewalk and Angel would approach her with the phrase *Try the mai tai at Tahiti Nui.* Tahiti Nui was a bar in the area, so that made sense, but not something a complete stranger would say to someone.

Ashlynn ended the exchange with a description of the clothing she'd be wearing, but when Angel assured her she knew what Ashlynn looked like, a whisper of fear tickled the back of her neck.

She sat for a few minutes staring at the screen. Could she trust Angel? Why not? There was no reason for Angel or anyone else to want to harm her. She didn't know anything about the case of the woman in the trunk...not yet. Angel wouldn't be probing her for information, as Angel was the one providing all the tips. Ashlynn was just a mouthpiece. Wasn't that what Sean always maintained?

Until he'd become the mouthpiece for a serial killer and lost his life.

Ashlynn bounded from the couch and snagged a denim jacket from the closet by the front door of the duplex she rented in Culver City. She didn't live far from Venice, but she didn't want to be late. If Angel didn't see her right away, she might think she'd gotten cold feet. Ashlynn didn't think she could muster up her courage again for this meeting.

She slung her purse across her body and tucked a canister of pepper spray in the outside pocket—just in case Angel was no angel.

As she closed her door, she waved to her duplex neighbors just pulling their car into the spot next to hers. Niles was a software engineer, and his girlfriend, whose name she'd forgotten, had just moved in with him a few months ago. They clambered from their car, weighed down with bags of food from the local Chinese place and waved back.

They knew what she did. Knew about *LA Confidential* and what had happened to Sean. They didn't hold it against her—of course, the blog had never accused their parents of murder. She'd tried to dismiss Denver from her mind, but she hadn't been successful. Even without the blog stuff, she'd have a hard time forgetting Denver Holt—tall, dark, handsome and...ornery.

She couldn't help herself. She'd always had a weakness for guys who were hard to get—or at least played hard to get.

She'd make a more concerted effort to block him from her mind, as he was probably married with a few kids and, well, he hated her. There was hard to get and then there was near impossible. She'd slot him into the latter category and forget about him.

She cruised west into Venice and the indigo sky that hung above the ocean, soaking up the last of the sun's rays that still floated on the water.

Parking was no picnic in Venice, and Ashlynn circled twice before waiting for a couple getting into their car. When they vacated the spot, she wheeled in.

She stepped out onto the sidewalk and adjusted her purse. She'd arrived fifteen minutes before the appointed meeting time and could squeeze in a stroll to the pier and back before expecting Angel to approach her.

She strode down Washington to the pier, looking straight ahead. She didn't want it to seem as if she were looking for someone, and she didn't want to catch the eye of any of the homeless people who mingled with the rest of crowd scooting in and out of the bars and restaurants that lined the street.

At least Angel had suggested a populated location, although Angel must've been wary of any cameras catching them inside one of the businesses. It sort of made sense to Ashlynn, which was one of the reasons she'd agreed to pounding the sidewalk aimlessly until Angel approached her with the code phrase.

Her gaze flicked toward Tahiti Nui, patrons with drinks in their hands crowding the patio in the front. Angel knew this area, unless she'd just looked it up on the internet. You could discover anything on the internet—including why the hot cop you'd immediately crushed on hated you.

She sauntered to the beginning of the old pier and inhaled the salty air. A few fishermen in silhouette packed up their gear, and an old man carefully navigated the wooden slats. She gulped in a few more breaths and turned to face the boulevard where someone calling herself Angel awaited.

She crossed the parking lot and started walking down the north side of the street. When she reached Pacific, she crossed to the other side of the street and headed back toward the pier. Before the parking lot as she crossed back over, a homeless woman approached her with her dirt-encrusted hand held out.

"Spare change?"

"Sorry, not today." Ashlynn moved past her

and, out of the corner of her eye, saw the homeless woman turn in her direction to follow her. Great. She should probably just slip her a dollar to get rid of her.

As Ashlynn plunged her hand in her purse, the woman whispered, "You should try the mai tai at Tahiti Nui."

Ashlynn spun around. "What did you say?"

The woman opened her mouth in a toothless grin and crooked her finger. "Try the mai tai at Tahiti Nui."

Stumbling after the shambling woman, Ashlynn asked, "Who are you?"

This couldn't be Angel, could it? Where would a woman like this get a computer? The library? It made sense. A transient might be more likely to witness a crime without someone noticing her. A transient might be less likely to contact the police for fear of being dismissed, or worse. Did homeless people read *LA Confidential*? Again, they could have access to computers at the library. Anyone could get access to technology today.

The homeless woman didn't turn right onto the sidewalk. She crossed the parking lot and started down Speedway.

Ashlynn hesitated. She didn't want to go this way. They were supposed to stay in a well-lit, crowded area. She licked her lips. "Hold on."

Sand scuffled on the ground to her right and a shadow loomed over her. She clawed for the pepper spray from the side of her purse and as her fingers curled around the canister, something whacked the back of her head.

She dropped to her knees. Dizzy and nauseous, she waited for the next blow that would end her life—just like Sean's.

Chapter Four

With adrenaline coursing through his veins, Denver broke into a jog and rounded the corner of Speedway, slipping and sliding on the loose sand. Ashlynn lay crumpled on the ground and a dark figure sprinted into the night.

"Hey!" Denver took a few steps toward the fleeing person but heard Ashlynn moan behind him. He cranked his head over his shoulder and skidded to a stop on the gritty pavement as a transient poked Ashlynn with an umbrella.

Denver roared. "Stop that, unless you want to wind up behind bars."

The homeless guy backed off and melted into the shadows.

Denver crouched beside Ashlynn. "Are you all right? What happened?"

Her long eyelashes fluttered and she opened one eye. "What are you doing here?"

"I'll get to that later." He wound an arm beneath her and hoisted her to a sitting position, propping her up against the dirty wall of the building. He hoped she wouldn't notice the stains. "Are you injured?"

She rubbed the back of her head, her fingers showing traces of blood. "Someone hit me on the head."

"That homeless woman you were following?" His gaze darted left and right, but he didn't see any sign of the female transient.

"How do you know…?" She shook her head. "Not her. Someone came at me from between the two buildings. Hit me with something."

"An umbrella?"

"Umbrella?" She wrinkled her nose and he noticed a few freckles scattered across her skin. "Heavier than an umbrella. Felt like a brick. Is it bleeding badly?"

Leaning over her, he parted some strands of her hair, sticky with blood. His fingers traced a small bump. "You have a lump on your head, but it's not gushing blood. I'll call the paramedics."

"No." She grabbed his arm as he reached for the phone in his pocket. "I don't need any medical attention. Just some ice and maybe a drink— no mai tais at Tahiti Nui."

He cocked his head. She must still be confused and dizzy. "You sure you don't want to get treated?"

"I'm sure." She flattened a hand against the

stucco wall and then snatched it away. "God, this is gross. Can we get out of here?"

He helped her up and she staggered against him. Tucking an arm around her waist, he led her back to the street, the lights and the people. What the hell had she been thinking, following that woman onto Speedway in the dark?

He walked her past Tahiti Nui and steered her across the street to Venice Whaler. They bypassed the hostess and he settled Ashlynn in a booth at the edge of the bar. "Do you want to use the restroom to clean that wound? It looks like it stopped bleeding. I'll get some ice from the waitress and a plastic bag. What do you want to drink? Anything but a mai tai?"

"Get me an Irish whiskey—Jameson, neat."

He raised his brows as she scooted out of the booth. Not what he'd expected, but she did look like an Irish lass with all that red hair. He kept his eyes on the dark recess where Ashlynn had disappeared—just in case someone followed her.

A waitress flicked a couple of napkins onto the table. "What can I get you?"

"Jameson, neat, and whatever light beer you have. Can you also get me a small plastic bag with ice?"

When the waitress quirked her eyebrow, he explained. "My friend bumped her head."

"Oh, is she okay?"

Denver tipped his head at Ashlynn making her way back to the table. "She's fine."

The waitress touched Ashlynn's arm. "I'll bring you that ice. Do you need anything else?"

"He ordered the whiskey?"

"He did."

"Thanks, I'm good." She slid into the booth across from Denver. "Now that my head is somewhat clear, you can start talking."

"Me?" He jabbed a finger into his chest. "Why don't you start by telling me what you were doing down here?"

"You obviously followed me or—" she narrowed her eyes "—whatever. You go first."

He held up his hands in surrender. "You got me. That's all there is to my story. I followed you here."

"From my house? You know where I live?" She winced and squeezed her eyes closed briefly.

"I'm a cop." He tapped the side of his head. "Is that wound giving you trouble?"

"Hurts, but I'm fine. You looked me up after you yelled at me on the phone and then drove out to my house to…what? What did you hope to see?"

"Exactly what I did see." He splayed his hands on the table, touching his thumbs. "You, out on some fool's errand. Just like—"

The waitress appeared just in time to stop him

from blurting out something insensitive. A serial killer had murdered her brother. He didn't need anyone to remind him what it felt like to lose a family member to murder.

He took a gulp of beer and toyed with the corner of a napkin. "You need to be careful."

Ashlynn took a tentative sip of her whiskey, and she still sniffed. "I know what happened to your father, and I know my brother covered his case in *LA Confidential*. I'm sorry."

His hand jerked and his beer frothed over the side. "Are you? Isn't that what you bloggers and podcasters do? Go after cold cases and find a killer—even if you're ruining people's lives?"

"I'm not sorry that he featured the case on his blog." She traced her fingertip along the rim of her glass. "I'm sorry you lost your father that way."

He clenched his teeth. Can't accuse this woman of soft-pedaling anything. He usually liked that, didn't he? He took a deep breath and another deep drink.

"I'm sorry about your brother, too. Losing a family member like that messes with your mind. I know it's no consolation to you, but at least you know who killed him. My father's case is still cold—despite your brother's efforts to implicate my mom."

"I had assumed it was the copycat who killed

my brother after tempting him with being his contact with the LAPD, but it was really The Player, who'd objected to his copycat working with a true crime blogger. That was a shock." She hugged herself. "Gave me the creeps."

"And this doesn't?" He flicked a finger at the window that looked out over the beach. "Is someone giving you a heads-up about this case? How do you know it's not the killer of that girl in the trunk? How do you know he's not just toying with you? Hoping for some publicity?"

The skin around Ashlynn's luscious mouth turned white and she took another sip of whiskey—not so tentative this time. Her blue eyes watered, and she dabbed her nose with a napkin.

"Who said I was meeting anyone here about the case? I came out to Venice for a walk and a drink." She lifted her glass and the light caught the amber liquid as it sloshed up the sides. "Someone decided to conk me on the head and mug me."

He narrowed his eyes. "That's the way you want to play it? Clicks or whatever you're after are more important than finding the killer of this girl?"

She swirled her drink. "I don't have anything to give you, Detective—no evidence, no clues. I can't solve this case for you."

"You got that right." He smacked his hand on the table, rattling the glasses. "So don't even try."

AFTER ESCAPING DETECTIVE HOLT'S dark stare and smoldering anger, Ashlynn slumped in the seat of her car, wedging the bag of ice against her bump with the headrest. She'd been annoyed that Denver had followed her, but he'd probably saved her life. Had she thanked him for that?

She'd been too busy trying to dismiss his suspicions that her contact was just some weirdo looking for publicity...or worse. She couldn't deny that her tipster had just led her into a very dangerous situation.

She tapped her phone and navigated to the blog, which still displayed her wrap-up to the Reed Dufrain case. Her lips turned down at the number of blog visits. You were only as good as your current case—and now she had one. She still had to write and post her first entry for the girl in the lake, but at least she had a name for the case: "The Girl in the Lake."

Now, if only her person of contact wasn't trying to kill her.

She glanced at the empty message in-box and then sighed and started the car. Sean had made it look so easy. But then, he'd made everything look easy.

As she pulled out of her metered parking

space, she glanced in her rearview mirror. She'd made it laughably easy for Denver to follow her here. She hadn't once checked for a tail on the way over.

And when had Detective Holt become Denver in her mind? Probably when she was mooning over his dark, liquid eyes across a couple of drinks. She still didn't know if he was married, but a surreptitious glance at his left hand said no, or maybe he didn't like rings.

Would he be chasing after witnesses on his off hours if he had a wife at home? If he were hers, she wouldn't let him out of her sight. She huffed through her nose. That's why her previous relationship had ended—too needy, too clingy. Who wouldn't be with parents like hers?

At least she had both of her parents. Denver's eyes had shimmered with loss when he'd talked about his father's murder—and her brother had added to his pain by suggesting Denver's mother had had something to do with the death.

She cruised up Venice Boulevard, back to her duplex, her eyes darting between her rearview and side mirrors. It had occurred to her there might be others who could be following her; others who meant her more harm than Denver—not that he posed any threat to her. He just wanted his case back, and whatever info she could give him. She could use that to her ad-

vantage. He wasn't a detective in LAPD's Robbery-Homicide division—but oh, he wanted
to be.

Ashlynn swung into the driveway next
to Niles's car. As she exited her vehicle, she
grabbed the bag of ice.

She fumbled with her key and, once inside,
made a beeline for her kitchen. Dumping out
the half-melted ice in the sink, she refilled the
bag from her freezer. She downed an ibuprofen with some water and scooped up her laptop
with one hand.

Let's see how her tipster wriggled out of this
one. She brought up the blog messages and asked
Angel what the hell had just happened.

Sipping her water, Ashlynn clicked back and
forth between Sean's archives and the blog messages until a ding indicated a new message. She
read the explanation from Angel, with a hand
at her throat.

Angel insisted she'd been followed and hadn't
wanted to put Ashlynn in danger, so she'd melted
away without approaching her. They went back
and forth, as Ashlynn described what had happened to her, including the code words the homeless woman had uttered—leaving out the part
about Denver coming to her rescue.

The fact that the transient had known the
phrase freaked out Angel. She couldn't under-

stand how that had happened, unless someone had hacked into her computer. As soon as Angel expressed that thought, she signed off.

Ashlynn nestled her fingers in her hair to trace the small bump on her head. Could she trust Angel? If someone had followed Angel, or had hacked into her computer, that someone knew she had information about the woman in the trunk, and she'd already put herself in danger. Now Angel had put Ashlynn in danger, too. She and Angel had never made contact in Venice, so the person who'd attacked her must've recognized her. Ashlynn had told Angel what she'd be wearing. She must've been easy enough to spot. If Angel were telling the truth, she had been hacked. How could Ashlynn hope to get anything more from her?

Maybe Denver was right. She should give up the whole thing. Who was she kidding? She didn't have Sean's talent, his drive, his courage.

She shoved the computer from her lap and put the glass in the dishwasher. She'd hang on to the bag of ice and give it another ten minutes before she went to bed.

She toed off her running shoes in the bedroom and crossed the floor to the master bath in her stockinged feet. She pushed open the door and blinked in the bright light.

As if in slow motion, her gaze tracked from

the lipstick cap on the floor, to the open tube on the vanity, to the letters in red scarlet slashed across her mirror.

Find Another Case.

Chapter Five

After receiving Ashlynn's frantic call about a warning on her mirror, Denver swore as he gunned it on the freeway. He should've followed her home. It's not like she would've known. He'd followed her to Venice tonight on a hunch, and she hadn't noticed him.

He'd had a hunch when she'd set off for her place tonight, too, but he hadn't followed through. After that attack in Venice, he'd known she'd put herself in a sticky situation—and now someone had broken into her house and scribbled a message on her bathroom mirror. Gutsy.

He careered down the off-ramp and ran a few red lights to reach her. When he rolled up her street, he saw the dome light in her car parked in the driveway. She'd been home for almost an hour before she'd discovered the message in the bathroom. The perpetrator would be long gone by now, but he could understand her reluctance to wait inside like a sitting duck.

As he pulled to the curb across the street, Ashlynn shot out of her car and waited on the sidewalk, practically hopping from foot to foot. She started talking before he was half-way across the road.

"Someone broke into my place. I don't know how they got in because as soon as I saw the message on my bathroom mirror, I fled. I don't know if they're still there, hiding."

"Good idea." His forehead creased. "Why didn't you call the police?"

"I did. I called you." She tipped her head at him, making him feel ten feet tall that he'd been her go-to guy.

He had an idea why she hadn't called 9-1-1. When he reached her, she spun around, leading the way to her house. He put a hand on her shoulder. "You can wait out here, if you want."

Her red hair flicked as she glanced over her shoulder. "I feel safe now that you're here."

Did she actually bat her eyelashes? And what was with all the compliments when, two hours ago, she couldn't even thank him for rescuing her from a street attack?

He kept a few paces behind her, not intentionally to watch her hips sway, but that was an added bonus. When she reached the door and unlocked it, he nudged her to the side and withdrew his weapon. "Let me go in first."

Her eyes widened for a second and she held up a canister of pepper spray. "I was going to use this, but that's much more effective."

He eased open the door and stepped into a small entryway, the kitchen branching off in one direction, a hallway in the other, and the living room spread before him.

"I'll check the windows." He tugged on the two snug windows in the kitchen, and studied the one in the living room. She'd locked up tight.

"Do you ever leave this unlocked?" As he walked up to the sliding-glass door that led to a small patio and grassy area, he noticed the drapes puckering inward. He whipped them aside. "Hello."

"What?" She'd been right on his heels and bumped into his back when he stopped.

With his fingertip in the air, he traced the square of glass cut from her door, right next to the handle and the lock. "He got in this way. I take it you don't have a lock on the track of the slider."

Clutching his arm, she bent forward to inspect the intruder's handiwork. "He used some sort of glasscutter to cut and lift that square out, and then reached in to unlock the door."

"Doesn't even have to be that fancy. Someone can just smash through the glass and unlock it if it's the only lock on the door." He jerked his thumb at what must be the wall she shared with her neighbors. "Probably didn't want to make that much noise."

"Damn." She kicked the metal door track with her bare foot. "I had a little screw-on device on here at one point."

"Weren't you in the living room before you discovered the note in the bathroom? You didn't notice the air coming in through this door?"

"The drapes were already closed, and I was sitting on the couch with my back to that door. Never even noticed it." She folded her arms and hunched her shoulders. "I guess I should've checked all the windows and doors myself after what happened tonight. I didn't think... I mean I didn't see anyone following me from Venice. Whoever this is, knows where I live."

"Unless he's followed you before...maybe home from the lake that day."

"So, now that we know how he gained entrance to my house—" she crooked her finger at him "—I'll show you the scary part."

As she led him through her bedroom, he skirted the king-size bed with one corner of the blue floral bedspread turned down, and his gaze flicked toward a pile of clothes on a chair, a lacy bra dangling off the arm.

She pushed open the bathroom door with a flourish. "He used my lipstick and didn't bother to put it away when he was finished. I actually noticed the lipstick before the words on my mirror."

The red warning leaped out at him immediately—block letters, no misspellings, intentional or otherwise, and no regard for Ashlynn's lipstick.

"I hope that wasn't your favorite color." He nudged the cap on the floor with the toe of his shoe. "Do you have a plastic bag?"

She loosened her grip on the doorjamb and ran a hand through her wavy hair that curled at the ends. "You mean like to bag this up as evidence?"

"I doubt we'll find any prints but yours, but it's worth a try." He met her eyes in the mirror. Two chips of ice stared back.

"I'm not reporting this." She folded her arms at her chest, crossing one leg over the other. She looked like a pretzel.

"You sort of did report it." He spread out his arms. "As you pointed out earlier, I am a cop."

Her gaze dropped to his backside, and he felt a coiling response in his belly. "You're not wearing your cop clothes and, besides, you're LAPD. The last time I looked out my window, I lived in Culver City. We have our own police force."

He turned to face her. "We work with Culver City all the time. I'm sure they'd be more than happy to help out with a homicide in LA."

"Who said anything about a homicide in LA?" She gave him a bug-eyed stare and an exaggerated shrug, like a cartoon character. "I got scared because someone broke into my place and scrawled a message on my bathroom mirror. I did what any girl would do who had the phone number of a hunky cop at her fingertips—called him."

She thought he was hunky? Did women even say hunky anymore? He stiffened his back and just managed to avoid puffing out his chest. "You're telling me you called me so you could check out my ass?"

"I was not…" Her cheeks matched her hair, and she knew it. She took a deep breath. "I called you because your number was handy and I was scared…and you already saved me once tonight."

He rubbed the back of his neck. "Let's start over. You are planning to feature this case on *LA Confidential*, and someone is already warning you off. I checked the blog, and you haven't posted anything about this case. How did your intruder know to warn you off? I think we can agree that the attack in Venice was another warning. How did that person know you were going to be down on Washington tonight?"

She drummed her fingers against the door. "Let's get out of the bathroom. Coffee? Water? Beer?"

"Did this turn into a social call?"

"Friendly business." She backed away from the bathroom. "I'll even get the baggie for the lipstick."

He had no choice but to follow her. Hell, even if he had a choice, he'd follow her.

She gestured toward the couch. "Have a seat, or help yourself to something to drink first. I'll bag the lipstick and cap, and don't worry, I won't touch either one."

She rummaged in a kitchen drawer and hustled back to the bedroom, a small plastic bag stuck to her fingertips.

Denver took her place in the kitchen and opened the fridge. He grabbed a soda from the top shelf. He could use a little caffeine right now but couldn't face coffee. He didn't want to be too wired for this friendly business meeting, but he needed to be on his toes.

Ashlynn sashayed back into the living room, swinging the baggie with the lipstick tube and cap. "Here you go. Just don't do anything official with it because I'm not reporting this break-in."

Cocking his head, Denver asked, "Why not?"

"What happens in the blogging world, stays in the blogging world. I don't want any official record of what I'm up to." She pretended to turn a key at her lips.

He supposed this was what he'd signed up for when he agreed to work with her. He circled his finger in the air. "Did you ever check to see if anything was missing?"

"Just made sure my laptop was still here— that's it. I don't have any expensive jewelry stashed away, no bundles of cash, no fancy electronic devices, and no guns—yet."

Denver rolled his eyes. "God, help us. I got a soda for myself. Did you want one?"

"I'm good." She dropped the baggie on the coffee table next to where he was perching on the arm of the couch. "What can you do with that...unofficially?"

"I can get someone to run prints...unofficially." He answered her raised eyebrows. "I know people."

"I'll bet you do." She took the other end of the sofa, bracing her back against the arm and stretching out her long legs toward him.

He glanced at her toes wiggling in her socks and slid down the arm so that he landed on a cushion of the couch, her feet inches from his lap. "What business could we possibly have together?"

She pulled her knees to her chest, wrapping one arm around them. "I need a case...and you need a case. This could be it for both of us."

His nostrils flared as some emotion thumped in his chest. Anger? Shame? Excitement? He couldn't even ID it, himself.

He ran his hands across his face, his day-old beard scratching his palms. "You're suggesting we help each other—I keep you apprised of the investigation and you give me what you're getting from the readers of your blog."

She nodded, blue eyes sparkling. Anyone looking in at her might think they were discussing wedding plans instead of murder.

He held up one finger and growled more fiercely than he'd intended. "I see one problem with that."

She flashed him her pearly whites. "Only one?"

"One major problem." He cleared his throat and took a sip of soda, the bubbles rushing to his nose. "The information I'd be giving you would be accurate. The stuff you'd be passing off to me...garbage."

She tipped her feet back on her heels and tapped them together. "Did I find garbage in Lake Kawayu? No. I found a car with a body in the trunk. Would you have found that body without me? Doubt it."

"Which brings us back to the beginning." He jabbed his finger into the couch at the edge of her toes, where the gesture lost all effectiveness as his finger sank into the cushion. "How did you know where to find the car? Why did you go to Venice tonight?"

"If I tell you, can you keep it to yourself? It's all garbage, anyway, right? Lunatics out in cyber land who want to play detective. If word gets around in law enforcement circles that I'm cooperating with a cop, I might not get any more information. If we keep this hush-hush between us, I might still get the info, I can feed it to you and you only, you can give me a little inside story and—" she clapped her hands "—I've got a blog worth reading and you're the hotshot detective who solved the case. That's what we both want, isn't it? Justice for that woman in the trunk?"

Denver circled his fingers around the can of soda and squeezed in one side of the aluminum. How pathetic and obvious he must've come across. Playing at being a homicide detective without really being a homicide detective. Ashlynn had spotted his desperation a mile off, must've smelled it coming from him in waves.

What did he have to lose?

He thrust out his hand. "Justice for the girl in the trunk."

A LITTLE THRILL fluttered through her veins as she clasped Denver's warm, strong hand. "It's a deal, Detective."

"If we're going to be working with each other, you can start calling me Denver." He squeezed her hand before releasing it.

She settled back against the arm of the couch, failing to mention she'd already been calling him Denver in her head. "I'll try."

His eyebrows knitted. "Start now. How did you know that car was going to be in the lake with a body inside?"

He wanted to get right down to business. She took a deep breath. "I got a tip on my blog."

"I figured that. How?" He hunched forward, elbows on knees. "Someone posted on the blog for everyone else to see?"

"I—Sean had a private message feature on the blog. People can hit the message icon and contact me directly, without anyone else seeing it."

He rubbed his knuckles against his stubble. "More private than emailing you because the person can mask his or her email address."

"Exactly. Sean thought that method would encourage more tips—and it has."

Nodding toward the laptop on the table, he asked, "Can you show me the message?"

"Yes." She swung her legs off the couch and flipped open her computer. She accessed the blog, clicked on her private messages, and scrolled back to her first contact with Angel.

She jabbed her finger at the screen. "That's the first time she contacted me."

"'She'?" He pulled the computer into his lap,

forcing her to scoot closer to him if she wanted to see what he was reading.

"She has since identified herself as Angel."

"Angel. *Angel.*" He pronounced the name the second time in Spanish. "Could be a Latino dude."

"Could be, but I have a feeling this is a woman."

He squinted at the screen. "She tipped you off to a car in Lake Kawayu and indicated you'd find a body in it, but she didn't mention the trunk."

"If she didn't know the body was in the trunk, that rules out Angel as an eyewitness or accomplice, right?"

The corner of Denver's mouth twitched, and she braced herself for sarcasm.

"Maybe, unless Angel saw this at night, knew there was a body somehow, but didn't know where the perpetrator had left it."

No sarcasm detected.

"Yeah, I see how that could happen. Same for an accomplice. She could've left the woman in the car with the killer at the lake and not watched or known what he'd done with the body."

He flicked his finger at the message. "Not much here. You got the message and hightailed it to the lake the next day to look for the car."

"That's how this works. True crime bloggers

take a lot on faith. We're not like cops—we don't have to verify, we don't have any rules."

"And that's what gets you in trouble." He brushed his thumb against the mouse. "Angel must've sent you something else to send you on your way to Venice tonight."

She waved her hand in the air. "Keep scrolling. She saw the news and knew I had acted on her tip. She wanted to meet me in person to give me more information. I was supposed to walk along Washington and wait for someone to approach me with a code phrase. That's why I followed the homeless woman—she had the code phrase."

Denver whistled. "Unless Angel is the culprit, somebody learned that code to preempt your meeting."

"I don't think Angel is playing me. Read on. She contacted me after the meeting went south. She thinks someone might be hacking into her computer, and that's how he knew our code phrase."

"That's not good." Denver tapped the keyboard to view the rest of the messages. "Someone reading this knows that Angel tipped you off. Angel put a target on your back...or two targets. Looks like they double-teamed you tonight. One person went to Venice to disrupt the meeting and, while they knew you were out, someone else came here to scribble a warning on your mirror—just in case getting whacked on the head didn't do the trick."

"It didn't." She rubbed the knot on the back of her head.

"Sounds like Angel isn't going to contact you via computer anymore, but that doesn't matter. We have a guy at the station who can track this IP address. We can talk to Angel in person."

"Wait a minute." She pulled the computer from his lap to hers and snapped it shut. "That's not our deal."

"Our deal—" he crunched his soda can in one hand "—is to find the killer of some poor woman stuffed in the trunk of a car."

"My contact is going to help us do it—on her own terms. If she'd wanted to call the cops, she would've done so. If she suspects I'm working with the LAPD, that'll be the end of the flow of information."

"That might be over now."

Denver's cell phone rang and he held up one finger.

"Holt." His dark eyes widened and his fingers tightened on the phone. "Well, isn't that something? I'll pay them a visit first thing tomorrow morning."

The call ended with nothing more than a few grunts on Denver's side. A crease formed between his eyebrows as he tapped the phone against his chin.

The call had something to do with the case... and it was big. She cleared her throat. "I gave you what I had. It's your turn now."

He smacked the phone against his palm, and she jumped. "That car you found in the lake?"

"Yeah?" She twisted her fingers into messy knots.

"It's part of a fleet that belongs to the Campaign to Re-Elect Mayor Wexler."

Chapter Six

The following day, Denver dipped into the parking structure beneath the sleek glass-and-steel structure that housed the offices for the Campaign to Re-Elect Mayor Wexler. Or, as Wexler's staff liked to call it, CREW.

Marino had thrown this case his way, as the detective was busy wrapping up another homicide. Denver was flying solo on this interview, but he had the weight of Chief Sterling behind him. The chief had already given the mayor's office a heads-up—hell, the two men were golfing buddies. As long as their tee time didn't interfere with his investigation, he'd use all the help the chief offered.

Twisting around, Denver grabbed his jacket from the back seat. He'd opted for his most expensive suit for this interview, courtesy of Cool Breeze himself, Detective Billy Crouch. Billy had hooked him up with his personal tailor, and Denver needed as much confidence as he could muster to go charging into the mayor's campaign headquarters asking questions about a dead body in the trunk of one of the campaign's official cars.

He stepped into the elevator, smoothing the lapels of his jacket and using the same motion on the sides of his hair. Either the chief trusted him with this case, or Sterling knew he could manipulate the sap. But this sap had a secret weapon—a redheaded blogger with a burning desire to prove herself.

He'd read some of the stories Ashlynn had written for that magazine she'd worked for, and he had no clue why she was so hell-bent on picking up where her brother had left off. Her brother had a reputation of being anti-police, and the department hadn't been a big fan. Detective Jake McAllister had only agreed to work with Sean Hughes because the guy had opened a channel of communication with one of The Player's copycats. But in the end, Hughes had gotten burned by that fire when The Player himself had killed him for interference.

He hoped like hell Ashlynn wasn't traveling down the same path as her brother. He hoped like hell he wasn't leading her down that path.

The elevator dinged on the ninth floor of the building, and Denver gave his tie a tug and exited onto a slick tiled floor. He swiveled his head in search of a reception desk or reception-ist, but the floorplan stretched into a large, light open space with cubbies here and there, exer-cise balls in front of desks in lieu of chairs and a few glass-walled offices hugging the perim-eter of the room.

As his gaze tracked among the busy worker bees, he cleared his throat. Not one of them looked up or even broke stride. If nobody was going to play nice, he'd be as intrusive as pos-sible.

Making a beeline for one of those offices, he squared his shoulders and plunged into the melee, skirting desks and charging past the ex-ercise balls, sending them skittering sideways. That earned him a few quick glances and open-mouthed stares.

Out of the corner of his eye, he saw a man scurrying toward him, a laptop clutched to his chest. "Excuse me. Excuse me, Detective Holt?"

Ah, so they *were* expecting him. Denver halted in midstride and swung around on the guy, causing him to stumble to a stop. A second minion careened through the desks to intercept them, her oversized glasses giving her a startled, bug-eyed look—or maybe she was startled.

Denver stuck out his hand to the man with the laptop. "Detective Denver Holt. You must be Christian Bushnell."

Bushnell juggled the laptop in his arms and shook Denver's hand, his mouth twisting up at the corner as Denver went in for the hard squeeze. "Nice to meet you, Detective Holt. This is my coworker, Amalia Fernandez."

Denver finally released Bushnell's hand and turned to Amalia, who was much better at navigating the handshake and the laptop, which was tucked under her left arm.

Did these people walk around with laptops and tablets attached to their bodies?

"Good morning, Detective Holt. I'm the mayor's campaign director and Christian is my assistant." She sure wanted to set the record straight. She swept an arm to the side. "We'll be talking in one of the offices for privacy."

"Looks like that's in short supply here."

Amalia drew back her shoulders and flicked her neat dark ponytail. "Mayor Wexler prides himself on transparency."

Always campaigning, this bunch. Must be exhausting. Denver gave a tight smile. "That's what I'm counting on."

He followed the two of them to an office with glass walls that looked out onto the controlled chaos of the rest of the room. If the Northwest Division had interview rooms like these, the cops wouldn't garner half the confessions they got.

He pulled out the chair Amalia indicated with a nod of her head and tried to perch on the edge. The slant and cushioning of the seat made that difficult. The cops would have even more trouble getting confessions out of anyone sitting in these chairs.

He grabbed the edge of the table to keep from sliding back into the black leather, and plucked a notebook from the front pocket of his shirt. He smacked it on the table, and Amalia and Christian both flinched.

Not as calm and collected as they appeared.

"You both know why I'm here. A body was found in the trunk of a car that belongs to this office, and the car was sitting at the bottom of Lake Kawayu."

Christian shook his head. "I had no idea that lake was so deep."

Amalia shot him a look and may have even kicked him under the table because Christian clamped his mouth shut and reddened up to his eyeballs.

"I—I mean, we were shocked when we found out."

"We heard the news, Detective Holt." Amalia folded her hands in her lap. "We, and that includes the mayor, were so distressed. What can we do to help? Mayor Wexler has instructed us to cooperate fully, of course, and has assured his good friend, Chief Sterling, that we're here to help."

"That's good to know." Denver held his pen poised above a clean sheet on his notepad. "Why did you tamper with the license plate and VIN on that car?"

Christian swallowed a big lump in his throat and Amalia's smile froze on her face. "Excuse me. We don't tamper with license plates or destroy the VINs on our cars, and didn't do so to that car. Whoever stole the car from our garage must've done that."

"That car was stolen?"

"Of course." Amalia spread her hands on the table. "This is LA, Detective, the car theft capital of the world."

Denver opened his eyes wide. "Even with Mayor Wexler at the helm?"

The smile stayed plastered on Amalia's lipsticked mouth, but had dropped completely from her eyes. "One of the many issues he's going to address in his second term."

Hunching forward, Denver placed the tip of his pen on the paper in front of him. "When did you report the car stolen?"

"We didn't." Amalia pursed her lips and jutted her chin out aggressively.

He knew they hadn't reported it stolen, and she knew he knew. He let his pen drop to the table, and Christian's reaction would've made you think he'd fired a shot instead of dropped a pen.

Denver screwed up his face. "Oh, I'm sorry. I misunderstood. I thought you said the car had been stolen from your lot."

Crossing her arms, Amalia said, "You didn't misunderstand, Detective Holt. You knew we hadn't reported it stolen, or you would've already had that report in your hand. We have a lot of cars in our fleet here at CREW. We don't always keep track of them as well as we should. We didn't notice this car was gone, but I can assure you, somebody stole that car out of our garage."

"You might've just solved the crime, Ms. Fernandez. You have cameras at the garage?" He scribbled some gibberish in his notebook. They were both too far away to read it anyway.

"We do have cameras, and I'm a step ahead of you, Detective. I've already ordered the security footage. Unfortunately, we keep it for seven days only, so if the car was stolen before that..." Amalia shrugged her shoulders.

Denver mumbled under his breath. "That's convenient."

"Excuse me?" Amalia narrowed her eyes.

"I said, how inconvenient, but we'll work with what we have." He rapped on the desk just because he liked seeing Christian jump. "I'm going to need a list of everyone who works on the campaign."

"What?" Christian had finally found his voice, and it had a decided squeak that had been missing before. "We have hundreds of people working on CREW."

"I hope you can print out all those names from a database. That'll make it easy." Denver snapped his fingers. "I'll do you one better. Get me the list of people who worked on the campaign *and* had access to the fleet of vehicles. I'll take that breakdown first, and then you can supply the names of all the campaign workers."

Amalia drummed a sharp set of talons on the table. "Waste of time, Detective Holt. I already told you the car was stolen."

She'd gone too far even for Christian, who shot her a worried look from beneath a creased brow.

Denver clapped a hand over his heart. "Thanks for your concern and, uh, expertise, Ms. Fernandez, but you let me worry about what's a waste of time and what's not." He picked up his pen again. "What do staffers use the cars for?"

To make up for Amalia's misstep, Christian launched in helpfully. "All sorts of things—delivering items to campaign stops, doing door-to-doors, providing transportation for the mayor's guests for speeches and events, e-even picking up lunch for the CREW."

"Do all these perks come from the city budget?"

Christian opened his mouth but Amalia cut him off with a slicing motion. "Absolutely not. That would be a campaign violation. The cars, the lunches, everything you see here is funded by the Campaign to Re-Elect Mayor Wexler."

Denver held up his hands in surrender. "Hey, sounds good to me. I'm here to investigate a homicide, not the mayor's finances."

Sitting perpendicular to the office door, Denver spotted a man in a cap with the parking service logo on the front approaching the office.

Amalia jumped up before the guy finished knocking. "Thank you, Gerardo."

She took something from his hand and started to close the door, but Denver pushed back his chair and lunged forward, putting his foot against the doorjamb. "Gerardo, can I ask you a couple of questions? I'm Detective Holt with the LAPD."

Gerardo slid a glance to Amalia before saying, "Yes, sir."

Denver pointed to the thumb drive swinging from a ribbon wrapped around Amalia's index finger. "That contains the footage from the garage for the past seven days?"

"Yes, it does. It covers both exits, so it catches any cars that left the parking garage by either exit in the last week."

"No way to get footage from more than seven days ago."

"I'm afraid not, Detective. It's taped over."

Denver felt in his front pocket and pulled out a card. He extended it to Gerardo. "Call me if you remember anything about the cars in Mayor Wexler's fleet, or anything unusual in the garage the past few weeks."

"I'll do that." Gerardo murmured something in Spanish to Amalia, and she gave a quick shake of her head.

Denver didn't know if he would've understood it even if he spoke fluent Spanish—which he didn't.

When Amalia closed the door after Gerardo, she dangled the thumb drive in front of Denver. "Here you go, Detective. I thought it would be easier for you to review the footage at the station. If you have any questions about it, you can call Gerardo."

He pocketed the thumb drive. "Thanks, Ms. Fernandez. Did, uh, Gerardo have something to add at the end there?"

She blinked her eyes, rapidly. "He just asked if he could use the restroom here on his way out."

"Oh, you didn't let him?"

She opened her mouth once and snapped it closed.

"I mean, you shook your head like no."

"We don't allow anyone but staffers to use the restrooms on this floor." She gave him a tight smile. "I think Gerardo understood. Now, is there anything else, Detective Holt?"

"One more thing." He held up a finger. "Do either of you know the name Tiana Fuller?"

Denver shifted his gaze to Christian, the weak link. The boy didn't disappoint. Christian's Adam's apple bobbed as if he'd just swallowed a golf ball.

Amalia didn't give Christian the chance to step in it, though. "Never heard that name before. Is she the…victim? A suspect?"

"Can't say right now." He tipped his head toward Christian. "You?"

"Wh-what?" The color rushed from Christian's throat to his cheeks. He'd never make it as a poker player.

"Have you ever heard the name Tiana Fuller or know who she is?"

Christian rolled his eyes to the ceiling. If he'd had a thinking cap, he'd have slapped it on his head. "No. No, I haven't."

"That's all I have—for now." He tapped his finger next to the card Amalia had left on the desk. "Give me a call if you think of anything else. I'll review the footage from the garage while waiting for you to send over the list of campaign workers. I expect that today, right?"

"Of course. I'll have Christian get right on that for you. Shouldn't take long." Amalia opened the door. "Mayor Wexler is anxious to clear this up, and his office will be sending condolences to the family—once we know the identity of the victim. Will you let us know, Detective Holt, or do we find out from the TV news like everyone else?"

"I'll let you know as soon as we get an ID—just in case."

"In case?" She narrowed her dark eyes.

"In case she's connected to the campaign… or Mayor Wexler."

Chapter Seven

After he'd mentioned Tiana's name in connection to Mayor Wexler, Amalia escorted him out of the CREW office so fast he could hear the wind whistling past his ears. When he reached his car, he shrugged out of his jacket and smoothed it out carefully in the back seat.

He'd like to get Christian alone, but Amalia had probably already schooled him in the proper responses to this investigation—we know nothing, the mayor knows nothing.

Denver checked his phone and his heart pounded as he listened to a voice mail from Captain Fields. Mrs. Edmunds had delivered her daughter's DNA to the station, and if he hurried, he might be back in time to learn whether or not Tiana Fuller was their victim.

He positioned his phone on the console for the Bluetooth and tamped down the disappointment he felt over the absence of a message from Ashlynn. Maybe she didn't want to step on his toes and expected him to take the lead. They had a business relationship, not a romantic one.

He tapped in her number and her phone rang through the speakers. She answered after the second ring, out of breath, as if she'd just jogged a mile or two.

Before he could even get through the niceties, she asked, "Did you read the blog post?"

"I did. It was good. You're a good writer."

She coughed. "Does that mean it grabbed you by the throat and left you wanting more?"

She left him wanting more.

He cranked up the AC. "Yeah, it was like a story, a mystery. Have you gotten any more tips? Hear from Angel?"

"I've gotten tons of public comments, and a few weird private ones that I'm still sorting through." She paused, taking a sip of something. "Do you have anything for me yet? Has she been ID'd?"

"Not yet. We're working on it." Denver glanced in his rearview and accelerated onto the freeway. "Weird tips? Do you feel safe?"

"Yeah. I had a locksmith come out and install a proper lock on the sliding door and got the glass replaced. I'm submitting everything to my insurance company. I mean renter's insurance has to cover something, right?"

At her breezy tone, he loosened his grip on the

steering wheel. He hadn't cared about anyone's safety for a long time. He'd made sure he never cared about anyone enough to worry about them. After his father's murder, he'd driven himself, and everyone around him, crazy with his hovering and double-checking. Had given himself an ulcer, too—at least, that's what the department-mandated shrink, Kyra Chase, had told him.

He licked his lips. "Wouldn't hurt to get a security system, maybe a camera. Lots of people have them these days."

"I'll look into it. If that lipstick message and the assault at Venice Beach meant to warn me off, I'm not heeding it. Who knows what this person will try next?"

Denver's palms broke out in a sweat and he wiped them, one by one, on his slacks.

He needed to back off. If she wanted to put herself in danger, that was her business. He had a job protecting people—strangers. Mom had a new husband, and his sister had married a guy with hundreds of relatives practically living on top of them. He'd relinquished the reins of their protection to others, and he had no intention of picking up another set. "Okay, keep me posted, and let me know if you hear from Angel again. I'll tell you what I can."

He ended the call abruptly and sped back to the station.

When he got there, he bypassed his new desk in Robbery-Homicide and went straight to the lab. The remodel of the Northeast Division had included a state-of-the-art lab where the techs could do DNA matching.

He sidled up next to Lori Del Valle, one of the fingerprint techs. "DNA match done yet?"

"No, it isn't." She shoved at his arm. "Watching the techs isn't going to make it go any faster, but nobody has located Tiana Fuller yet."

He sucked in his lower lip. "It's not looking too good for Tiana. Her mother tentatively identified the top our victim was wearing as Tiana's."

"We know you're lead on this case, Denver. We're going to tell you first." The nudge at his arm turned into a pat.

"Too eager, huh?"

"Understandable." She tossed him a baggie. "But, hey, I processed the tube of lipstick and there are no prints at all—none. That means it was probably wiped."

"I figured." He put his finger to his lips. "Just between us, right?"

"Discretion is my middle name."

"Don't wanna get you in trouble again." He meandered back to the Robbery-Homicide room with a little less spring in his step and dropped his bag next to his desk.

Detective Falco nodded as she walked past

him. "How'd it go at the mayor's re-election office?"

"As you'd expect—closemouthed groupies doing their best to protect their guy."

"You know the chief's going to want you to back off as soon as the CREW is cleared of any association with this woman."

"I'm aware, and I plan to back off when no more arrows point in that direction."

"Good answer."

When she dove to answer a phone, Denver inserted the thumb drive from the garage into his computer. Detective Falco obviously didn't envy him this assignment. The chief could've assigned this to the golden boys—McAllister and Crouch—but there's no way he could control those two. Could the chief control him? Denver could think of a few ways Sterling might try.

He queued up the footage to the very first minute that was available and hunched forward to watch the flickering images on his monitor. He had the gate to Santa Monica Boulevard on the top of his screen, and the one to the side street on the bottom. Seemed like most of the CREW's cars used the side street. The sedans all looked the same, and he kept his eyes on the license plates. Although the plates on the car in the lake had been swapped, he knew the real plate number from the VIN and doubted someone had spent time in the garage removing the plates before driving it out of the garage. And if someone had done that? He'd locate the car without the plates.

When he made it through day one without a hit, he snatched a bag of chips from his desk drawer and popped it open. He rubbed his eyes, and then stuffed several chips in his mouth, crunching as he watched the first car of the next day roll under the parking arm.

He jumped when someone clamped his shoulder. "Boy does not live by chips alone. That footage isn't going anywhere while you get some lunch."

Denver twisted his head around, glancing at Billy's smiling face. Easy for him to say. "One day down, six to go."

"My guess?" Billy circled his finger in the air over the monitor. "You're not going to see that car on camera. The person who took it had to know that it was going to be ID'd sooner or later, even without the correct plates, registration and a scratched-up VIN. He either knew about the footage being taped over every week, or he did something to the cameras."

Denver clicked the mouse to stop the footage and licked salt from his lips. "Tell me something, Cool Breeze. How come you and McAllister aren't on this case? A murder of a young woman, found in a public place, in a car belonging to the Campaign to Re-Elect Mayor Wexler? Sounds right up the alley of the dynamic duo."

Billy brushed his knuckles down his tie, as if worried some of the salt from Denver's chips had attached themselves to the silk. "If you don't know the answer to that, my man, you're probably never going to make permanent detective in Robbery-Homicide."

Denver nodded. The chief couldn't pressure J-Mac and Crouch like he could the new guy. Denver crumpled a napkin in his left hand. "Any advice?"

"Just do your job, Rocky."

"Rocky?" Denver lifted an eyebrow. Like all squads in the LAPD, Robbery-Homicide was notorious for assigning nicknames to the detectives.

"You know—Denver? Rocky Mountain High?"

Denver groaned and shot the balled-up napkin at the sharp crease in Billy's impeccable slacks.

He spent the next two hours speeding through the remaining days, too. As he watched the last car on the footage roll beneath the parking arm, he slumped in his chair. Billy had nailed it. The killer hadn't made this easy. He'd either taken the car in advance, without reporting it, or he'd tampered with the camera or footage. Denver had been watching the counter on the footage and hadn't noticed anything hinky.

Someone had taken the car in advance of the murder—either planning the murder or planning something else he or she hadn't wanted tracked. Or maybe it was dumb luck. Someone took the car without planning anything at all.

Denver pinched the bridge of his nose as his stomach rumbled. A bag of potato chips didn't cut it for lunch.

His desk phone rang and he grabbed it. "Holt."

Lance from the lab said, "We have the DNA match to Tiana Fuller. She is the victim in the trunk of the car."

"Thanks, Lance." Denver's eye twitched.

The ID of a victim always cut both ways. Knowing the victim allowed the investigation to progress in a valuable way, but it also meant ripping apart another family. He'd personally notify Mrs. Edmunds. In most of the homicide investigations he'd worked, he'd become the go-to guy for family notifications, given his own background.

He almost felt it his duty to take on the notifications to protect the other detectives from sinking into the grief pit with the families. He'd already visited that pit, had already been scarred by it.

Taking a deep breath, he swiveled his chair

toward the wall and stared at a spot near the ceiling. Then he called Mrs. Edmonds.

She answered after the first ring. She'd been waiting for his call. "Hello? Detective Holt?"

"It is, Mrs. Edmonds. We identified the victim in the trunk of the submerged car as your daughter, Tiana. There is no doubt. The DNA matches the sample you submitted." He held his breath.

Other cops might dance around, might try to couch the news in soft, pretty words. The families of victims didn't want or need that.

Mrs. Edmonds let out a sob. "I knew it."

His chest tightened, and he loosened his collar. "I'm sorry for your loss. I'm going to need to talk to you and your husband. Get a list of Tiana's friends, boyfriends, roommates—but not now. Tomorrow okay?"

She sniffled. "Tomorrow is fine, Detective."

She ended the call before he could respond, but he really had no response. There were no words, and sometimes words made it all worse.

He studied the spot on the wall and flicked the pad of his thumb beneath his eye. Then he spun his chair back to his computer. The garage footage had held his attention all afternoon, although from the corner of his eye he could see emails popping up every so often at the bottom of his screen. Now, he scanned through them, the last of the bunch from Lance with the DNA report, and cursed under his breath.

Christian at the CREW had failed to send the database of campaign workers. As he grabbed his jacket, he tapped Christian's number on his phone. He left the guy a not-so-civil voice mail reminding him what he owed him.

After he left the message, he listened to one from Ashlynn on his way out of the station, inviting him for dinner tonight. Probably wanted to pick his brain some more, find out if he'd learned the identity of the victim.

He'd promised to play ball with her and, as long as Tiana's family knew first, he didn't have a problem releasing Tiana's name to Ashlynn. Her identity would be all over the news and social media by tomorrow morning anyway.

And his rumbling stomach told him the invitation couldn't have come at a better time. He texted her Tiana's name and accepted the invite to dinner, asking if she wanted him to bring anything. Picked brain or no, he never went to anyone's house empty-handed.

A half hour later, as the freeway spit him out onto one of the boulevards bordering Culver City, he stooped over his steering wheel, looking for a liquor store. Ashlynn had promised stir-fried beef and veggies, so he picked up a Pinot

Grigio. He also grabbed a bag of trail mix just in case he had to wait for dinner.

He pulled up to the curb across the street from her duplex, opened his door and dusted the salt from the peanuts from his hands and slacks. He still had on his good suit and didn't want to spoil the effect. To top it off, he reached for his jacket in the back seat and slid his arms into the sleeves. Might as well maintain the appearance of a business meeting—with stir-fry.

He knocked on her door, and he heard a chain slide and a dead bolt click. When she opened it, he said, "I'm glad to hear you're taking your security seriously."

She stepped back to let him over the threshold. "When the guy from the lock and key shop came out to install the contraption on the sliding door, I asked him to install a new dead bolt and a chain—just in case."

He sniffed the air and while the smell of ginger didn't do anything for him, he knew it heralded more savory tastes. He held up the bottle in the bag. "Pinot Grigio?"

"Sounds good." She took the bag from him and peeked inside. "Is it cold by any chance?"

"No, sorry. The liquor store had only the cheap stuff refrigerated."

"That's okay. I'll stick it in the freezer and it should at least be chilled by the time we eat."

He nodded, grateful for the trail mix rattling around in his empty stomach. "Have you already released the news about Tiana Fuller on your blog?"

"I have, thanks." She sidestepped into the kitchen and ducked into the refrigerator. "Terrible news for her family."

He clasped the back of his neck. "Yeah, it was."

Waving a hand over his clothes, she said, "Straight from work. I'll take your jacket, and you can lose the tie. You can even lose the shoes, if you like."

"I can just hang it over a chair." He shrugged out of the jacket and made a move toward a kitchen chair pulled up to the small table, already set for two.

She snatched it from him and held it up, giving it the once-over. "It looks expensive. I used to write about fashion. I know, it's hard to believe."

"It's my one really good suit." His gaze swept across her skinny jeans that hit right above her ankles, a pair of gleaming white tennis shoes and light green top that dipped into a V on her chest. She'd swept her red hair into a half up, half down ponytail. She looked neat and crisp, and good enough to eat.

He swallowed. Man, he really was hungry.

She rested her cheek against the material of

his jacket and ran one hand down the sleeve. The gesture twisted his stomach into knots. He had a hunger for more than just food.

"It's nice. I'll hang it up." She crossed back over to the hallway and opened a door to the closet. "Don't forget it."

"Do you need some help?" He jerked his thumb at the wok on the counter, next to a cutting board filled with a colorful array of veggies.

She snapped her fingers. "You can warm up the lumpia and eat it."

"Lumpia?" His mouth instantly watered.

"I know I'm sort of crossing cultures here, but my friend Mercy made the lumpia and dropped some off today. It's in the fridge and just needs some heat. Microwave will do."

He opened the fridge and slid a plastic container from the shelf. He popped the lid. "Homemade and everything, huh? My buddy's mom was from the Philippines and always whipped up homemade lumpia when I went to his house. My favorite deep-fried snack. Looked just like this."

She pointed to the microwave. "Not too long. Maybe a minute. You can start eating that while I'm cooking this."

As he put the container in the microwave, Ashlynn peeled the foil from a bowl of beef strips, marinating in some sauce that made his eyes sting. "You were planning this dinner for a while?"

She cranked up the heat under the wok, and her cheeks sported two red spots. "I was planning to cook this for myself tonight after Mercy dropped off the lumpia. Some of us single people still eat more than takeout and pizza."

"We do?" The microwave beeped and he punched the button with his knuckle to open the door. "I know every pizza delivery place within a five-mile radius of my place in the Marina."

"You live in Marina del Rey? Apartment?"

"Condo."

"Must be nice." She jumped back as the meat sizzled and popped in the pan. "I figured you might live closer to the police station up north."

He'd bought the condo with the proceeds from his dad's rental property in Oregon. Dad had left that property to him and his sister, with his mom's blessing.

"I, uh—" he carefully removed the container from the microwave with the tips of his fingers and dropped it on the counter "—used to work Pacific Division. Transferred to Northeast a few years ago for Vice. The commute's not that bad."

"I have chopsticks on the table, and Mercy included some spicy red chili sauce for dipping. Why don't you dig in while I finish this?"

She prodded the vegetables in the wok and they hissed back at her.

She didn't have to tell him twice. He backed up to the table, grabbed a pair of chopsticks and fished the red sauce from the fridge. He maneuvered a piece of lumpia between his chopsticks and dipped it into the sauce. He closed his eyes while he chewed.

Ashlynn laughed and nudged him with her elbow. "That good, huh?"

"It would be nirvana even if I weren't starving."

"I knew it. You had that rangy, feral look about you." She puffed a lock of hair from her face. "You wanna give me one of those? I'm a little busy here."

He plucked up another lumpia, dunked it in the sauce, and held it out toward her puckered lips, almost as red as the sauce. She took the snack with her teeth and sucked it into her mouth.

Rolling her eyes at the ceiling, she said, "Yummy."

He devoured two more while she finished the stir-fry and the rice cooker clicked off.

Ashlynn grabbed two plates, piled both high with sticky white rice, and ladled the beef and veggies on top. "There's more, if you want seconds."

"I probably will." He brought the wine and the lumpia to the table while she set down the plates.

She collapsed in a chair and then hopped up again. "A corkscrew would be nice—I mean, since you said it wasn't the cheap stuff. The bottle probably doesn't have a screw top."

"It does not." He took the corkscrew from her and did the honors. "Only slightly chilled."

She held the glass to her lips and the reflection of the wine rippled in her eyes as she gazed at him over the edge. "You seem more…human tonight."

He took a swig of the wine and felt the warmth flow through his veins. "I had to tell Mrs. Edmonds today that we'd ID'd Tiana as the body in the vehicle. That kind of conversation tends to awaken your humanity, no matter how far you've buried it."

She cocked her head and ran a finger around the rim of her glass where she'd left a sticky print from her lips. "Why is yours buried?"

He concentrated on scooping up some rice and meat with his chopsticks. "What's the internet saying about Tiana? I'm sure you've already taken a peek in between marinating meat and chopping veggies."

She blinked at his abrupt change of subject and tapped the side of her plate with her chopsticks. "Just the usual speculation—sex worker, trafficking, drugs, online dating gone wrong. Nobody knows about the car yet."

"I'm glad you didn't release that information on your blog. I'm sure it'll get out soon enough, though. Everyone at CREW must know it now, and everyone in parking services at that building."

She raised her eyebrows. "You told me not to release it. I'm still trying to gain your trust, here. It seems like an important detail to withhold, doesn't it? I may be just a blogger, but I have my protocols, as well. If you spew out too much information, you can't discern the crackpots from the people who really know something."

"That's exactly how *we* operate. I figured the more crackpots, the better for you."

She crossed her chopsticks on the edge of her plate. "We really do want to help, you know. It's not all about the clicks. My brother's proudest moments as a true crime blogger were when he actually got to help an investigation."

"Like he thought he was doing with The Player."

"Exactly, even though it cost him his life."

He toyed with a grain of rice on his plate. "That guy I talked to at the mayor's campaign office was supposed to send me a list of campaign workers, highlighting the ones who had access to the vehicles."

"He didn't do it?" She widened her blue eyes, and the smattering of freckles stood out on her nose.

"Nope. I left him a strongly worded voice mail. Now, I'm wondering if they're cleansing the records."

"To protect their own? Why would they want to protect a killer?"

He shrugged. "Their job is to re-elect Wexler. They don't want him to look bad."

"Once it becomes common knowledge that a CREW campaign car is connected to Tiana's death, it's not gonna help. They'll have to go into ultra-spin mode."

"I think they're in that mode right now. Maybe Tiana even worked for the campaign. She was old enough to vote." He dangled a piece of meat over his plate. "This is really good, by the way."

"Thanks. I'm glad you accepted my invitation, though I have a feeling you did so because I caught you at the right moment. No time for lunch today?"

"Busted." He stuffed the meat into his mouth.

They, or rather he, finished the rest of the food, and he washed it down with another half glass of wine. He poured her another glass and volunteered to clean up the kitchen.

As he rinsed the plates at the sink, Ashlynn settled on the couch with her laptop. He said,

"I'm assuming you didn't get anything from Angel since I talked to you today."

"Angel has been mum." The keyboard clicked as her fingers raced across it. "Denver?"

"Yeah?" The tone of her voice caused a dish to slip through his soapy fingers and fall into the sink with a clatter. "Angel?"

"I don't think so, but an important bit of evidence just the same—if it can be believed."

He shut off the water. "What is it?"

"You're not going to find Tiana on the rolls of the campaign workers for Wexler."

"Why is that?"

"Because she worked for his opposition—the Campaign to Elect Veronica Escalante."

Chapter Eight

Ashlynn watched Denver through narrowed eyes, not moving a muscle, her hand hovering over the keyboard. Would he discount her information? Ridicule her sources?

He turned from the sink and wiped his hands on the dishtowel, his eyebrows creating a vee between his eyes. "You're sure it's not from Angel?"

"Funny how you trust Angel all of a sudden. This is from my blog post where I released Tiana's name. It's among the responses." She squinted at the screen. "It already has over a hundred up-votes and a few theories attached to it."

He balled up the towel in his hands and tossed it onto the counter. "Theories but not corroborating proof. Who is this person who posted the link between Tiana and Escalante's campaign?"

"You really wanna know?" She wedged the soles of her sneakers against the edge of the coffee table and expelled a breath. "It was Lil' Snoop."

Denver snorted and cranked on the water to finish the dishes. "We're supposed to believe a statement from someone called Lil' Snoop?"

"It's more than anything coming from someone called LAPD Detective."

"Ouch."

"Think about it, Denver. The LAPD didn't release the information that the car in the lake belonged to the CREW. That's a hell of a coincidence that Lil' Snoop knows Tiana worked for the opposition campaign without knowing she was found in a CREW car."

He retrieved the dishtowel and carefully dried the wok as if it were made of priceless crystal. "The LAPD didn't release that information, but like I said, someone else could have."

Ashlynn's blood boiled and she smacked her palm against her chest. "Me? Is that what you're saying? You think I released that info?"

He waved the dishtowel like a white flag. "I didn't say that."

"You didn't have to. I got the message." She shoved off the couch, clutching the sides of her laptop. "Do you want to see? You read my blog today. I didn't mention the connection to Mayor Wexler."

"I believe you, but there are others who

knew. The CREW knew—at least, Amalia and Christian."

"You said they wanted to hush it up. That's not something they're going to voluntarily release." She perched on the arm of her couch, balancing her laptop on her knees, her temper cooling. "Even if that information did get out, it doesn't mean Lil' Snoop is wrong."

"Okay, what cred does this… Snoop have? Is he or she a regular poster on the blog?" Denver shook out the towel and hung it over the oven door handle.

"He is a regular poster and seems to have inside information. He won't tell us his profession, but he has connections in the city. He's usually right. He posts publicly, but he's never messaged me privately." She slid onto a cushion of the couch and crooked her finger at Denver. "Come here. I'll show you how it looks, and you can read the theories with me."

He joined her on the couch, the sleeves of his dress shirt rolled up, exposing strong forearms corded with veins and muscle. He looked as if he were capable of doing a lot more than the dishes.

He hunched over her shoulder, smelling of dish soap and hot chilies. "Okay, let me see what Snoop has."

She scooted the laptop closer to his legs and jabbed a finger at the screen. "This is his first post—a comment to my blog update naming the victim as Tiana Fuller."

Denver's shoulder pressed against hers as he bent forward for a closer look. "He made that comment less than an hour after your post. That's fast work. I'm still waiting to get the list of names from the CREW."

"Looks legit, right? He doesn't mention the car from Wexler's campaign because he doesn't know about it."

Denver rubbed his knuckles across his sexy stubble. "If this guy's so plugged in, why doesn't he know about the car?"

"That's the beauty of the citizen sleuth." She drew a circle in the air over the screen. "It's small pieces coming together. One person knows one thing. Someone else knows something else. There are people from all walks of life chiming in."

"What I want to know is why these people aren't coming to the police. Why didn't this Lil' Whoever call the LAPD with this information?" He sat back against the couch and shoved a hand through his dark hair.

"There are lots of reasons, Denver. In Lil' Snoop's case, it could be that he'd get in trouble for releasing information. Some people don't want to go on record. Some people don't want the cops sniffing around."

"Great." He slumped, kicking out one leg, resting his shoe on her coffee table. "I'm going to have to make a visit to the Escalante campaign tomorrow to check this out, after I talk to Tiana's parents. I need to get a list of her friends, boyfriends, her phone carrier—that is, unless you can get all that from your blog."

"Silly." She slugged his hard bicep. "Even I know this stuff isn't admissible evidence for a search warrant."

He raised an eyebrow. "Ever hear of anonymous sources? I'm not going to serve a search warrant on Councilwoman Escalante's campaign headquarters, anyway. I'll just drop by for a friendly visit."

"Weird, isn't it?"

"That Tiana worked for one campaign and was found dead in the car of another? Yeah, weird." He tipped his head toward the computer. "What's the theory online?"

"That someone from Wexler's campaign murdered her to make Escalante look bad."

"And stuffed her in a Wexler car? How's that gonna work out for them?"

"The posters don't know she was found in a CREW car, though, do they?"

"But we do." Denver chewed on his bottom lip, his dark eyes unreadable.

Did the *we* mean him and her, or the LAPD?

She asked, "Do you have a theory of your own?"

"Not yet. I want to talk to her parents first. I want to get to know Tiana."

"Sadly, it's too late for that." Her bottom lip trembled as she thought about that poor young woman in the trunk of the car.

Denver sat up sharply. "I can't save her now, but I can find her killer and get her and her family some justice. That's the thing with being a homicide detective. We come in after the damage has already been done. We're not expected to save anyone, except by getting a killer off the streets."

His vehemence had startled her, as if he were defending his role in the criminal justice process.

"That's huge. You are saving countless, nameless, faceless others by tracking down a killer. Look at The Player copycats. Each time the task force apprehended one of the copycats, it saved the lives of others in their murderous paths."

"That's the idea. Even if Tiana's killer has no intention of striking again, he needs to be brought to justice. I'll get him."

His jaw hardened, and she believed him. She just hoped he'd let her help.

THE FOLLOWING MORNING, Ashlynn rolled onto her side and opened one eye. She stretched her arm across the other side of the bed and smoothed her hand over the undisturbed bedspread. She slept in a king-sized bed, but she barely moved in her sleep. Making the bed consisted of flipping up the covers and tucking in the side of the sheet.

It had been a long time since someone had messed up that other side of the bed. Her ex-boyfriend had been a cheater, and she hadn't felt like venturing into the dating world since. Then Sean had been murdered, and dating had slipped further down her list of priorities.

Her hand bunched the smooth sheets next to her. Didn't mean she didn't miss a body next to hers—especially a body like Detective Denver Holt's.

Despite the sexual tension between them last night, Denver had kept things professional. Or maybe the tension was hers alone.

Sighing, she scooted from the bed and flicked up the corner. Before she even hit the bathroom, she pulled her laptop onto the bed and accessed her blog.

People had gone crazy over the "The Girl in the Lake" story. Her scoop on the victim's name last night had resulted in an overload of comments. The LAPD had sent a news release to the mainstream media, and Tiana's name and picture were all over the internet now...but she'd been first with it.

She owed Denver, big-time, and she had to

deliver more than dinner if she hoped to keep the flow of information coming. She sent a private message to Angel, asking if she was okay and if she'd known Tiana. Ashlynn didn't expect a response, but she wanted Angel to know she still trusted her even after the debacle in Venice.

One idea of how she could help Denver had come to her as she'd drifted off to sleep last night. The plan looked even better in the light of day, and she'd put it into action as soon as she could.

She showered and dressed young—jeans, T-shirt, tennis shoes—pretty much how she usually dressed, leaving off the makeup and scooping her hair into a high ponytail. The sun had come through early this morning, and one of those warm, So Cal spring days called out to everyone to abandon the office and stick their toes in the sand.

Her office didn't resemble most nine-to-five joints, but she couldn't ditch work anyway.

As she nibbled on the edge of a piece of toast spread with crunchy peanut butter, her cell phone buzzed. She wiped her fingers on a napkin and studied the display. Sean always said unknown numbers were the best kind.

She answered with a cautious note to her voice. "Hello?"

"Ashlynn Hughes?" The woman on the line

didn't wait for confirmation before launching ahead. "This is Megan Wright with KTOP. Your blog, *LA Confidential*, published Tiana Fuller's name as the victim in the submerged car in Lake Kawayu before the LAPD released its news item to the press. How did you get that information?"

Ashlynn swallowed. As a news reporter, Megan should know all about confidential sources, and Detective Denver Holt was the most confidential source she'd ever had.

She took a small sip of orange juice. "Hi, Megan. I have my sources, just like you do, and they are every bit as confidential. I'm not at liberty to release the name of my source."

"Got a live one, huh?" Megan chuckled. "Good for you. I, and everyone else, am going to be keeping my eye on the blog. You also found the body. Did that come from this source, as well?"

"No comment." Ashlynn dabbed at a few crumbs on her plate and sucked them into her mouth.

"Are the cops all over you on this yet?"

"No comment."

"Okay, okay. Just keep me in mind for…anything." Megan coughed and lowered her voice. "And I want to tell you how sorry I was about Sean's death. I almost feel responsible."

Ashlynn's hand moved up to her throat. "You?

How? The Player killed Sean for working with one of his copycats."

"I knew your brother, had collaborated with him on a few things. I'm the one who suggested his blog as a means of communication between the copycat killer and Detective McAllister." The polished reporter sucked in a breath and her voice wavered. "I wish I had never done it."

"Don't blame yourself. Sean would've killed for that opportunity. You knew that, and gave it to him. Instead, *he* got killed, but you couldn't have predicted that. Nobody could."

She sniffed. "Just know I considered your brother a friend, and if there's anything I can do for you, just ask."

Sounded like she could do a lot more for Megan than the reporter could do for her. "I'll keep it in mind, and thanks for your condolences."

Ashlynn dumped her plate in the sink, checked her locks and grabbed her keys.

Wouldn't Megan Wright like to know where she was headed right now? Wouldn't Detective Denver Holt? She had no intention of telling either one.

Forty-five minutes later, she breezed through the double glass doors of Veronica Escalante's campaign headquarters. She surveyed the room, bustling with phones and computer activity, but that lasted only a few seconds as a man emerged from one of the offices with a view of the room. He barreled toward her, a used-car-salesman smile on his lips and suspicious beady eyes drilling into her.

"Can I help you?"

She cocked her head, her ponytail swinging behind her. "I hope I can help you. I'm Jenny Cochrane. I'm a poli-sci major at UCLA, and I'd love to volunteer for Councilwoman Escalante's campaign for mayor."

"Excellent. I'm Jed Gordon, Veronica's campaign manager." He snapped his fingers in the air. "You can fill out a form with a few details about yourself, and we'll put you to work."

"Sweet." Ashlynn clasped her hands in front of her. "I have some time now before my classes start. Is there something I can help out with?"

Jed's snaps had produced a decidedly less enthusiastic campaign volunteer, who shuffled toward them, brushing long, black hair from her face and pouting with a pair of collagen-injected lips.

Jed spared the volunteer a quick glance and said, "How are your envelope-stuffing skills?"

Ashlynn held her hands up and wiggled her fingers. "Top-notch."

The dark-haired woman snickered and asked, "What do you want?"

Jed's lips stretched into a smile. "Lulu, this is Jenny. She's a new volunteer. Can you get a form for her to fill out and show her what we're doing with the envelopes?"

Lulu grunted and turned on her heel.

Jed rolled his eyes at Ashlynn. "Follow Lulu. She'll show you what to do."

Ashlynn nodded and joined Lulu at a table where two other people were stuffing a folded sheet of paper into a preprinted envelope.

Lulu sat and shoved a chair toward Ashlynn with her foot. "Sit down. I don't know why Jed thinks someone needs to learn how to stuff envelopes, but if I sit here for a while with you, he'll stay off my back."

Ashlynn took the chair next to Lulu's. The longer she kept the surly campaign worker at the table, the longer she could avoid filling out any form.

Picking up a sheet of paper and an envelope, Ashlynn asked, "Don't you want to be here? I'm so excited about Councilwoman Escalante's chances. I think she'd be great for this city."

Lulu dug her elbows into the table and propped up her chin with her hands. "I'd rather be anywhere else, but my last name is Escalante. Veronica's my sister, so I sort of have to be here."

Ashlynn's pulse ticked up. Lulu could be a great source of information about the campaign and her sister. She shoved the paper into the envelope and raised her eyebrows. "Escalante? I thought the councilwoman was married."

"She's married to Kent Meadows. Can't get more Anglo than that." Lulu tapped her long, purple nails on the table. "But she keeps her maiden name to pretend she still cares about *la raza*. As if anyone from the old neighborhood is fooled. She's married to a freakin' billionaire."

Veronica's husband must be the same Meadows as Meadows Developments, who had signs and projects all over the city.

Lulu couldn't be a worse ambassador for her sister—and a better source of dirt. "What do you do when you're not helping your sister run for political office?"

"Mostly get into trouble." Lulu flipped her hair over her shoulder and laughed. "That's why she wants to keep me busy, but I don't think old Jed likes me here."

Ashlynn couldn't imagine why. "Oh, really?"

Lulu wasn't listening. Her gaze had traveled over Ashlynn's shoulder and her dark eyes sparkled. "*Hay, papi*. He's fine."

Ashlynn twisted her head to the side and froze as her gaze collided with Denver's stormy eyes.

Chapter Nine

Denver almost tripped over his own feet as he walked into Escalante's campaign headquarters and saw Ashlynn sitting there stuffing envelopes and chatting with a woman who looked like an escapee from the Kardashian compound.

But he didn't break his stride as he followed Jed Gordon to an office in the back of the room. What the hell was Ashlynn doing here? He hoped she'd planned on telling him about this little undercover stint—they had a deal.

"Please, have a seat, Detective. What can I do for you?" Gordon pointed to a chair across from a desk piled high with papers and folders.

Escalante's campaign headquarters buzzed but had nowhere near the activity of Mayor Wexler's office, and it didn't warrant his good suit. He fished his notebook from his pocket. "We have reason to believe Tiana Fuller, the victim of a homicide, worked for Councilwoman Escalante's campaign."

Gordon's black eyes flickered. Then he skimmed a hand over his shaved head. "That's terrible. Is this the same young woman who was found in the trunk of that car in the lake?"

"It is." Denver dropped his chin to his chest but didn't break eye contact with Gordon. "Did you know Tiana?"

"No." Gordon steepled his fingers and peered at Denver over the point. "We have a lot of volunteers, Detective. Some just wander in and out of this office, happy to do what they can to ensure a victory for Veronica."

Denver winced as he recognized one of Escalante's campaign slogans—Victory for Veronica. These political types never took a break.

"Maybe you'd recognize her face?" He slid the picture of Tiana her mother had provided from his pocket and positioned it on the desk, facing Gordon. "Does she look familiar?"

Gordon squinted at the picture as if bringing it into focus. "Pretty girl, but she doesn't look familiar to me. Like I said, we have a lot of volunteers coming off the streets to help out. Can I ask who gave you the information that this young woman worked for Veronica's campaign?"

"You can ask, but I can't tell you." Denver snatched the picture back. "Maybe some of the volunteers might recognize her."

Gordon blinked but not before his gaze shifted

to the window on the busy room. "Sure. You can leave her picture here, and I'll ask around."

Denver pressed the picture to his chest. "I just got this from her mother, and I have only one. I'll do the asking."

"Of course." Gordon pushed back his chair, all feigned eagerness.

"Before we go out there, can you provide me with a list of people who work for Councilwoman Escalante's campaign? Do you have a database of names or something?"

"We do." He brushed his fingers across his computer's keyboard. "I can have someone provide that for you."

"It must be a small list." Denver rested his hand on the doorknob and made a half turn.

"Small?" Gordon rubbed his hands together. "I assure you, we have a lot of volunteers on our team. We're much more grassroots than Mayor Wexler's campaign."

Denver wrinkled his brow, practicing his best dumb cop look. "Oh, you were so sure Tiana didn't work for Escalante's campaign, I thought you must know the names of all the volunteers."

Gordon's lips tightened for a second. "I'm sorry if I gave you the impression that Ms. Fuller never worked here. I just meant I'd never heard of her, nor seen her around the office."

"Okay. Maybe someone else has, or maybe

her name will be on your list." Denver stepped out of the office and ignored Ashlynn.

He started on the other side of the room and flashed Tiana's picture to the volunteers, as Gordon stayed close, breathing down his neck.

He saved Ashlynn's station for last. He placed Tiana's photo in the middle of the table. "Have any of you ever seen this woman working here or at any events for Councilwoman Escalante?"

As they all shook their heads and murmured, a chair scraped against the floor. The woman Ashlynn had been talking to earlier, bumped against the table, shifting it.

She covered her mouth with her hand. "Oops, sorry."

Denver asked, "Have you seen her?"

"Me?" She flicked a long fingernail against what had to be fake eyelashes. "No."

Denver stepped back. "Okay. Thanks for your cooperation."

Gordon walked him to the door. "I'll email you that list of volunteers as soon as I get it, Detective Holt."

"Thank you for your cooperation." Denver shook the other man's hand.

As soon as he slid into his sedan, he texted Ashlynn to meet him for lunch someplace far far away from Escalante's campaign headquarters and the beady eyes of Jed Gordon. She had some explaining to do.

A half hour later, when he got to the almost-empty Mexican restaurant, he had the luxury of selecting a booth in the back. The waitress approached the table with a basket of chips and salsa. "Water?"

"Two, please, and I'll take a coffee."

By the time Ashlynn showed up, peering at him through the dark restaurant, he'd munched through half the chips and downed his black coffee.

She paused at the table and studied the picture of Pancho Villa over their table. "Out of all the Mexican restaurants in LA, you picked this one?"

"Serves our purposes—big, dark, and nowhere near Escalante's headquarters." He pointed a chip at the seat across from him. "You wanna tell me what you were doing there?"

She plopped onto the vinyl banquette and gulped down some ice water. "Thought I'd do a little undercover investigation work."

"You're not afraid of getting recognized?"

"Did you see my picture anywhere on *LA Confidential*? It's not there for a reason. I don't do social media. Or, at least, I don't post any pictures of myself on my accounts." She grabbed a chip and dipped it in the salsa. "I'm not visible like a Megan Wright. Nobody there recognized Jenny Cochrane, or I'm sure Jed wouldn't have allowed me to stick around stuffing envelopes."

"He didn't ask you for ID or anything?"

"In case you didn't notice, that room wasn't exactly a beehive of activity, was it? Looks like they're a little short on volunteers." She waved her second chip in the air. "I was supposed to fill out some form with my name, address—that kind of thing—but I avoided it, and I'll keep on avoiding it."

"Keep on?" He stopped when the waitress hovered, asking if they were ready to order. He'd already studied the plastic menu and ordered a chicken burrito and a refill on his coffee.

Ashlynn ran her finger down the lunch specials. "I'll have the two chicken tacos, but can I get a side salad instead of rice and beans? And a diet whatever."

He leaned forward once the waitress left. "You plan to go back there?"

"I'm going to work the sister."

His hand holding the water glass jerked and the ice tinkled against the sides. "Sister?"

"Lourdes Escalante, goes by Lulu—black hair, long nails, eyelash extensions—total Kardashian vibe."

"That woman is Veronica Escalante's sister?"

"Sort of the black sheep, from what I can

gather. No fan of her sister's." Ashlynn tilted her head and her ponytail swung over her shoulder. "Didn't you see what happened when you showed her the picture of Tiana?"

"The business with the chair?"

"That wasn't Lulu. That was Jed kicking the leg of her chair. I guess you couldn't see it because you were on the other side of the table. He was obviously warning her off talking about Tiana."

Denver wiped his hands on the napkin and dropped it back in his lap. "It didn't seem like the others knew Tiana because Jed didn't have to warn any of them."

"I don't know." She shrugged. "Lulu's going to be closer to the inner workings of the campaign, whether she likes it or not—and she doesn't. She hates working there."

Denver chewed on his bottom lip. "They might be hiding the fact that Tiana worked there to distance themselves from her murder, but wouldn't Tiana have told someone about working for the campaign? I'm meeting with her parents this afternoon. I'll ask them about it."

The waitress returned with their food, sliding his burrito in front of him and refilling his coffee.

As Ashlynn fluffed up her salad with her fork,

she wrinkled her nose. "That's a huge burrito, and it's almost too early for lunch."

"Tell me about it, but I figured it would be less crowded here at eleven, and I wanted to talk to you before I met with Mr. and Mrs. Edmonds." He sliced the end off his burrito and steam rose, warning him to back off. "I'm glad I did. I didn't even notice Jed nudging Lulu's chair. She complied, though, didn't she? Kept mum about Tiana."

"Not for long." She poked her chest with the end of her fork. "I'm going to get it out of her."

"How do you plan to do that? Especially if Jed is hovering in the background."

"He's busy in the office, on the phone. He doesn't have time to watch Lulu, and he has no reason to suspect I'm after anything but the thrill of working on a political campaign."

He smirked at her fresh face. "Laid it on thick, huh?"

"I did, and I know just how to get Lulu to open up. I pretended to be slightly shocked by every little thing she said today, and she enjoyed the effect her words had on me. I'll keep that up. Keep supplying the drama for her and she'll keep opening up more and more. Lulu doesn't much like her brother-in-law, either, Kent Meadows. *The* Kent Meadows."

Denver whistled. "His name is plastered all

over the city. You'd think Veronica would want to use it for name recognition alone."

"Not sure about that, but according to Lulu, Kent is backing his wife's political aspirations."

"You *did* get a lot out of Lulu. Maybe you missed your calling. Instead of a journalist, you should've been a therapist."

The corner of her eye twitched. "No, thanks. I've had enough of those."

He avoided her gaze and sawed off another piece of his burrito. She seemed too well adjusted to require the services of a therapist. But what did he know? The department had been telling him for years to see a shrink, and he thought he was pretty balanced, too. At least once he stopped caring about anyone enough to obsessively worry, he'd been fine.

"Nothing more on your blog? Anyone talking about Lil' Snoop's claim that Tiana worked for the Escalante campaign?"

"Just more political intrigue theories. Wait until they find out about the CREW car. Are you releasing that information?"

"We are. It's going to get out anyway. The parking attendant in the building where the CREW is located already knows something is up. And once the mainstream media—no offense—pick up the story about Tiana possibly working for Escalante, things are going to heat up in the mayor's race."

She held up her taco, which dripped onto her plate. "No offense taken. If the LAPD can't verify that Tiana worked there, though, they may drop the story. If Jed doesn't have a record of Tiana being a volunteer or her parents don't confirm she worked there, it may be a nonstory."

"Or people will confuse the campaigns when they find out the car was from Wexler's. They might think she volunteered for Wexler."

She crunched into her taco and a shower of shredded lettuce fell to her plate. "It is a coincidence, though, isn't it? I mean, maybe her death has nothing to do with the campaigns."

"Maybe." He lifted his shoulders. "But even if another campaign worker murdered her for personal reasons, it ain't gonna look good for the candidate."

"Politics is a dirty business." She dabbed her mouth with a napkin, leaving a string of lettuce in the wisps of hair framing her face.

He reached forward and plucked it free. Holding it up on his finger, he said, "Lettuce in your hair."

"Yikes, can't take me anywhere."

He'd take her anywhere and everywhere. Maybe he needed to take a step back and evaluate why he'd agreed to cooperate with her. Was it because of Tiana and the case, or because he just wanted to be close to her?

He didn't need to be close to her—or anyone.

"Almost done?" He pushed away his plate with the half-eaten burrito.

She had just crunched into her second taco and waved her hand in front of her mouth as she chewed. She swallowed and took a sip of her soda. "You're done already? I'd like to finish this taco."

"You were right. It is too early to eat lunch. I'll take this with me and finish it at my desk." He checked his phone. "I gotta go back to the station right now and write up a few things before meeting with Tiana's mom and stepdad."

Ashlynn's face blanched and her lush lips tightened into a frown. "You go ahead. I'm going to finish my lunch."

As he tossed his napkin on the table and reached for his wallet, she held out her hand. "That's okay. I'll take care of the bill."

He plucked out a twenty and a ten and dropped them on the table. "I got it. You paid for dinner last night, and you gave me some good info today."

She dragged her napkin from her lap and pressed it against her chest. "You don't have to pay me for information."

"I didn't mean it like that. I'll touch base later,

if I have anything else to share." He stood and raised his hand. "Take care, Ashlynn."

He spun around and walked blindly toward the exit as Ashlynn called after him. "You forgot your burrito."

He'd forgotten more than his burrito. He'd forgotten his vow never to care for anyone ever again—at least, nobody alive.

Chapter Ten

Ashlynn's nose stung as she dabbed the tip of her finger on a drop of hot sauce in her plate. "Jerk."

The guy had done a one-eighty on her—one minute scarfing down chips and salsa and discussing the case with her, the next throwing down his napkin and practically running for the exit.

She sighed and poked her fork at her unfinished taco. He'd probably prefer to work with Sean, too. She'd had no business taking over *LA Confidential*. She would never reach the heights Sean had reached.

She dropped the fork and squared her shoulders. *Stop doing this to yourself, Ashlynn...and eat.* Detective Holt wasn't anything special—arrogant, hostile—and she could see through it all to the part of him that desperately wanted to be a full-fledged homicide detective.

She scooped up her taco and took a big bite with a smile on her face. She'd uncovered a lot more about this case than he had. What had he given her? The pleasure of his company, that's it. And that hadn't turned out to be much.

Shoving the rest of the taco in her mouth, she waved to the waitress. "Can you please bring me a box for this burrito?"

"Sure." She pointed at the money on the table. "Do you want me to take this?"

"Yes." Ashlynn leaned back against the banquette and patted her full stomach. He'd just paid for her lunch *and* her dinner.

BY THE TIME she'd made it home after running a few errands, proofreading her freelance article on public art spaces in LA, and having an online meeting with her web designer, Denver's burrito had turned into a soggy mess. She'd dumped the whole thing in her sink and run the disposal with gusto.

He hadn't contacted her the rest of the day, so she didn't know how his meeting with Tiana's parents had lasted—not that he owed her anything. In fact, it seemed as if he didn't think he owed her anything at all.

This relationship had been a one-way street—in many ways.

She swung open the fridge door and surveyed the packed shelves. After she'd recovered from her eating disorder, her therapist had recommended that she keep food in her kitchen—healthy stuff. She just figured she'd have some of that stir-fry left, so she wouldn't have to cook again tonight. But Denver Holt had gobbled up everything in sight last night—everything but her. She slammed the fridge door shut.

One night of In-N-Out with animal fries wasn't going to make her relapse. As she grabbed her keys, her cell phone buzzed.

Her heart flip-flopped in her chest when she saw Lulu's name. The two of them had exchanged numbers while working together today. She'd given Lulu her real number, as she didn't mention *LA Confidential* on her voice-mail greeting for this phone. She kept a separate phone for the blog.

She pitched her voice higher with an excitement she didn't have to fake. "Hi, Lulu. Wassup?"

"Girl, you left the building so fast, I didn't get a chance to tell you about the fundraiser tonight."

"Fundraiser?" Her voice positively squeaked.

"It's the best part of working for this stupid campaign—the only good part. All the volunteers are always invited to the fundraisers. I'm not saying we don't have to run around like gofers sometimes, but the food's usually good, there's valet parking, and the booze is first rate… and free. Can't get better than that."

"Perfect. I'm always down for free booze. Where and when? And are you sure it's okay if I'm there? I just started today. For all you know, I might never come back."

"I don't care about that, and Jed's not gonna notice you one way or the other—not with my sister in the room." Lulu huffed out a breath. "The fundraiser is at my sister's house in Sherman Oaks. It's up in the hills, off Beverly Glen with all the other mansions. I'll text you the address. It starts at seven, but show up closer to eight when it'll be more crowded."

"So I can sneak in? Are you sure it's okay?" she asked again, unsure.

"You're not sneaking. You're a volunteer. Grassroots and all that. It's just that the food will be circulating by then, and it's easier to snag drinks without certain people watching you."

All of a sudden, Ashlynn was starving. "Sounds dank. What should I wear?"

"If you're looking for a sugar daddy, you can go slinky cocktail. If you wanna come off as the dedicated kiss-ass, dress down from there."

"Thanks for thinking of me, Lulu. I can squeeze in a little more studying by eight. You'll be there by then?"

"I'm already here. I live in this hellhole known as my sister's house."

As soon as they ended the call, Lulu texted her Veronica's address. Lulu had just presented her with the perfect opportunity to get close to the Escalante campaign. Nobody there would know her face.

She scanned through her contacts for Denver's personal cell. Her finger hovered over his name for a second, and then she tossed the phone onto the kitchen counter. If he wanted to cool things down, she could be ice cold.

In the end, she dressed somewhere between sugar baby and earnest young volunteer. She straightened the hem of her little black dress and stepped into the black sandals, waiting in front of the mirror. She released her hair from her ponytail and fluffed it around her shoulders.

When she slid behind the wheel of her car, she tapped in the address for Veronica Escalante's house. If the GPS took her by way of the Valley, she'd force it to change. Even at this time of night, she didn't want to chance traffic out to the Valley. She'd go up the back way and take Mulholland.

Forty-five minutes later, Ashlynn negotiated the hairpin turns on Mulholland to reach Escalante's house in the hills. She rolled to a stop behind a line of cars waiting for the valet parking attendants.

How much money would Escalante raise to ultimately lose to Mayor Wexler? What would her campaign do to make sure she didn't lose?

An attendant in a white shirt and red vest jogged up to her car and she popped the locks. He opened her door. "Good evening, miss."

That was a nice touch. "Hello. Just leave the keys in the ignition?"

"Yes, miss. We'll take care of your car."

She surveyed the gleaming luxury vehicles ahead of and behind her in the line. She had a lot less to worry about with her VW than the rest of these well-heeled donors. "I'm sure you will. Thanks."

As she exited the car, she hitched her small black purse across her body. Her heels crunched the gravel as she made her way toward the gates of the house until she hit the pavers on the circular driveway.

The double doors stood open and lights bathed the beautiful garden in front. Ashlynn inhaled the heady scent of jasmine and ducked behind a couple approaching the broad steps fronting the Tudor-style mansion.

Who knew sitting on the LA city council paid so well? But then, Veronica had her own, private wealthy donor.

As soon as she and the couple made it over the threshold, a waiter appeared, bearing a tray of champagne flutes glimmering with the golden liquid. Ashlynn lifted a glass and took a small sip while sidling against a wall to take in the spectacle.

She'd never moved in political circles and neither had her parents, despite their wealth, but these folks knew how to live it up. She snatched a little pastry puff of something from a tray that floated by and stuffed it into her mouth. Shrimp. She hadn't eaten since she'd forced herself to finish that taco from her early lunch with Denver.

She zigzagged her way through the crowd to reach the pretty display of food and lifted a small plate from the stack.

"Told you." Lulu appeared next to her, dressed to kill in a slinky red number with cutouts along the sides and a deep V, clinging to all of Lulu's dangerous curves. "The food is worth the boredom."

"You don't look like you're planning on boredom." Ashlynn piled a few shrimp puffs on her plate, some bacon-wrapped scallops, a couple of tiny ribs and a piece of bruschetta.

Lulu winked. "Sometimes you get lucky."

"Does your sister know you troll for—" Ashlynn waved the bread in the air "—luck at her fundraisers?"

"How do you think she snagged her rich husband? He's gotta have at least twenty years on her. So, as long as I keep it hush-hush, she doesn't care what I do." Lulu narrowed her heavily made-up eyes. "She hates publicity—the bad kind."

Like a campaign volunteer showing up dead in the trunk of a submerged car.

"Who doesn't?" Ashlynn licked some barbecue sauce from her finger and grabbed a napkin. "You don't have to babysit me. I'm gonna make my way through this food, grab a few more glasses of champagne, and flirt with that bartender."

"Don't sell yourself short. You're cute in a wholesome kind of way. These older guys vibe on that." Lulu smoothed her dress over her hips and shimmied her shoulders. "I got a line on one now."

Ashlynn watched Lulu sashay across the room toward a huddle of men old enough to be her father. At least Lulu's game plan would leave her alone long enough to snoop around.

As she stood with her plate, shoveling enough little appetizers in her mouth to make up a three-course meal, Ashlynn sized up the room. She could distinguish the donors from the hangers-on or charity cases by their clothing, and Veronica Escalante was no slouch as a clotheshorse.

Ashlynn could spot the councilwoman's designer shoes with the red soles, as she worked her way through the crowd schmoozing.

Ashlynn hadn't been lying to Denver when she'd told him she'd written fashion articles for an e-magazine, but she hadn't told him she knew clothes inside and out because her mother had been a model. Her mother had lived and breathed fashion, and had tried to make it the center of Ashlynn's life, too.

She'd fallen short, literally by one inch, of her mom's willowy five-foot-ten-inch frame, which had only increased her mother's pressure on her to stay thin.

She'd showed her. Ashlynn had become a pro at staying thin.

Ashlynn had left her champagne glass at the end of the table where she'd started, but had no desire to finish the drink. She stashed her empty plate on a tray by the door and asked the cute bartender for a Coke with a lime on the side.

She'd already spotted the other volunteers and made her way to where they stood in a clump by the patio door, which led to a sparkling pool. She hung on the edge of the group, her hand curled around the highball glass.

A lull in their conversation offered her an in. She cleared her throat. "What did you all think about that cop flashing that girl's picture around this afternoon?"

One of the guys glanced her way, and a spark of recognition lit his dark eyes. "Oh, you just started today, huh?"

"Yeah, that's me." She raised her hand as if she were sitting in a classroom. "The new girl."

The man patted his chest. "I'm Andre. This is Sydney, Bryant, and Karis."

"I'm Jenny." Ashlynn nodded to the group, raising her glass.

Sydney, a young woman with a sleek, blond ponytail, definitely dressed for eager political asset, asked. "You work fast. Your first day and you made it to a gala."

"Lulu invited me today."

Sydney's eyes widened. "Lulu invited you here?"

"Y-yeah. Should I not be here?"

"No, we're always invited. It's just that Lulu isn't the friendliest person in the office." Sydney cupped a hand around her mouth. "You know she's Veronica's sister, right?"

"I do. She was friendly to me." Ashlynn plucked the lime from the edge of her glass and squeezed it into the Coke. "I guess nobody knew the girl in that picture."

Andre patted the side of his short Afro. "We didn't know her, but we knew who she was—

that murdered girl. We still can't figure out why the po-po came around asking questions."

Ashlynn tipped her head and wrinkled her nose. "I think I heard the cop say something to Jed about that girl working for Veronica's campaign."

Karis, the petite Latina, grabbed Sydney's arm "No way. She worked for Veronica? I never saw her in the office."

"That's crap." Bryant finally spoke, pushing his hipster black-rimmed glasses up on his nose. "None of us ever saw her. She didn't work for the campaign. Maybe she was one of those wannabes who get all excited and then lose interest after they make one phone call. They come and go. How about you, Jenny? You a wannabe?"

"Me?" Ashlynn put her hand over her heart. "I'm all-in."

She jiggled the ice in her drink and took a sip. No Jed here to coach them. They honestly didn't know Tiana, had never seen her at the office, but that didn't mean Lulu didn't know the dead woman. She hadn't imagined Jed's nudge to the chair when Denver showed Lulu Tiana's picture.

"If you are sticking around, here's a pro tip." Karis tapped her finger against her head. "Stay away from Kent."

Ashlynn widened her eyes as her pulse jumped. "Kent Meadows, Veronica's husband."

"Yeah, he's a creeper." Karis hugged herself. "Right, Sydney?"

The blonde nodded solemnly. "Total manther."

"'Manther'?" Ashlynn had to show her ignorance if she wanted the answer.

Karis giggled and tossed her dark curls. "You know. Instead of a cougar, an older woman going after young guys, he's a manther. Cougar…panther…manther."

Ashlynn wrinkled her nose. "Yuck."

Sydney waved her drink toward the patio. "I see someone lighting up on the other side of the pool. Anyone want to keep me company?"

Bryant answered, "Only if you let me bum a ciggie off you."

As the two of them wandered off, Ashlynn jerked her thumb over her shoulder. "I'm going to get some more free booze before they cut us off."

If Lulu was the one who knew about Tiana, then she should be talking to Lulu. She propped up the wall next to the bar and scanned the room, her gaze meeting Jed's for a split second.

His ankle-length slacks and no-socks ensemble screamed, *I'm trying hard to look fresh*. But at least he glanced away, not recognizing her, and she turned her head so he wouldn't catch her on the double-take—not that she didn't have every right to be there. The other volunteers had showed up, and she'd been personally invited by Lulu, although there didn't seem to be any love lost between Lulu and Jed.

She spied Lulu chatting up an older man in a pair of nice slacks, a black T and a mustard-colored jacket. It worked. He looked put together with a personal twist. He stroked his salt-and-pepper beard, while leaning toward Lulu and her cleavage.

Ashlynn gripped her glass and threaded her way through the crowd to reach Lulu and her conquest.

Attaching herself to the duo, she said, "Great turnout."

Lulu's seductive stance changed in a second as she gave Ashlynn a pointed look. "Yeah, great. Jenny, this is Syngin Parish. Syngin, one of our volunteers."

"Nice to meet you, Jenny." Syngin gave her hand the briefest of squeezes before dropping it. He wanted her gone as much as Lulu did.

"You, too. Thanks for supporting Council-woman Escalante. She'll do great things for the city."

Syngin's blue eyes sparkled with amusement. "I've known Veronica's husband, Kent Mead-ows, for years. I'm afraid I'm not very political."

"Everyone needs the support of friends." She winked.

Lulu drilled a knuckle into Ashlynn's back. "You should go find Jed and show him your face for a few brownie points."

"Oh, I will." She put a finger on her chin. "Speaking of the office, did Lulu tell you that a LAPD detective came to the campaign headquarters today asking if we knew that murdered girl, Tiana Fuller?"

Syngin's face didn't register any change at all, but Lulu stiffened beside her.

"I didn't hear that. I heard about the body in the lake, but I didn't know she was connected to the campaign."

"Because she's not." Lulu squeezed Ashlynn's upper arm, her long nails digging into her flesh. "If you actually want to help the campaign, Jenny, you won't talk about murders."

Ashlynn covered her mouth with her hand. "I'm so sorry. I just thought it was weird he was there. Nobody knew her, so he must've been wrong."

Syngin flashed his very white teeth. "You don't have to worry about me. As I said, I'm apolitical. I'm just here to support Kent and Veronica—and because I have lots of money."

"I knew there was something I liked about you." Lulu tugged on the sleeve of the mustard jacket, fluttering her lash extensions.

Ashlynn had never felt more like a third

wheel. "I'm going to find Jed, grab some more food and head out. Thanks for the invite, Lulu."

Syngin and Lulu barely noticed her departure as she slipped back into the crowd. She didn't want to draw Jed's attention to her, but it sounded like Lulu would tell him she was at the party, anyway. She might as well touch base.

She studied each knot of people and those wandering in and out of the house. Was Jed a smoker? She stepped outside onto the patio and stood at the water's edge, squinting at the smokers across the pool.

A leaf drifted from one of the trees, which must create a natural umbrella for the patio, and landed in the water. Ashlynn meandered around the curve of the pool and ducked down, scooping the leaf from the lapping water with her hand.

Before she rose from her crouch, she heard whispers from the clump of trees. Holding her breath, she stayed down and strained to hear the voices. A man and a woman went back and forth in heated conversation, but she couldn't make out the words.

Twisting her head, she peered to the side, just getting a glimpse of two pairs of legs. She made out a man in high-cut black slacks, no socks and brown loafers, and a woman in a dress or skirt, long bare legs, her feet in a pair of expensive stilettos. Ashlynn could see the red soles in the dark.

She crawled a few feet away from the trees and rose to a standing position, brushing off her knees. She didn't want to get caught eavesdropping on Jed and Veronica.

Why were they arguing in secret? Better than arguing in public, but why would those two be arguing? Jed was her campaign manager. Veronica's word should be law.

She heard the bushes rustle behind her but she didn't turn around. Instead, she adjusted her purse across her body and dug inside for her valet ticket and a five-dollar bill.

She cruised through the house, giving a quick wave to Lulu and then landing on the front porch. Clutching her ticket and cash, she approached the valet attendants.

"Hey, can I get my car, please?"

One of the young men sprang forward with his hand held out, and she placed the ticket in his palm. His shoes crunched against the road as he scurried off to find her car.

This neighborhood in the hills south of Ventura Boulevard didn't need sidewalks. These streets were for residents only, not scraggly pedestrians who didn't have any business in this hood. Apparently, they didn't need streetlamps, either.

Ashlynn rubbed her arms as she waited for her

car, Ranchera music thumping from a speaker where the valets huddled.

She stepped forward as the attendant pulled her car up in front of her. He left the engine running and the door open.

"Thanks." She slipped him the five and got behind the wheel. Hopefully, the parking attendants would be getting better tips from the likes of Syngin, but she knew rich people. They could be cheaper than anyone. She hoped, for Lulu's sake, Syngin wasn't one of those stingy ones.

She pulled onto the road and turned toward Mulholland Drive again. Even with the twists and turns on this part of the road, she preferred it to going through the Valley. And she'd had only two sips of champagne and a boatload of food. She'd be fine.

She negotiated the first few turns with ease before noticing the headlights behind her. Damn. She was more comfortable driving these kinds of roads if nobody was behind her. She tapped her rearview mirror and said, "You're gonna have to relax, buddy. I'm not whizzing around these curves."

She eased off the accelerator at the next bend but instead of backing off, the car behind her got right on her tail. There were no immediate turnouts for her to allow him to pass. She muttered, "Moron."

She came out of the turn and sped up a little, but the next curve greeted her all too soon. She slowed again, and the guy behind her was not having it.

His headlights flooded her car as he rode her bumper.

"What is your problem?" She hugged the shoulder on the right in case he wanted to risk passing her. Sure enough, he moved into the opposing lane of traffic, but instead of roaring ahead like she'd expected, his car bumped the back of hers.

She grabbed the wheel but her tires were already on gravel and they spun to gain purchase on the shifting surface.

The last thing she saw before rolling down the canyon was the other car's taillights as it sped away.

Chapter Eleven

Denver slid down further in his seat and shielded his eyes against the oncoming headlights of Ashlynn's car. Either she'd found what she'd needed or realized she wasn't going to get anything out of Escalante's donors—and she hadn't even told him about her plans.

He didn't deserve to know after the way he'd treated her at lunch. His scheme had worked the way he'd intended: give her the cold shoulder, make her dismiss him as a jerk and throw cold water on whatever they had going on.

Another vehicle crawled out from a shallow turnout, its parking lights barely illuminating the road. Had the valet attendants been using that space for the guests' cars?

His senses percolated as he watched the low-key car roll past the valet stand and Escalante's house. Why was the driver creeping around? Taking license numbers?

He flicked his rearview and watched the car

make the same turn toward Mulholland as Ashlynn had made. He swallowed against his dry
throat. Was someone tailing her?

He cranked on his engine and made a tight
U-turn in the road, waving out the window at
the valets who'd let him park across the street
after he'd flashed his badge and given each of
them a twenty. He made the turn onto Mulholland just in time to see the taillights of the sedan,
which had taken off after Ashlynn's, disappear
around the first bend of a winding section of
the boulevard.

He sped up, but the car was keeping well
ahead of his. Crazy driving.

Coming out of the next curve, Denver blinked
his eyes. The reverse lights of the black sedan
he'd been following glowed as the driver backed
up on the road. Beyond the trunk, Ashlynn's car
poked over the edge of the canyon at a forty-
five-degree angle.

The stealth car switched into Drive and started
rolling toward Ashlynn's precariously situated
vehicle. Denver flashed his headlights and
flicked on his blue and red revolvers.

The driver of the sedan jerked to the right and,
with a squeal of tires, shot off down the road.

Denver had gotten a partial plate, but he
couldn't leave Ashlynn's vehicle at the preci-
pice of the canyon. He hadn't seen any move-

ment from the VW, and his heart pounded as he parked his own vehicle, killing the lights, and clambered out of it.

He rushed to the edge of the road where Ashlynn's car pointed toward the canyon, his shoes slipping on the gravel, almost carrying him past the car and into the trees.

Grabbing on to her door handle, he peered inside the window. Her head turned toward him, her eyes wide and glassy, her hands still gripping her steering wheel.

All four of her wheels were still on solid ground—just—and he yanked open her door. "Are you hurt?"

"I—I don't think so."

"Turn off your engine. Put the car in Park. Can you do that?" He reached across her body and unhitched her seat belt.

She shoved the gearshift into Park and switched off the ignition. Then she placed her hands back on the wheel.

He touched her wrist gently. "You can get out of the car, Ashlynn. It's okay. It's not gonna go over or shift if you move."

She released the steering wheel as if it burned her hands and whipped her head around to face him, her hair dancing at her shoulders like flames. "A car forced me off the road and took off."

"I figured that. I saw the tail end of the accident." He didn't tell her he thought the car was getting ready to push her into the canyon. "The sedan took off."

"Bastard." Her anger broke through her shock and she scrambled out of her car, landing on her knees.

"Steady." He took her arm and helped her to her feet. He glanced at her high-heeled, strappy sandals and swept her into his arms to carry her up to the road.

"I can walk." She kicked her legs.

He set her down on the side of the road. "I know that, but that's some rocky ground. I slipped myself, and I'm not wearing sexy sandals."

Her chin dropped and she stared at her black dress, as if she'd forgotten what she was wearing.

"Are you all right?" He fished into his pocket for his phone. "I'm calling 9-1-1."

"Don't!" She grabbed his arm. "If you make a fuss here, the people from the party might find out about this. I attended that fundraiser as Jenny, ingenue college student and starry-eyed political volunteer. I'd have to give the police my real name."

"You can't leave your car there. You can't back it out of there without risking it tumbling down the canyon—with you in it."

She covered her mouth. "That's what he wanted. He pushed me off the road. He just didn't push hard enough."

"What happened in there?" He jerked his thumb back toward Escalante's house.

"Wait." She ran a pair of unsteady hands through her hair. "What are you doing here? Did you follow me again?"

"I didn't follow you. I didn't even know you were going to be here." He waved at a car slowing toward them to go ahead. Ashlynn was right. They didn't need a collection of cars and people up here. "I knew about the fundraiser and thought I'd do a little surveillance to see who showed up. I saw you arrive, and figured you were here as your alter ego. Then when I saw you leave, I noticed a suspicious car hot on your tail. I'm glad my instincts kicked in."

"Me, too." She folded her arms and kicked some pebbles with her toe.

She still thought he was a jerk, and that was okay.

"But we need to make sure you're okay…and get your car out of here."

"Don't I look okay?" She spread her arms wide, and his gaze swept over her body in her short black dress, long, slim legs up to there.

He dragged his eyes to her face. "You look fine. Why didn't your airbags deploy?"

"No clue. Maybe because I didn't hit anything? It was like a roll down the hill." She rubbed the back of her neck. "Just noticing a little soreness back here, maybe whiplash."

"Probably. You need to a see a doctor."

"I'll see my own doctor, in my own time. Are you gonna help me get my car out of here?"

"What? Push it up the hill with my bare hands?"

"You know…people, don't you? Can't we do this on the hush-hush? If the cops come out here with their lights and sirens and tow trucks and ambulances, it's going to cause a scene. People leaving the party are bound to stop. I'll have to tell the cops where I was. They might even give me a breathalyzer."

He cut her off. "Have you been drinking?"

"Do two sips of champagne count? No, I haven't been drinking, but the cops might want to check out the party. I can't afford that, Denver. I can't afford to blow my cover."

"You already did." He clenched his teeth. He'd like to get his hands on the person driving that sedan.

Ashlynn caught her bottom lip between her teeth. "You're right about that. Either someone followed me to Escalante's, or someone made me there."

Another two cars wound down the road, and

Denver waved them past. "We need to get out of here before more people leave the party. My guess is the majority won't take Mulholland, but enough will."

"So, you agree we shouldn't create a scene here."

"Do you promise me you'll see a doctor about your neck?"

"Promise." She drew a cross over her heart.

"Okay, hop in my car, and I'll get you home, as long as you tell me what you discovered at the fundraiser." He took her arm to guide her to his vehicle tucked into a small outlet.

She slipped from his grasp when she reached the car. "So, now there are two conditions? I go to the doctor and give up what I discovered? When do I get something out of this relationship besides a ride home?"

Opening the passenger door, he held up two fingers. "If we're keeping track here, I've rescued you twice now—three times if we're counting the break-in at your house and the message on your mirror."

"That wasn't a rescue. That was moral support." She dropped onto the seat and slammed the door.

He blew out a breath and circled to the driver's side. When he got in behind the wheel, he slid a gaze to the side. Ashlynn had her eyes closed.

"You're sure you're okay?"

"I probably could use some ibuprofen." She massaged her temples.

"You're in luck." He flipped up the console and felt around for the small bottle every detective kept in every car. His fingers closed around it and he shook it before handing the bottle to Ashlynn. "You can take it down with my lukewarm coffee, if you like."

"Thanks." She popped the lid, shook a green gel cap into her palm and slapped her hand against her mouth. She plucked his cup from the holder and took a small sip, leaving a semicircle of red lipstick on the lid.

He maneuvered his car back onto the road. "I'll call the tow service we use tonight. I don't think anyone's going to see your car off the road in the meantime. I only knew it was there because I saw you roll over the edge and your lights were still on."

"I hope nobody calls it in." She settled into the seat and tucked her hands between her knees. "You wanna know what I discovered at the party?"

"If you're ready." His muscles tensed. Had she been asking too many questions at the fundraiser?

She held up her hand and ticked off each item on her fingers. "I don't think any of the volunteers know about Tiana Fuller. I think Lulu does know something about Tiana, and so does Jed. Jed and Veronica seem to have something more going on than candidate and campaign manager."

"How'd you determine that last bit?"

"I heard them in a heated discussion out by the pool, under cover."

A muscle twitched in his jaw. "Did you hear what they said?"

"Nope. Whispers, and I didn't want to get too close."

He released a breath. "They didn't see you?"

"Not sure about that."

"That's all you got?"

"That and the definition of manther."

He snorted. "Enlighten me."

"A manther is like a male cougar—an older man who hits on younger women. The volunteers said Kent Meadows was a manther." She slugged his arm. "Don't ever become a manther."

"Don't worry about that. I prefer women to girls." He cleared his throat. "Anything else?"

She pulled her skirt over her thighs. "That and a closer relationship with Lulu. She's the one who invited me to the party. She called me."

"Do you think you can get more out of her?"

"Maybe." She gathered her hair in one hand,

dragging it over her shoulder. "But I'd kind of like to get more out of you."

His head jerked to the side. "What do you mean?"

"Don't get excited." She patted his forearm. "I don't mean more warmth or humanity. I'm talking about your meeting with Tiana's parents. You met with them after lunch and didn't bother to fill me in at all. This is beginning to feel like a one-way street."

Should he tell her he'd changed his mind about their deal? Or at least he had until he'd seen her glide up Escalante's driveway like she owned the place. He couldn't deny having a source like Ashlynn might help him solve Tiana's murder.

He cleared his throat. "I'll tell you about it when we get back to your place."

Closing her eyes, she nodded. "Deal."

And just like that, Ashlynn Hughes was back in his life.

BY THE TIME Ashlynn pushed open the door to her place, she could barely move her head on her stiff neck. She'd taken an ibuprofen in the car, but she needed another.

"Do you want something to drink? I'm going to pop another pill and put some ice on my neck." She hung on to the freezer door. "Ice or heat?"

"I'd start with ice, but I'm no expert." He sidled up next to her at the fridge and said, "Bottled water or tap?"

"I use the water from the refrigerator. I figure it's filtered, and I haven't grown any horns yet."

He brushed past her and lifted two glasses from her cupboard. "Ice to go with your ice?"

"No, thanks." She crouched next to the fridge and pulled a plastic bag from a drawer. "I'm going to fill this with ice and deposit it against the back of my neck. I guess it could've been worse, huh?"

"Are you going to tell me what happened at that fundraiser to make someone come after you and try to run you off the road?"

"I told you everything that happened. I did not draw attention to myself." She punched the button on the ice maker to release the ice and fill her bag.

"Someone noticed you, or someone recognized you. You run one of the most popular blogs in the city. Why do you think you can run around incognito?" He took her place in front of the fridge and filled up two glasses with water.

"*LA Confidential* is not really my blog. I didn't make it popular. That was Sean's doing."

He cocked his head at her. "Take credit where credit is due. Your brother is gone, and you've done a helluva job in his place. That series you did on Reed Dufrain and the shenanigans at the

Brighter Day Recovery Center was top-notch. That drug lab sounded like something from a TV show. You did that, Ashlynn. Why are you selling yourself short?"

She shrugged and her bag of ice crackled against her neck. "Just feels like it's Sean's baby, like it'll never be mine."

"Make it your own, or do something else. I thought you said something about a podcast?"

"Yeah, Sean intended to turn *LA Confidential* into a podcast. I had started helping him."

"Take the idea and run with it." He placed his hand on the small of her back and steered her toward the couch. "Sit down, and I'll tell you what I found out from Tiana's parents."

She lowered herself to the cushion on the end, positioning the bag on her neck. "Was it hard talking to them?"

"Hard for me?" His eyebrows shot up to his hairline and the dark lock of hair that had a habit of falling across his forehead. "What I feel is nothing compared to what they're going through."

She nodded. "I remember when the detective came to tell me about my brother's murder. He was so uncomfortable, I almost felt like I was supposed to comfort him. I didn't want to break down too much because I was afraid of what it would do to him."

"It shouldn't be that way. As difficult as it is for us, it's not our tragedy, not our story." He coughed and gulped back some water. "Tiana's parents couldn't tell me much, but I got the impression that she *was* working for the Escalante campaign."

"Just an impression?" The ice slipped to her shoulder and she left it. "They couldn't tell you for sure?"

"They didn't know for sure, but Tiana was a political science major at Cal State Long Beach. She was very interested in local politics, and was looking forward to applying for an internship with the city of Long Beach her senior year. It would make sense that she'd volunteer for a campaign like Escalante's."

"But she never specifically told her parents she was working for Escalante?"

"Nope." Denver scratched his jaw. "I wonder why. If she were so excited about politics, you'd think she'd tell her parents about her volunteer work."

"She was keeping it a secret for some reason." She snapped her fingers. "What about Wexler's campaign? Did they ever get back to you with a list of their volunteers?"

"They did, but her name wasn't on the list. I wasn't anticipating it. If she'd been working for them, I would expect them to scrub her name from the database. Tiana is already connected to one of their cars, they don't want to compound the problem by linking her to the campaign."

Ashley wrinkled her nose. "Tiana is working for Escalante and winds up dead in a vehicle tied to the Wexler campaign."

"Doesn't make any sense." Denver massaged his temples. "Oh, and her mother said Tiana had a boyfriend up here, or maybe just a guy who was a friend—Tony Fuentes."

"He hasn't contacted you?"

"No, but I'm going to run him down and find out why." He pointed to her plastic bag. "That's slipping down your arm. I thought you had whiplash."

"It's too cold." She snatched the bag from her shoulder, cupping it in her palms.

"That's kind of the point." He took the ice from her hands and said, "Turn around."

She presented her back to him, tucking one leg beneath her and tugging her dress over her thighs.

Denver swept her hair over her shoulder, his fingers trailing along her bare back.

A warm flush suffused her body. If he put that ice against her skin now, it would melt in a matter of seconds.

The ice clacked as he positioned it on the back

of her neck. He kept his hand on the bag, pressing it against all the stiff spots. She closed her eyes as a chilling numbness seemed to freeze her twitching muscles.

"Okay, yeah. I see the point here." She lifted her shoulders and shivered. "It hurts so good. I mean I kind of can't stand it, but the ice is definitely numbing the area."

"I think we were right to ice instead of heat." He blew out a warm breath that tickled her flesh. "I was relieved to see you weren't hurt—at least not seriously. When I saw that car take off after yours, I didn't think he was going to run you off the road. Follow you, maybe, but he could've killed you."

Ashlynn jerked her head to the side and clamped her neck with a wince. "Do you think whoever is threatening me graduated to violence?"

He dropped the bag of ice to the coffee table. "I think he already did that in Venice."

"I'm talking about mortal violence. You think someone wants to kill me?"

His hand skimmed down her back. "He pushed you into a shallow dip, not off the edge of a canyon. He could've picked a more dangerous spot on Mulholland to start playing bumper cars with you. I think you're still in the warning stage. It's not like you've discovered anything about Tiana yet. Neither have we."

He'd been rubbing a circle on her back, and her eyelashes fluttered when he stopped. "Could you keep doing that?"

She felt his warmth behind her as he gathered her hair in her hand and lifted it from her neck. He pressed his lips against her cool flesh and she could almost feel the sizzle.

"Yeah, like that." She dipped her head and his lips trailed to her collarbone.

Turning to face him, she grabbed the lapels of his denim jacket. "You always seem to be in the right place at the right time to rescue me."

"Right place, but always two beats late." His lips crooked into a smile and the unexpectedness of it took her breath away.

She smoothed her hands against the front of his T-shirt, and his heart thumped beneath her palms, matching the pulse in her fingertips. She raised her eyes to his face and whispered, "Why'd you blow me off at lunch?"

"I realized I had stuff to do." His dark eyes shifted to the hand he was running through her hair.

You didn't have to be a homicide detective to spot that tell. The lie was so obvious, Denver didn't even try to cover it.

She didn't need honesty right now. She'd never

demanded that much from the men in her life anyway. Stroking his cheek, she said, "Kiss me."

The fingers sifting through her hair wove around the strands and he pulled her closer. When their lips met, she tasted peppermint and possibilities.

His hand slid to the back of her head and he broke their connection. "I don't want you hurting your neck—even for a kiss."

"If you can't risk it all for a hot kiss, there's something missing in your soul." She touched his bottom lip with the pad of her thumb. "I forgot all about my whiplash for a minute."

"Let me help you forget some more." He wrapped his hands around her waist and pulled her into his lap. Her dress rode up her thigh, and he ran his rough palm across its curve.

"I don't know how you could've believed you were flying beneath the radar at that party in this dress."

She burrowed into his lap and hung an arm around his neck. "I was a moth among butterflies. Believe me. The flash and glitz in that room could've blinded you."

"That's why you probably stood out. You don't need flash and glitz. You have something more indefinable than that—style, sexiness without hitting people in the face with it."

She must be her mother's daughter after all.

"Can we stop talking now? I thought you were the strong, silent type."

He gently took her face between his hands and kissed her mouth, his tongue slipping between her lips. She'd wanted him from the moment she'd seen him at the lake, but she always did go after the unattainable ones.

As she peeled herself from his chest, she whispered against his lips, "Let's take this to my bedroom."

His dark eyes searched her face. "Are you sure?"

"My neck is fine."

"I wasn't talking about your neck, I—"

She knew exactly what he meant, but the ring from her phone cut him off. She held up her finger. "Normally, I wouldn't take a call at a moment like this, but under the circumstances..."

Rolling from his lap, she grabbed her phone from the coffee table. She held it in front of him. "It's Lulu."

"Take it."

"Hi, Lulu." She carefully pressed the button for the speaker.

"Girl, are you all right?"

"Why wouldn't I be all right?" The blood thumped in her ears.

"You bounced out of here so fast I thought maybe someone recognized you."

"Recognized me? I thought you said it was okay for me to be there."

"Cut the crap, Ashlynn. I know who you are and, if anyone else does, you could be in big trouble."

Chapter Twelve

Ashlynn licked her lips and flicked a quick glance at Denver, who avoided giving her the *I told you so* look. "Do you think anyone else knows?"

"I'm not sure, but that's not the point. I've been reading the blog, so I know what you're after. I don't know who killed Tiana Fuller, but I do know for a fact that she was working for my sister's campaign. That cop will never find her name on any paperwork here, but I've got proof…if you want it."

"I do want it." Ashlynn rubbed the back of her neck. "Can you email or text it to me?"

Lulu paused. "I wouldn't chance it. Meet me tonight and I'll hand over the proof."

Denver jabbed her hip and shook his head.

She rolled her eyes at him. "How about to-morrow?"

"I want to unload this as soon as possible.

I stole it, and I don't want it in my possession anymore. Come get it tonight, or I'm tossing it."

"Wait, wait. I'll meet you. Tell me where." She pointed to Denver and then herself. He could come along. In fact, she wanted him at least in the vicinity.

Lulu said, "There's a dog park at Mulholland and Laurel Canyon. I'll meet you in the parking lot in an hour."

Ashlynn ignored Denver's furious slicing motions in the air and answered Lulu. "I'll be there. It's going to be safe, right?"

"You don't have to worry about me. I want to help you, but nobody can know what I'm doing. I didn't make you fill out that paperwork today, did I? That's because I recognized you right away. I just wanna be part of the blog."

"I'm not going to call you out."

"God, no. Don't do that, but I'd still know I was part of the blog."

"Okay. I'll see you in an hour."

When she ended the call, she held up her hand against Denver's protests. "She's right. She kept quiet about me today at the campaign headquarters when she could've outed me, and she invited me to the fundraiser, knowing who I was."

"You don't even know if she's telling the truth. Maybe she had no idea who you were earlier. She just found out at the fundraiser because someone told her, and now she'd luring you out with promises of proof that Tiana worked for the campaign." He sat forward and grabbed her hands. "Someone just tried to bulldoze you off Mulholland and now you're returning to... Mulholland. Not a great idea."

"You're coming with me." She drilled her finger into his chest, regretting she'd never even gotten to take off his shirt.

He captured her finger. "This time. I can't be protecting you twenty-four seven, Ashlynn. I do have a job."

"I don't need protection all day, every day. This is one situation that might be a little sketchy, and this *is* your job."

He squeezed his eyes closed and pinched the bridge of his nose. "If Lulu has this proof that Tiana worked for her sister, why not just call me?"

"You're kidding, right? If Veronica Escalante or her top dog, Jed, knew Lulu even had this information, never mind turning it over to the cops, they'd go ballistic."

"Why? Why the secrecy?" He slammed his fist into his palm. "If they didn't have anything to hide, why would it matter that Tiana worked for the campaign? They must be involved in her death or know something about it."

"Or they just don't want the campaign to be

associated with a murder." She pushed up from the couch, tugging on the hem of her dress. "I'm going to change for this meeting. It's probably better if she doesn't see you. She'd recognize you, anyway."

"You think?" He pinched the material of his cotton T-shirt between his fingers. "I'm not wearing my suit, and I have a baseball cap in the car."

"Oh, she noticed you today. I doubt she's going to forget what you look like, regardless of your clothes." She headed for her bedroom and spun around. "Dodgers, Angels or Padres?"

"What?" He glanced up from his phone, his brows knitted over his nose.

"The baseball cap—Dodgers, Angels or Padres?"

"Are you serious? The Dodgers, of course."

She nodded and slipped into her bedroom.

"LULU HAD BETTER not be here early. One look at me and she'll probably bolt—if what you said was true and she'd recognize me." The knots in Denver's gut tightened as he took the last curve toward the dog park.

"Lulu thought you were hot. She's not going to forget." Ashlynn glanced at the phone in her hand. "Besides, we got here in thirty-five minutes. There's no way she'd be this early."

"If Lulu's not alone, take off."

"And leave you out in the park?"

"You can swing by and pick me up later. Get out of here if something feels off." His hands gripping the steering wheel, Denver turned into the lot for the park.

It was really a playground for kids, with equipment and everything, but it was also an off-leash dog park for part of the day. The edge of the common area rushed downhill in a tangle of bushes and undergrowth. He didn't want to hide that far away from the car. He didn't want to be here at all. When people had to meet in secret to give up information they shouldn't have, it all screamed danger.

He let out a long breath as he scanned the empty parking lot. A few lights beamed down on the asphalt, and Denver pulled in under one of them.

He cracked open the driver's-side door. "You could leave the engine running, just in case you need to make a quick getaway. If you see any other car besides Lulu's BMW pull in, take off. If you see anyone in her passenger seat, take off."

"I got it, Denver." She pushed at his arm. "You'd better find your hiding spot before Lulu gets here. She might take off herself if she sees you."

"I'll be behind that clump of bushes at the edge of the playground. If worse comes to worst, run toward me and I'll have you covered."

"You mean with a gun?"

He patted his hip where he'd clipped his holster back onto his belt at her place. "Yeah."

"And I've got my pepper spray." She pulled her purse into her lap.

"Then we've got all bases covered." He tugged on a lock of her hair. "Be careful, and don't do anything stupid."

"I'll be fine. Go."

He stepped from the car, and Ashlynn didn't even bother getting out on her side. He watched through the window as she crawled over the console and slid into the driver's seat.

He loped toward the swing set and ducked behind the bushes bordering the play area. He crouched on his haunches and played with the branches of the bush to get a clear view of his car and Ashlynn's silhouette.

That phone call from Lulu had saved him from making a big mistake tonight. As much as he wanted Ashlynn, he didn't need the emotional entanglement right now—or ever. Would he be crouching behind a bush in the middle of the night if they hadn't almost wound up in her bed?

He sucked in a breath as a pair of headlights

swept into the parking lot. Squinting into the darkness, he made out the BMW logo on the front of the car, but he couldn't tell who was driving or if the driver had company.

The car pulled into a space two down from Ashlynn, and the dome light illuminated the interior as the driver got out of the vehicle. His muscles relaxed a little when he recognized Lulu, tossing her long dark hair over her shoulder. She obviously hadn't changed from the party, and the light from the lamp above caught the sequins on her dress, which shimmered as she approached Ashlynn.

As Ashlynn popped her own door, Denver murmured to himself, "No, no, no. Stay in the car."

The two women met in the parking lot, and he strained to hear their voices, rising and falling in a conversational cadence. He covered his mouth with his hand and said, "Get the proof and get out."

As Denver massaged a cramp in his thigh, he caught sight of a shadow moving into the parking lot from the road. His nostrils flared. Was that an animal? Coyotes and even mountain lions roamed this area. The park had closed for a while a few years ago after a coyote had attacked a few dogs.

He blinked at the spot where he'd noticed the

movement. The shadow had taken the shape of a dark figure—a man-sized figure. Denver grabbed his gun from the holster, the muscles in his legs coiled.

People came to this park all the time at night for a variety of reasons, but they usually drove cars. A walk from one of the nearby residences would be a tricky proposition, and it was a bit late for a stroll.

Had Ashlynn and Lulu noticed the man? Denver whistled in what he hoped was an approximation of a night bird's cry. He didn't even care at this point if Lulu made him.

Ashlynn turned her head to the side.

Had she noticed the man yet?

Lulu had. She jerked back and grabbed Ashlynn's arm as the man emerged from the shadows, his arm outstretched as he approached them.

The light glinted on an object in the stranger's hand and his voice carried all the way to the playground. "Hand it over."

Gripping his weapon, Denver lunged from his hiding place. "Get down, get down, get down."

The adrenaline coursing through his veins propelled him into the parking lot.

Ashlynn dropped to the ground and grabbed Lulu's hand, dragging her down with her.

The man spun around and ran for the edge of

the park, speeding across the grass flattened by countless dogs over the years.

Denver gave chase, shouting over his shoulder, "Get in the car and leave—now."

He slammed into the side of a picnic table that had come out of nowhere, his knees hitting the attached bench, his palms slapping the top of the table. Cursing, he pushed off and scanned the edge of the canyon that dipped away from the park.

The man had disappeared into the foliage. Had probably rolled down the hill. Denver didn't want to play hide-and-seek in the canyon, even if he had the superior weapon.

He gave up the chase and limped back to the parking lot, the gun still in his hand. This guy could have an accomplice.

He tripped to a stop, his heart thundering in his chest. Lulu's BMW was gone, but his car sat in the same spot…empty. He'd told Ashlynn to get in the car and take off, but maybe someone had prevented her from leaving.

The breath rasped in his throat as he yelled, "Ashlynn! Ashlynn!"

A head popped up on the driver's side of the car, and he stumbled again, his knees weak. He circled around the vehicle and yanked on the handle of the passenger side. The locks clicked and he tried again, swinging the door open so hard it almost closed again.

He dropped onto the seat and asked, "Are you okay?"

"I'm fine. What happened out there?"

"Move." He smacked the dashboard with his hand. "Move."

She cranked on the engine and peeled out of the parking lot, the back tires fishtailing on the loose dirt.

When she steadied the car, he smoothed a hand over her arm. "What happened? Is Lulu all right?"

"She's okay, but she's not happy with me."

"With you? Is she the one who invited the goon with the knife to the meeting?"

"If she was, she's a good actress. She was as surprised and scared as I was when he showed up."

"What did he want? What did he say? I heard 'hand it over' at about the same time I saw the glint of the knife in his hand."

"H-he said he wanted our phones, cash, jewelry."

Denver said, "He was pretending to be a common mugger, but we know better, and Lulu knows better. The whole thing could've been a setup, designed to lure you into another dangerous situation."

"I don't think so, Denver. I don't think Lulu knew about the man with the knife."

"Really? She gets you to meet her at a deserted park in the dead of night on the pretense of giving you proof that Tiana worked for the Escalante campaign and, instead of getting the proof, you almost get knifed. And *she's* mad at *you*?" He plowed a hand through his hair.

"But it didn't play out like that."

"What do you mean? I saw it unfold right in front of me. I chased the guy before he disappeared into the canyon."

"Yeah, that all happened, but I didn't walk away empty-handed." Ashlynn reached into the cup holder and dangled a thumb drive from her fingertips. "Lulu delivered the goods."

Chapter Thirteen

Denver jerked his head to the side, almost giving himself whiplash. He held out his hand and she dropped the thumb drive onto his palm. "Did she say what was on it?"

"Nope." Ashlynn carefully negotiated the last curve and pulled up to a red light at the bottom of the hill. "Just told me it contained proof that Tiana worked for the Escalante campaign."

"How'd she get a copy? They must know she has it."

"Slow down a minute." Ashlynn rubbed the back of her neck. "I can't drive, talk and think at the same time, not when I can't even turn my head."

"Take the turn onto Hollywood Boulevard. We'll get coffee. I have a lot of questions for you."

She slid a gaze to the side. "I have a few for you, too. Why are you limping?"

"I tripped over a picnic bench in the dark.

Once that happened, your assailant had disappeared into the canyon that borders the park. I had no chance of finding him." He tapped on the windshield. "Pull into that diner."

Ashlynn signaled a left turn and cruised into the lot of an all-night diner. Patrons for the nearby clubs and bars packed the place, and they grabbed a table in the corner that hadn't been cleared yet.

A busboy swept up the clutter as they sat and ordered two coffees.

Denver, having pocketed the thumb drive, drew it out and dangled it over the table by its ribbon. "This is the proof, huh?"

"That's what Lulu said—before we were rudely interrupted."

"Lulu seemed surprised by the intrusion?"

"Surprised, scared, mad. It was legit. She didn't know." Ashlynn spread her hands on the table, her thumbs touching. "Besides, why would she hand off evidence to me while she was planning to have someone take it right away?"

"To cover herself." He bobbled the drive. "We don't yet know what this contains. It could be garbage."

"One way to find out. Don't know why we're wasting our time here." She circled her finger in the air.

He closed his hand around the device. "Because you—we both just had a scare. The information on this thumb drive isn't going anywhere."

The waitress came to their table and poured coffee into their upturned cups. "Anything else?"

Denver asked, "Do you have blueberry pie?"

"We do, hon. Ice cream with that?"

"Ice cream and two forks." Denver held up two fingers.

Cupping her chin with her hand, Ashlynn tilted her head. "I thought most cops dealt with stress by drinking whiskey. Your poison is blueberry pie à la mode?"

He blew on his coffee before taking a sip. "Don't knock it until you've tried it. A lot of people eat when they're stressed out."

"Or don't."

"Sorry?"

"Never mind." She rubbed her hands together. "I'm ready for your questions. I'm anxious to see what we have here."

"What were you and Lulu talking about for so long? I thought you'd grab whatever she had and we'd get out of there."

"I wanted to ask her how she knew who I was."

"And?"

"She's a big fan of the blog—was a big fan of my brother's."

Denver trapped his sigh in his throat. Couldn't she just once take credit for the blog without bringing her brother into it?

"You said before, your picture's not on the blog and you keep a low profile otherwise. How'd she know you were Ashlynn Hughes?"

"Just my luck, she's kind of obsessive about true crime in general and *LA Confidential* in particular." She folded her hands around her cup and stared into the steam rising from it. "When Sean was murdered, Lulu followed everything about the case and, somewhere in the coverage, my name was mentioned. She looked me up. She saw my picture and recognized me that first day. That's why she didn't follow up with Jed's instructions to have me fill out paperwork, which would've meant a copy of my driver's license."

"You dodged a bullet. Is that why she didn't turn you in to Jed? Because she's a super fan of the blog?"

"That's one reason, or maybe it's the main reason. She invited me to the fundraiser and offered me this info because she wants to be involved in the blog."

"Why didn't she just give you the proof tonight at the party?"

She crinkled her nose. "She wasn't sure she was going to turn it over. Then when I left so suddenly, she thought I might be in trouble and figured she needed to reveal the truth. She swears neither Jed nor Veronica knows my identity."

"Someone does." He smacked his fist on the table, sending tiny ripples through the coffee.

"Does that mean you want more coffee?" The waitress delivered the pie, two scoops of vanilla ice cream already melting into the crust."

"Sorry, just making a point. This looks great, thanks." Denver aimed a smile at the waitress. He didn't want her to think he and Ashlynn were fighting.

She glanced at Ashlynn's full cup. "Do you want something else, hon?"

"Water would be great."

Denver plucked a couple of paper napkins from the dispenser on the table and dropped them onto his lap. He pointed his fork at Ashlynn. "You'd better eat some of this pie, or that waitress is going to think this is some kind of domestic situation."

"Only a cop would think something like that." She plucked up a fork and ran the tines through the ice cream, scooping up a berry from the plate.

The tart berries exploded in his mouth as the sweet ice cream melted down his throat. He closed his eyes, and Ashlynn nudged his foot under the table.

"Earth to Denver."

"See? Just relaxing." He swiped a napkin across his mouth. "When the stranger approached you, did Lulu seem to recognize him? Did you?"

"He was wearing a ski mask." She asked, "You didn't notice that?"

"I never got a good look at his face He stayed out of the light. How about his voice? Did it sound familiar?"

"No. Didn't jolt any memories for me." She held up her hand. "And before you ask me about race, hair color or anything like that, I couldn't tell you. He had a black turtleneck that met the ski mask, jeans, black gloves. All I can tell you is that he was average height because he was about as tall as me and a little shorter than you."

"Great." He dug his fork into the pie. "And he was a fast runner."

"Are you done with your questions?" She pulled her phone from her purse. "I'm going to check on Lulu."

"Not yet. We need to look at what's on the thumb drive first. If it's junk, she set you up. You need to know that before you communicate with her again." He picked up the other fork, lopped off a piece of pie and held it in front of her lips. "Try it. I can't eat the whole thing."

"Looks like you're doing a great job." She

eyed the pie as if it were going to bite her instead of the other way around.

He tipped the fork back and forth. "Going, going…"

Ashlynn opened her mouth and closed her lips around the fork. She chewed for a few seconds and said, "Gone."

He pointed his fork at her phone on the table. "Lulu didn't text you, did she?"

"She didn't. When she heard you shouting, her eyes shot daggers at me. She hadn't expected me to bring company, even if she didn't recognize you as the hot cop from before."

"Even though I could've been saving your lives at that point? What did she think was going to happen? What did you think was going happen?"

"I figured we'd hand over our money, phones, jewelry, and then he'd ask me for the thumb drive, like, 'by the way, give me that, too,' even though we'd all know that's what he'd wanted in the first place."

"He could've hurt you. He had a knife. That's no joke. Yeah, it wasn't a match for my gun, but when someone is that close to you, a knife can do fatal damage."

"I'd transferred my pepper spray from my purse to my pocket. Before you stormed out of your hiding place, I'd planned on using it."

Denver's heart skipped several beats. That could've been a deadly move on Ashlynn's part. He opened his mouth and then nipped it shut. She hadn't had to use the pepper spray—no point in lecturing her.

He pushed away the plate, which had become a swirling mess of purple and white. "We know we weren't followed to the park. I made sure of it on the way over. The only way that guy shows up is if the meeting was a setup, or he followed Lulu."

"He followed Lulu. There's no way that was a setup, or Lulu should stop wasting her time stuffing envelopes and become an actress. She was clearly shocked." Ashlynn ran the tip of her finger through the blueberry swirl and sucked it off.

Denver followed the action and swallowed a gulp of lukewarm coffee. "Why is Lulu being followed? Is it because Jed or her sister don't trust her, or is it because someone saw her talking to you and knows she invited you to the gala?"

"I don't know. Did the pie do its job? Are you done unwinding?" She fingered the thumb drive he'd left on the table. "I'm dying to find out what's on this thing."

"That—" he slipped the drive into his pocket

and slapped a ten on the table "—is a bad choice of words."

HE'D TAKEN OVER the driving duty from Ashlynn and forty minutes later, he pulled into the driveway of her duplex.

As they'd turned onto her block, Denver had driven slowly and studied every car. Maybe they hadn't been followed, but the people after Ashlynn had already proved they knew where she lived. A few new locks might not be enough to keep them out, especially if they believed she had proof that Tiana had volunteered for the campaign in her possession.

When he put the car in Park, he reached for her arm. "Do me a favor and sit in the car until I come around and let you out."

"Is this a sudden spasm of chivalry, or do you think someone's watching us?"

"Chivalry all day, baby."

"Right." She smirked but stayed put as he hustled around to her side, his hand hovering over his gun.

He cracked open the door. "Okay, let's move"

Luckily, Ashlynn's long legs kept up with his stride as he propelled her to the front door. While she unlocked the dead bolt, he did a half turn and blocked her body with his, his gaze scanning the sidewalk and probing the bushes.

He followed her inside and locked up as she headed straight for her laptop.

"You finally ready to see what we have here?"

"Sated with blueberry pie and ready." He pulled the thumb drive from his pocket and handed it to her.

When she woke up her computer, she inserted the drive into the port on the side. A folder opened, containing a video from a phone. Ashlynn double clicked on it.

When the video launched, it displayed a blurry thumbnail of the side of a desk.

"Play it." Denver said the words at the same time Ashlynn clicked the play button.

They both huddled forward to watch, their heads almost touching.

A man's voice came over the computer's speakers as the video showed a table with a couple of cans of soda and a woman's arm, her fingers tapping the table. "So, you're good with that, Tiana?"

Ashlynn sucked in a breath. "That's Jed's voice."

A female voice responded. "Sure. I'll do whatever it takes to stop a second term for Mayor Wexler."

Jed said, "Hold on. I need to answer this text."

The view of the camera shifted upward as Jed held up the phone, pretending to answer a text.

As Tiana Fuller came into focus, Denver said, "Stop it."

Ashlynn clicked the mouse. "Tiana doesn't know she's being filmed, does she? Jed was holding the phone in his hand and secretly turned on the video. Now he's pretending to answer a text just so he can hold up the phone and capture Tiana on camera."

"Exactly." Denver's jaw tightened as he looked at Tiana, vibrant and very much alive. "Let's hope Jed reiterates what he just suggested to Tiana, and what she just agreed to do."

When Ashlynn tapped Play, Tiana came to life and tucked a strand of light brown hair behind her ear, presumably waiting for Jed to stop texting.

The camera view shifted to the side, as if Jed were still holding it up but not pointing it directly at Tiana. Jed continued. "It's just a few dirty tricks, right? Nothing too serious, nothing against the law. Campaigns do it all the time. Hell, we might have a Wexler mole in our own office."

Tiana laughed; a high, tinkling sound that made Denver flinch. "You never know, huh? This could be fun. This is the side of politics that interests me—the behind-the-scenes stuff, what makes a campaign tick."

"I'm with you on that. The upside is that Veronica Escalante is a great leader. You'll be providing a great service to the city if you can help get her elected as the next mayor of LA."

"I can't wait to start. Will you invite me to all the war room meetings? I feel as if I have a lot to learn from you, Mr. Gordon. You're the best." Tiana gave a flirtatious giggle.

Jed coughed. "I think I can teach you a few tricks."

The video ended and Ashlyn turned to face Denver, her eyes wide. "Sounds like Jed recruited Tiana to spy on the Wexler campaign. Why would he lie to you about knowing her, and why'd he take this video?"

"I'm not sure about any of that yet, but after watching that video—" he tapped the laptop's screen "—I'm starting to wonder who was playing who."

Chapter Fourteen

"Something sounded off to me, too." Ashlynn sat back and jabbed a finger at the video still on the screen. "Was Tiana *flirting* with Jed? He sounded all in control, and then she turned on the feminine charm to flatter him when she didn't need to. She'd already gotten the gig, right? Sounds like she'd got it even before the video started."

"I'm glad you heard it, too. I didn't know if I was picking up on her tone because I'm a guy or because I'm a detective. But the dynamic shifted at the end." He shoved that lock of hair from his forehead. "One thing that is clear from this video is that the Escalante campaign was using Tiana to get some dirt on the Wexler campaign."

Ashlynn bit the side of her thumb. "Maybe she got the dirt, someone from the CREW found out and killed her for it."

"Why would the Escalante campaign be hiding that information?" He spread his hands.

"If Jed's right and everyone plays these tricks, what's the problem for them? I'd say murder is a little more serious than campaign dirty tricks. You'd think he'd want to point the finger at the Wexler campaign."

"You'd think. I mean that's not a good look for Escalante, either. Set up a young girl to pull a fast one on a political campaign, and then she gets murdered."

"Why?" Denver jumped up from the couch and circled the room. "What exactly did Tiana find out about Wexler? And if she did dig up some serious infraction, why wouldn't Escalante use it? That info should be all over the news by now."

Ashlynn flopped back against the cushions of the couch, suddenly exhausted. "Something's not adding up, but I guess it explains why Tiana never told her parents she was working for Escalante. She must've been there in an undercover capacity. That's why the other volunteers didn't know her—and I believe them."

"Lulu knew about Tiana because Lulu, whether she likes it or not, is in the inner circle. Maybe that's why Lulu gave you the video. She thinks it's going to help her sister's campaign." Denver finally stopped pacing and propped his shoulder against the wall, folding his arms.

"I'm not sure Lulu is all that interested in

helping her sister's campaign, but I'm wondering why she decided to color outside the lines and copy this video. Just to be part of *LA Confidential*?"

"And why did Jed make the video?"

"That makes no sense to me, either." She patted the couch next to her. "Have a seat. You're making me nervous, and you're still limping."

"Maybe he made it to have proof that Tiana agreed to the spying, in case things went sideways and she accused the campaign of coercing her." Denver sliced his hand through the air, still standing against the wall. "That doesn't make sense. Jed still looks complicit in that video. He's not doing himself any favors."

"Maybe he didn't make the video for protection but as proof he asked Tiana. Maybe he made the video for Veronica."

Denver shrugged and then crossed the room to perch on the arm of the couch, his leg brushing her arm. "Whatever his motives, Lulu got hold of the video and gave it to you."

"Speaking of Lulu, now that we know her proof was legit, I'm going to text her and make sure she's okay."

Denver warned. "Keep me out of it. Even if she thinks she recognized me, don't cop to it—and tell her to be careful. She has an enemy in the campaign."

Ashlynn snatched up her phone from next to the computer on the coffee table, and typed a message to Lulu. She waved the phone at Denver. "I just told her thanks for the video and asked if she was okay."

"How about you?" He stroked her hair. "Are you okay? The threats seem to be building against you—two in one day. How's your neck?"

She squeezed the back of her neck. "The car wreck seems like it happened days ago. I feel all right. Did you happen to hear from the tow service about my car?"

He patted his pocket. "Forgot to tell you. They towed the car and tested it at the yard. It started just fine. I can take you there tomorrow morning to pick it up. They mentioned a few scratches on the body and sent pictures. I'll send those to you."

"Now I'm feeling even better."

He asked, "Anything from Lulu yet?"

"No. My phone dings when texts come through." She turned over her phone and glanced at the display, just in case. "I hope she's okay, too. She must've risked a lot to get that video and then hand it off to me."

"What is it with Lulu, anyway? Does she hate or love her sister?"

"A little of both, I think." Ashlynn picked up her laptop and carried it to her kitchen table.

She plugged in the charger. "She doesn't like the phoniness of politicians, but Veronica basically supports Lulu in a style that she enjoys—mostly from Veronica's husband."

"I looked him up. The dude's a high roller. He's putting up buildings all over downtown LA. Even if Escalante loses, and I think she will, she won't be hurting for money."

Ashlynn ran her fingers through her hair. "I'm glad you were there tonight. I don't know if that guy would've hurt us, but he would've taken the thumb drive for sure."

"I wasn't about to let you meet Lulu on your own, not after what happened on Mulholland." He rubbed his knee. "Even if I missed the guy."

"Maybe *you* need some ice." She tipped her head toward the fridge. "Can I get you some?"

"I'll survive, but you can give me the thumb drive."

She dropped her lashes and wound an errant strand of hair around her finger. "You're leaving already?"

"Already? It's late. I thought you were exhausted." He stretched, and her gaze meandered down his body.

"I thought maybe...before..." She covered her warm face with her hands. "I was hoping you'd stay, and we could finish what we'd started earlier, before Lulu's text."

The silence from across the room rolled over her in waves. She spread open her fingers and peered at him through the narrow spaces.

He rose slowly from the couch, as if in slow motion, his gait halting, which had nothing to do with his knee.

His eyes kindled with a dark seductiveness that she felt as a tremble through her body. Her toes curled into the floor.

"You're sure?" His voice sounded gruff, as if he hadn't used it in years. Or maybe there was something else he hadn't used in years.

"You don't want me to sign a contract, do you?" Without expending conscious effort in the act, she'd been moving toward him and the invitation in his eyes.

"No, but—" he spread his hands "—I don't have any protection."

She flicked her fingers. "I do."

At the quirk of his eyebrows, she said, "I—I mean they're leftovers. Could even be expired by now."

His lips curled, and they were close enough now that she could see the slight flush on his throat. "I'm willing to take my chances, if you are."

She exhaled, and he took the final step toward her and gathered her into his arms. His kiss burned hotter than it had before, as if he'd been warming up and now it was full-steam ahead.

She wrapped her arms around his neck and sagged against his body. She didn't have the energy to play any games with him. If he could take her right now, she'd gladly face her next brush with death.

As if he sensed she'd never let him go, he swept her up into his arms and murmured against her lips, "Bedroom?"

"Uh-huh." Her place was small enough that he remembered the way, and her body jostled against his as he carried her to her room.

He actually had to kick open the door, which only added to the deliciousness of this moment. His next move had to be tossing her across the bed, but he must've figured her body had endured too much trauma tonight.

He backed up to the bed and sat on the edge, still holding her, folding her into his lap, her long legs awkwardly hanging over his thighs, her toes brushing the carpet.

She ran her hands beneath his shirt, the texture of his warm skin causing her fingertips to buzz. Lulu could keep her smooth sugar daddy. She'd take this slightly tangy, rough-around-the-edges cop any day.

Denver fell back on the bed and toed off his shoes.

Rolling to his side, she yanked open the drawer of her nightstand, feeling around for the foil packets of condoms.

She dragged out a strip and waved them in the air. "I think they're still good."

He unbuckled his belt and unzipped his jeans. "I think they have a shelf life of a hundred years, just in case."

She curled her hand over his as he hooked a thumb in his fly. "Let me undress you a little at a time. I'm not sure my system can withstand the shock of seeing a totally naked man in my bed all at once."

"Watch what you're calling little."

She giggled like a virgin schoolgirl and tugged at his shirt. As it rolled up his body, her hands replaced the material and she caressed his flesh, feeling him shiver beneath her touch.

She planted a kiss at the base of his throat where his pulse throbbed and slid her hand down his belly to his open fly. She peeled back his jeans and he lifted his hips to help her do the honors.

Suddenly, she lost all patience, hooked her thumbs beneath the elastic of his boxers and yanked them down to his muscular thighs along with his jeans.

She sighed and smoothed her hands over him. "Nothing little about it."

He kicked off his pants. "Your turn and, unlike you, I'm looking forward to seeing a totally naked woman all at once. I'll get over the shock quick enough."

She unbuttoned her shirt and shrugged out of it. Presenting her back to him, she said, "Can you unhook my bra? It sort of hurts my neck when I reach around."

With a twist of his fingers, he unhooked her and didn't even wait for the bra to come off her arms before he reached around and cupped her breasts.

He sucked in a breath. "Pretty and pert, just as I'd imagined them."

She cranked her head over her shoulder despite the pain. "You were imagining my breasts."

"Among other things." He stroked her cheek. "Turn around."

She shimmied around to face him and then lay on the bed next to him. He pulled off her jeans and underwear as she twisted this way and that—anything to facilitate his access to her body.

He trailed his fingers from her neck to her belly, and she arched her back. Placing a finger against her throbbing lips, he said, "Don't hurt your neck. I'll do all the work."

She narrowed her eyes. "Do you think making love to me is going to be work?"

"Some of us love our jobs."

And she approved of the tools of his trade as he used his lips, tongue and fingers to push all the right buttons.

When he had her breathless and panting, he entered her fully.

Her hands clawed through his thick hair and then she dug her fingernails into his shoulders as he moved against her, in her, with her. Her muscles tightened, and she wrapped her arms and legs around his frame, drawing him further inside.

Ashlynn broke apart when she reached her climax, which gave him the signal to release. As she came down from her high, he thrust into her, building to his own peak.

When he came inside her, she felt his pleasure in every shiver and tremble of his body. Spent, he shifted to her side and growled in her ear, "Was that worth all the pain and suffering you've been through?"

Speechless, she nodded and turned toward him, molding her body to his side.

When the lethargy left her body and Denver's breathing no longer sounded like he'd just run a marathon, Ashlynn scooted off the bed. "I'm going to brush my teeth and splash some water on my face."

"I'll dispose of the evidence and put some

toothpaste on my finger and run it across my teeth." He gathered up the used condom with a tissue from her nightstand and planted his feet on the floor.

"I may even have an extra toothbrush from my dentist, so you don't need to rough it."

As Denver went to the kitchen to get some water, Ashlynn brushed her teeth, washed her face and found a brand-new toothbrush for him.

He handed her a glass of water and disappeared into the bathroom. By the time he came out, she'd straightened the covers and fluffed the pillows.

"Come join me." She patted the bed. "This is the part where we cuddle. Do you mind?"

"If that means I get to relish the touch of your bare skin against mine and wrap my fingers in your red-gold hair as I drift off to sleep, you can call that anything you like."

The bed dipped as he slid in beside her. He hadn't been kidding about the skin-on-skin contact or the hair, but there was no drifting for Denver. Within minutes of his head hitting the pillow, he was out.

She soaked in the feel of his heavy arm around her waist, his warm breath against the back of her neck. It felt good to have someone on that side of the bed again—she'd even deal with the messed-up covers in the morning.

He took a few shuddering breaths and rolled away from her, onto his other side.

A few minutes later, she hoisted herself up on one elbow and peered over his shoulder. That pesky lock of hair lay plastered against his forehead. Lifting it with one finger, she kissed the skin beneath it, her breasts pressing against his arm.

He stirred and mumbled in his sleep, and she held her breath until he settled again, his breathing slow and steady.

Then she slipped out of the bed. She bent at the waist and picked up his T-shirt from the floor, pinching it between two fingers. Dangling the shirt by her side, she tiptoed from the bedroom. She pulled the door almost closed behind her.

She dragged his T-shirt over her head, thrusting her hands through the sleeves. Her nostrils flared as she inhaled his scent—a mixture of citrus and spicy, his body wash and deodorant at war with each other.

With the T-shirt brushing her thighs, she padded to the kitchen, the cold tile shocking the soles of her bare feet. She settled into a chair at the kitchen table, and flipped open her charging laptop, the thumb drive still jutting out from the side.

She right-clicked the video icon on the screen and made quick work of copying the recording to her laptop. She ejected the drive and tugged it from the computer port. Swinging the thumb drive from its ribbon, she crept to where Denver had left his jacket draped over the back of the chair and tucked it into his pocket—so he wouldn't forget it in the morning.

She returned to the laptop, eyeing it as if it were a dangerous snake ready to strike. Then she plopped down on the chair and brought up *LA Confidential.*

Biting her bottom lip, she glanced down the hallway at the bedroom door behind which Denver lay slumbering like a man with no reason to suspect a betrayal. She shook her head and brushed her hair out of her face. Denver hadn't told her *not* to post this video.

The people of LA had a right to know the dirt about the campaign of one of its mayoral candidates. Her online sleuths had a right to know. Maybe with this video out there, someone else might step forward with more information. As far as Ashlynn could tell, her readers were the ones bringing the heat on this investigation—not the LAPD.

She clicked on the button for a new post and began to type, the words of the blockbuster story pounding against her temples. She read the first few sentences aloud in a harsh whisper. "'Escalante campaign busted. Proof surfaces that murdered student Tiana Fuller had volunteered for the campaign in a covert role.'"

Ashlynn's fingers flew across the keyboard, each click a nail in the coffin of her budding relationship with Detective Denver Holt.

Chapter Fifteen

Denver woke up with a start, his body bolting upright in the bed. For a second, he couldn't remember where he was. Then his fingers smoothed a lock of Ashlynn's bright hair against her pillow. But he sure remembered who he was with.

He eased out of the bed and crept from the room on silent feet. Ashlynn seemed to have a well-stocked fridge, unlike most single women he knew, so maybe he could whip up some breakfast for them before they had to take off.

He couldn't let her sleep much longer. He had to get home and change before work, and drop off Ashlynn at the tow yard to pick up her car. He couldn't exactly go into the station looking like this.

He swept his boxers from the floor and stepped into them. Then he snatched his neatly folded T-shirt from the top of her dresser. He cocked his head as he shook out the shirt. Had he placed it there while in the throes of lust? If so, he'd exercised more self-control than he remembered. He shrugged and pulled it over his head. After tugging up his jeans, he made a beeline for the kitchen.

Ashlynn's laptop sat on the kitchen table, charging. His heart skipped a beat as he brushed his hand across the side of the computer where he'd expected to find the thumb drive sticking out.

Then his heart skipped another beat as Ashlynn stood, framed in the hallway, naked from her head to her toes, a grin lighting up her face. "Good morning."

"Morning, you." He jabbed a finger at the laptop. "I was looking for Lulu's thumb drive."

"I put it in your pocket, so you wouldn't forget it this morning." She stretched her arms over her head, tangling her hair in her fingers, just as he'd done last night. "Are you making breakfast, or what?"

He made a sweeping motion with his hand. "Go do your thing. I'll whip up something."

While Ashlynn showered and dressed, Denver scrambled some eggs and shoved a couple of pieces of bread in the toaster. She'd run out of coffee, but he could always drink the swill at the station.

He glanced at her closed laptop on the table.

She was usually glued to that thing first thing in the morning. Shower must've been more important than the blog this morning.

"Smells great." She bustled through the room, her long legs in a pair of dark jeans, her red hair vibrant against an emerald-green sweater. She joined him in the kitchen. "Sorry, I don't have any coffee. Tea?"

"I'll get some coffee at the station." He nodded at her plate on the table and jabbed a fork into his own eggs. "I forgot to tell you yesterday in all the excitement, Tiana's parents mentioned a boy. A young man Tiana was hanging out with ever since the beginning of the new semester. They figured he lived nearby because she saw him when she was home."

"You already told me about him. Tony Fuentes, right?"

"Good memory. I must still be rattled." He shook his head as if to clear it, but he didn't think he'd ever dismiss the memory of Ashlynn's body beneath his hands. "With any luck, we'll get his number from Tiana's phone records. Weird that he hasn't called us if he was that close to Tiana."

"If he was her boyfriend, it's strange that he hasn't stepped forward." She crunched her toast.

"Not sure it reached that level, but parents are usually the last to know with these new dating rules."

"Are there new rules?" She blinked. "No wonder I can't get lucky."

He cleared his throat. "What would you call last night?"

"Luck had nothing to do with that." She fluttered her eyelashes. "I set my sights on you from the start."

Had she? Instead of feeling flattered, wings of anxiety took flight in his belly. He'd stumbled right into her web by playing the hero to the rescue. She'd been in real danger, though. She hadn't faked any of that.

She nudged him. "I'm joking."

"We'd better get moving." He shoved the last bite of toast in his mouth and chewed. "After I drop you at the tow yard, I have to go home and shower and change." He took his plate to the sink and rinsed it off before putting it in the dishwasher. "The thumb drive is in my pocket, right?"

"Yeah." She bumped his hip with hers in front of the sink. "I'm going to finish these delicious eggs, and then I'll put away the rest of this stuff. You should collect your gun. You don't wanna leave that here."

He tugged at the ends of her hair and kissed the crumbs off her mouth. "I'm glad you're safe. I'm glad Lulu's safe. How's your neck?"

"In need of pain relief. How's your knee?"

Reaching down and squeezing it, he said, "Just another war wound."

He left her in the kitchen and clipped his holster onto his belt. He felt the side pocket of his jacket, his fingers tracing the oblong shape of the thumb drive. Jed would have some explaining to do today and, with any luck, so would Tony Fuentes.

Ashlynn had been unusually quiet on the drive to the tow yard. Had they made a mistake sleeping together? How could a mistake feel so good? But the act had introduced a level of awkwardness between them that hadn't existed before.

Maybe once this case was over, they could date like normal people. He didn't even know what that looked like anymore. Other women he'd gone out with in the past had accused him of being cold and aloof.

He'd tried that with Ashlynn, but she'd poked through his reserve. He huffed out a breath as he pulled onto the freeway. He'd better get a grip. He couldn't be detached when he'd found Ashlynn in danger—and she always seemed to be in danger. The heightened stakes had them colliding together. She'd wanted him last night because he'd rescued her, and he couldn't deny it to himself that he'd wanted her for the same reason.

Coming to the rescue still gave him a charge,

but only if he succeeded. If he were to fail...
again, he'd wind up in a very dark place.

After showering and changing at home, he
drove to the station. He parked and burst inside
with purpose driving his steps. He'd call Jed
Gordon first thing and ask him about the video.
Then he'd circle back to the Wexler campaign
and ask them what they knew about Escalante's
dirty tricks. Christian had finally sent over the
list of volunteers, and it was no surprise that
Tiana wasn't among them.

As he jogged upstairs, he passed Detective
Marino, who slapped him on the back. "Good
deal when the journos do our work for us, isn't
it? I'm glad I let you take lead."

Denver almost tripped on the next step.
"What?"

Marino waved his hand without answering,
and Denver continued to his desk in Homicide,
his steps decidedly slower. Was Marino directing that comment to him?

He yanked out his chair and fished the thumb
drive out of his pocket. As he booted up his
laptop, Captain Fields poked her head into the
room. "Holt, my office."

With his mouth dry, he glanced around the
room, but nobody met his eyes. He was being
paranoid. He was lead detective on the Tiana

Fuller case. Of course, the captain wanted to talk to him.

He tossed the drive in the air and caught it, clenching his hand around it. He had something to show her.

Captain Fields was already behind her desk when he approached the door. "Captain?"

"Have a seat, Holt."

He kicked out the chair in front of her desk and sat back. He didn't want to put his anxiety on display. He waited while she tapped her keyboard.

When he heard Jed Gordon's voice talking to Tiana Fuller, the blood drained from his face and his hands gripped the arms of the chair like claws.

Captain Fields spun her laptop around to face him, but he didn't need to look at the video. "How is it that a blogger is getting more information about the Tiana Fuller case than you are, Holt?"

He relaxed his clenched jaw and tipped his closed fist over, dropping the thumb drive on the blotter in front of her. "I have the same thing. That's Jed Gordon, Councilwoman Escalante's campaign manager, and he's talking to Tiana Fuller."

Her gaze flicked to the thumb drive. "I know that already and so does half of LA. My question to you is, why did half the city know this before I did?"

He lifted a stiff shoulder. "I guess my source delivered this video to me and... *LA Confidential.*"

"You say *LA Confidential* as if that's a person. Your source didn't deliver it to *LA Confidential.* He or she delivered it to Ashlynn Hughes—the enemy."

His eyebrows jumped. "Enemy. That's kinda strong. I—I mean, she's not her brother. Her brother was murdered, for God's sake."

Hadn't Ashlynn just become the enemy to him? A person who'd used him, slept with him, to pull a fast one. The captain was right.

"Don't get me wrong." Captain Fields ended the video. "What The Player did to Sean Hughes was despicable. Nobody in this department would say otherwise, but when you play with fire, you can expect to get burned."

He rubbed his knuckles along his jaw, feeling the singe. "I don't think Ashlynn is as bad as her brother."

She just might be worse.

"Nevertheless, I don't like being blindsided, Holt."

"I'm sorry, Captain, but I can't control my sources. If they want to communicate with the press, they have a right to do that." He swept up the thumb drive and rapped his knuckles on the desk. "I was about to get right on this. I interviewed Jed Gordon yesterday, and he told me at the time he'd never heard of or seen Tiana Fuller. He might just be my first suspect."

"Get to it, Holt. I just hope the blogger didn't spook Gordon."

"If he runs now, we have even more reason to suspect him."

"Don't make me regret taking a floater and making you lead detective on this, Holt." She waved her hand in dismissal.

"No, ma'am." So, he had Captain Field to thank for his position, not Marino.

As he walked back to his desk, he ground his back teeth. Why the hell was he defending Ashlynn to Captain Fields? She'd betrayed him.

Ashlynn hadn't been interested in her laptop this morning because she'd already written her blog and posted the video. When did she have time for that? Between kisses?

He slumped in his chair and brought up *LA Confidential* on his phone. He'd be damned if he'd let the other detectives catch him reading the blog on his laptop.

He didn't need to play the video, but he read the blog, his breath coming in short spurts as he cupped his hand over his cell. Damn, Ashlynn was a good writer.

The post had already garnered hundreds of

comments. He'd cull through them for anything useful. What had Marino said... *journos do our work for us*? That might be good enough for Marino, but Denver wasn't about to let it happen on his watch.

He pulled Jed Gordon's card from the file on his desk, flicked the corner and then tucked it into his breast pocket. If Jed had any intention of running, Denver didn't want to give him a head start by calling him first.

Grabbing the keys to his department vehicle, he called out to nobody in particular. "Heading out for an interview."

Billy yelled back at him. "Get there before the blogger."

Denver held up his middle finger as he strode out the door, a chorus of laughter erupting behind him.

Wait until they found out he'd slept with that blogger last night. That wouldn't come from him, but who knows what Ashlynn had planned in her quest for blog world dominance.

When he got to his car, he shrugged off his jacket, feeling warm under the collar already. He smoothed it onto the front seat and took off for the Escalante campaign headquarters. He didn't expect to find Ashlynn there. She'd been made.

He'd better find Jed there.

This time when he burst through the door,

heads swiveled and eyes darted. Before he had a chance to open his mouth, demanding to see Jed Gordon, the man himself glided out of his office, hand outstretched.

"Detective, I expected to see you this morning. Please join me for coffee down the street."

Denver gripped the other man's hand and searched his drawn face, the eyes pleading for... something. Was there fear in that look?

Nodding, Denver said, "Just so happened, I missed my morning coffee."

Jed's shoulders sagged in relief before his lips stretched into a smile. "Excellent. We can walk."

Jed barked a few orders to the staff on the way out, and heaved a long breath when they hit the sidewalk.

Denver looked over at him. "Everyone see that video?"

Jed said through gritted teeth, "Yes, and I'd like to know where that...blogger got it."

"Why'd you lie, Gordon?"

Jed put his fingers to his forehead and closed his eyes. "Can we wait until I'm sitting down with some coffee in front of me?"

Denver sealed his lips and walked beside Jed in silence until they reached a coffeehouse on the corner. Jed ordered a complicated concoction while Denver opted for the daily brew—black. He picked up the tab to get on Jed's good side.

When they sat across from each other at a large table, Jed slurped from his coffee cup. A thin layer of foam coated his upper lip, but he didn't seem to notice. "I lied to you yesterday. I knew Tiana Fuller and asked her to spy on the Wexler campaign for us."

"Yeah, I know that now." Denver popped the lid on his cup and blew on the steaming liquid. "The question is why."

"Why do you think?"

"Let me ask the questions, Gordon." Denver drilled his finger into the table, and Jed jerked back, his coffee sloshing over the rim.

"I asked a young woman to put herself at risk by pulling a few dirty tricks on Wexler, and she was found in the trunk of a Wexler car in a grungy lake. That makes me, the campaign and Veronica look bad."

"Yeah, you should've seen how it made Tiana look."

Jed's eyes bulged. "I never meant that young woman to come to any harm—none of us did. These things happen between political opponents. A little mudslinging here, a little defamation there—it's all part of the political landscape. The voters believe what they want to believe anyway."

"Whose idea was it to enlist Tiana Fuller's help?"

"It was hers."

"Sure it was." Denver crumpled a paper napkin in his fist. "She came up with that plan all by herself."

"Not the actual plan, but the suggestion." Jed swirled his coffee, his tongue darting out to capture some foam from the surface of the liquid. "Why do you think I videoed it on my phone?"

Denver leaned forward, spreading his hands on the table. "Explain it to me like I'm real stupid."

"I—I figured if I had Tiana on record agreeing to the plan, if anything happened, I'd have proof that she was a willing participant."

"What did you expect to happen?"

"Not *murder.*" Jed's hand trembled so much, he had to set his cup down. "What could Tiana have possibly found out about the Wexler campaign that led them to murder her?"

"'Them'?"

"Wexler's people." Jed waved his hands in the air. "Isn't that obvious? The CREW found out Tiana was spying and took care of her…in one of their own cars."

Denver tented his fingers. "What *did* Tiana find out? Did she report anything to you?"

"She filed a few reports with me, but it was stupid, petty stuff. She discovered some of the Wexler volunteers were ripping down Escalante posters, creating fake social media accounts to bolster Wexler and criticize Escalante—that kind of thing. Do you think anything like that warrants murder?"

"Not one for politics, but I can't imagine it would. Was she working on something? Did she ever indicate to you that she'd discovered something big?" Denver's phone dinged in his pocket, signaling an incoming text, but he ignored it. He wasn't ready to hear Ashlynn's excuses or apologies.

"Never. Like I said before, all minor league stuff."

"Did Councilwoman Escalante know about Tiana's role in the campaign?"

"No!" Jed folded his hands around his cup, his face reddening. "She called me this morning and read me the riot act when she saw that video."

Denver traced a finger around the rim of his cup, his eyes downcast to the dark liquid he'd barely tasted. "Was she mad that you recruited Tiana to spy, or was she mad that you made the video and got caught?"

"Veronica is clean." Jed pounded his fist on the table and the little packets of sugar danced.

Denver held up his hands. "She's a politician. You just said this was common practice."

"Among the campaign workers."

"Oh, okay." Denver nodded slowly. "How did Tiana get all this information for you?"

Shrugging, Jed said, "I don't know. I didn't ask, and she didn't tell."

"What did you mean earlier when you said this spying was Tiana's idea?"

"Just that. She's the one who suggested it. Said she had some contacts in the CREW and she could use them to get some dirt on Wexler."

"That's not on the video." Denver drummed his fingers on the table. He still didn't get why Jed had lied to him about Tiana's role in the campaign if she'd just discovered minor infractions.

"I—I couldn't get my phone in place fast enough to record the beginning of our meeting, but trust me. Tiana came on as a volunteer, bumped into me at a lunch spot down the street and made her case. Of course, I jumped on it."

"How come none of the other volunteers know Tiana, or were they lying, too?"

"Lulu gave Tiana the tour." Jed took a sip of his coffee and choked on it.

Had he just realized who'd stolen the video from his computer?

Jed cleared his throat. "Lulu got her signed up, and then destroyed Tiana's paperwork on my command. If Tiana got caught Watergate-style, I didn't want it to come back and bite us."

"If that's all that had happened." Denver fished his phone from his pocket after the second insistent ping and glanced at the unknown number, and the beginning of a text with his name.

"Are we finished here?" Jed pointed to Denver's phone. "Looks like you're busy, and I have to get back to it. I'll tell you anything you want, Detective. I don't have anything to hide, and neither does Veronica."

"Good, because I plan to pay her a visit." Denver lifted his cup. "You can leave. I'll stay and finish my coffee."

He watched Jed exit the coffeehouse, already on his phone. Was Jed warning Veronica? He seemed to worship the woman. The two of them had probably been discussing Tiana at the fundraiser last night when Ashlynn had seen them by the pool.

He tapped the insistent text, and adrenaline pumped through his system. Tiana's friend, Tony Fuentes, had finally surfaced and wanted to meet with him. He called the number on the text, but it went straight to a generic voice mail.

Two minutes later, Tony texted him that he couldn't talk on the phone but would meet with him in Venice by the pier. Why did everyone want to meet in Venice all of a sudden?

They arranged a meet location, and Denver took his coffee to keep him company on the long trip to the west side of the city. He could stop by Escalante's place on the way back to the station.

When he slid behind the wheel, he reached for his phone to text Ashlynn to tell her about Tony. He dropped it in the cup holder instead. Ashlynn Hughes could wait.

By the time he reached the Venice Pier, he had the AC blasting. They'd just come off a week of scattered showers, but the sun had been making a stronger appearance ever since and had hit peak Southern California spring beach day.

He parked in the lot next to the strand and left his jacket in the car. He stepped onto the asphalt, the sand crunching beneath his shoes. He couldn't do anything about his wingtips, but he could lose the tie.

He loosened his tie, pulled it over his head and undid the top buttons of his shirt. He dropped his tie on top of his jacket and locked up. He usually didn't leave anything on the seat of his car, especially in an area like this, but he figured the local beach transients wouldn't be interested in stealing his jacket and tie.

As he clumped through the dry sand, he rolled up his sleeves. Tony couldn't have picked a worse location, but Denver didn't want to spook the skittish boyfriend.

He spotted a figure beneath the pier and trudged over the beach toward him. As he drew closer, another person appeared next to the pilings, red hair streaming behind her in the breeze.

Denver's heart rattled his ribs. What the hell was Ashlynn doing here—at his meeting?

He picked up the pace and hit wet sand, veering to his right. "Tony Fuentes?"

The young man with a beard gathered his shoulder-length dark hair with one hand. "That's me. Detective Holt?"

Denver gripped Tony's hand and said, "Now that we've established who we are, can I ask why she's here?"

"Why do you think, Denver?" Ashlynn released her hair to put her hands on her hips, and the red locks caught fire from the sun as they whipped around her face. "This is my source."

Tony raised his hand. "Anthony Angel Fuentes, at your service."

Chapter Sixteen

Ashlynn sucked in her bottom lip. Denver looked ready to explode. She hadn't planned on contacting him today, hadn't even told him about this meeting with Angel, but when she'd seen Denver scuffing through the dry sand and realized Angel had called him, too, she wasn't going to run away. She wanted to hear what Angel had to say.

Denver closed his eyes for a second and wiped the back of his hand over his gleaming forehead. She felt for him. He must be burning up in that suit, or half a suit. He certainly *looked* hot.

"Why did you contact a blogger about Tiana's murder instead of the police, and I mean right from the beginning?"

Tony hunched his thin shoulders, his T-shirt billowing around his gaunt frame. "I was scared, dude. I wasn't sure you'd connect me to T, and I didn't want to expose myself. I don't wanna be next."

Denver held up his phone. "I'm recording this interview."

Not waiting for Tony's approval, Denver recorded the date and time, along with Tony's name. Then he went straight for the jugular. "Do you know who killed Tiana?"

"I don't know who did it." Tony ran his fingers through his beard. "I—I only know how they disposed of her body."

Ashlynn asked, "How do you know that? How did you know about the car in the lake?"

Denver had turned his back to her, as if he could cut her out of his exchange with Tony. As if Tony hadn't contacted her, too. As if she wasn't a part of this investigation just as much as he was.

She pushed her way into their circle.

"I saw it happen." Tony ducked his head and his long hair curtained his face. When he looked up, he had tears in his eyes. "I knew T was meeting someone. I told her not to go. I warned her. She wouldn't listen to me."

"I know the feeling." Denver's jaw formed a hard line. "Who was she meeting? What did she find out about the Wexler campaign that led to her murder?"

"Dude, I don't know. She wouldn't tell me."

Ashlynn curled her toes into the wet sand.

"How did you and Tiana know each other, school?"

"Yeah, we had a few poli-sci classes together." Tony wiped his face and sniffled. "I'm the one who got her to volunteer for the campaigns in the first place. It's my fault she's dead."

"Hold on a minute." Denver unbuttoned another button of his shirt. "Campaigns? How many campaigns did Tiana work for?"

Tony blinked. "Just the two."

"Two? What two? You lost me."

Denver finally glanced at her, a question in his eyes, but she quickly lifted and dropped her shoulders. Tony hadn't told her a thing.

"The Escalante and Wexler campaigns. She worked for both of them."

Denver's wide eyes and open mouth reflected her own feelings, and she took advantage of his momentary loss for words.

"Tiana wasn't very dedicated to either candidate, was she? Or was she just trying to get as much experience as possible?"

"Oh, no. She was dedicated to re-electing Mayor Wexler. We both were—are."

Denver had recovered and got in the question hovering on her own lips. "If she was pro Wexler, why was she working for the Escalante campaign and in that particular capacity?"

"Dude, I thought you knew." Tony turned his

head and spit into the sand. "She was working for the Escalante campaign as a mole. She was team CREW all the way."

Folding his arms, Denver said, "Dude, I didn't know that. How was I supposed to know that with you playing hide-and-seek and slipping tips to a *blogger* instead of the police?"

Ashlynn's blood simmered as Tony's eyes darted between her and Denver. "I figured you already talked to the CREW."

"I did talk to them—Amalia Fernandez and Christian Bushnell, to be precise. Both denied knowledge of Tiana Fuller."

"Dude, that sucks." Shaking his head, Tony covered his face. "I don't know why they're playing that game. Christian knows Tiana. He's the one T told about her plan to infiltrate Escalante's campaign."

Denver ran a hand through his hair. "Was that all Tiana's plan or Christian's?"

"That was all T, man." Tony grinned through his beard. "That girl was fearless. She suggested it to Christian and he gave his stamp of approval, but even if he hadn't, she would've done it, anyway. Then she joined the Escalante campaign and suggested to *them* that she spy on Wexler."

"How do you know she wasn't really working for Escalante and spying on Wexler?" Ashlynn glanced at Denver. "She was found in a Wexler car, not an Escalante car."

"I thought about that, but no way. She was all-in for Wexler. She was especially in favor of his slow-growth policies for the city. You see what Escalante and her husband are planning for downtown?"

"Slow down." Denver drew a line in the sand with the toe of his shoe. "That could've been her plan, but maybe she actually discovered some dirt about Wexler—dirty enough to result in murder."

"I can't believe that." Tony had the ring of the true believer in his voice.

"Let's go back to the car in the lake." Denver wiped the face of his phone on his pant leg. "How did you manage to witness that?"

"T had shared her phone's location with me weeks before her murder. Maybe she forgot, because I did. But when she didn't call me after her meeting, I freaked. Then I remembered she'd shared her location, and I brought it up on my phone. I couldn't figure out why she was heading out toward Angeles Crest, but I had a bad feeling. I followed the phone, and it took me to Lake Kawayu. The phone stopped working at that point, but I got there just in time to see two guys pushing a car into the lake."

Ashlynn covered her mouth. "Why didn't you call 9-1-1? Tiana could've still been alive."

"She wasn't!" Tony grabbed his hair at the roots, looking like a wild man. He turned wide eyes on Denver. "Tell me she wasn't. Tell me she didn't drown in that trunk while I watched from my safe distance."

Denver's voice had a rough edge when he answered the feverish question. "She wasn't. They shot her before they put her in the trunk. The coroner didn't find any water in her lungs. Did you get a good look at the two men?"

"No, but I swear they heard me. They definitely heard my car. I think they might be after me." Tony sank to his knees in the wet sand and sobbed. "I'm such a coward. Maybe I could've saved her."

Denver dropped his hand to the young man's shoulder. "I don't think so, Tony. You're doing the right thing now. We're going to find out who did this, and you're going to do the right thing by T and testify, right?"

"I will, I will." Tony dragged a hand across his runny nose. "Dude, I gotta go now. My ride's coming."

Denver ended the recording on his phone. "I can reach you at the number you used to text me?"

"Yeah, it's a burner, but I'm keeping it." Tony

staggered to his feet. "Don't put this in *LA Confidential*. The CREW will know it's me, and I just can't right now."

"I'll figure out something. You're helping Tiana now, Tony." She squeezed his arm. "Just keep cooperating with Detective Holt."

That earned her a quick glance from Denver.

"For sure." Tony wiped his face on his T-shirt and jogged down the beach on the packed sand.

Ashlynn pulled her sweater around her as the breeze from the ocean picked up. "Wow, this is a tangled web. Tiana was playing with fire any way you look at it—a double agent."

"Maybe, but she didn't get murdered for being a mole. She discovered something more serious than dirty tricks that someone wanted to keep quiet."

Ashlynn licked her lips, tasting the salt from the air. "I'm sorry I didn't tell you about posting that video on the blog. I had to do it, and I knew you'd object."

Denver shoved his hands in his pockets and stared at the ocean, roiling and spitting just a few feet in front of them, the spray clinging to his dark hair, making it curl at the ends.

"I have to hand it to you. You pulled a fast one, seducing me, getting me into bed so that you could sneak back and copy the video to your laptop."

Her jaw dropped. "Th-that's not… I didn't…"

"Save it for your readers. It might even make a good post for the almighty blog—how you tricked an LAPD wannabe homicide detective into leaving important evidence in your possession."

Tears stung her eyes as she reached out for him. "That's not why I slept with you. Making love with you last night was the first real joy I've felt since my brother died. The first time I've felt real and whole."

"Good for you."

As she watched him trudge through the sand back to the strand through blurred vision, one tear fell over the rim of her eye and ran down her cheek.

Looked like her brother had won again.

Chapter Seventeen

Denver's lead foot pressed against the accelerator in his zeal to get away from the beach and Ashlynn as quickly as possible—before he changed his mind about her.

Funny thing was, he'd felt the same way about last night—a connection with her, something solid and real after dozens of dates where he'd been afraid to scratch beneath any surface level.

He muttered to himself. "That's what she wanted you to feel."

He cruised down the freeway to the house of Veronica Escalante and her husband Kent Meadows. Meadows was a fat cat who had supported his younger wife's political aspirations. Escalante had recused herself from a few city council votes that had involved city planning where her husband could directly benefit. Still seemed shady to him.

He pulled up to the same drive he'd sat across from last night, but the valet attendants and lights were gone. In their place, gardeners worked the landscaping in the front of the house, the noise from their leaf blowers reverberating in the air.

When Denver got out of his vehicle, he waved and the gardener wielding the blower cut the motor. Denver called out, "Thanks."

He ascended the steps to the front door and pressed the doorbell, stepping back in case someone wanted to get a look at him from the peephole or the cameras in the corner.

A female voice came over a speaker. "Who is it, please?"

Denver unclipped the badge from his belt and held it up. "Detective Holt, LAPD, ma'am. I need to talk to Councilwoman Escalante."

"Just a minute, please."

At least she was polite as she left him out on the porch in the heat. A minute later, the door opened and a woman, her hair in a tight bun, with a tighter smile, stood before him. "Come in, Detective. Would you like something to drink? Iced tea? Coffee? Water?"

"Nothing, thanks."

She bowed her head. "This way, please."

He followed her, the heels of his shoes clicking on the tile floor behind her crepe soles. She pushed open another door off the great room, all signs of the party vanished.

She took one step into the room, a library or office, and said, "This is Detective Holt, Kent."

"Thanks, Mom." A fit-for-his-age man stood behind the desk, smoothing a hand along the side of his silver hair. He looked about the same age as *Mom*. "Detective, have a seat. I'm Kent Meadows."

Denver strode into the room and leaned across the desk to shake Meadows's hand; the older man's grip firm and practiced.

"Your wife isn't home?"

Meadows smiled, his blue eyes twinkling. "Ah, the demands of a campaign. I didn't want you to waste your time, Detective. Who knows? Veronica might show up before we're finished here."

Denver jerked his thumb over his shoulder. "Mom?"

"Rita is my mother-in-law."

"She works for you?"

Meadows waved his hands, his fingers tapering to a polished manicure. "Unofficial hostess. She lives in the appropriately named mother-in-law quarters in the back of the property—her own house—that she shares with Lulu, Veronica's sister. What can we help you with, Detective? I'm sure you're here about that unfortunate incident with that girl in the lake."

"Incident? It was a homicide, and your wife's

campaign manager is on video with that girl in the lake, asking her to spy on Wexler's campaign."

"Of course, of course." Meadows folded his hands on his desk. "Tragic. I assume you've talked to Jed Gordon."

"I spoke with him. He couldn't deny the video, but said Veronica had nothing to do with the request."

The nostrils of Meadows's patrician nose flared. "Jed would say anything to protect Veronica."

Denver raised his eyebrows. "You don't believe him? Do you think your wife knew about Tiana Fuller?"

"Oh, I believe him. My wife doesn't concern herself too much with the volunteers or the nuts and bolts of the campaign. I take care of the financing and Jed takes care of the details, and Veronica does what she does best—connects with the people."

"I was hoping to talk to Veronica to find out if Jed told her anything about Tiana or what she may have discovered about the Wexler campaign."

Meadows eased back in his chair and flicked the drapes behind him, revealing a view of the meticulously tended garden in front of the house. "You're in luck, Detective Holt. My wife just pulled up to the house, but she looks busy. She's on her cell phone and she's not even out of the car yet."

"I won't take up too much of her time." Denver pushed back from the desk to get a view of Veronica Escalante stepping from a Porsche, teetering on a pair of stiletto heels, her phone to her ear, a bag slung over her shoulder.

Denver's gaze shifted from the window to a credenza behind Meadows, boasting several photos of construction sites. He pointed to one. "That's the Meadows Plaza downtown, right?"

Meadows's eyes flicked like a lizard's in his tanned face. "I hope it will be. Construction has stalled for the moment, but it should resume shortly."

"Shortly, as in when your wife gets elected mayor of LA?"

Meadows's lips stretched into a smile, but this time there was no twinkling of the eyes. "That's not how it operates, Detective."

"Are you waiting to see me?" Councilwoman Escalante's voice sounded different from her commercials and speeches. She'd lost the Spanish accent she put on for public appearances.

As Denver turned toward her, Meadows said, "This is Detective Holt, Veronica. Of course, he has some questions about that idiot Gordon and the video of him and that murdered girl. Why did he try to hide it in the first place?"

"You know Jed, my love." Veronica strode forward, her heels sinking into the thick carpet. She shook Denver's hand with a feminine hold, which she ended quickly.

She skirted him and placed a kiss on her husband's forehead. "Thank you for filling in for me, *mi amor*."

Meadows hopped up from his chair, his wife in those heels besting him by about three inches. "You two use my office. I've had a long day. I'm going to rustle up a drink before dinner. I'll be out at the pool, *mi vida*."

The Meadows kissed again, and Denver felt in danger of choking on saccharine sweetness if he stayed in their presence much longer. Was this lovey-dovey stuff for his benefit? He didn't even vote.

Meadows touched his fingers to his forehead as he left the room. "Nice meeting you, Detective. Good to see my donations to the Police Protective League not going to waste."

Whatever that meant.

Veronica sat in a leather love seat against the wall, crossing her shapely legs. "Only my husband sits behind his desk, Detective Holt. Have a seat and let me know how I can help. I feel terrible that Tiana worked for our campaign and that Jed knew it and wasn't forthcoming when you first questioned him. I've already talked to

Jed about that, but surely any dirty tricks Tiana played on the Wexler campaign didn't result in her murder. That's just crazy to think that. Nobody gets murdered over tearing down flyers."

Typical politician. He'd have to talk fast to get a word in. "Did you ever meet or talk to Tiana?"

"No, I usually don't interact with the volunteers except to give pep talks or maybe buy pizzas." She flashed a fake smile. "They're invited to certain events, like our fundraiser last night."

"Have you seen Tiana's picture? Did you recognize her from any of those occasions?"

She squinted her dark eyes. "I did see her picture—pretty girl—but I had never seen her before, and if Jed was using her for undercover work, he probably wouldn't have invited her to any of the events."

"Did Jed tell you what Tiana had discovered about Wexler?"

"I told you, Detective. I didn't know anything about Tiana until after the video, and Jed told me what I'm sure he told you—petty tricks. We don't know anything about Wexler, except that he's not for LA at this time, and we're going to turn things around, including with the LAPD. Mayor Wexler and Chief Sterling are too cozy. The LAPD needs more oversight." She winked. "Although I'm sure you don't."

Denver held out one hand. "I'm not here to

discuss LAPD policies, Councilwoman. I suppose Jed had no inkling that Tiana was actually a mole."

"What?" Veronica's confidence wavered with her voice. "What are you talking about?"

"According to one of my sources, Tiana didn't support you at all. She was all for Wexler and was playing Jed to get into your campaign."

Veronica's face paled. "That little…bi…sneak. She really wanted to get down and dirty, didn't she? If you're suggesting she might've discovered anything about our campaign, I can shut down that line of thinking right now. We play by the rules."

"Of course." Denver rose, leveling a finger at the photo of the Meadows Plaza construction site. "Too bad that project is stalled. Would be nice for downtown."

Veronica flicked a strand of dark hair over her shoulder as she rose from the love seat. "I'll let you know if I learn anything else about Tiana. Does Jed know she was a mole?"

"Not yet, but I'm sure you'll tell him. I'll see myself out." As Denver transitioned from the office to the great room, he let out a breath.

He sure hoped Escalante came across better with her constituents. She put him on edge.

The gardeners were planting a new bed of flowers under the direction of Veronica's mother as he maneuvered down the walkway. When he reached the gate, Mrs. Escalante touched the sleeve of his jacket.

He jerked his head around and she put her finger to her lips. "You're here about that murdered girl?"

"I am. Do you know something about her, Mrs. Escalante?"

She glanced over her shoulder at the house. "Just that she was here several times, *muchos tiempos*."

Chapter Eighteen

Ashlynn glanced between her phone and the door of the high-rise office building, as she sipped an iced tea on the patio of the office complex. The tall buildings created a wind tunnel and bits of debris swirled in mini tornadoes. She pushed her hair out of her face and replied to Lulu's text.

Veronica's sister had contacted her earlier to let her know she was okay and to inquire about her well-being. Once they'd assured each other that they were unharmed, Lulu had pressed her for information about her friend.

Ashlynn had Lulu half convinced already that he was just a friend looking out for them. He hadn't even known why they were meeting.

She had asked Lulu if she'd been followed to the dog park and if she'd recognized the man who had accosted them, and now she sat tapping her toe, waiting for a reply.

Glancing up as the office door swung open,

she stuffed her phone in her purse. Lulu's response would have to wait.

She jumped to her feet, her ponytail swinging behind her, and caught up with the fresh-faced young man hurrying from the office building, a stack of folders beneath one arm.

"Christian?"

He swung around, almost dropping the files. "Y-yes. Do I know you?"

"Not yet." Ashlynn gave an encouraging smile. Christian needed kid-glove handling, which was probably why Denver hadn't gotten anything out of him. Had he tried again after their meeting with Tony? He wouldn't have had time—or at least Christian wouldn't look so carefree if he'd just come from a meeting with Detective Holt.

Christian tipped his head, a shy smile curling one corner of his mouth. "I'm sorry?"

She hated to disrupt the happy vibe here, but someone had to do it. Taking a few steps in his direction, she thrust out her hand. "I'm Ashlynn Hughes from *LA Confidential*."

You would've thought she'd told him she was from the IRS with an audit request the way the color drained from his face and then all came rushing back, staining his cheeks in a crimson tide.

"I—I don't have anything to say to you. We

already talked to that detective, gave him our volunteer list. That's all." He pressed his lips together, as if willing himself to be quiet.

"You talked to Detective Holt today?"

"Today?" He gulped, his Adam's apple bobbing in the slim column of his throat. "A few days ago. Is he coming back?"

"He just might." Ashlynn shifted her gaze to the side without turning her head, indicating they could expect him at any time. "But you can talk to me instead…and it's all confidential. I won't report your name. You don't have to testify to anything. Just between us."

"What do you want from me?" He hugged the folders to his chest, a poor substitute for armor. "I don't know anything about Tiana Fuller."

"I know that's not true, and Detective Holt's gonna know soon enough." She didn't have to terrify him any more by letting him know Denver already knew.

She took a step back toward the table and her iced tea. "Let's sit down a minute. I'm not going to record you or report your name. I just want to verify some information for my blog. It doesn't have to be about you, or even the Wexler campaign."

He followed her to the table, his gait stiff, and sat across from her, folding his thin frame in half. "What do you know? Or what do you think you know?"

She wrapped her ponytail around her hand and sucked in her bottom lip. "I know that Tiana did work for the CREW, that she was dedicated to re-electing Mayor Wexler—just like I am. I know that she offered to infiltrate the Escalante campaign as a spy, and then she pretended to fulfill the same role there as she actually had with the CREW. How am I doing so far?"

Christian's head dropped once. "That's what she was doing, but I didn't tell her to do it. Nobody did. That was just Tiana. She wanted to do it, thought it would be fun."

"Okay, okay." She folded her hands in front of her. "Tiana was an adult. I'm sure she made her own decisions. But what happened? What did she discover?"

"It wasn't about us." Christian crossed his hands over his chest. "I swear. She didn't find anything on Mayor Wexler. She wasn't even looking. She was digging into Escalante, not the mayor. She had no access to anything at our campaign headquarters. She never even came in."

"You think she found out something about Escalante?" She tapped her fingernails against her plastic cup.

"She must have, but she didn't tell me." He

snapped his fingers. "She might've told one of the other volunteers—Tony. They were tight."

Been there, done that.

"How did she wind up in the trunk of one of your cars?"

"I can't tell you. I couldn't tell the cops, either. Honestly, nobody keeps tabs on those cars. I've known volunteers to take them out to pick up lunch and bring them back four days later, nobody the wiser. Tiana herself used the cars sometimes."

"She never gave you any hint about what she was working on? What she might've found?"

"Nothing, but she seemed…"

"What?" Ashlynn hunkered forward. "Go on."

"Secretly satisfied?" He rubbed his clean-shaved chin, which looked as if it had never experienced razor burn. "You might think she'd have been worried with all the subterfuge, but she seemed pleased about something. That's how I'd describe it. That's why I was so shocked when I found out she'd been murdered. She was happy, not scared."

"Maybe she didn't know enough to be scared, but she should've been." Ashlynn rattled the ice in her cup. "How come you didn't tell Detective Holt any of this?"

"First of all, he interviewed me with my boss.

If I had said one word, I would've been fired. This is a paid gig for me. I got the feeling Detective Holt wanted to get me on my own. He's been leaving me messages, and I've been avoiding them."

"This is a woman's life here, Christian. It's not fun and political games."

"You don't think politics are life and death? Neither did Tiana, and look what happened to her." He straightened the files on the table. "Amalia doesn't want it known that one of our volunteers was murdered. It's bad enough that Tiana was found in one of our cars. Looks like the Escalante campaign didn't want to claim her, either."

"Poor Tiana. Both campaigns were eager to use her, and then disowned her when she needed them."

After she assured Christian she wouldn't use his name in her blog, he escaped to where he was headed when she'd waylaid him.

She checked her phone for Lulu's response to her most recent text, but she hadn't answered the all-important question of whether or not she'd been followed last night. She had assured Ashlynn that she had left town and was keeping a low profile, especially as Jed had accused her of stealing and then leaking the video.

She sucked down the rest of her tea and took

a big breath. Before running to her blog to release this latest piece of information, she had
some amends to make first.

She couldn't believe Denver thought she'd se-
duced him just to post that video before he could
question Jed. It looked bad, but she'd wanted that
man from the get-go, and it had nothing to do
with *LA Confidential*—for once.

She called Denver and held her breath as his
phone rang. Would he brush her off?

He picked up after the third ring. "Yeah."

"I'm going to apologize without saying sorry."

He huffed out a long breath. "You like playing games, Ashlynn. I don't."

"Yeah, like dissing me at lunch the other day
after we'd been getting along great was not some
kind of maneuver?"

"I think I made up for that, or I thought I did.
Didn't realize I was getting handled."

"Now I'm going to make it up to you. I have
some information from Christian Bushnell, and
I'm coming to you first instead of splashing it
all over my blog."

He caught his breath. "I have some information, too."

She smacked her palm on the table for her
own benefit. "Then let's get together and return
to our original purpose."

"Dinner tonight?"

Her heart fluttered in her chest. "I'd love to have dinner with you and compare notes."

"Marina, The Warehouse, seven o'clock."

He ended the call before she even had a chance to respond. There was only one response to give. Whether Denver Holt believed her not, she might be ready to put something or someone ahead of the blog.

For once, she was more excited to see Denver than to hear the information he had about the case. Would he believe her?

DENVER TOOK A sip of beer through the thick head on the top. He had to be out of his mind. He should be sharing this information with Marino, not Ashlynn, even though she had worked harder on this case than Marino had. Could he trust that she wouldn't run off to post it for her followers?

She wouldn't if he explained to her how it could compromise the case. The video of Jed and Tiana hadn't done that. He'd had no intention of tiptoeing around Jed Gordon, but this piece of knowledge demanded a certain level of secrecy.

He spied Ashlynn on the edge of the bar, surveying the dining tables. When their eyes met, he felt an electric shock.

She raised her hand and strode toward him with those long legs, her hair bright against a black top. Her black jeans and boots just made her look like one long, lean line of sexy.

She slid into the booth, across from him, and lifted the purse slung across her body over her head. She nodded at the big window overlooking slips of bobbing boats. "This is…touristy."

"It's kind of my local. I can walk here." He tapped the side of his glass. "Sorry I started without you. It's been a helluva day."

"Tell me about it. I can't believe Tony watched while two men stuffed his friend's body in the trunk of car, and then pushed that car into a lake, and didn't do one thing about it." She glanced up as the waitress approached. "Glass of chardonnay, house is fine."

"I could see where he was coming from. Even if he called the police at that point, nothing could've been done for Tiana." He sat back and folded his arms. "At least he contacted you."

She folded the corner of the napkin the waitress had tossed in front of her. "I saw Christian Bushnell today."

"Let me guess." He caught a bead of moisture from the outside of his glass with the tip of his finger. "You got more out of him than I did."

"I caught him alone, without his boss hovering. I think you would've gotten to him eventually. He's not a very good liar, and I don't think he likes lying."

"He's in the wrong business. What did he tell you?"

"Not too much. He verified Tony's story about Tiana working for the CREW. Just like Jed, Christian maintained that the spying angle was Tiana's idea."

"Hmm." He scratched his chin and gulped down some beer as the waitress delivered Ashlynn's wine.

She wrapped a finger around the stem. "Hmm, what?"

"You told me over the phone that you had some news for me. That's hardly news. We already got that from Tony."

She blinked and took a careful sip of her wine. "There's more. He said Tiana wasn't scared or worried, that she seemed pleased about something. He also said anyone could've taken one of the vehicles. Tiana herself could've taken one of the cars."

"Okay, but he didn't know what she'd discovered over there?"

"He didn't have a clue. Sounds like she was keeping things to herself. Honestly?" She pinged her glass and the golden liquid inside shimmered. "I just wanted to see you. To apologize for how my actions appeared to you. Sure, I didn't want you nixing my post with the video, but I swear I did not use sex to get one over on you. I would've found a way to copy that video to my laptop, whether you spent the night with me or not."

"You're not apologizing for posting the video on your blog?"

Her eyebrows jumped. "Absolutely not. It drove people to the blog, and it didn't hurt your case. You know it didn't, Denver."

"It got me in some hot water with my captain, it gave Jed a heads-up. He could've bolted."

"Leaving Veronica? Never."

"There are some tips that aren't meant for public consumption. You know that, right?"

"I never revealed that Tiana was found in a CREW car, did I?"

"Ready to order?" Their waitress had finally taken the plunge after hovering every time she passed their table.

Ashlynn's gaze flicked over the menu. "I'll have the crab cakes appetizer and a side salad."

"Sea bass for me, please."

After the waitress clarified a few more details about their order and left, Denver hunched forward. "If I tell you something now, you have to promise to keep it out of *LA Confidential*. This is too important, Ashlynn. More important than the blog."

"I understand." She pressed a hand to her chest. "I promise, Denver."

"It has to do with something you mentioned earlier, on the night of the fundraiser. That's why I want to run it by you."

"The argument between Veronica and Jed?"

"No, an offhand comment by the volunteers. They said Kent Meadows was a manther."

Her giggle ended in a choke when she realized he was serious. "Kent Meadows? What do his personal preferences have to do with anything?"

"I went out to the house to talk to Veronica about that video and to find out what she knew about Tiana's role in the campaign. She denied knowing of Tiana's existence."

"She's lying. She and Jed were arguing about something that night, but what does this have to do with her husband?"

"I'm getting there. Did you know Veronica's mother lives with them?"

Ashlynn nodded. "She lives in a guest cottage in the back, with Lulu."

"Mrs. Escalante was there today and, when I was leaving, she pulled me aside and told me that Tiana had been to the house."

"Well, that sort of proves Veronica was lying, doesn't it?"

"Maybe not." Denver drummed his fingers on the table. "Mrs. Escalante told me Tiana was there to see Kent."

Chapter Nineteen

Ashlynn covered her mouth with her hand. "Kent? Tiana was there to see Kent?"

"That's what Mrs. Escalante told me. She said Tiana had been to the house several times, and I just assumed she meant to see her daughter. But she corrected me, and said only Kent was home when Tiana was there."

"Unless Mrs. Escalante was lying to protect her daughter." Ashlynn toyed with her napkin. Denver was right. This information didn't belong in the blog...not yet.

"I thought about that, but then why tell me anything at all? I wasn't questioning Mrs. Escalante. I was on my way out the front gate when she grabbed me. She didn't have to say a word."

"What does it mean? I don't think Kent is even that involved with the campaign. He's strictly the money guy."

"Strictly the money guy and the guy who hits on young women. What better source of young, eager women than your wife's election campaign?" He moved his beer to the side to make room for the plates in their waitress's hands.

"Anything else? Refill on the drinks?"

They both declined the second drink, and Ashlynn shook out her napkin. "You think Kent and Tiana were hooking up?"

She wrinkled her nose as she asked the question, and he didn't think it had to do with the savory smells coming from their food.

"Hooking up might be too strong. Maybe they were having some kind of flirtation." He dragged a fork through his garlic-mashed potatoes. "You picked up on that vibe in the video with Jed, right?"

She waved her fork at him. "Hold on. You're not blaming the victim here, are you? Whatever Tiana did or whatever methods she may have used to get information, none of that deserves a death sentence."

A muscle twitched in his jaw. "I did not say that, and I'm not implying it at all, but it might explain what she was doing with Kent Meadows. She saw his weakness and went in for the kill. We already know she was willing to take risks for the thrill of the hunt."

"She cozies up to Kent, gets invited to the house while the candidate is campaigning, and discovers...what?"

"We already established that Kent wasn't interested in the nuts and bolts of the election, but it doesn't mean Tiana couldn't discover things in that house that could benefit Wexler—maybe something so big, Kent had to keep her quiet."

Ashlynn scooted up to the edge of the booth. "And what's so big to Kent right now? We've been thinking politics all this time, but maybe Tiana found out about something else."

"Meadows Plaza. The project is currently on hold. Why?"

"I can write a post tomorrow about Meadows Plaza, see what my readers know about it."

"We don't want to tip off Meadows. So far, he believes we think he's Veronica Escalante's Mr. Moneybags, nothing more. If you and your readers go snooping around Kent Meadows and Meadows Plaza, we're giving him a heads-up." He pointed his fork at her. "You're not the only one with sources. I know a guy in Building and Planning. I'm sure he can give me the lowdown on Meadows Plaza."

Ashlynn poked at her salad, a shiver of excitement giving her goose bumps. "I think we're really on to something, Denver. Thank you for sharing that with me."

"The other night—" he dragged a napkin across his mouth "—it felt like you used me to post that video on your blog. I don't like being used, and it made me look like a fool in front of my captain."

"I know." She gripped the edge of the table. "I didn't think how it would look for you, being in the dark. At that point, it was more important for me to get that blog out."

"Why is it such a big deal for you to prove yourself with that blog? It's kind of toxic. I think you need to strike out on your own." He threw back the rest of his beer. "And that's as far as I'll go."

"I know you're right. My parents were perfectionists in everything they did when Sean and I were growing up—still are. It's just that Sean seemed to do everything right, and I was the eternal screw-up. So, I started controlling the one thing that was all mine—eating. I became anorexic and my supermodel mom didn't even realize it until I fainted. Even after family therapy, my mom didn't acknowledge her role in my eating disorder—not that I'm blaming her." She held up her hand. "That was all me, and I was no angel."

Denver reached for her hand and smoothed his thumb across the inside of her wrist. "Having an eating disorder doesn't make you a bad person."

"How about outing your own brother?"

He cocked his head. "What do you mean?"

"I found out Sean was gay. I knew he wanted

to tell my parents in his own way and time, and I should've allowed him that space, but I thought I could finally get one over on him. I figured my parents would be upset when they found out their only son was gay, so I blabbed it to them. I felt terrible when Sean found out what I'd done. And the funny thing is? My parents didn't care at all, which is how it should be, and I'm glad they reacted the way they did. The whole thing blew up in my face. I was the bad guy."

"Not cool, but how old were you?"

"A teenager—no excuse. I just wanted to be the chosen one for a change."

"How did Sean react to all of this? From what I've heard about him, he was no angel, either. I mean he called out my mom as a murderer based on some life insurance and an extramarital affair."

Ashlynn had read that whole blog series and could see where Sean was coming from, but she'd never admit that to Denver. "You're right. Sean had his issues. He knew he was the favored one. He didn't exactly lord it over me, but he reveled in it. We made our peace before he died. I'm thankful for that."

"Now this blog is hanging over your head as a way to prove yourself worthy in your parents' eyes and maybe to make up for what you did to Sean. But just like the food was controlling you, not the other way around, this blog is controlling you."

"Your father's murder doesn't control you to an extent?"

"It does, but it also dovetails with what I want to do with my life—solve homicides. I'm not sure the blog is what you want to do with your life."

"I'm not sure about that. I'm really pumped about the direction we're going with this case. It feels good." She sawed into her crab cake and held it up. "And I no longer have an eating disorder, in case you haven't noticed."

"I'm glad." He pointed to his plate. "Maybe you can help me with some of this."

"Ugh, you're not going to start watching what I eat, are you? Whenever I tell people I had anorexia, they start counting my calories for me."

"I'm sure you can handle your own food intake. It's your obsession with *LA Confidential* that worries me."

THE NEXT MORNING, Denver updated both Marino and Captain Fields, letting them know he was going to look into Kent Meadows, as he'd gotten a tip that the councilwoman's husband may have known Tiana. Marino was happy he didn't have to do anything today except talk to some of Tiana's school friends in Long Beach, and Captain Fields was glad Denver had seemingly wrested control of the investigation from the blogger.

He didn't tell the captain about dinner last night.

Both he and Ashlynn had made the decision to sleep in their own beds. His ego needed some time to recover, and Ashlynn wanted a chance to prove herself to him.

Her blog today had focused on Tiana, paying tribute to a bright and energetic young woman lost too soon. She hit all the right notes and had managed to draw even more people into the story of "The Girl in the Lake."

Maybe he was wrong and this blog was her true calling. He just hated seeing her try so hard for validation from her parents that would most likely never come.

As soon as he sank into his chair and reached for the mouse, his contact at the Building and Planning office called him. He snatched up his phone. "Ebert, what do you have for me?"

Greg Ebert whistled across the line. "That Meadows Plaza project is in big trouble. Kent Meadows is never going to get that done. The dude owes money, he's being sued, we just rejected his most recent set of diagrams. He's going to lose a bundle."

"That's common knowledge, though, right?

Or it could be if someone wanted to investigate the project."

"Sure, what are you getting at?"

"Secrets."

"I can tell you this, Holt. If that wife of his gets elected mayor, she could make a lot of his problems go away. It would have to be done on the sly, but this type of quid pro quo happens all the time."

"Okay, thanks, Ebert. I appreciate it."

Seemed like he needed to have a talk with Kent again—and this time he planned to get personal. He placed a call to Meadows and left a voice mail.

He spent the rest of the afternoon reviewing the ballistics report for the bullet that killed Tiana. He'd also gotten forensics for the car—all prints wiped clean, most evidence washed out in the lake—but the forensics team had discovered a few hairs in the trunk that didn't belong to Tiana and a few fibers.

Nobody had any idea where Tiana had been murdered, including Tony, and with the pithy evidence from the car, Denver needed something big. He needed a confession from Kent Meadows.

When his phone rang, his heart pounded when he saw Ashlynn's name. They hadn't touched base all day, and he still couldn't stop worrying about her although she'd abandoned her undercover gig at the Escalante campaign headquarters.

He picked up and said, "Is this the hot blogger who's breaking the case of the girl in lake?"

She laughed with a nervous edge. "You read the blog today, right?"

"It was good, and I appreciate your discretion. I know it wasn't easy, knowing what you do about Meadows."

"I just want you to know I'm all about solving this crime. I won't do anything to jeopardize that."

"I can see that, so I think I can tell you that Meadows is in trouble over that project."

She huffed out a breath. "That's apparent, though, isn't it? That building site has been sitting there for months with no progress."

"You're right, but my guy at Building and Planning seems to think all of Meadows's problems can magically disappear once his wife gets elected."

"If Tiana knew that, or maybe how that was going to play out, it might be motive enough for Meadows."

"Maybe. I reached out to him today. I need to do a little probing."

"I might be able to help you with that. Lulu

texted me today. She's okay. She's in hiding, and she wants to meet with me."

A sharp pain lanced the back of his neck. "Is that a good idea? Have you forgotten what happened the last time you two had a meeting?"

"This is different. She's aware of the danger now, and she's in a secure location. I might be able to get her talking about Kent. I don't think there's any love lost between those two."

"Be careful. No meetings in vacant dog parks."

"I promise I'll be careful. I think I took some heat off myself with this latest blog. Nobody can feel threatened by a tribute to the victim. I think I proved the threats intimidated me into backing off. Nobody knows we're working together."

"Nobody on my end knows." Denver glanced around the room. He'd catch hell if they did. "Keep me posted, anyway, and we'll touch base later."

"You, too. Denver…"

A pulse throbbed in his throat. "Yeah?"

"Let's get justice for the girl in the lake."

He let out a breath. "You got it."

When he ended the call, he tapped the edge of the phone against his chin. He jumped when it buzzed again. Had she decided to tell him what she'd really wanted to tell him?

He glanced at the display, disappointment

bursting his bubble. "Mr. Meadows, thanks for calling back."

"Call me Kent, please. What can I do for you, Detective?"

"I want to talk with you again, Kent—in person."

"I'm busy today."

"It needs to be today."

"Do you mind coming downtown? I'm going to be having a meeting at my building site here, and I can chat with you when I'm done."

A muscle ticked in Denver's jaw. *Perfect.* "I can be there. What time?"

"Let's make it seven o'clock."

"In the dark?"

"We just switched to daylight savings. It's not that dark at seven, and the construction site is lit up like a Christmas tree most of the time."

"I'll be there."

Denver didn't have any intention of meeting with Kent Meadows at a half-finished construction site downtown without telling someone first. He notified Marino and told Billy Crouch, just in case Marino didn't remember or care.

With downtown LA on the way home to the Marina, Denver decided to put in some extra time and get a bite to eat before his meeting. Could he break Meadows at the place that had the power to break Meadows?

At around ten minutes to seven, Denver drove right onto the construction site, spitting up sand and gravel with the back tires of his sedan. Other cars dotted the flat area next to a giant hole, cement pylons and steel beams crisscrossing the vast space. Definitely stalled.

He pulled into the same row as two Teslas, a Porsche Cayenne and a classic Corvette. If Kent couldn't get money out of these people, he needed a new plan.

Denver waited in his car and sucked down the rest of the soda he'd got with his burger and fries. His phone pinged, and he read a message from Ashlynn that her meeting with Lulu was on. His thumb hesitated over the keyboard on his phone. He didn't have to tell her to be careful. She already knew that. They could trust Lulu, and Lulu knew to be careful, too.

Instead of sending her a cautionary text, he gave her a thumbs-up emoji.

A few minutes later, a woman and two men emerged from the bowels of the construction site. The woman picked her way over the gravel and slid into the Corvette.

One of the guys gave Denver a hard look before claiming one of the Teslas, and the other man turned and waved at the gaping hole in the earth as he unlocked his Porsche.

Denver exited his vehicle before the others drove

away, just so that they could get a good look at him in case he wound up with a bullet in the back of the head at the bottom of that pit. As he walked closer to the site, he saw a small gray building with the Meadows Construction logo plastered all over it. Now he saw what the other guy had been waving at. Kent Meadows stood framed in the doorway of the outbuilding, casual in a pair of slacks and a cashmere sweater, his arms crossed.

Lights did illuminate the construction site, and a little porch lamp cast a yellow glow over Meadows, making his silver hair glint. Denver raised his hand as he strode forward, avoiding the potholes and dips.

"Welcome to my folly." Meadows spread his arms wide.

Jerking his thumb over his shoulder, Denver asked, "Any luck with that bunch?"

"Not really." He shrugged his sweater-clad shoulders. "Office? There's light and coffee and maybe a few snacks left over from the last construction workers who were here."

"How old would those snacks be?"

"About six months old, but this stuff has enough preservatives in it to last until the project gets completed."

"When will that be?" Denver crossed the threshold of the office and knocked over a pile of folders on his way to take a seat. "Sorry about that."

"That's all right." He waved a hand. "Someone will clean this up at some point." Meadows's thin lips twisted. "Probably won't be me."

"Unless your wife gets elected mayor."

Meadows chuckled. "Is that what this is about, Detective? You found out what a bottomless pit this project is for me and how much I need saving?"

"Something like that."

"Shh." He put his finger to his lips. "Don't tell anyone, but my wife doesn't have a chance."

"Does she know that?"

He shook his head. "That campaign manager of hers keeps blowing smoke up...you know, in her face, and she believes him."

"But you weren't always so resigned, were you? You thought Veronica had a chance, and you thought this project had a chance."

"Not really." Meadows steepled his fingers. "Do you really think I killed a young woman to keep her quiet about my failing project? She wouldn't know about that, anyway. Meadows Plaza is not part of Veronica's campaign strategy, and that young woman was working for the campaign. I'd never met her. I don't involve myself with my wife's campaigns, except to foot the bills."

"You're sure you never met Tiana when she was at your house with you when your wife wasn't home?"

Meadows's face froze and the corner of his eye twitched. "Where did you hear that?"

"From a member of your household."

"Did that little snitch Lulu tell you?" He patted the side of his expensive haircut. "And after I set her up with a few of my friends, too."

"Set her up for what?"

"Exactly what she wanted, Detective. Look—" Meadows flattened his hands on the small dingy desk "—you don't have any proof that Tiana was at the house. I made sure any of our security footage showing her there was erased—and not because I murdered her but so that my wife wouldn't murder me. I had a fling with the girl. That's it. I was horrified when I learned of her death, but I wasn't involved. No motive."

"I can think of a few." Denver held up his hand and ticked off his fingers. "To keep your affair a secret. To keep her quiet about your plans for Meadows Plaza. Anger because she played you."

Meadows's head jerked up. "Played me? What do you mean?"

"Your wife didn't tell you? You haven't been following the news? Tiana Fuller was working for the Wexler campaign. She was a mole in your wife's campaign, looking for dirt. Seems that she found some."

Denver's words had sobered Meadows. His jaw tightened and his eyes narrowed. "That makes sense now. One day at the house, Tiana and I had drinks and I blacked out. I think she got into my computer that day."

"And discovered what?"

Meadows folded his hands, his knuckles white. "I'm not telling you any more, Detective Holt. You have no proof of anything and if Lulu told you about me and Tiana, she won't be able to testify to that."

Denver shot up in his chair, his fingertips buzzing. "Why is that? Did you kill her, too?"

"I didn't kill anyone, but we did send her away."

"Sent her away?" Denver's heart was pounding so hard, the buttons on his shirt were bouncing.

"After her stunt with that video, Veronica and I agreed it would be best if Lulu took a trip, so we sent her to Italy. She'd been wanting to go, anyway. She's sunning on the Italian Riviera about now, so she's not going to be telling tales about me."

Denver fumbled for his phone and jumped to his feet, sending the chair crashing behind him.

If Lulu was in Italy, who the hell was Ashlynn meeting tonight and why?

Chapter Twenty

Ashlynn crept along the path on the side of the Escalante mansion, the sparkling pool beyond the bushes to her right. She hadn't even seen the back quarters when she'd been here before. Then the path dipped to a clearing and a cozy house that merged with the canyon around it appeared like a cottage in a fairy tale. No wonder Lulu put up with her sister and the campaign. She had a sweet spot here.

Ashlynn knocked on the door, calling out, "Lulu? It's Ashlynn."

The door swung open and the other sister greeted her. "Hello, Ashlynn. Lulu had to go out, but when she told me she'd been expecting you, I thought we could meet instead. *LA Confidential* is a powerful force in the city, and I'd like to do a sit-down with you and discuss Tiana's role in the campaigns. Would you want to include a post like that? An exclusive with me?"

Ashlynn blinked. What a coup. "Of course I would, Councilwoman Escalante. Right now?"

"Sure, I'm actually free for a change." She gave a little laugh. "Call me Veronica. It's a nice night. Let's sit by the pool."

"Will Lulu be joining us later? Is she okay? Did she tell you about being followed?"

"Lulu is safe now. She'll be by later. She did mention that she'd been followed and the two of you had been accosted. I can't believe the Wexler campaign would go to those lengths." She rolled her shoulders. "Amazing what some people will do for power."

Ashlynn started to turn to take the path back to the patio of the main house, and Veronica touched her arm. "Can I have your phone, Ashlynn? I don't want this recorded, at least not now. You can take notes, if you like."

Ashlynn patted her purse. "Okay. I understand. I won't record."

"I'd feel better if you left the phone here." Veronica shook a finger at her. "I know how you journalists are, so I have to insist just for my peace of mind."

"I suppose." She slipped her phone from her purse and handed it to Veronica.

Veronica tapped the case with a long fingernail. "I'll leave this in the cottage for safekeeping. Lulu and my mother also keep a fully stocked kitchen and bar. Can I get you something to drink?"

"Nothing alcoholic. I still have to maneuver my way down Mulholland."

"Such a pain, isn't it? We pay a price for living in the hills. I'll get us a couple of sodas."

Ashlynn traipsed back to the pool area, her step light. She'd come here just to touch base with Lulu, and she'd leave with an exclusive interview with a candidate for mayor.

As she sat on one of the lounge chairs, she dug in her purse for some paper and a pen. Was Veronica afraid she'd say something that could be used against her in the campaign and that she'd splash it over the blog? Ashlynn wasn't interested in the campaign, only as it related to Tiana's death.

As she settled a piece of paper on her knee, Veronica emerged from the path carrying two glasses in her hands. "Found some soda in the fridge. Will this do?"

"Thank you." Ashlynn took the drink from her and downed a few gulps before placing the glass on the little teak table between them. "What do you know about Tiana's spying on your behalf, and did you realize that she was a mole for the CREW?"

Veronica's generous lips tightened and her nostrils flared. "Jumping right in, aren't you?"

She'd agreed not to record the interview, but if Veronica expected softballs, she'd contacted the wrong blogger. Would anyone ever try to put one over on Sean?

She tapped the paper with her pen. "I'm sorry, Veronica. I'm not interested in how you got your start in politics or why you think you'd be better than Wexler for the city. *LA Confidential* is a true crime blog, and my readers and I are investigating the murder of a young woman who was involved in your campaign and in Mayor Wexler's. I want to know what she discovered."

Veronica raised her glass to Ashlynn. "Cheers to strong women getting down to business."

Ashlynn grabbed her glass and clinked it with Veronica's. "Cheers to strong women answering tough questions."

Veronica took a tiny sip of her drink and then ran her thumb up and down the condensation on the outside. "I didn't even know Tiana Fuller was working as a volunteer for our campaign…until she started having an affair with my husband."

Ashlynn sucked in a breath and took another gulp of her drink. "You knew about that?"

"I knew about all of Kent's affairs. I had a spy of my own—my mother. She kept an eye on things."

"Y-you didn't care?" Ashlynn rubbed her eye as the lights over the pool blurred.

"Look at this house. Look at my clothes, my car, my vacations." She snorted delicately. "Not bad for a girl from the barrio. I use Kent, and he does what he wants."

"That doesn't sound like a very good recipe for a marriage."

"It works. What would you know about it? Rich girl from San Marino."

Ashlynn swallowed against her dry throat. She took another sip of her drink, cupping the ice cube on her tongue. "I didn't realize you knew anything about me."

"When we found out Lulu had given you that video, Jed and I did a little investigating of our own—mostly Jed. Anyway—" she flicked her fingers "—the arrangement worked for me and Kent, or it had worked until Tiana Fuller showed up."

Ashlynn's heart thudded in her chest as her brain struggled to make sense of Veronica's words. This was important. This meant something. "Tiana? Why was she different?"

"Feeling okay?" Veronica leaned forward and stroked Ashlynn's hand, which could barely grip the pen. "Tiana became different the day I realized she'd gotten into Kent's computer—the idiot."

"Wh-what'd she find on Kent's…?" The pen

dropped from Ashlynn's fingers and rolled off the table. She watched it dumbly, without reacting.

"She probably discovered that I'd been facilitating Kent's projects in the city for years—dummy corporations, money from phony sources, votes cast to grease the wheels of Kent's moneymaking machine." She clicked her tongue. "If any of that stuff ever came out, not only would I lose the mayor's race, I'd probably be heading to federal prison. I'm not doing that."

Ashlynn should probably feel more excitement, more horror at Veronica's pronouncements, but she felt only fatigue. She opened her mouth and tried to move her thick tongue. "You…you…"

"Well, not me personally." Veronica placed a hand over her heart. "I hired a couple of professionals to take care of the matter."

"Jed? K—?" Ashlynn couldn't remember the name of Veronica's husband. Blackness hovered on the periphery of her vision. This woman had drugged her.

Veronica tossed back her thick mane of brown hair. "Neither Jed nor Kent was involved, although I think Jed suspects something. Strong women—right, Ashlynn? I don't need a man to make power moves."

"Murder." Ashlynn screamed at her muscles

to move, but all she could manage was to lift one finger.

"Murder is the biggest power move of all, and I'm done with this interview. On the bright side, just think of all the hits your blog's going to get when you go missing or when some hikers discover your body in six months or a year. You'll put *LA Confidential* on the national map."

DENVER LOOMED OVER Kent's desk, and the older man reached for the top drawer. Denver lunged toward him, slamming the drawer on his fingers. Kent wailed, clutching his bloody hand to his chest, the gun in the drawer forgotten. Denver grabbed the gun and pocketed it. "Where is she? Where's your wife?"

Meadows gasped. "She wouldn't. She couldn't."

"Liar. You know what she's capable of." Denver shoved Meadows's phone into his chest. "Call her. Text her. And I'll be watching and listening, so don't tip her off."

"My wife did nothing." Meadows wiped his injured hand on the sleeve of his expensive sweater. "I'm not going to find her for you."

Denver slid his gun from his holster and leveled it at Meadows's head. "You're going to get on your phone right now, or I'm going to splatter your brains all over the plans for Meadows Plaza. You got me?"

"Y-you can't do this. I don't have a weapon. I'll sue you."

"You can't do that if you're dead." Denver smacked the phone on the table in the blood, and drops of it went airborne.

Meadows peered at him and then grabbed his phone. He entered the pass code with a misshapen finger and tapped the screen.

Denver growled. "Speaker."

The call rolled right to voice mail and a robotic voice answered.

"Text her."

Denver peered over Meadows's shoulder, the gun still aimed in Meadows's direction, as Meadows typed out a message to his wife, asking her whereabouts. The message hung there, undelivered.

Meadows coughed, cradling his hand. "She must have it turned off."

"Because she's committing a crime." Denver snatched up the phone before it could go into lock mode and scrolled through the apps until he found the one he wanted. "I knew you'd be tracking your wife's phone. Wouldn't want her surprising you with one of your sidepieces, right? Of course, she knew Tiana, figured out that she'd gotten some dirt on you—enough to sink you both."

Denver dashed the sweat from his eyes and squinted at the phone's display. He recognized the last location before she'd turned off her phone as her home in the hills above Sherman Oaks.

"Who's at the house now? Where's your mother-in-law? Do you have live-in staff?"

"I…"

Denver circled in front of Meadows, repositioning his gun to his Meadows's forehead, right between his eyes. "Not fast enough."

"We don't have live-in staff. My mother-in-law is in Mexico. We sent her there yesterday." Meadows choked. "Veronica's home alone. She'd do it there."

Denver pocketed Meadows's phone and handcuffed him to the desk so he couldn't warn his wife. He may have just ruined his chances with Homicide, but nothing mattered now but getting to Ashlynn.

As his car screamed from the construction site, he placed a call to the LAPD watch command. He ordered a unit to Escalante's address, claiming an assault in progress. At least, he prayed whatever was happening there was still in progress and not a done deal.

He turned on his blue and red revolvers and left the twinkling lights of downtown behind him as he sped down the 101, his adrenaline pumping through his system, his hands clenching the steering wheel.

Twenty minutes later as he careened off the freeway and hit Coldwater Canyon Boulevard, his phone rang and he flexed his fingers on the steering wheel. In his anxiety, he barked out, "What did you find?"

The sergeant on the other line said, "That's Councilwoman Escalante's house."

"I know that. What did you find?"

"Nothing. Nobody's home."

"Send them back."

"Detective, this isn't the Northeast Division, and we have no cause to barge into the empty house of a member of the LA city council. Don't know about you, but I value my pension."

Denver cut him off and stomped on the accelerator, his tires squealing as he took a sharp curve. If he had to save Ashlynn himself, he would.

He cut his lights and cruised to a stop in front of the Escalante mansion. Lights embedded in the flower garden lit the front of the house and guided him to the double doors. The cops had probably already rung the doorbell. They didn't get an answer, and he didn't expect one, either.

He slid his weapon from its holster. He crept

around the side of the house and spotted a side gate standing open.

He sidled through the space sideways, not trusting that the hinges on the gate would stay silent. He avoided the flagstones, and his shoes squished against the dirt and grass. As he peered around the corner of the house onto the patio, his heart stuttered in his chest.

LA City Councilwoman Veronica Escalante knelt by the side of the pool, both hands in the water, pushing something beneath the surface. Had Ashlynn given up the fight? Had Escalante already killed her?

Denver charged forward, leaping over a chaise longue, his gun aloft. "Stop what you're doing! Stop!"

With her arms in the water up to her elbows, Veronica cranked her head to the side and her mouth dropped open. "I—I'm trying to save her. She fell in."

"Get away from the pool, and put your hands up where I can see them."

"I'm Councilwoman Escalante. This woman tried to drown herself in my pool." She sat back on her heels, her arms hanging by her sides, dripping water.

Oh, God. Was Ashlynn dead already?

Denver ran to the side of the pool, knocking Veronica backward. Ashlynn was floating on her stomach, her arms splayed to the sides, her hair creating a red fan in the water. He shoved his gun in his waistband and reached to pull her toward the edge.

Grabbing handfuls of her clothing, he rolled her from the pool and onto her back. He pumped her chest and listened for her breath. "C'mon. C'mon, Ashlynn."

He applied another compression and she coughed up water, her eyelids fluttering. "That's my girl."

"Sh-she drugged me." Her eyes opened and then widened at the same time he felt Veronica snatch his gun.

He spun around, staring down the barrel of his own weapon.

Veronica's hand trembled. "I told you I tried to save her. She's one of my husband's lovers, a volunteer. When Kent broke things off with her, she came here to kill herself."

"Did you kill Tiana Fuller yourself, or did you hire someone?" Smiling slowly, he nodded at her shaky grip on the gun. "You farmed that one out, just like you hired someone to intimidate your own sister and Ashlynn at the dog park that night. You don't even know how to hold a weapon properly. It's a lot different from drugging someone and holding her head under water, isn't it?"

"I—I told you what happened."

"I know exactly what happened. You didn't care that your husband was seeing Tiana until you discovered she'd stumbled onto your little personal money train where you were funneling funds into Kent's shell companies."

Her dark eyes smoldered. "You're crazy. You came barging in here, demanding answers from me, demanding answers from Ashlynn Hughes from *LA Confidential*. When you didn't get what you wanted, you shot Ashlynn. While you were pushing her into the pool, I got your gun and shot you."

"That's a lot of setup to manage, Councilwoman, especially as it's clear you know nothing about guns and Ashlynn will have drugs in her system. How are you going to explain that?" He inched closer to her, still in a crouched position, sliding his hand up his pant leg and curling his fingers around the handle of his knife.

"Just because she's a blogger doesn't mean she wasn't having an affair with my husband. I'll stick to my original story. She came here to kill herself. I was reasoning with her until you crashed the party, desperate to solve this case, desperate to wrest it back from the blogger. It's no secret that the LAPD hates *LA Confidential*. I can pull it off." She tossed her head. "Do you know who I am?"

He lunged toward her, yanking the knife from its sheath around his leg. As she stumbled back, firing wildly into the air, he swung the blade, making contact with her side.

She screamed and dropped the gun, clutching her wound as it gushed blood.

He kicked the gun out of her reach and twisted around toward Ashlynn, her chest rising and falling, despite the paralysis of the rest of her body. He pulled her into his lap. "You're going to be okay. Everything's going to be okay."

Then he grabbed his phone and pointed it at Veronica, writhing on the patio, blood oozing between her fingers. "I know exactly who you are. You're the suspect under arrest for the murder of Tiana Fuller."

Epilogue

A few days later, Ashlynn answered her door and pulled Denver into her place. "How'd it go?"

"When Veronica saw the evidence we had against her—Kent's computer, her prints on my gun, your testimony against her, the drugs she used on you in the guest cottage—she confessed from her hospital bed. She gave up the two hitmen who killed Tiana, too. If she's going down, she's bringing everyone with her."

"I had no doubt you'd nail her either with the evidence or a confession, but I meant how'd that other thing go?" She held on to his hands, lacing her fingers through his.

"Suspended." He lifted his broad shoulders that had carried so much.

She squeezed his hands. He'd given up his career aspirations to save her. "I'm sorry, Denver. Even though you solved this case, does that mean they're not going to bring you on to Homicide?"

"I wouldn't say that." He raised her hands to his lips and kissed her fingers. "I could use a beer."

She disentangled herself and scooted past him into the kitchen. "So, there's still hope for you?"

"Let's put it this way. Billy Crouch and Jake McAllister, the two superstars of Robbery-Homicide, took me aside today, congratulated me on the case, and said, if anything, the way I questioned Meadows to get to his wife was a bright golden star next to my name, as far as they were concerned."

"Is Meadows going to sue the department?" She dipped into her fridge to grab two bottles of beer.

As he took a bottle from her, he snorted. "He can try…from federal prison. I think he's going to be busy with his high-priced attorneys for a while."

She grabbed his hand again and led him to the couch. "Poor Tiana. She craved the excitement of a political campaign and got in over her head. She never slept with Kent, you know. It was all a big tease to get into the house. Lulu told me that."

"I think Tiana watched too many TV shows. She had this unrealistic view, and didn't realize how far people would go to protect their interests."

"One thing that's been bothering me is how did she wind up in a Wexler vehicle? Did Veronica order her thugs to steal a Wexler car to frame the mayor?"

He combed his fingers through her hair. "That just fell into their laps. Tiana already had that car. She'd taken it herself and used it for her covert operations. She drove out in the car to meet who she thought was someone from the Wexler campaign. She was ambushed by the hitmen, dumped in the trunk, and pushed into the lake."

"Convenient for Veronica, but also a mistake. In the end, if Tiana hadn't been in a CREW car, she never would've been connected to either campaign. Neither campaign would've claimed her, and Tony would've been too afraid to step forward. Maybe Lulu would've come through."

"How is Lulu?" Denver rubbed a circle on her back. "At least she tried to do the right thing, regardless of her motives."

"She's fine. She's still in Italy. She wasn't that surprised about the turn of events. She always knew her sister was ruthless, even though Lulu was supposedly the black sheep of the family."

"Is that why you two connected?" Denver tapped the neck of his bottle against hers.

"Maybe." Ashlynn scraped a nail through the foil label on her damp bottle. "What did you think of the blog?"

She hated asking, but it still mattered to her.

She'd proved that by stumbling into a dangerous situation with Veronica just to get an exclusive.

"It was great. Your writing is top-notch, but is that you? Scrabbling for a story almost got you killed—several times."

Turning toward him, she traced a fingertip along his jaw. "It also brought you into my life."

He captured her finger and sucked it into his mouth. "As much as I get a thrill out of rescuing you, I want to make sure I stay in your life and you stay in mine. You're sure you don't want to go back to writing about fashion?"

"But we did it, didn't we? We did it together."

He wiggled his eyebrows. "We've done several things together. Which one do you mean?"

"Justice for the girl in the lake." She held out her fist for a bump. "Justice for Tiana."

He tapped her fist with his and then pulled her into his arms to kiss her long and hard. When he released her, he put a finger against her lower lip. "Does that mean fashion is out and true crime stays?"

"I'm ending the blog and starting a podcast." She curled a leg beneath her and cupped his face with both hands. "It's going to be all mine, something Sean never did. I'm going to put my own spin on it, my own stamp."

He encircled her wrists with his fingers. "You're going to need a contact, someone on the inside, someone not afraid to break a few rules. You're going to need me."

And then he showed her just how much she did need him.

* * * * *

Look for more books in Carol Ericson's
The Lost Girls series coming in 2023.
And be sure to look for the first title,
Canyon Crime Scene, *available now*
wherever Harlequin Intrigue books are sold!

Get 4 FREE REWARDS!

We'll send you 2 FREE Books plus 2 FREE Mystery Gifts.

FREE Value Over $20

Both the **Harlequin Intrigue®** and **Harlequin® Romantic Suspense** series feature compelling novels filled with heart-racing action-packed romance that will keep you on the edge of your seat.

Get 4 FREE REWARDS!

We'll send you 2 FREE Books plus 2 FREE Mystery Gifts.

FREE Value Over $20

Both the **Harlequin® Desire** and **Harlequin Presents®** series feature compelling novels filled with passion, sensuality and intriguing scandals.

ISBN-13:978-0-373-29440-4
ISBN-10: 0-373-29440-9

EAN

HHIFCART840

Diane Gaston

INNOCENCE and IMPROPRIETY

"Mr. Flynn, why do you tie this up in pretty words?

"Do you not mean the Marquess is wishing me to be his mistress? Is that not what this is about?"

A muscle flexed in Mr. Flynn's jaw, but his gaze held. "To be such a friend of this man has many advantages. He can assist you. Protect you."

Rose's gaze slipped to the door that hid her father and Letty. They both certainly wanted her to accept the Marquess's protection. And his money.

He looked to the door, as well. "Will you need protection, Miss O'Keefe?" His voice was soft and low. And concerned.

"I'll be needing no help. Thank the Marquess for me. It was good of you to come."

He grasped her hand in his. "Welcome or not, Miss O'Keefe, you do have a friend."

He released her and swiftly took his leave. Rose brushed her hand against her cheek, wishing the friend were not the Marquess but Mr. Flynn himself.

* * *

Innocence and Impropriety
Harlequin® Historical #840—March 2007

Praise for Diane Gaston

"The art of romance writing should be the art of seduction. A good romance book must be about seduction, lust, and desire….Diane Gaston is an author who understands this."
—*Historical Romance Writer*

The Mysterious Miss M
"Wow...it's a real emotional roller-coaster ride…you simply cannot put [it] down—absolutely mesmerising!"
—*Historical Romance Writer*

"This is a Regency with the gutsiness of a Dickens novel. It's not always pretty, but it's real and passionate. Gaston's strong, memorable debut provides new insights into the era and characters that touch your heart and draw you emotionally into her powerful story."
—*Romantic Times BOOKreviews*

The Wagering Widow
"The protagonists were so deeply sculpted into living-breathing individuals that the reader will immediately be feeling their emotional turmoil…. The entire tone of the book was steeped in sensuality... reading of the highest order!"
—*Historical Romance Writer*

A Reputable Rake
Winner of RITA® Best Regency Romance Award 2006
"A delightful and thought-provoking look into a side of London we don't usually get to see."
—*Romance Junkies*

"Brilliant writing, a classic reformed-rake plot and vivid depictions of the Regency period make this a compelling read."
—*Romantic Times BOOKreviews*

Diane Gaston

Innocence and Impropriety

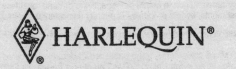

TORONTO • NEW YORK • LONDON
AMSTERDAM • PARIS • SYDNEY • HAMBURG
STOCKHOLM • ATHENS • TOKYO • MILAN • MADRID
PRAGUE • WARSAW • BUDAPEST • AUCKLAND

ISBN-13: 978-0-373-29440-4
ISBN-10:   0-373-29440-9

INNOCENCE AND IMPROPRIETY

To the "Roses" in my life:
my sister, Marilyn Rose
(though she was never fond of her middle name)
and
my sister-in-law, Rosemarie

Chapter One

London—July 1817

Vauxhall Gardens was not a place Jameson Flynn would have chosen to spend his night hours, but his employer, the Marquess of Tannerton, required his presence.

To Flynn, Vauxhall was all façade. Mere wooden structures painted to look like Greek temples or Chinese pavilions. Revellers were equally as false, wearing masks to disguise whether they be titled, rich, respectable, or rogue, pickpocket, lady of ill repute.

'Have some more ham.' Tannerton handed him the plate of paper-thin ham slices, a Vauxhall delicacy of dubious worth.

Rich as Croesus, Tanner—as he liked to be called—ate with as much enthusiasm as if he were dining at Carlton House instead of a supper box at Vauxhall. Flynn declined the Vauxhall delicacy but sipped his arrack, a heady mixture of rum and Benjamin flower that redeemed Vauxhall only a little in his eyes. It was not unusual for Tanner to seek Flynn out for companionship, but Flynn had no illusions. He was Tanner's secretary, not his friend.

To look at them, you might not guess which one was the marquess. Flynn prided himself on his appearance. His dark brown hair was always neatly in place, his black coat and trousers well tailored. Tanner, a few years older and lighter in colouring, took less care, often giving the impression he'd just dismounted from his horse.

Flynn placed his tankard on the table. 'You brought me here for a purpose, sir. When am I to discover what it is?'

Tanner grinned and reached inside his coat, pulling out a piece of paper. He handed it to Flynn. 'Regard this, if you will.'

It was a Vauxhall programme, stating that, on this July night, a concert of vocal and instrumental music would be performed featuring a Miss Rose O'Keefe, Vauxhall Garden's newest flower.

Flynn ought to have guessed. A woman.

Ever since returning from Brussels, Tanner had gone back to his more characteristic pursuits of pleasure in whatever form he could find it. Or, Flynn might say, from whatever woman. And there were plenty of women willing to please him. Tanner had the reputation of being good to his mistresses, showering them with gifts, houses, and ultimately a nice little annuity when his interest inevitably waned. As a result, Tanner usually had his pick of actresses, opera dancers and songstresses.

'I am still at a loss. I surmise you have an interest in this Miss O'Keefe, but what do you require of me?' Flynn usually became involved in the monetary negotiations with Tanner's *chère amies* or when it came time to deliver the *congé*, Tanner having an aversion to hysterics.

Tanner's eyes lit with animation. 'You must assist me in winning the young lady.'

Flynn nearly choked on his arrack. 'I? Since when do you require my assistance on that end?'

Tanner leaned forward. 'I tell you, Flynn. This one is exceptional. No one heard of her before this summer. One night she just appeared in the orchestra box and sang. Rumour has it she sang again at the Cyprian's Masquerade, but that is not certain. In any event, this lady is not easily won.'

Flynn shot him a sceptical expression.

Tanner went on, 'Pomroy and I came to hear her the other evening. You've never heard the like, Flynn, let me tell you. There was nothing to be done but try to meet her.' He scowled and took a long sip of his drink. 'Turns out she has a papa guarding her interests. I could not even manage to give the man my card. There were too many ramshackle fellows crowding him.'

Flynn could just imagine the top-lofty marquess trying to push his way through the sorts that flocked around the female Vauxhall performers. 'What is it you wish of me?'

Tanner leaned forward eagerly. 'My idea is this. You discover a way to get to this father and how to negotiate on my behalf.' He nodded, as if agreeing with himself. 'You have the gift of diplomacy, which you know I do not.'

Flynn suspected all the negotiating required was to have said, 'How much do you want?' and the lady would have fallen, but he kept that opinion to himself. He would act as broker; he'd performed such tasks for Tanner before, but always after Tanner made the initial conquest. The way Flynn looked at it, he was negotiating a contract, not so different from other contracts he negotiated for Tanner. Flynn negotiated the terms, the limits, the termination clause.

The orchestra, playing some distance from their supper box, its strains wafting louder and softer on the breeze, suddenly stopped. Tanner pulled out his timepiece. 'I believe it is about time for her to perform. Make haste.'

Flynn dutifully followed Tanner's long-legged stride to the

Grove in the centre of the gardens where the two-storeyed gazebo held the orchestra high above the crowd. Tanner pushed his way to the front for the best view. He was filled with excitement, like a small boy about to witness a balloon ascent.

The music began, a tune familiar to Flynn, and, amid cheers and applause, Miss O'Keefe took her place in front of the orchestra. She began to sing:

> *When, like the dawning day*
> *Eileen Aroon*
> *Love sends his early ray...*

Her crystalline voice filled the warm summer air, silencing the revellers. Flynn lifted his gaze to her and all the glittering lamps strung on the gazebo and throughout the surrounding trees blurred. Only *she* filled his vision, dressed in a gown of deep red that fluttered in the light breeze.

Her hair, dark as the midnight sky, dramatically contrasted with skin as pale as clouds billowing over mountaintops. Her lips, now open in song, were as pink as a summer garden's rose.

This was Rose O'Keefe, Vauxhall's newest singing sensation? She seemed more like some dream incarnate. Flynn watched as she extended her arms towards the audience, as if to embrace them all. Hers was a graceful sensuality, but earthy and deeply arousing.

> *Were she no longer true*
> *Eileen Aroon*
> *What would her lover do...*

Flynn swallowed against a sudden tightness in his throat. The Irish tune—'Eileen Aroon'—sung with the tiniest lilt, created a wave of emotion such as he'd not felt in years. He squeezed shut his stinging eyes and could almost see his mother at the old pianoforte, his father by her side, his brothers and sisters gathered around. He could almost hear his father's baritone booming loud and his sister Kathleen's sweet soprano blending in harmony. He could almost smell the rich earth, the fresh air, the green of home.

He'd not crossed the Irish Sea in the ten years since he'd sailed for Oxford, filled with ambition, but this singing temptress not only aroused his masculine senses, but also gave him an aching yearning for just one evening of song, laughter, and family.

'Is she not all I said she would be?' Tanner nudged him on the shoulder, grinning like a besotted fool.

Flynn glanced back to her. 'She is exceptional.'

...*Never to love again...Eileen Aroon...*

Tanner also gaped at Rose O'Keefe, unmindful that his frank admiration showed so plainly on his face. Flynn hoped his own reaction appeared more circumspect, even though the heat of frank desire burned more hotly with each note she sang.

She seemed to represent all Flynn had left behind. Country. Family. Joy. Pleasure. It made him wish he'd answered his mother's monthly letters more than three times a year, wish he could wrap his arms around her and his father, roughhouse with his brothers, tease his sisters. He missed the laughter, the gaiety. How long had it been since he'd laughed out loud? Embraced a woman? Sung 'Eileen Aroon'?

Flynn's ambition had driven him away from his past. He'd been the marquess's secretary for six years, but the position was a mere stepping stone. Flynn aimed to rise higher, in government, perhaps, or—his grandest aspiration—to serve royalty. Tanner supported his goals, taking Flynn with him to the Congress of Vienna and to Brussels, where powerful men learned Flynn's name and recognised his talent. The marquess assured him the time would soon come for a position suitable to Flynn's ambitions.

Which was why Flynn was shocked at his reaction to Rose O'Keefe. She propelled him back, not forwards, and her clear, poignant voice left him very aware of his manhood. Carnal desire and thoughts of home made an odd mixture indeed, and a thoroughly unwanted one. Still, at the moment, he seemed helpless to do anything but let her voice and vision carry him away.

Later he would plant his feet firmly back on the ground. He must, because this woman who had temporarily aroused his senses and unearthed a buried yearning for home was also the woman he must procure for his employer.

Rose glanced down at the crowd watching her, so silent, so appreciative! Her audience had grown larger with each performance, and she had even been mentioned favourably in the *Morning Chronicle*. She loved hearing her voice rise above the orchestra, resounding through the summer night air. The magic of Vauxhall seemed to charm her as well, as if singing an Irish air in this fanciful place were merely some lovely, lovely dream.

Mr Hook himself watched from the side of the balcony, smiling in approval. Rose tossed the elderly musical director a smile of her own before turning her attention back to her audience. She was so glad Miss Hart—Mrs Sloane, she meant—had seen her perform before leaving for Italy on her wedding trip. Rose's brief time living with Miss Hart had taught her many lessons, but the one she treasured most was to be proud of who she was. And Rose was very proud this day. Proud enough to feel all her dreams were possible. She believed that some day she would be the celebrated singer all of London raved about. She would sing at Covent Garden, at Drury Lane or—dare she hope?—King's Theatre.

Rose scanned her audience again. Most of the faces lifted toward her in admiration were masculine ones. Since she'd been ten years old, men had been staring at her. At least now she knew how to hold her head up and be unafraid of their frank regard. She'd learned how to talk to gentlemen, how to encourage their interest—or, more importantly, how to discourage it.

Rose's eye was drawn to two gentlemen in the audience below her. They stood close to the balcony, so that the lamps illuminated them. One was very tall, at least as tall as Mr Sloane, but it was not he who drew her attention as much as the one who stood so still, gazing up at her. This man's rapt expression made her heart skip a beat.

She sang the last bar.

Truth is a fixed star. Eileen Aroon…

Applause thundered skywards as the music faded. Rose stole a peek at the gentleman who had captured her interest. He continued to stand, statue-still, his eyes still upon her. She felt her cheeks go warm.

She bowed and threw a kiss, eyes slanting towards her quiet admirer, before beginning her next song. As she continued through her performance, her gaze roved over all her admirers, but her eyes always returned to him.

Soon the orchestra began her final tune of the evening, 'The Warning'.

'List to me, ye gentle fair; Cupid oft in ambush lies…' Rose began softly, animating her facial expressions and her gestures. 'Of the urchin have a care, Lest he take you by surprise…'

She let her voice grow louder and had to force herself not

to direct the song at the mysterious gentleman, who still had not moved. She could neither distinguish his features nor see what colour were his eyes, but she fancied them locked upon her, as she wished to lock hers upon him.

Flynn tried to shake off his reaction to Rose O'Keefe, tried to tell himself she was merely another of Tanner's many interests, but he could not make himself look away from her. Had his grandfather been standing next to him and not in his grave these last twenty years, he'd have said, ''Tis the fairies t'blame.'

Perhaps not fairies, but certainly a fancy of Flynn's own making. It seemed to Flynn that Rose O'Keefe was singing directly to him.

An illusion, certainly. There could be nothing of a personal nature between him and this woman he had not yet met. All he experienced while listening to her was illusion, as fanciful as believing in fairies. His role was clear. He must approach Miss O'Keefe's father and convince the man to allow him to plead Tanner's suit directly to the daughter. Perhaps he would also be required to deliver gifts, or to escort her to Tanner's choice of meeting place. He'd performed such errands in the past without a thought.

It was unfortunate that this rationality fled in the music of her voice, the allure of her person. She sang of Cupid, and Flynn understood why the ancients gave the little fellow an arrow. He felt pierced with exquisite pain, emotions scraping him raw.

With one more refrain, her song ended, and, as she curtsied deeply to the applause that erupted all around him, he roused himself from this ridiculous reverie.

'Bravo!' shouted Tanner, nearly shattering Flynn's eardrum. 'Bravo!'

A moment later she had vanished as if she'd been only a

dream. Tanner clapped until the principle performer on the programme, Charles Dignum, began singing.

Flynn stared at Tanner, feeling suddenly as if this man who employed him were Cromwell come to seize his lands and take his woman, an even more ridiculous fancy. Flynn's mother was English, though she'd spent most of her life in Ireland. He had as much English blood in his veins as Irish. What's more, Flynn embraced his. England was where his life was bound. England was where his ambitions lay.

He shook his head, trying to rid himself of this madness. Rose O'Keefe had been a mere fleeting reminder of home, nothing more.

He pressed his fingers against his temple. He would soon recover his sanity and return to serving Tanner with dispassionate efficiency.

But as Tanner grabbed his arm and led him back to the supper box, the sweet voice of Rose O'Keefe lingered in Flynn's ear, an echoing reverie:

List to me, ye gentle fair; Cupid oft in ambush lies...

Chapter Two

Rose peeked through the curtain at the throng of men outside the gazebo, some carrying flowers, others waving their cards, all calling her name. There were so many, she could not see them all. If *he* was there, the man who had watched her with such rapture, she could not see him.

She turned to her father. 'There are more tonight.'

'Are there now, Mary Rose?' Her father placed his oboe in its case.

The woman at his side, a robust creature with ample décolletage—the woman who shared his bed—added, 'We have our pick, I'd say.'

Rose frowned. 'I do not wish to pick, Letty. I am content merely to sing.'

She had known nothing of Letty Dawes when Rose had surprised her father by appearing on his doorstep four months ago. The letters her father had sent to her at the school in Killyleagh made no mention of Letty, but then his letters had never been very informative.

Her father had been very surprised and perhaps somewhat disappointed to see that Rose had come to London with the ambition to sing. He had always told her to stay in Ireland, to remain at the school he'd sent her to after her mother died, the school that had kept her on as a music teacher. But teaching was not for her. Rose burned with the passion to perform, to sing.

Like her mother.

Rose's most treasured memories were of sitting by her mother's sickbed, listening to her tales of the London stages, the excitement of the music, the lights, the applause, the glory of her finest hour, performing at the King's Theatre. Even seven years of schooling and four more of teaching could not extinguish the fire that had been ignited so early within Rose to follow in her mother's footsteps. Rose had saved her pennies until she had enough to make the journey to London.

But any fantasies she'd had about a loving reunion with her father had been thoroughly dashed in those first few minutes of his surprised hugs and kisses. Letty Dawes had appeared from behind him, lamenting the sacrifices they would have to make to house and feed her, laughing at her desire to sing on the London stage. What theatre would employ an Irish country lass? Letty had said.

At first Rose thought her father had married again, but her father explained that entertainers lived by different rules from those she learned in school. He and Letty did not need marriage to share a bed. Then her father offered to pay Rose's way back to Ireland, and Letty exploded in rage at how much it would cost. A huge row broke out between them, and Rose walked out to escape hearing it, knowing she had caused it. She was glad now that she had walked out, because otherwise she would never have met Miss Hart.

It was Miss Hart who brought her to Vauxhall Gardens that glorious night when Rose had another tearful reunion with her father, and he introduced her to Mr Hook. Mr Hook let her sing one song and, seeing as she was not yet twenty-one, asked her father if he might hire her. So when it came time to leave Miss Hart's house, Rose returned to her father and Letty, who suddenly perceived her as a source of more income. To sing at Vauxhall, Rose would endure anything, even living with Letty.

It seemed she must also endure this frenzy of interest from gentlemen, all pressing her father to meet her. It was all part of the profession, her father told her.

He glanced out of the window. 'Perhaps there will be some titled gentlemen among these fellows. That is who you must court if you wish to move ahead.'

'Yes, indeed,' Letty added, putting an arm around Rose's shoulders as if in affection. 'A titled gentleman would be grand. There is no telling how much you might make, Rose. Why, some men even buy houses for their…'

Rose wrenched away. She knew much more about what men expected of women who performed on stage than she had when she first arrived in London. But what of love? Of romance? That was what Miss Hart had found with her Mr Sloane. That was what Rose coveted for herself.

'What men are expecting in exchange for those houses, I have no wish to give,' she told Letty.

Letty broke into shrill laughter. 'Give? If you don't give it, men will just take it anyway. Better to profit, I always say.'

Her father walked up to her and tweaked her chin. 'Never fear, Mary Rose.' He spoke gently. 'Your papa will make certain you are set up like a fine lady. I wouldn't let my little girl go with some penniless rogue, now would I?'

Rose pressed her hand against her throat. All part of the profession, her father had told her.

He hurried away, and she heard him shout, 'Give me your cards, gentlemen...' before the door closed behind him.

Letty shook a finger at her. 'You obey your father. He has your best interests at heart.'

To escape having to talk to her further, Rose peered through the curtain. The men outside flocking around her father appeared spectre-like in the dim light, like a flock of bats in a moonlit sky. She shivered. She loved her newfound singing success. After Vauxhall's season was over, she was certain she could find more employment. She could support herself. She could afford to wait for love to find her.

Rose gripped the curtain in determined fingers. Until she discovered for herself the sort of true love she'd witnessed at Miss Hart's, she must merely sing her songs and fend off all other plans her father and Letty had for her.

As she stared through the gap in the curtain, she wondered if one of the shadowy figures would materialise into the man who'd drawn her attention when she'd performed. Would he be the one? she wondered. The one who might love her? But as her father collected the cards and gifts, she didn't see anyone who could be *him*.

Letty walked up behind her and opened the curtain wider. 'Your father is a smart man to put them off. They'll be willing to pay more if they must wait to win you.' She paused as if wheels turned slowly in her head. 'But not too long. Too much waiting and they will lose interest.'

Her father's arms were filled with small packages and bouquets of flowers. One hand was stuffed with cards. He turned to come back in, but another man stepped forward. Rose could not make out the man distinctly in the dim light, but he was dressed in a dark coat and seemed of similar size to her man in the audience.

She had a melting feeling, like when she'd watched Miss Hart with her Mr Sloane.

Her father and the shadowy gentleman spoke a few words before the man bowed and walked away, and her father re-entered the gazebo.

He dropped the heaps of fragrant flowers and small, ribbon-wrapped packages on to a nearby table and turned to Rose. 'Mary Rose, pull this last card from my hand.'

She pulled the card sticking out from the stack and read, 'The Marquess of Tannerton.'

He let the other cards cascade on to the table. 'I told the fellow he could call tomorrow at four o'clock.'

Letty's eyes lit up. 'That was the Marquess?'

'I'm not sure of it.' Her father smiled sheepishly. 'I was half-stunned, to be sure. Didn't heed what the fellow said, but I heard "marquess" and told the man he could call.' He gave Rose a patient look. 'You must see a marquess, Mary Rose.'

It should hearten her that the marquess might be the man who so captivated her, but somehow it did not. Whatever could exist between a marquess and a songstress would not be love.

Rose sighed. She would just have to discourage this man. She was confident she'd learned enough about gentlemen to fend off unwanted attention. Her priority at the moment was to finish out her summer singing at Vauxhall, and to have Mr Hook put her forth with the highest recommendations to others who might hire her. Rose wanted to keep singing, perhaps on a proper stage this time, part of a real theatre. She wanted to rise some day to the principal roles, to have her name always in the newspapers, her image on playbills, theatre managers clamouring for her to sing for them.

In the meantime, she wanted coin enough to pay her keep so Letty would not complain that her father allowed her to stay. Until she found where she truly belonged—or with whom—she would not settle for less. She would not engage her heart to a marquess who wanted her for mere amusement. Even if he was handsome. Even if her blood stirred when he looked upon her.

She merely would let her father believe otherwise.

'I will receive the marquess, Papa,' she said.

Flynn stepped out of the hackney coach and walked the short distance up Langley Street to the lodgings where O'Keefe had directed him, a plain enough building from the outside. He took a deep breath and nodded, telling himself again that the previous night's infatuation with a Vauxhall singer had been due to too much arrack. He was clear headed now.

Rose O'Keefe, like Tanner's many other conquests, would be a woman of business, savvy enough to work out that making herself into a hard-won prize would drive up the price. It was Flynn's job to see that Tanner did not pay one pence more than she was worth—and she ought to be worth no more than the others had cost the marquess.

Flynn stared at the door of the building and tugged at his cuffs, straightening his coat. Appearances were always important in negotiations, he told himself. He cleared his throat and opened the door, stepping into a dark hall.

Letting his eyes adjust to the dim light, he waited a moment before ascending the wooden staircase. One flight up, he turned and knocked upon a plain wooden door. As its knob turned and the door began to open, his chest tightened, exactly as if he had run from Mayfair to Covent Garden.

But the sensation passed when Mr O'Keefe admitted him into a small parlor with threadbare furniture, adorned by luxurious bouquets of flowers on almost every surface.

Flynn congratulated himself for forgoing a bouquet of rare blooms. He patted the inside pocket of his coat that held Tanner's offering.

'Good day to you, sir.' Mr O'Keefe bowed repeatedly. 'Good of you to call.'

'How do you do, sir.' A garishly dressed woman curtsied deeply.

Mr O'Keefe took his hat and gloves and gestured to the woman. 'This is Rose's very dear friend and mine, Miss Dawes.'

She curtsied again.

Their deference was extreme. It dawned on him that they thought he was Tanner. 'I did not give you my name last night. I am Mr Flynn, the Marquess of Tannerton's secretary—'

Mr O'Keefe suddenly relaxed. 'Yes, yes,' he said in an almost normal voice. He thrust his hand out to Flynn. 'Good of you to come.'

Flynn accepted the handshake. 'It was good of you to allow me to call.'

O'Keefe gestured to the sofa. Flynn indicated that Mr O'Keefe must sit as well, and the older man, thin as a reed and a good head shorter than Flynn, lowered himself into an adjacent chair.

'I come on the marquess's behalf,' Flynn began. 'The marquess has had the pleasure of hearing your daughter's lovely voice. He is most anxious to meet her.'

Mr O'Keefe nodded, listening intently.

Flynn continued, 'I should like to convey the marquess's high regard to Miss O'Keefe directly, if that is possible.'

'I'll fetch her,' Miss Dawes piped up. 'I have no idea why she has not showed herself.'

'I would be grateful.' Flynn watched her bustle through an interior door.

'Rose!' he heard Miss Dawes say sharply.

Flynn frowned.

'She'll come,' Mr O'Keefe said in a reassuring tone.

Flynn did not wish to negotiate with the father. Experience had taught him that it was preferable to deal with the woman herself.

'Here she is,' chirped Miss Dawes from the doorway. She quickly stepped aside.

Rose O'Keefe entered the room, so graceful she seemed to glide above the floor. Up close, with daylight illuminating the room, her beauty robbed his lungs of air. Her face, so fair and fine, was framed by raven-black tendrils, her skin translucent. But it was her eyes that captured him and aroused him again. They were as green as the rolling hills of County Down.

He stood.

Before he could speak, she said, 'You are?'

Her father rose from his chair and walked over to her. 'Mary Rose, Mr Flynn is secretary to the Marquess of Tannerton.'

Her glorious green eyes widened slightly.

Flynn bowed. 'Miss O'Keefe.'

She seemed to recover from any surprise, saying coolly, 'You were wanting to speak to me, sir?'

Flynn heard the lilt of Ireland in her speech, not quite as carefully eradicated as his own. He began, 'I come on behalf of the marquess—'

'I see,' she interrupted. 'What is it a marquess wants of me that he cannot be asking himself?'

Flynn blinked.

'Mary Rose!' her father pleaded. 'Mind your tongue.'

'Obey your father!' Miss Dawes scolded.

Miss O'Keefe darted Miss Dawes a defiant glance. This was going badly, Flynn thought. It was beginning to seem as if her father and this Dawes woman were forcing her into this. Tanner never desired a woman be compelled to share his bed. Flynn needed to deal directly with Miss O'Keefe. He must be assured she would be a willing partner.

And, at the moment, Miss O'Keefe looked anything but willing.

'I will speak with Miss O'Keefe alone, sir,' he said in a smooth voice.

Mr O'Keefe looked uncertain.

Miss Dawes wagged her finger towards the daughter. 'Talk to him, Rose. Be a good girl.' Then she hustled the father out of the room.

Flynn turned back to Miss O'Keefe. Her green eyes were strained.

'I would not distress you, miss,' he said softly.

She waved a graceful hand in the air. 'It is of no consequence.'

He paused, composing his next words.

She spoke first. 'You came for a reason, Mr Flynn?' Her voice was high, and tiny lines appeared at the corners of her perfectly sculpted lips.

His brows knitted. This girl seemed not at all eager to hear an offer. 'Indeed. About Lord Tannerton.'

'Would you care to sit, sir?' she asked with forced politeness.

He inclined his head, waiting for her to sit opposite him before he lowered himself into the seat.

'You were saying, Mr Flynn?'

He began again, 'I was saying, the marquess has heard you sing—'

'And you, Mr Flynn? Have you heard me sing?' She seemed bent on interrupting him.

'Yes, Miss O'Keefe, I have had the pleasure.'

A genuine smile fleetingly appeared. 'Were you liking my

singing?' She dipped her head and he noticed that her lashes were long and luxurious.

'Very much,' he said, regaining his wits.

She folded her hands in her lap. 'Flynn…it is an Irish name. Where are you from, Mr Flynn?'

Flynn did not usually lose such total control over a conversation. It disturbed him, nearly as much as perceiving her reluctance disturbed him. Nearly as much as her eyes disturbed him.

'Where am I from?' he repeated.

'Yes, where in Ireland are you from?'

He could not remember the last time he'd been asked this. 'County Down, near Ballynahinch.'

Her bewitching eyes sparkled. 'I attended school in Killyleagh.'

'So did my sister.' Those words slipped out.

'Oh!' She turned thoughtful for a moment. 'Could she be Siobhan Flynn, by any chance? There was a Siobhan Flynn two years ahead of me.'

Siobhan's name propelled him back to Ballynahinch. Little Siobhan. She'd been eleven when he'd last seen her. How old was she now? Twenty-one?

It meant Miss O'Keefe was naught but nineteen. No wonder her papa hovered near.

'She may have been the same,' he said.

Miss O'Keefe's eyes danced with excitement. 'How does she fare? I rarely heard news of any of the girls after they left.'

Flynn realised he had barely heeded news of Siobhan in his mother's letters. 'She is married and has two sons.'

Miss O'Keefe sighed. 'How nice for her!'

Flynn began again. 'About the marquess—'

'Oh, yes, the *marquess*.' Her false tone returned. 'He sent you. You did not come to speak with me about home.'

Home. Home. It repeated in his ears.

'The marquess is anxious to make your acquaintance, Miss O'Keefe. He is prepared to become your friend.'

'My friend?' She glanced away. 'He knows so much after listening to a few songs?'

He opened his mouth to respond with lavish compliments.

She spoke first. 'Are your friendships so easily made, Mr Flynn?'

'My friendships?' He was repeating again. He disliked that she distracted him from his intent, making him think instead of friends, long-ago boys who explored crumbling castle ruins with him or fished in crystalline streams.

He forced himself to meet her gaze directly. 'I assure you, Miss O'Keefe, the marquess chooses his friends judiciously, and none would complain about the connection.'

She did not waver. 'And is he usually sending you to inform his new friends of their good fortune?'

Flynn wrinkled his brow. She did not seem pleased at all at Tanner's interest. Why? Her father and that other female certainly relished the potential connection.

He must convince her she would do well under Tanner's protection. She would certainly have more freedom than she appeared to have in her father's house, with the shrill Miss Dawes bullying her.

But the image that rose in his mind was not of her with Tanner, but of her standing on a green hillside, wind billowing through her skirts and hair.

He mentally shook himself. Somehow he maintained his direct gaze. 'The marquess involves me if he feels it would best please the lady to do so.' He reached into his coat pocket. 'To show his good intentions, the marquess wishes to bestow upon you a small gift.'

Flynn pulled out a velvet box. She glanced in alarm at the door behind which her father and Miss Dawes were certainly eavesdropping. She stilled his hand. 'No gifts,' she whispered, slanting her eyes towards the door again. 'Please.'

Flynn's hand paused in mid-air, her touch branding his skin. Silently he nodded, slipping the box back in his pocket.

'A gift would be very nice indeed,' she said, raising her voice.

'Then you shall have one very soon,' he said.

Rose returned her hand to her lap, her breath coming rapidly. Her hand still tingled from touching him, and all her insides felt like melted candle wax.

He had played along with her wish not to have her father or Letty hear of a gift. If he had not, Letty would be badgering her for days to get her hands on a gift from a marquess. And to keep peace, her father would implore her to give in. The other gifts gentlemen left for her—gifts that ought to have been returned—made their way into Letty's possession or were sold to buy some other trinket she desired.

Rose tried to show Mr Flynn her gratitude with a look, but had to avert her gaze from the intensity of his startling blue eyes.

When Letty had come to fetch her, saying the marquess's secretary had arrived, Rose had been relieved she would not have to refuse a marquess to his face, especially if he were indeed the man who'd so captivated her. But the man who captivated her was his secretary and was Irish, and, even more wonderful, he'd become a momentary ally.

He was very handsome up close, with his commanding gaze. His hair and brows were nearly as dark as her own. She loved the firmness of his jaw and the decisive set to his sinfully sensuous mouth. What would it be like to touch her lips to his?

Rose mentally shook herself. She was thinking like a romantic, making this into a story like the novels she enjoyed reading, the ones that wove wonderful stories of love. This man had not come to court her, but to procure her for his employer.

Even so, his blue eyes continued to enslave her.

'The marquess is a good man, Miss O'Keefe,' he said.

She peered back at him. 'Mr Flynn, why do you tie this up in pretty words? Do you not mean the marquess is wishing me to be his mistress? Is that not what this is about? Is that not the kind of "friend" he wishes me to be?'

A muscle flexed in Mr Flynn's jaw, but his gaze held. 'To be such a friend of this man has many advantages. He can assist you. Protect you.'

Rose's gaze slipped back to the door that hid her father and Letty. They both certainly wanted her to accept the marquess's protection. And his money.

He looked to the door, as well. 'Will you need protection, Miss O'Keefe?' His voice was soft and low. And concerned.

She glanced back in surprise and gave a light laugh. 'I shall experience no difficulties, I assure you.'

Letty was as unpleasant as a woman could be, and her father was completely under her thumb, but Rose did not feel they yielded that much authority over her. She liked living with her father, making up a little for all the years that had separated them.

'You could allow the marquess to help you,' he said.

She reached over to grasp his hand in reassurance but stopped herself midway. 'I'll be needing no help.' She added, 'All I want is to sing…'

He seized on those words. 'Lord Tannerton could help you—'

She put up her hand, regretting she had spoken. 'I require no help. Do not be worrying yourself over me.'

Their eyes connected, and it felt like butterflies took possession of her insides.

'Thank the marquess for me,' she said in a loud voice. 'It was good of you to come.' She stood and walked towards the door.

It took a moment for him to follow her. 'I do not understand you, Miss O'Keefe,' he said, his voice no more than an urgent whisper. 'Why do you hesitate?'

She handed him his hat and gloves. 'Good day to you, Mr Flynn.' She opened the door.

He started to walk through it, but turned and grasped her hand in his. 'Welcome or not, Miss O'Keefe, you do have a friend.'

He released her and swiftly took his leave. Rose brushed her hand against her cheek, wishing the friend were not the marquess but Mr Flynn himself.

Chapter Three

Flynn paused a moment when he reached the street, puzzled by this experience. The times he'd risked huge amounts of Tanner's wealth on some tenuous business matter, he'd been in better control. Nothing had gone as he'd expected. Worse, his senses were still awhirl. Merely looking at the girl had been enough to throw his rationality out of the window.

With no idea what to tell Tanner, he straightened his hat and started walking in the direction of Covent Garden to find a hack.

'Mr Flynn!' he heard behind him.

Turning, he saw Mr O'Keefe running toward him. Flynn stopped.

The older man caught up to him, breathing hard. 'Letty said—I mean—I wanted a word with you.'

Flynn merely waited.

'Tell…tell the marquess how flattered we are—my daughter is, I mean—at his kind interest.'

'I will tell him.' Although, if Flynn did tell Tanner this, he'd be lying. The daughter did not seem flattered in the least.

Mr O'Keefe's mouth twisted into an apologetic smile. 'My Rose is a sensible girl,' he said, a fond look appearing in his eye. 'She'll just need some persuading.'

Flynn regarded this man who looked as if a strong wind might blow him away. Flynn could not see him persuading his daughter about anything. The unpleasant Miss Dawes, however, was another matter.

'I must leave.' Flynn turned away.

'Do try again, sir,' Mr O'Keefe cried as Flynn walked away.

Flynn looked over his shoulder. 'I shall tell the marquess you said so.'

Mr O'Keefe nodded vigorously, and Flynn hurried on his way to a row of waiting hackney carriages.

He soon reached Tanner's Audley Street town house, returning to the familiar opulence, the order, the civility.

The footman who opened the door said, 'His lordship wishes you to attend him in the game room straight away.'

Not even a moment to collect himself, nor to plan an explanation of his incredible meeting with Miss O'Keefe.

'Thank you, Smythe.' Flynn handed the man his hat and gloves and made his way to the game room.

When he entered, Tanner was leaning over the billiard table, lining up a shot. Flynn stood in the doorway until the ball cracked into another one, sending it rolling across the green baize and landing successfully in the pocket.

'Flynn!' Tanner waved him in. 'Come, tell me all about it. I am most anxious. Could think of nothing else since you left.'

Tanner settled himself in one of the leather chairs by the window and gestured for Flynn to pour them some claret from the decanter on the side table.

'Well, did you see her?' Tanner asked as Flynn handed him a glass of claret. 'Of course you did or you'd have been back sooner. What did she say? Did she like the gift? What the devil did you purchase for her?'

Flynn poured wine for himself, but did not sit. 'I purchased a matched set of gold bracelets.'

'And?' Tanner grinned eagerly.

Flynn took a sip before speaking. 'She refused the gift.'

Tanner half-rose from his seat. 'Refused?'

'I fear so, my lord,' he admitted.

Tanner waved his hand dismissively. 'It was the wrong gift, then, but I am sure you assured her there would be more gifts. What of a meeting?'

Flynn averted his eyes.

The marquess sank back in the chair. 'Do not tell me she refused to meet me?'

'She did not refuse exactly, but neither did she agree.' Flynn's powers of diplomacy had escaped him with Miss O'Keefe, but perhaps they would hold him in better stead with Tanner.

Tanner raised his brows. 'What the devil happened then? What did you talk about?'

Of home. Of Ireland. But Flynn was not about to provide this as an answer. 'I explained the advantages of your…friendship, and she listened.'

'That is all?' The marquess's forehead wrinkled in confusion.

'That is all.'

Tanner slowly sipped his wine, finishing it, while Flynn could not even put a glass to his lips.

He placed his still-full glass on the table and reached for the decanter. 'More, sir?'

Tanner shook his head, still silent.

All of a sudden Tanner burst into a wide grin and thrust out his glass. 'She is playing a deep game, is all. Gold bracelets? You were too cheap, man. The girl wants more and she knows she can get it!' He laughed. 'You must deliver a more valuable gift.'

Flynn refilled Tanner's wine glass, not wanting to explain that giving Miss O'Keefe a gift was not so simple a task.

'Give her emeralds next time, to set off her eyes. An emerald ring!' Tanner's own brown eyes sparkled. 'What the devil, offer her patronage as well—an allowance. A generous one. Show her I am willing to pay her price.'

As a business move, Flynn typically would have advised against this. The next offer in a negotiation ought not to be so high. But in Rose O'Keefe's situation, he was more than willing to try to get her away from the bullying Miss Dawes.

Flynn nodded. His heart raced at the prospect of seeing her again, even though to see her was merely a function of his duty to Tanner. Still, he could not erase from his memory the sensuous grace of her figure, the irresistible tint of her lips, the eyes that beckoned him home.

He took his leave from Tanner. There was much to be done to carry out the next phase of the marquess's plan.

The very next night Flynn stood below the gazebo's balcony at Vauxhall Gardens, again listening to the crystalline sound of Rose O'Keefe's voice filling the evening with song. He'd secured a private box and supper for Miss O'Keefe, leaving a message to her father to escort her to the box when the orchestra broke and Signor Rivolta, the man who played six or eight instruments at once, performed. He trusted her father would approve of the meeting.

She wore the wine-red gown again, the colour of passionate nights, and her fair skin glowed against its richness. Flynn convinced himself he merely admired her beauty, the way he might appreciate the beauty of a flower or a painting or how the house in Ballynahinch shone golden in the light of the setting sun.

He watched until she made her final curtsy and disappeared into the dark recesses of the balcony. He then made his way to the supper box to ensure all was as he'd planned—a supper of light delicacies, nothing too fancy, but all very tasteful. Assured everything was prepared and ready, he spent the rest of the time pacing, his breath catching whenever the music ceased, and easing when it resumed again.

Finally the orchestra was silent. Flynn continued pacing until he heard the O'Keefes approach. Unfortunately, it was Miss Dawes's piercing voice that gave him warning. He ought to have expected her.

'Behave yourself, miss. I'll not have you ruining this for your father—' The woman's speech cut off when she saw Flynn. 'Mr Flynn!' She switched to a syrupy tone.

'Good evening,' Flynn said to them all, but to the one who wore a hooded cape that nearly obscured her face, his voice turned husky. 'Miss O'Keefe.'

She nodded. 'Mr Flynn.'

'This is so very kind of you, sir.' Mr O'Keefe tiptoed into the box and hesitated before accepting Flynn's outstretched hand. O'Keefe's hand was bony, but his handshake warm.

'So kind,' O'Keefe murmured. He turned to his daughter. 'Is that not so, Mary Rose?'

She merely glanced at her father before turning to Flynn. 'Is the marquess here?'

Both Mr O'Keefe and Miss Dawes wore hopeful expressions, but Miss O'Keefe seemed anything but eager.

'He regrets not being at liberty to come,' Flynn prevaricated. He directed them to the table. 'But please sit and have some supper.'

Mr O'Keefe and Miss Dawes hurried to the round table set with porcelain china, crystal glassware and silver cutlery. Flynn pulled out the chair for Miss O'Keefe, and she glanced into his eyes as she sat down. He signalled the footman to bring another chair and place setting, after which the food was served: tender capons and a rich assortment of cheeses and fruit. The footman uncorked a bottle of champagne, pouring it into all four glasses.

'Oooh, bubbles!' exclaimed Miss Dawes in her coarse voice. 'I love the bubbly wine.'

Rose picked up her glass and took a sip. She had tasted champagne before at Miss Hart's, so its fizzy taste was not a surprise.

She watched Letty dig into the prettily displayed food as if she had not consumed a large dinner a few hours before. Mr Flynn's food was fine, Rose thought, nibbling more delicately. The cheese tasted good with the strawberries and cherries.

Mr Flynn sat himself next to her and she discovered that she was very aware of each small movement he made. In a way she was glad she could not see his eyes. It was hard to be thinking when she could see his eyes.

Signor Rivolta's lively music drifted over to their ears, his gay tune seeming out of place in the tension-filled supper box.

'When is the marquess going to make his offer for our Rose?' Letty bluntly asked.

Rose stilled, hating that Flynn would be associating someone so ill mannered with her.

Flynn paused, just one beat, before directing his answer to her father. 'To speak of an offer is premature, sir, but I should like to discuss with Miss O'Keefe a possible meeting.'

'Oh, there will be an offer all right,' Letty broke in, waving her fork at Rose. 'Look at her! What man could resist our lovely Rose?'

She reached over and not so gently patted Rose on the cheek. It was all Rose could do not to flinch.

'I am most interested in my daughter's welfare,' her father added in an earnest voice. 'This must be worth her while.'

Rose disliked being discussed like this, as if she were goods to barter.

Mr Flynn put down his fork. 'I am instructed to tell you, Mr O'Keefe, that the marquess insists I speak with the lady herself in such matters. He must be assured his interest suits her before he proceeds in the negotiation. I am sure you understand.'

Her father's brows knitted. 'But I must also agree to any arrangements. She is still my responsibility, sir.'

'She knows what is expected of her,' added Letty.

Rose knew exactly what Letty expected. Letty expected a great deal of money to come into her pocket by way of this marquess. She glanced at her father. His motives were more unselfish, but still distasteful.

'We will speak later,' Flynn said to her father.

Rose rather liked the way Flynn simply passed over Letty, as if she had no say in the matter, which she certainly did not.

'She's still young, Mr Flynn,' her father added, sounding genuinely worried.

Flynn turned to Rose with a question in his eyes, but Rose had no idea what he was asking. 'I will see no harm comes to her.' His gaze changed into something that made her feel like fanning herself.

She glanced down at her food. Imagine that a mere look from a man could make her feel like that.

Signor Rivolta's music ended and the faint sound of applause could be heard. Soon the orchestra would play again.

'I must get back.' Mr O'Keefe rose.

Flynn stood as well. 'Miss Dawes will wish to go with you, I am certain.' He walked over to help Letty from her chair, giving her no oppportunity to argue. 'I will safely deliver Miss O'Keefe to you before the night is done.'

Mr Flynn escorted them both out of the box, then returned to the table, sitting opposite her this time.

Rose gazed at him with admiration. 'You do have the silver tongue, do you not, Mr Flynn? I believe Letty thought she wanted to go with Papa.'

He frowned. 'Only one of many talents,' he said absently.

He'd rattled her again, making her wonder what had suddenly made him frown. She picked up a strawberry and bit into it, slowly licking its juice from her lips.

Mr Flynn's eyes darkened and he looked even more disturbed.

Rose paused. Could it be she had captured Mr Flynn's interest? That idea made her giddy.

She took another sip of champagne and lowered her eyes to gaze at him through her long lashes. He reached over to retrieve his glass, downing the entire contents.

Rose felt light headed.

He gave her an intent look. 'We must talk, Miss O'Keefe.'

But she was not finished flirting with him. She leaned forward, knowing it afforded him a better glimpse of the low neckline of her gown. 'Will you not call me Rose?'

His eyes darkened again. 'Rose,' he repeated in a low voice that resonated deep inside her.

Their heads were close together, his eyes looking as deep a blue as the Irish Sea. The air crackled between them and he leaned closer.

A reveller, one who no doubt had been drinking heavily, careened into the supper box, nearly knocking into the table.

The footman quickly appeared and escorted him out, but it was enough to break the moment between them.

He frowned. 'I apologise for that.'

She hoped he meant the drunken man. 'You could not help it.'

He gazed at her in that stirring way again. 'I could not help it.' He set his jaw. 'About the marquess—'

But Rose could not bear losing this new, intoxicating connection between them. She daringly put her hand upon his arm. 'Let us not speak of the marquess. Let us simply enjoy this beautiful night.'

He stared at her hand for a moment. Slowly he raised his head. 'Your father—'

'I will tell my father that I put you off, but that you will be back.' She squeezed his arm. 'What say you? Can we walk through the gardens? I have seen so little of Vauxhall. I have been confined to the gazebo, really.'

He stared at her, then released a long breath. 'Very well.'

With a leaping heart, she finished the rest of her champagne. She grasped his hand in hers and led him out of the supper box. He offered his arm. 'Hold on to me, Rose. I must keep you safe.'

It was a fair warning. Vauxhall could be a dangerous place for a woman alone, but that did not keep Rose from enjoying the feel of his muscle beneath his sleeve.

They joined the throngs of people enjoying the clear, warm night. The music of the orchestra filled the garden, the sound ebbing and flowing on the summer breeze. Night had fallen and the lamps glowed like bright stars. Flynn escorted her through the arches painted to look like the Ruins of Palmyra. He showed her the Pavilion with its allegorical paintings. They strolled down the Colonnade past the fountain sparkling in the lamplight. What had seemed false to him two nights ago now seemed magical. He was under her spell again, he had to admit, but that last exchange with her father gave him pause. Her father treated her as if she'd just come out of a schoolroom.

As if she were an innocent.

If she were an innocent, negotiations were at an end. Even if Tanner would accept a girl who'd been untouched—and he would not—Flynn could never involve himself in such an arrangement. It was almost a relief. An end to this madness.

They paused by the fountain, and she dipped her fingers into the cool water, a gesture so sensuous it belied his earlier thought.

'Rose! Rose!' A young woman ran towards her, bosoms about to burst from a revealing neckline, flaming red hair about to tumble from a decorative hat. A rather mature gentleman tried to keep pace with her. 'Rose, it is you!' The two women embraced. 'I've been here every night you've sung. I thought I'd never talk to you.'

'Katy.' Rose pressed her cheek against her friend's. 'I have missed you so much.'

This Katy broke away to eye Flynn up and down, making him feel like a sweetmeat in a confectioner's shop. 'And who is this?'

'This is Mr Flynn, Katy.' Rose turned to him. 'My dear friend, Katy Green.'

Flynn somehow managed to keep the shock from his face. Her friend could only be described as a—a doxy. No innocent would greet a woman like Katy Green with such undisguised affection.

He bowed. 'I am charmed, Miss Green.'

The young woman gave a throaty chortle and turned to
Rose. 'Where did you find this one? He's quality, I'd wager
a guinea on it.'

'Oh, Mr Flynn is a very important man.' Miss O'Keefe
slanted an amused look at him. 'But, it is not what you are
thinking, Katy.'

'Isn't it?' The doxy's expression was sceptical. 'What a
shame…'

As the two young women talked of even more acquain-
tances, Flynn was left standing with the older gentleman.

He recognised the somewhat ramshackle fellow who
was said to be one step from River Tick. 'Good evening,
Sir Reginald.'

The man was still catching his breath. 'Flynn, isn't it? In
Tannerton's employ, am I right?'

'You are, sir.'

Sir Reginald poked him in the ribs. 'Doing very well for
yourself, ain't you, my boy? Rose is a looker.'

Flynn did not reply. He was still in the throes of confusion.
Rose O'Keefe could not be an innocent. Sir Reginald, a man
on the fringe of society, knew her. A doxy knew her. She
must be of their world. It made sense—the way she moved,
the expression in her eyes, the timbre of her voice. That sort
of sensuality made for arousing a man's needs, enough to
bewitch him, that was for certain. But she also brought him
an aching yearning for the green hills of Ireland, the warmth
of family, and the pure, unspoiled days of his boyhood in Ballynahinch. How did he explain that?

Illusion, he told himself. Again. In any event, none of this
should matter to him. Rose O'Keefe could be nothing to him.

'I am working for Tannerton,' he explained to Sir Reginald.

'Aha!' The man wagged his brows knowingly, but this only

disturbed Flynn more, as if by his innuendo the man were crushing the petals of a flower. A rose.

A bell sounded, announcing the illuminations were about to begin.

'Come,' cried the red-haired Katy. 'We must get a good spot!' She seized Sir Reginald's arm and pulled him through the crowd.

Flynn held back until Katy and Sir Reginald disappeared. He wanted Rose to himself, wanted the illusion to return, even if she was not supposed to mean anything to him.

But he was thinking only of himself. He turned to Rose. 'Do you wish us to find your friend?'

She shook her head and gripped his arm again. Together they walked to the illuminations. People jostled and pushed them, all trying to find the perfect spot to see the fireworks. It seemed natural for Flynn to put his arm around her and hold her close, so that she would not become separated from him.

The whoosh of a rocket signalled the first of the bursts of light and colour, and the explosions sounded like several muskets firing at once.

'Oh!' Rose gasped as the sky lit up with hundreds of shooting stars.

She turned her smiling face towards him, the hood of her cape falling away. Their gazes caught. The illuminations reflected in her eyes, and he was truly bewitched, lost, drowning in the sparkling lights. He bent his head and she lifted hers so that there could be no more than an inch separating their lips. Flynn wanted, ached, to close the distance, to feel the soft press of her lips against his, to taste her, to hold her flush against him. His body demanded more of her, all of her.

But he forced himself to release her, to break the contact with her eyes.

What had he been thinking? This was Tanner's woman, as sure as if Tanner had given her his name. What sort of suicide was it for Flynn to even gaze at her as he had done?

Tanner might appear affable, but he was a formidable adversary if crossed. If Flynn, a mere secretary, a mere employee, took liberties with a woman Tanner had selected for himself, not only his position would be lost, but his entire future.

Her smile disappeared and she turned her head to watch the pyrotechnic display. Flynn kept his arm wrapped around her. Indeed, he could not bring himself to move it. She felt soft and warm against him, and he wanted to hold her through eternity.

The illuminations, however, came to an end.

'I must return you.' He slipped his arm from her back as the crowd dispersed, and glimpsed her friend strutting away, Sir Reginald in tow.

Rose—Miss O'Keefe, he should call her—nodded, taking his arm in a more demure fashion. Still, he could not hurry to the orchestra's gazebo where he must leave her. He did not wish to let her go.

She stopped when they reached the door. 'Thank you, Flynn, for the lovely tour of the park and the illuminations. I am most grateful to you.'

No, he could not release her yet. It was too soon.

Flynn remembered he had not given her the emerald ring still in his coat pocket. He had not spoken to her of Tanner's willingness to be a generous patron. He had done nothing that his employer had sent him to do.

But even Tanner's disappointment in him could not compel him to rectify this lapse in efficiency at the present moment.

'Miss O'Keefe, may I call upon you tomorrow?' Tomorrow he would do his duty, what his employer required of him.

She stared into his eyes, not answering right away. She

inhaled sharply as if her decision had been a sudden one. 'Not at my lodgings. Take me for a drive in the park.'

He nodded. 'Two o'clock?' Neither of them belonged in the park during the fashionable hour when the highest rung of society took over. Two o'clock should be early enough.

'Two o'clock,' she repeated.

'There she is!' a man's voice shouted, and other voices joined him.

A throng of men started towards them. Flynn quickly rapped loudly on the door. It opened immediately, and she disappeared inside.

Flynn faced the group of men, unreasonably angry at their pursuit, unreasonably wanting to claim her for himself. Had he been alone that first night, not with Tanner, he might have been among men such as these. 'She is spoken for, gentlemen. Abandon your pursuit.'

There were grumbles and arguments, but they all eventually dispersed. Except one man, elegantly attired in a coat that could only have been made by Weston. Flynn recognised him as the Earl of Greythorne.

'You are Tannerton's man, are you not?' the earl asked.

'I am,' Flynn responded. He started toward the Grand Walk.

The earl fell in step with him. 'And is the alluring Rose O'Keefe claimed by Lord Tannerton?'

'She is.'

Flynn tried to remember what he knew of the gentleman, besides the fact that Tanner thought him a 'damned prig.' Greythorne's estate was in Kent, but he possessed properties in Sussex and somewhere up north as well. He frequented the *ton* entertainments. Belonged to White's. Still, there was something he was forgetting. Some rumour about the man.

Greythorne chuckled. 'A pity. I fancy her myself.' His arm

swept the area. 'As do others. Tannerton may be in for a serious contest.'

Greythorne possessed enough wealth to pose a threat. If he offered a great deal of money to put Rose under his protection, Flynn had no doubt Miss Dawes would bully O'Keefe into accepting. She'd have no qualms about selling Rose to the highest bidder.

Flynn regarded the man. 'I am certain, as a gentleman, you would not covet what another man has claimed as his.'

Greythorne's slippery smile remained. 'Her father does not seem to agree with your perception. He seemed to indicate the game was still in progress.'

It was as if dark clouds suddenly gathered. 'The deal is all but made,' Flynn said.

Greythorne continued walking. 'I would be the last man to encroach,' he assured Flynn. 'But if the deal is not made, I'm prepared to play my hand.'

Chapter Four

The next day was as sunny as any summer day could be in London as Flynn navigated the streets of Covent Garden on the way to Rose's lodgings. Tanner had wholeheartedly endorsed this escapade, especially after hearing of Greythorne's interest.

'Something about that fellow,' Tanner had said. 'I have always detested the man. Damned natty, for one thing. Never a speck of dirt, or a wrinkle in his coat. Every hair in place. Devilish odd.' Tanner had shuddered. 'Something else, though. I shall endeavour to discover what it is.'

Tanner had insisted Flynn take his curricle and the matched chestnuts, which had cost him a fortune at Tattersalls.

Flynn brought the curricle to a halt in front of Rose's building. He tossed a coin to a boy passing by, asking the lad to hold the horses. As he climbed the stairs to knock upon Rose's door, his excitement grew, an excitement he had no right to feel.

The door opened and there she stood, green paisley shawl draped over the same dress she'd worn when he last visited these rooms, hat and gloves already on. If she could appear this beautiful in a plain dress, think of how she would look in all the finery Tanner could buy her.

He frowned as she turned to close the door. He must keep Tanner in mind. Wrest control over this tendency to be bewitched.

But his resolve frayed as his hands spanned her waist to lift her into the curricle. And frayed more when she smiled down at him.

He climbed up next to her, and the boy handed him the ribbons. 'Hyde Park, is that correct?' he asked her.

'It does not have to be Hyde Park,' she replied in a breathless voice.

'Where then?'

The sun rendered her skin translucent, and he had the urge to pull off his gloves and touch her with the tip of his finger.

'Anywhere you wish,' she whispered.

They stared at each other.

'Hyde Park, then,' he said finally.

He flicked the ribbons and the horses started forward. He drove through the riders, wagons, carriages, and hacks on Long Acre towards Piccadilly. 'Your father gave you permission for this outing, I trust.'

'He and Letty are out,' she responded. 'So there was no objection.'

She had not really answered him, he realised. He thought of asking for an explanation. Why did she appear to be under her father's control, yet also out in the world with the likes of her friend Katy Green?

'It is a fine day,' he said instead.

'Yes, it is.' She changed positions and her hand brushed his leg as she readjusted her skirt.

He felt her touch long after her hand closed upon the bench to steady herself.

Flynn mentally shook himself, and concentrated on what

he intended to accomplish. He must give her Tanner's gift, the finest emerald ring Flynn could find at Rundell and Bridge. He must offer her Tanner's patronage and propose a time and place for her to meet Tanner.

And he must ensure she spurned Greythorne.

As the curricle reached the Hyde Park gate, Flynn felt back in form. 'Have you driven through the park before, Rose?'

'Oh, yes,' she replied, with no elaboration.

He was again reminded that she was no green girl, but it only forced him to wonder who her former escorts had been.

The fine day had brought many others to the park. Governesses with young children, servants and shopworkers, all taking respite from their toil. Fine gentlemen drove carriages accompanied by gaily dressed female companions—their mistresses, no doubt. Flynn knew some of these men, though he knew better than to nod in greeting. Later in the day some of these same gentlemen would return to this same carriage path to drive their wives or some respectable miss they were courting.

It occurred to Flynn that, if he did his job successfully, Tanner would soon be sitting in his place in this same curricle with Rose beside him. He frowned.

'What makes you unhappy?' she asked.

He started and looked over to see Rose staring at him, her lips pursed with concern.

'I am not unhappy, I assure you.'

One brow arched. 'You looked unhappy, I was thinking.'

With effort he composed his features into their usual bland expression. 'I am not unhappy. Merely concentrating on driving.'

She faced forward again to watch the few carriages approaching them at a leisurely pace. 'Yes, it is so treacherous here.'

He ignored her teasing and changed the subject. 'Do you enjoy carriage rides?'

'I do,' she replied, smiling again.

'The marquess has several carriages,' he said, dutifully promoting Tanner's interest. 'This one, of course, and a phaeton, a landaulet—'

'How nice,' she said without enthusiasm.

He persevered. 'He also has been known to purchase carriages for special friends.'

'Yes. Special friends.' She showed no increased interest.

Flynn gave her a sideways glance. Most women would leap at the chance to receive this man's regard. The advantages were inestimable. 'He is a generous man, Rose. I can provide you many examples to prove it, if you wish.'

She gave him an imploring look. 'Please do not.'

He frowned again, pretending to concentrate on the horses and the carriage path. Finally he asked, 'What is it, Rose? Every time I mention the marquess, you put me off. Perhaps if you could explain why, I would proceed in a manner to please you.'

Two spots of colour dotted her cheeks. 'Oh, I have nothing against the man…'

Flynn waited for her to say more. The horses waited, too, almost slowing to a stop. He flicked the ribbons and they moved again. The Serpentine came into view, its water glistening in the afternoon sun.

'It is pretty here,' she said after a time.

He forgot about Tanner. Against the green of the grass, lushness of the trees and blue of the Serpentine, she looked like a Gainsborough portrait. He wished he could capture her image, frame it and hang it upon a wall to gaze at for ever.

He closed his eyes. This was madness, coveting his employer's intended conquest.

He drew a breath, steeling himself again to perform his

task. 'I should like to speak for Lord Tannerton, if you will permit me.'

Rose wiped an escaped tendril from her forehead. She'd been pretending Mr Flynn had called upon her like a suitor. A foolish notion. He merely wanted to talk of the marquess.

The rhythmic sound of the horses' hooves on the gravel path seemed louder while she delayed her answer. How could she explain to him that she was not wanting a marquess's money? She was wanting what every girl wanted.

Love.

She set her chin firmly. 'Later perhaps we can speak of the marquess.'

'But I ought—' he began, but clamped his mouth shut. He blew out a long breath and continued in a resigned tone. 'What do you wish to talk about, Rose?'

The knot inside her uncoiled. She could pretend a bit longer. 'Oh, anything…' She smiled at him, suddenly light hearted. 'Things people talk about.'

Things she longed to know about him.

She took a breath. 'Have…have you been in England long, Flynn?'

It took him a moment to respond. 'Since I was eighteen.'

'And how long is that, then?' she persisted.

'Ten years.'

She had discovered his age! Twenty-eight. 'What brought you to England, then?'

'I came to attend Oxford.'

'Oxford? That is where gentlemen go, is it not? To become vicars and such?'

He laughed. 'Yes, and other things.'

'Your family was high enough for Oxford?'

He stiffened. 'It was.'

She'd offended him. 'I should not have spoken so.' She blinked. 'I hope you'll forgive me.'

His expression softened. 'My father is gentry, Rose, a fairly prosperous landowner. He was well able to send me to Oxford.'

Rose relaxed again. 'And what after Oxford?'

'I came to London in search of a position. Lord Tannerton took a risk hiring me.'

'You must have impressed him.'

He gave a half-smile. 'More like he took pity on me, I should think. But I have learned much in his employ.'

She felt bold enough to ask more. 'Have you been back to Ireland, then?'

He shook his head, and the frown reappeared on his face.

Oh, dear. She'd made him unhappy again. She cleared her throat. 'I've only been in England a few months.'

'And why did you come, Miss O'Keefe?' His response sounded more automatic than curious and, oh, so formal.

'The school was willing to keep me teaching. The school near Killyleagh, I mean. But I had this desire to sing, you see.' She paused. 'Like my mother.'

'Your mother?'

She nodded. 'My mother sang in London in her time. She died long ago.'

He looked at her with sympathy, pricking a pain she usually kept carefully hidden.

She swallowed. 'In any event, my father was working in London, so I came here.' She glanced away. 'He could not afford to keep me at first, but then Mr Hook hired me to sing.' She skipped over a lot of the story, perhaps the most important parts. 'And when I'm done singing at Vauxhall, I'll find another place to sing.'

'Where?' he asked.

'Oh, somewhere. I'm thinking there are plenty of theatres in London.'

'There are theatres in Ireland as well,' he said.

She shrugged. 'Not like in London. London has King's Theatre and Drury Lane and Vauxhall nearby. Plenty of places. My mother once performed in King's Theatre.'

'That is impressive,' he said.

She laughed. 'Not very impressive, really. She was in the chorus, but she did sing on the stage at King's Theatre.'

'Do you wish to sing in the King's Theatre?' he asked.

She sighed. 'I do. More than anything. It must be the most beautiful theatre in the world.'

He smiled. 'It is quite beautiful.'

'You've seen it?' She turned to him eagerly.

'I've accompanied Lord Tannerton there on occasion.'

'You have?' She would have loved to just walk inside the building, see the boxes and the curtain and the stage. She sighed again.

He continued to smile at her.

She could not help but smile back at him, thinking how boyish he looked when he let his face relax.

A carriage came in the other direction and he attended to the driving again. They lapsed into silence.

She searched for something else to ask him. 'What work do you do for Lord Tannerton, then?'

'I manage many of his affairs—' He cleared his throat. 'His *business* affairs. Tend to his correspondence, arrange his appointments, pay bills, run errands and such.'

'Ah, I see.' But she really did not understand the business of a marquess.

He went on, 'You might say I attend to all the tedious

details, so the marquess is free for more important matters, and so his life runs smoothly.'

Such work would give Rose the headache. 'Are you liking what you do?'

He nodded. 'I have learned much about the world through it. About politics. Money. Power—'

Such things were mysteries to her.

'I have even been to Vienna and Brussels and Paris with Lord Tannerton.'

Her eyes widened with interest. 'Have you now?'

'The marquess assisted in the diplomacies, you see. And I assisted him.' He spoke proudly.

She liked seeing his pride. 'Were you there for the great battle?'

'In Brussels, yes, but we were not at Waterloo.' His face became serious. 'The marquess helped with the aftermath, assisting in the logistics of the wounded and in any other way of being at service.'

Rose did not know what 'logistics' were, but she knew there were many wounded in the battle. Many Irish soldiers had fought and died at Waterloo. She was glad Flynn had been there to help those who survived.

He gave a dry laugh. 'But it must be tedious to hear of such things.'

'Oh, no,' she assured him. 'I confess I do not understand all of it, but you were meaning, I think, that you were in important places, doing important things.'

'That is it,' he agreed. 'In the centre of things. A part of it all.'

'I'm supposing it is a little like being a performer, isn't it? Performing is not so important, perhaps, but it is being a part of something. I mean, the singing is only one piece of it.

There are the musicians, too, and the conductor and all. Everyone together makes the performance.'

He looked at her so intently her insides fluttered. 'Yes, it is precisely like that. One feels good about one's part in it.'

'Yes.' She quickly glanced away and spied a man crossing the park with a bundle on his shoulder. 'And that man there is doing his part, too, isn't he? We don't know what it is, but without him it would not happen, would it?'

A smile flitted across his face, disappearing when he gazed into her eyes again. 'Yes, I expect you are very right.'

Her breath quickened, like it had when he'd almost kissed her under the illuminations the night before.

'So what, Flynn, is your King's Theatre?' she asked, needing to break the intensity, just as he had broken away when he almost kissed her. 'Or have you reached it already?'

'My King's Theatre?'

'What you want more than anything.'

His eyes darkened, making her insides feel like melting wax again.

The horses stopped, and his attention turned to them, signalling them to move.

'What I want more than anything...' he repeated as if pondering the question. 'To be a part of something important,' he finally replied. 'Yes, that is it.'

She waited for more.

His brow furrowed. 'Lord Tannerton is an excellent employer, an excellent man, Rose, but...' His voice faded, although his face seemed lit with fire.

'Something more important is what you are wanting?' she guessed.

He nodded. 'To work for government. For a diplomat, perhaps. Or the Prime Minister. Or for royalty.'

'Royalty?' she exclaimed.

He flicked the ribbons and shook his head. 'It is daft.'

She put her hand on his arm. 'It is not daft! No more daft than me wanting to sing in King's Theatre.' But it did seem so impossible, and somehow it made her sad. 'It would be important, wouldn't it? So important you'd not be seeing the likes of me.'

He covered her hand with his and leaned towards her. The horses drifted to a stop again.

'Move on!' an angry voice shouted.

A young man driving a phaeton approached them from behind. Flynn put the chestnuts into a trot, but the phaeton passed them as soon as the path was wide enough.

They finished their circuit of the park, not speaking much. Their silence seemed tense, holding too many unspoken words, but Rose still wished the time to go on endlessly. Soon, however, other carriages entered the park, driven by gentlemen with their ladies. The fashionable hour had arrived, and they must leave.

As Flynn turned the curricle on to her street, he was frowning again. 'What is it, Flynn?' she asked.

'I have not talked to you of Tannerton,' he said. 'My reason for seeing you. And there is something else, Rose.'

She felt a pang at the reminder of his true purpose. 'What is it?' she asked in a resigned tone.

He gave her a direct look. 'Another man will be vying for your favours. He is Lord Greythorne. He is wealthy, but some unpleasant rumour hangs about him.'

'What rumour?' She had no intention of bestowing her favours on whoever it was, no matter what.

'I do not know precisely,' he said.

She shrugged. 'I thank you for the warning, Flynn.'

'It is important that you not choose Greythorne.'

She did not wish to choose any man, not for money or the gifts he could give her. She wanted to tell Flynn he could tell them all to leave her alone. Let her sing. That was all she wished to do, even if he were making her imagine other possibilities.

Her father had been drumming it into her that to be a success on the London stage, she must have a wealthy patron. It seemed all anyone wanted of her—her father, Letty, the marquess, this Greythorne.

Flynn.

He was still talking. 'Lord Tannerton would be good to you, Rose. I would stake my life on it.'

But she did not *love* Lord Tannerton. That was the thing.

With such a lofty man, she could never have what Miss Hart had with Mr Sloane.

She needed time. 'I will think on it some more, Flynn.'

Langley Street was empty in front of her building. He jumped down from the curricle and held her waist as he lifted her down.

She rested her hands on his shoulders a moment longer than necessary, not wanting to say goodbye to him. Wanting to see him again. 'I…I will be singing at Vauxhall tonight. If you've a mind to come.'

He stood still, but it seemed as if his eyes were searching hers. 'I will be there.'

'Come to the gazebo door. You'll be admitted, I promise.' Her spirits were soaring again. He wanted to see her. *Her.*

He grasped her hand and held it a brief delicious moment. 'Tonight, then.'

Feeling joyous, Rose entered the building and climbed the stairs to her father's rooms.

When she opened the door, Letty stood there, hands on her

hips. 'Were you with that Flynn fellow? Has he given you a meeting time with the marquess?'

She ought to have been prepared. 'It is not set, Letty. But soon, Mr Flynn tells me.'

'Where did you go, Mary Rose? I was wondering.' Her father sat in the chair near the fireplace.

Rose walked over and gave him a kiss on the top of his bald head. 'A drive in the park, is all.' She headed for her room.

Letty blocked her way. 'This Flynn. Did he tell you how much the marquess will pay?'

Rose looked her in the eye. 'I thought you would be proud of me, Letty. I put him off. Did you not say that would increase the price?'

'Well, I—' Letty began, but Rose brushed past her to disappear into the little room that was her bedchamber.

Returning from the mews where he'd left Tanner's curricle and horses, Flynn ran into Tanner walking back from St. James's Street.

Tanner clapped him on the shoulder. 'How fortuitous! You have been on my mind all the afternoon. What progress, man? Do tell.'

Flynn had nothing to tell.

'Out with it, Flynn. What the devil happened?'

As they walked side by side, Flynn used what Rose had called his *silver tongue.* 'You must trust me in this matter, my lord. The lady is not the usual sort. You were correct about diplomacy being required.'

Tanner put a hand on his arm, stopping him on the pavement. 'Do not tell me she disliked the emerald ring!'

Flynn had forgotten it was in his pocket. 'I did not present it to her, sir.'

'You did not present it?' Tanner looked surprised.

It was difficult to face him. 'She would have refused it.'

Tanner started walking again. 'My God, she is a strange one. What woman would refuse such a gift?'

One who bewitches, thought Flynn, but he replied, 'She is a puzzle, I agree.'

'You do not think she prefers Greythorne, do you?' Tanner asked with a worried frown.

'She was unaware of Greythorne's interest.'

Tanner looked aghast. 'And you told her of him? Now she will know there is competition!'

Flynn countered, 'Now she knows to come to us to top any offer he makes.'

After a few paces, Tanner laughed. 'She is a rare one, isn't she? I am unused to exerting myself. This is capital sport.'

Tanner, of course, had not exerted himself at all beyond charging Flynn with the work. 'I need some time to gain her trust, I think. I shall see her again tonight at Vauxhall.'

Tanner clapped him on the shoulder again. 'Excellent! I have a previous engagement, otherwise I'd join you.'

Flynn felt only a twinge of guilt for being glad of Tanner's previous engagement.

'Did you discover anything about Greythorne?' Flynn asked.

'Not a thing,' replied Tanner.

Later that evening when Flynn strolled down the Grand Walk of Vauxhall Gardens, he thought about Greythorne, trying to place his finger on who'd spoken ill of the man.

He had at least an hour to ponder the puzzle before the orchestra played. He knew she would have arrived by then, and he could then present himself at the gazebo door.

He thought about simply knocking on the door now, but he

really did not want to chance encountering her father, or, worse, being plied with questions about Tanner by Miss Dawes.

Flynn stopped at one of the restaurants in the gardens instead. Sitting at an outside table, he sipped arrack amid the laughter and buzz of the people walking by. He could feel the velvet box containing the emerald ring still in his pocket. It kept him grounded. A reminder of Tanner, of Greythorne, of what his duty must be.

As he idly watched the passers-by, he let his mind drift to how it had felt to walk through the gardens with her, her arm through his, how the illuminations lit her face, how tempting her lips had been.

He took a longer sip of arrack.

'Well, look who is here!'

Flynn glanced up to see Rose's friend, Katy, striding his way.

'Mr Flynn! Fancy meeting you here again!' She flung herself into a chair even before he could rise. 'You must be here for Rose. Imagine, our little Rosie catching the eye of a marquess! Not that I'm surprised. She barely needed lessons with that face and figure. Just enough to get rid of the accent and learn to put herself forward.' She reached for his glass and took a sip.

Flynn felt as if he were caught in a whirlwind. 'Lessons?'

Katy laughed, patting his arm. 'Never mind that.'

Showing no signs of leaving, she commandeered his glass for herself. He signalled for more for both of them.

She rested her elbows on the table. 'Tell me about this marquess. Sir Reginald says he is an important man.'

Flynn pursed his lips, wishing he'd said nothing to Sir Reginald. 'You must understand, Miss Green, this is not a matter I am free to discuss.'

'Miss Green?' She laughed again. 'Well, aren't you the high-and-mighty one! Call me Katy. Everyone does. I tell you, it's a marvel how well Rosie's done. Here I thought I was the only one. Not that Sir Reginald is anything. He takes me around and I meet people. I'm going to rise higher myself, I am.'

Katy's words were like puzzle pieces scattered on a table. They made no sense. 'How do you know Miss O'Keefe?'

'Rose, you mean?' She grinned, then tried to compose her animated face. 'You might say we were…schoolmates.' Her voice trembled with mirth on this last word, and she dissolved into gales of laughter, slapping the table and causing several heads to turn their way.

He raised his brows, but she did not elaborate. Their arrack came and she finished his first glass before reaching for the next one.

'Are you here to see Rose?' she asked.

'Yes,' he answered, somewhat reluctantly.

'And where is this marquess? I've a fancy to set eyes upon this paragon.' She looked around as if Lord Tannerton might suddenly appear.

'He is not here.'

She shrugged, taking another gulp of arrack. 'I'll be on tenterhooks 'til I see him, I expect. I might fancy a marquess myself, though I didn't aim to look so high. Miss H— Well, I mean, we were told to think high of ourselves, but I keep my feet on the ground, so to speak.'

Flynn was no closer to understanding her. Rose and Katy schoolmates? Not in Killyleagh.

The discordant chords of the orchestra tuning up reached his ears, and he interrupted Katy's unrestrained volubility. 'Forgive me, Miss Green. I must go.' He stood.

'Go?' She rose as well. 'Where are you off to, Mr Flynn?'

He hated to tell her, but feared she would follow him no matter what. 'Miss O'Keefe said to meet her at the gazebo.'

'Oh?' She clapped her hands. 'That is splendid. I'll go with you. Give her another hello.'

So, with the gaily dressed, red-haired young woman hanging on his arm, Flynn strolled to the orchestra's gazebo.

Miss Dawes opened the door. 'Mr Flynn! Come in. Come in.' She noticed Katy behind him and gave a scowl.

Katy grinned at her. 'How do you do?'

Some mischief took hold of Flynn, making him give precedence to the obvious harlot, Katy. 'Miss Green,' he said in his most formal voice. 'May I present Miss Dawes, a friend of Mr O'Keefe's.'

Miss Dawes looked like thunder, but Katy rose to the occasion. 'A pleasure, ma'am,' she said in an uncannily lady-like voice.

Miss Dawes ignored her. 'I'll fetch Rose.' She huffed out of the room, almost tripping over a jumble of instrument cases the musicians had left.

A minute later Rose walked in, the lamplight softening her lovely features.

'Katy!' she said in surprise.

Katy danced up to her and gave her a hug. 'I hope you don't mind, Rosie. I talked Mr Flynn into bringing me here. Met that dragon, Miss Dawes, too. Who does she think she is?'

Rose looked bewildered. 'Are…are you here with Mr Flynn?' Her glance slid over to him.

Katy laughed, but it was Flynn who answered, 'She merely wished to say hello to you.'

Katy released her. 'That I did.' She chattered on about Miss Dawes and how all the men would admire Rose when she sang.

Rose turned to Flynn, anxiety in her eyes. 'If you wished to spend time with Katy—'

'Goodness!' Katy exclaimed. 'I am meeting Sir Reginald,

who has promised to introduce me to some rich fellow.' She swayed up to Flynn and pressed herself against his arm. 'Unless that marquess would be interested in me?' Without waiting for his reply, she returned to Rose to give her a peck on the cheek and flounced out of the door.

Rose looked at him. 'I…I thought you were with her.'

'I was not,' Flynn said.

Her face relaxed. 'Would you like to stand in the balcony while I'm singing?'

'I should like that,' he responded truthfully.

They talked of inconsequential things until she was called to perform. Flynn stood in a dark corner of the balcony, able to see her in profile, though she turned to smile at him before beginning her first tune, an old Irish ballad he remembered his sisters singing as a duet. She continued with 'O Listen to the Voice of Love.'

His gaze wandered to the audience. It was still light enough to see the people staring spellbound as she sang. She captivated them all, he thought, scanning the crowd.

He caught sight of Lord Greythorne and scowled. But Greythorne was not looking at Rose. Flynn followed the direction of the man's gaze across the span of people. He froze. At the edge of the crowd stood a familiar tall figure, arms crossed over his chest, face tilted toward the lovely Rose O'Keefe.

Lord Tannerton.

Chapter Five

Flynn listened to Rose's final notes drift into the night air and watched her take her final bow. Tanner's 'Bravo!' sounded above all the other voices.

It was good he was here, Flynn told himself determinedly, because Flynn needed to remember that his task was to get Rose to accept Tanner's protection. He needed to be certain Tanner won her over Lord Greythorne. The more time Flynn spent alone with her, the more bewitched he became, as if he were also vying for her regard.

Rose came over to him, smiling. She grasped his hand. 'We must go below.'

He let her lead him to the room below stairs.

'How was I?' she asked him, as the voice of Charles Dignum reached their ears. 'I felt myself straining here and there. Was it noticeable, do you think?'

She still held his hand. He stared at it a moment before answering. 'I noticed no imperfection.'

She smiled and squeezed his fingers. 'What shall we do now? The night is lovely and I must wait for my father and

Letty. I know you wish to talk to me, but could we do so while we explore the gardens again? Go see the hermit?'

The hermit illusion was located at the far end of one of the darker, less crowded paths well known for dalliance. Flynn could just imagine leading her into one of the private alcoves, holding her in his arms and finally tasting her lips.

He forced himself to face her. 'Lord Greythorne is here,' he said. 'As is Lord Tanner.'

Her eyes flashed. 'Lord Tanner? You did not tell me he would be here.'

'I did not know,' he quickly explained. 'He was engaged elsewhere, but I saw him in the audience. He is here.' Flynn held her shoulders. 'Allow me to present you to him. You might see for yourself the man he is.'

She stared into his eyes. 'Oh, Flynn.' It took her a moment to go on. 'Not so soon. I mean, I…I am not ready to meet him. I have not decided yet that I should.'

He tilted his head toward the stairway leading to the orchestra's balcony, to where her father played his oboe. 'Your father wishes it, does he not? The marquess will not wait for ever, and Greythorne is very willing to step in.'

Her eyes turned anxious. 'Time, Flynn. Can you be procuring me a little more time?'

He nodded, knowing he should not.

Tanner would take care of her. Take her away from the unpleasant Miss Dawes and the drab set of rooms shared with her father. Tanner would protect her from men like Greythorne, anyone who might mistreat her. It would be best for her to simply meet Tanner. See the man he was, and make her decision. Then Flynn could go back to a sane life.

'I shall see you have more time,' he said.

'Thank you.' She grasped his hand. 'Call on me tomorrow,

Flynn. Share supper with me. I do not perform tomorrow. You could come after my father and Letty leave. I will be more prepared to think.'

He stepped closer to her. What could one more day matter? Her beautiful face turned up to his. It seemed natural to slide his hand down her arm, lift her hand to his lips. Even through her glove he could feel its warmth, taste the allure of her.

He released her. 'I will call tomorrow, then.'

'Eight o'clock? Papa and Letty will have left by then.'

He nodded.

He walked over to the door, but before he opened it, he turned back to her. 'I had forgotten. I must give you this tonight. From Lord Tanner.' He pulled out the small velvet box from his coat pocket.

She held up her hand to refuse it.

'Accept it, Rose. It is a trifle to him, but I can no longer find excuses for not giving it to you.' He placed it in her hand.

She opened the box, revealing the ring, a sparkling emerald surrounded by tiny diamonds, in a setting of carved gold. 'This is not a trifle, Flynn,' she said, trying to hand it back to him.

'It is to Tannerton.' He closed her fingers around it. 'Take it, Rose. It does not obligate you to him, I promise.' He kept his hand over hers for too long. 'I must leave.'

He quickly pulled away and opened the door.

'Goodnight, Flynn,' he heard her say as he hurried through the doorway into the night.

Adam Vickering, Marquess of Tannerton, sat in a supper box with his friend Pomroy and the party of high flyers and dashers Pomroy always seemed to collect.

Pomroy filled his glass with arrack. 'You're like a besotted fool, Tan—' He paused to belch. 'Never thought you the sort who let a woman lead him by a string.'

Tanner gulped down half his arrack. 'I'd be dashed pleased to be led by this one, if I could only get near enough to secure her.' He looked heavenwards. 'You heard her, Pomroy. She is an angel.'

'Ha!' his friend barked. 'I'd say she's devilish crafty. Has you eating out of her hand and all without speaking a word to you. She's going to play you against Greythorne, you know, like bidders at Tattersalls.

'Got to admit, it is good sport.' Tanner's grin turned to a scowl. 'What have you discovered about Greythorne?'

'He courted Amanda Reynolds, all the rage a year ago. Everyone thought they would marry. She spurned him, though.'

'Left him for another man?' Tanner asked.

'Some soldier, I believe.' Pomroy shrugged.

'Her head turned by a man in regimentals?' Tanner concluded. 'Not unheard of, you know.'

'Yes, but there was more to it, I'm certain,' Pomroy said. 'She could have had anyone. Don't you remember her? She was perfection.'

Tanner conjured up an image of a cool blonde, the sort who would pine for routs and balls and dreadful *musicales*. He took another mouthful. 'Always disliked that fellow Greythorne. Looks the whole day like he'd just left his valet.'

Pomroy was summoned by one of the prime articles he'd found in the Gardens. Pomroy would no doubt enjoy her company all night through, but such females held no interest for Tanner. While his friend attended to the pretty thing, Tanner leaned back on his chair, balancing it on its rear legs. He raised his drink and gazed out into the crowd.

With any luck he'd catch sight of his secretary and have

him wrangle a meeting with Miss Rose O'Keefe. Even if luck
was not with him, he could still congratulate himself for
escaping Lady Rawley's tedious *musicale*. Half an hour of the
soprano she'd hired had nearly done for him. He wished half
the fashionable set would leave Town and go rusticate in the
country. Leave him free of their tiresome invitations. Let them
all go rusticate, in fact.

Not that he had any intention of burying himself in such
boredom. He paid his managers well so he would not have to
put in an appearance at any of his properties until hunting season.

Tanner swished his arrack in the glass. Ordinarily he'd be
in Brighton this time of year, but the elusive Rose O'Keefe had
kept him in town.

Tanner's eyes narrowed as a pristinely attired gentleman
swinging a walking stick strolled up to the supper box.

'Why, if it is not Tannerton.' Greythorne tipped his hat in
an elegant gesture that seemed to mock Tanner's boyish balancing act.

Tanner perversely accentuated his lack of gentility by
stretching his arms to the back of his head. 'Greythorne.'

Behind Tanner Pomroy laughed and one of his female
companions squealed. Greythorne eyed them with ill-disguised contempt.

He directed his gaze back to Tanner. 'I hear we are rivals
of a sort.'

'Rivals?' Tanner gave a dry laugh. 'I highly doubt that.'

Greythorne ignored his barb. 'For the captivating Rose
O'Keefe. I quite covet the girl, you know.'

'Really?' said Tanner in a flat voice.

Greythorne tapped the wall of the supper box with his
stick. 'Your secretary tells me she is yours, but I confess I see
no signs of it.'

'Eyes bothering you?' Tanner remarked.

Greythorne brushed at his coat, as if a piece of dirt dared mar his appearance. 'You are amusing, Tannerton.' He glanced in the direction of the Grove where Miss O'Keefe had performed. 'Perhaps I shall amuse you when the young temptress is mine.'

'No fear of that.' Tanner lifted his glass to his lips. 'Doubt you've ever been amusing.'

Greythorne's lips thinned and Tanner actually fought the need to laugh.

'To the victor go the spoils,' Greythorne said, making a salute before strolling off.

'Trite bastard,' Tanner muttered to himself.

Pomroy twisted around. 'Did you say something?'

Tanner did not reply, because he saw someone else in the crowd. He propelled himself out of his chair, sending it clattering to the ground, and vaulted over the supper-box wall.

'Flynn!' he called, pushing through the people to catch up. He grabbed Flynn's arm and pulled him to the side. 'When do you meet with her, Flynn?'

His secretary regarded him in his usual unflappable manner, not even showing surprise at his presence. 'I have done so already,' Flynn answered.

'To what result?' Tanner asked eagerly.

Flynn paused, only briefly, but enough to try Tanner's patience. 'I was able to give her the ring,' Flynn finally said.

'Excellent!' Tanner's eyes lit up. 'Did she like it?'

'She said it was more than a trifling gift.'

That was all? 'Well, I suppose that is something.' Tanner grasped Flynn's arm. 'We need more progress, man. That snake Greythorne is slithering around. He just spoke to me.' Tanner gave a mock-shiver. 'I'd hoped for a meeting tonight.'

'I did not expect you tonight, my lord,' Flynn said in a bland voice.

Tanner grinned. 'That is so. I escaped some ghastly *musicale* with some equally ghastly soprano to come here. I could not resist. I tell you, Miss O'Keefe's sweet voice was balm in comparison.' He rubbed the back of his neck. 'This business is taking an intolerably long time.'

'Patience is required.'

'Well, we both know how little of that commodity I possess.' Tanner clapped him on the arm. 'That is why I depend upon you, Flynn. If it were up to me, I'd go there now and demand she see me, but I suspect you would advise against it.'

'I would indeed.'

Tanner blew out a frustrated breath. 'I wonder what Greythorne will do. I trust him about as far as I can throw him.' He thought about this. 'Make that as far as he could throw me.'

'I can assure you she shows no partiality toward him,' Flynn said.

Tanner grinned. 'That is good news. What is next for us then?'

'I shall dine with her tomorrow.'

Tanner gaped at him. 'Dine with her? Well done. Very well done, indeed.' His secretary was clocking impressive amounts of time with her. Things were looking up.

Flynn gave him a wan smile.

'Tanner!' Pomroy was standing in the supper box, waving him over.

Tanner glanced at him. 'Pomroy beckons. I suppose I must go. He's managed some entertaining company, no one to remark upon, but anything is better than that ghastly *musicale.*' He rolled his eyes. 'Enjoy yourself, Flynn. Might as well see what pleasures the garden can offer, eh?'

'Thank you, sir,' Flynn replied.

Tanner headed back to the supper box, not noticing his secretary did not heed his advice. Flynn turned towards the Kennington Lane gate where he could catch a hackney carriage back to Audley Street.

The next evening Rose said goodbye to her father and Letty, watching from the window until they were out of sight. Waiting a few minutes longer to be sure they had time to get in a hack, she donned her hat and gloves, picked up a basket, and hurried outside. She walked the short distance to the Covent Garden market past youngbloods who whistled and made lewd remarks. The theatres had not yet opened their doors, but the street was teeming with well-dressed gentlemen casting appraising glances at gaudily dressed women who only pretended to have some destination in mind.

Rose listened for the pie man's call and made her way to him to purchase two meat pies. She also bought strawberries, a jug of cream, and a bottle of Madeira wine. It would be simple fare, but the best she could manage without the means to cook and without her father and Letty suspecting. She returned home, setting the pies near the small fire in the parlour fireplace. She moved the table they used for eating and found a cloth to cover it. She set two plates, two glasses, and cutlery and stood back to survey her work.

It was not elegant, nothing, to be sure, like a marquess's table set with porcelain china and silver, but it was the best she could do.

All the day she'd felt out of breath, not from nerves at hiding this from her father, but anticipation of seeing Flynn.

She'd been so disappointed at Lord Tannerton's appearance the night before, forcing her to forgo Flynn's company. She'd had girlish fantasies of walking with Flynn down the Dark Walk, where lovers could be private, where lovers could kiss. Tannerton had spoiled it.

She was determined Tannerton would not spoil this evening, even if Rose must talk about him with Flynn. She intended to spend some part of the evening merely enjoying being alone with him. In school she'd learned it was not proper to entertain a man alone in one's lodgings, but here in Covent Garden no one expected proper behaviour. She planned to take advantage of that fact.

While she checked the kettle to see if there was water enough to heat for tea, the knock sounded at the door. Rose wheeled around, pressing her hand against her abdomen to quiet the flutters. She hurried to the door and opened it.

Flynn stood with a small package in his hand. 'For you, Miss O'Keefe.'

She hesitated. Another present from Tannerton. Letty had already discovered the ring and was at this moment wearing it on her finger. Rose took the package into her hand and stepped aside so Flynn could enter.

Flynn placed his hat and gloves on the table near the door and turned to her, pointing to the package. 'It is a token,' he said. 'From me.'

From Flynn? That made her happy. She eagerly untied the string and opened the box. Inside was an assortment of sweet-meats, all prettily arranged. She thought she had never seen anything so lovely, nor received such a wonderful gift.

She smiled at him. 'Thank you. I will serve them with our tea.' Or leave them untouched to treasure for ever. 'Please come to the table.'

She poured him a glass of Madeira. 'I know it is customary

to have conversation before dinner is served, but I thought it best for us to eat right away.'

'Whatever you desire, Rose,' he said, still standing.

He waited until she had fetched the meat pies from in front of the fire and placed them on the plates, then held her chair for her. She smiled up at him.

'Our meal is rather plain,' she apologised.

'I do not mind.' He settled in his seat and took a forkful. 'I do not know when I last ate meat pie.'

She felt her cheeks warming. 'I am sorry to serve you such poor fare.'

'Oh, no,' he said. 'I meant it is a rare treat.'

She gave him a disbelieving glance. 'There goes your silver tongue again.'

'Truly, Rose.' He looked so sincere she was tempted to believe him.

She glanced back down at her plate. 'You know, in my grandparents' house this would have been a luxury. There's more meat in my pie here than they ate in a week sometimes.'

A faint wrinkle creased his brow. 'Their lives must be difficult.'

'Oh,' she said, 'they died a long time ago, soon after my mother. After that my father put me in school in Killyleagh.'

He glanced up again. 'You had other family, certainly.'

'Not of my mother's family, but there are plenty of O'Keefes.' She took a sip of her wine. 'My father's family never was accepting of him being a musician, so I never really knew them.'

Flynn took another bite of the pie he was truly enjoying. He remembered how poor some were in Ireland. He had not realised she'd been one of them. Tanner's generosity could give her a secure, comfortable life. This was the perfect opportunity to convince her of the advantages of accepting his offer. If he could even convince her to meet Tanner, she would learn this for herself.

'We need to discuss your meeting with Tannerton, Rose,' he ventured.

She stared down at her plate. 'Yes. I have promised you we would do so.' She looked up at him. 'So speak. I shall listen.'

The force of her eyes drove all words from his mouth. 'Perhaps after our meal,' he said.

She smiled. 'Tell me more of King's Theatre, then. Tell me of its interior.'

So he talked of King's Theatre, Drury Lane, Covent Garden, as well as other smaller theatres he'd attended. He told her of the sopranos he'd seen: Catalani, Camporese, Fodor, among them. She listened, eyes dancing in delight at his descriptions, and he found himself wishing he could share such experiences with her.

She served him a simple dessert, strawberries and cream, and after she cleared the dishes away, she said with a twinkle in her eye, 'Shall we retire to the drawing room, then?' She gestured to the two cushioned chairs near the fire. 'I'll make tea.'

He sat while she poured hot water from the kettle into a teapot. Though their conversation had been comfortable before, they now lapsed into a strained silence, broken only by her questions of how he took his tea.

She sat opposite him and poured, placing one of the sweet-meats he'd given her on the saucer.

'Rose…' he began.

She attempted a smile, but it vanished quickly. 'I know. We must talk.'

His brow furrowed, and he felt like whatever silver tongue he might possess had been badly tarnished. 'Let me arrange a meeting with Lord Tannerton, Rose, before Greythorne becomes more of a problem.'

She frowned at him. 'Do you mean *meet* Lord Tannerton, or something else?'

He picked up the sweetmeat, but could not bite into it. He returned it to the saucer. 'A meeting only. You are not obligated for more.' It was becoming torturous to think about the *more* that would eventually transpire once she accepted Tanner.

She stared into her teacup. 'And later?'

He could not look at her. 'If you find him…agreeable, there is no limit to what he might do for you.'

'Ah, but it is what I must do…' she murmured, her voice trailing off.

He gave her a puzzled look. What was her reluctance? She was not without experience in such matters. She was friends with Katy Green, after all, whose station in life was very clear. Katy seemed to take the marquess's interest in Rose as nothing unusual. And Rose had alluded to other liaisons—those gentlemen who drove her in Hyde Park, for example. A connection with a wealthy marquess ought to be eagerly sought after. Unless…

He straightened his back. 'Rose, is there another man…?'

'Interested in me, do you mean?' She pointed to a tray of cards on the table where he'd placed his hat and gloves. 'Those fellows, I suppose.'

He shook his head. 'I mean a man who interests you.'

'Me?' It took a moment for comprehension to dawn. 'Oh!' She blinked rapidly, then raised her liquid emerald eyes to his. 'No, Flynn,' she said in a soft, low voice. 'There is no one else.'

He stopped breathing.

Finally she averted her gaze. 'Why do you ask such a thing?'

He picked up his cup. 'You have persistently avoided talking about the marquess.'

'So you thought it must be another man.' She regarded him with an ironic expression. ''Tis not enough I might not fancy being bartered like some fancy item in a shop.'

He stared at her. 'You are not being bartered.' Though he feared she had captured the essence of the matter.

'Of course I am,' she said, her tone pragmatic.

But why did she dislike it, if she would come out the winner?

She stood. 'Never mind it. I'll meet your marquess.' She crossed the room. 'Tell me when.'

He walked over to her, making her look at him. 'Are you certain?'

She cocked her head. 'I'm certain. But I'll not be obligating myself further than that. And I'd prefer Letty and my father not be a part of it.'

He had no difficulty agreeing with that.

'And no gifts, if you please.'

That was unexpected, but easily done.

'And you must be present.'

He gave her a surprised glance. 'I?'

'Yes, and it would not look very well if I were the only woman with two gentlemen, so I would like Katy Green to come as well.'

He nearly winced. 'Miss Green?'

She looked up at him through her thick lashes. 'I do not want to be alone.'

'I will arrange it,' he said in a resigned tone. He'd not imagined being forced to watch Tanner charm her.

She gave him a brave but false smile. 'Good. That is settled. No need to talk of it further.'

She drummed her fingers on the long wooden box that

rested on a table in the corner of the room where they stood. 'Let me show you something,' she said suddenly.

He raised his brows.

She smiled with mischief. 'Watch.' She opened up the box to reveal a small pianoforte. 'Isn't it a treat?'

He laughed. 'Yes, a surprise as well.'

She ran her fingers lightly over the keys. 'It belonged to my mother. To take with her when she travelled in those days she was singing. It is in fine sound, too. Listen.'

She pulled up a small stool and rested her fingers on the keys, playing random chords until she began a tune he recognised only too well, though he had not heard it for over a decade: 'Shule Agra.' She sang:

> *His hair was black, his eye was blue*
> *His arm was stout, his word was true*
> *I wish in my heart, I was with you…*

He'd sung the song of a sweetheart slain for the Jacobite cause with the rest of his family at his mother's pianoforte. When Rose came to the chorus, Flynn could not help but join her.

'Shule, shule, shule agra…'

He closed his eyes and let the sound of their melding voices float around him and seep into his skin, sending him back to Ballynahinch, to home and family.

'Go thee, thu Mavourneen slaun,' they sang, holding the last note for several extra beats.

She rose and turned to him and their gazes held. 'Beautiful,' he said, bewitched.

Without thinking, he brushed his fingers across her cheek. Her eyes darkened and she leaned closer to him. His nostrils gratefully inhaled her sweet clean scent, like the flowers in his mother's garden. She tilted her face to him, so close he could feel her breath against his skin.

He lowered his head slowly, wanting for just one brief moment to find home again in her lips. She remained perfectly still, waiting. His lips came closer, so close their breath mingled. A half-inch more and he would taste her—

Voices sounded in the hallway, someone entering one of the other rooms, but enough to jar him from his reverie.

He dropped his hand and stepped away.

'Flynn?' she whispered. Her eyes reflected his own wrenching need.

'This is madness,' he rasped. Madness for him to covet the woman his powerful employer laid claim to.

She tried to come closer, but he held up his hand. 'I must go.'

She blocked his way to the door. 'Why is it madness, Flynn?'

He had no choice but to touch her. He put his hands on her arms and eased her aside so he could collect his hat and gloves.

She stepped closer again. 'Why is it madness?' She scooped up the calling cards that had been piled next to his gloves. 'It is what Tannerton and Greythorne and all these gentlemen want, is it not?' She let the cards cascade from her fingers. 'Why can it not be between you and me?'

'Because of my employer, Rose.' He pulled on his gloves. 'It would be the ruin of my future. Yours as well. Do you not see that?'

'But he need never know,' she countered.

'*I* would know. After all he has done for me, I would not repay him so.' Did she think he could make love to her one day and face Tanner the next?

He opened the door, but turned back to her. 'You are indeed like your friend Katy, are you not? Do not tease me further with talk of needing time. I will not believe you.' He started through the door but swung around again, leaning close to her face, as close as when he almost kissed her. 'You are just what you seem, Rose. A fancy piece.'

Her lips parted in surprise, but they remained as enticing as before. With a growl of frustration, he wrenched himself away and hurried down the staircase.

Rose leaned against the doorframe, arms wrapped around herself. She squeezed her eyes shut. His words stung, but she knew he'd been correct. She'd behaved badly. Wantonly.

She re-entered the room, shutting the door behind her and hurrying to the window. She watched him leave the building, his pace as quick as if pursued by lions.

Leaning her forehead against the cool glass, she sang, 'I wish in my heart, I was with you…'

Vauxhall was not nearly as pleasant this night without Rose O'Keefe singing. Greythorne grimaced as Charles Dignum began. He stalked out of the Grove and strolled towards the Transparency. Out of the corner of his eye he glimpsed one of Vauxhall's many delights—a woman with flaming red hair, laughing on the arm of that fool Sir Reginald, pulling him through the crowd.

He sucked in a breath. That laughter gave him a twinge.

He blew out the breath and walked on, scanning the crowd. He wanted a woman. Needed a woman. It had been a long time since he'd invited a woman into his den of pleasure. What harm to pluck another flower while he waited to win the elusive Rose from that—that—*Corinthian* Tannerton?

Blood surged through his veins. He'd win Rose O'Keefe and show her his special set of delights, and once under his control, she would forget all about Tannerton's pursuit.

Greythorne wiped his face, grateful to the Diamond,

Amanda, who had spurned him and lost the opportunity to experience his special talents. Because of the Diamond, he'd pushed himself to dare new delights. New heights. Nearer and nearer the brink.

He'd also had to take more care. There were some who knew his brand of pleasure, and he dared not risk more exposure. He rubbed his hands together. The more secretive he became, the more daring as well. There were no limits in anonymity.

He grinned, imagining this girl's laughter fading, her eyes widening, mouth opening, cries ringing against the walls of his special room.

He donned the mask he kept in his pocket, the mask that protected him, the mask that freed him. The red-haired woman might be occupied this night, but there were other blooms to be plucked.

And Greythorne loved to cut flowers.

Chapter Six

The message from Flynn arrived for Rose the following afternoon, delivered into her father's hands. 'Mary Rose, it is from that marquess's fellow,' he said.

Letty, interrupted from admiring how the emerald ring sparkled on her pudgy hand, ran to his side. 'Well, what is it? What does he say?'

Letty snatched the letter from her father and walked over to read it by the light from the window. 'He wants to meet her! Two days hence.' She dropped the letter on the table. 'Did I not say it would be so?'

Rose picked up the paper, reading that the selected meeting place was King's Theatre, to see a performance of Don Giovanni. She pressed the paper against her beating heart. Flynn was giving her King's Theatre. A real opera, too, with performers singing out the whole story. It was almost exciting enough to forget that he'd pushed her away, accusing her of acting like a harlot. Or that she must meet the man who wanted her to be his harlot.

Letty snatched the paper from Rose's hand. 'Let me read it again.' Her lips moved as she went over the words. She handed it back to Rose. 'He is saying that Miss Green must come with you.'

'I asked that she be invited. She is one of the girls I lived with.' Rose had never explained much to her father about living in Miss Hart's house. She never explained anything to Letty.

'Where do you meet the marquess?' Her father took another sip of gin.

'She will ruin it, I know she will,' Letty grumbled, crossing the room to pour more gin for herself, drinking it alone in a sulk.

'At King's Theatre, Papa,' Rose replied.

He smiled at her. 'Your mother sang at King's Theatre. Did you know that, Mary Rose?'

'I did, Papa.'

He put his hands on her shoulders. 'Daughter, you are saying you want to sing. Here is your chance!'

She laughed. 'Papa, I am to watch the opera. And the marquess will not be asking me to sing.'

'I keep trying to tell you the way of things.' He put his arm around her and sat her down in one of the chairs. He sat opposite, still holding her hand. 'A woman in the theatre gets work by pleasing the right people, if you get my meaning. This is the life you chose.' He reached over to pick up his glass of gin from the table. 'The marquess has a lofty title and money. 'Tis said he is very generous to his girls.'

'Papa,' she entreated. 'I'm certain I can make money singing. The newspapers said nice things about me. I'm sure to get another job after the Vauxhall season is over.'

Her father took a sip, then shook his head. 'You'll be hired to sing if you have someone asking for you. Like I could ask Mr Hook for you, being in the orchestra and all. But in the theatres, you need a patron, Mary Rose. And if this marquess wants you to sing, you will be finding work.' He took her hand again and made her look at him. 'If you displease such a man, if you spurn him, you'll never work again. All he has to do is say the word.'

Rose glanced away. Flynn had said as much. The marquess had the power to dash her dreams.

Her father squeezed her hand until she looked at him again. 'Listen, your own darling mother might have risen to greatness. She had the voice, the prettiest voice you'd ever be wanting to hear, and she was as lovely—you favour her, Mary Rose.' He smiled sadly. 'She caught the eye of such a man as your marquess. An earl, I'm remembering he was. But she was wanting me, instead.' He shook his head as if he could still not believe it. 'The earl was mighty angry, as you can imagine. And then neither of us could find work anywhere. By then you were on the way, and I took her back to Ireland. It was a long time before the earl forgot, and I could return to England to earn good money again. And then, of course, your mother got sick…' His voice faded.

Rose bowed her head, her emotions in a muddle. Her beautiful mother had been faced with such a choice? Her mother had chosen love. Had that not been right?

Her father's eyes filled with tears. 'She got sick, but I was here in London. Working. Never to see her again—' He lowered his head, his shoulders shaking.

Tears poured down Rose's cheeks as well. If she had not been born, perhaps her mother might have returned to the stage. Perhaps she would have become the darling of the London theatre. But her mother had chosen marriage and childbirth and poverty. If she had chosen that earl, perhaps she would have lived.

Rose put her arms around her father. 'Well, I'm meeting the marquess, so there's nothing to fear.'

He lifted his head again and gave her a watery smile.

Rose returned a fond look. She wanted to sing, not only for herself, but for her mother. Let her mother live again through her.

Letty called from her corner of the room. 'What are you talking about, Alroy? I hope you are telling your daughter to get off her duff and take what this marquess wants to offer us.'

'I have convinced her, I think.' Her father sniffed and patted Rose's hand again.

'I'll meet the marquess, Papa,' she repeated.

He smiled again and raised his glass to his lips. Rose left her chair and went to her bedchamber to don her hat, gloves and shawl. When she returned to the parlour, Letty was busy talking with her father of where they might live when the marquess's money was in their pockets.

'Henrietta Street, I'm thinking,' Letty was saying. 'But a proper house, not three rooms—'

'I'm going out, Papa,' Rose broke in.

Her father looked up. 'There's a good girl, Mary Rose. Watch out for yourself.'

'That's right.' Letty laughed. 'We don't want you damaged.'

Rose walked out the door and down to the street. It was a grey day, and she hoped it would not rain. She headed for Covent Garden to find a hackney carriage.

She had never visited Katy, who now lived at Madame Bisou's gaming-house. Madame Bisou had invited Katy to live there after they left Miss Hart's. The other girls had chosen love, Rose reminded herself.

Rose wanted success, now more than anything.

She found a carriage and told the coachman, 'Bennet Street, please.'

He let her off at the junction of Jermyn Street and Bennet

Street and she walked to a sedate-looking house where anyone might have lived. A large footman answered her knock.

'Good day to you,' Rose said. 'Would you please be telling Miss Green that Miss O'Keefe has come to call?'

The footman put a finger to his cheek. 'Miss Green?' His confusion suddenly cleared. 'Oh. Katy. Just a moment.' When he returned he said, 'Follow me.'

He led her above stairs to a sitting room. Both Katy and Madame Bisou sprang to their feet when she entered.

'Rose! How good to see you.' The *madame* kissed Rose on both cheeks. 'You've not been here since Katy moved in.'

'Forgive me, Madame,' Rose responded, only now realising how much she had missed this woman with her false French accent. The girls had quickly figured out Madame Bisou was not really French. The *madame*'s hair colour, an unnatural red, was false as well.

There was nothing false about her large breasts, pushed up to show to best advantage in her low-cut dress, nor about her generous, loving nature. Rose gave her a heartfelt hug.

Katy came over and Rose also hugged her. 'Who'd have thought you would visit? Vauxhall's newest flower doesn't need a gaming hell.'

Madame Bisou stepped out of the room to arrange for tea and Katy pulled Rose on to a settee.

'So why are you here?' Katy asked. 'Have you met up with the marquess? Have you come to tell us about it?'

'Not exactly,' Rose said. 'But you are not far wrong.'

'I knew it!' said Katy.

Madame Bisou walked back in. 'Tea will be coming, but I must not stay, Rose. I must get back to Iris.'

Katy turned to Rose. 'Iris was badly hurt last night.'

Rose did not know the girl. 'I am sorry to hear of it.'

'She went with me to Vauxhall,' Katy cried. 'But I left her with some fellows when Sir Reginald showed up.'

'It was not your fault, Katy,' Madame Bisou said. 'These things happen.'

'What happened?' Rose asked.

Katy's eyes flashed. 'She went with some man. A gentleman, she thought, because he had fine clothes, but he tied her up and used a whip on her—'

'Used a whip!' Rose exclaimed.

Madame Bisou crossed her arms over her chest, squeezing out even more décolletage. 'I ought to have told you girls of this, but, how could I?'

'Told us what?' Rose asked.

Madame Bisou sat down, facing them. 'Some men seek their pleasure not in the usual way.' She paused. 'Some get their senses aroused by inflicting pain.'

Rose glanced to Katy. 'Pain?'

'Oh, I see,' Katy said. 'Whips and things.'

Rose looked to Madame Bisou. 'Men get pleasure from using whips?'

'Well, it's a rare one that does—not that you don't find plenty, mind you,' Madame Bisou went on. 'Most men, you know, are easily led if you make them think they are seducing you, but some…some get an arousal when they hurt a girl. It is their pleasure to inflict pain. Like a bully, *n'est-ce pas?*'

Rose felt sick at the thought.

'A Frenchman wrote a book about it,' Madame Bisou added.

Rose put her hand on her chest. 'Oh, Katy, you must take care!'

Katy waved a hand. 'I can handle myself.'

'Do you know who hurt the poor girl?' Rose asked the *madame*.

She shrugged. 'Iris said he wore a mask.' She patted Rose's hand. 'I assure you, we do not allow such men in this gaming hell. If we hear of such a man, or if one dares mistreat one of the girls, Cummings tosses him out.'

Rose shook her head. 'But Katy is out and about. At Vauxhall, where so many men wear masks.'

Katy laughed. 'Do you think I cannot spot a viper like that?'

Madame Bisou cautioned her. 'It is sometimes difficult. You cannot tell merely by looking at a man.' She stood. 'I must go.' She took Rose's hand briefly. 'Katy has told me of your marquess. That is good for you, Rose. Tannerton is a good man.'

Even Madame Bisou sang his praises.

Katy settled back in her seat. 'Tell of the marquess. That is what I wish to hear.'

Rose could not help but think that Katy needed the marquess more than she did, no matter what her father said of the theatre. If Katy had enough money, she could abandon this dangerous life.

'I hope you will like it,' Rose said. 'I am to meet with him in two days. His guest at King's Theatre.'

'At a theatre?' Katy seemed unimpressed.

Rose continued. 'The best news is, you are to accompany me.'

Katy's mouth dropped open. 'Me?'

'Yes. I asked if you could come with me.'

Her friend looked at her as if her wits had gone begging. 'But why?'

Rose hesitated before answering. 'I was not wanting to go alone. Mr Flynn is to be there, too. If you do not come, I'll be the only woman with two gentlemen.'

Katy laughed. 'You did not want two men all to yourself? If your marquess is half as handsome as your Mr Flynn, it would be heaven to have them all to yourself.'

Rose felt her cheeks grow hot.

Katy's eyes filled with mischief. 'Why not bring Letty Dawes with you?'

Rose returned a withering glance. 'You must be jesting.'

Katy laughed. 'Oh, I'll go. I have a fancy to meet this marquess who pines for you so strongly. Wish I could play it cool like you do, Rose. Never could disguise wanting a man as much as he might want me.'

Rose gave her a stern look. 'Did not the *madame* always instruct you to dampen such liveliness? Do you not remember?'

'That's like asking a tiger not to have spots,' Katy responded.

Rose could not help but smile.

When the night arrived to attend the opera at King's Theatre, Rose went to Madame Bisou's to dress. The *madame* had insisted on hiring a hairdresser to fix their hair, and Rose and Katy each wore Paris gowns Miss Hart had given them. Katy's was a rich green silk gown that set off her red hair to perfection. Rose wore silk in a pale blush with white lace adorning the bodice and hem. The hairdresser threaded a strand of pearls through her hair, and Madame Bisou lent her pearls to wear around her neck and on her ears.

As Rose and Katy stood next to each other, surveying their images in a full-length mirror, Rose thought they looked tasteful. She had no wish to look like a harlot, even if that was what everyone wished her to be, what Flynn had accused her of being. She looked pretty, but she was nothing compared to Katy. What man could resist Katy's vibrant beauty? Perhaps, if Rose were very lucky, the marquess would transfer his interest to Katy. And Flynn would forgive her.

Gentlemen were already arriving at the gaming-house at the time the marquess's coach was to pick them up. Perhaps they would think her a new girl at this place, not much better than a bawdy house.

She shook her head. She must accustom herself to men thinking of her in this carnal way. It was part of being in the theatre, her father would say. She glanced at Katy, whose excitement just enhanced her lively beauty. How could she not impress the marquess?

Soon the footman came to tell them a gentleman waited for them in the hall.

'Well, you are off, then,' Madame Bisou said, nearly as excited as Katy. 'I wish you good luck.'

She squeezed both their hands, and the two young women descended the stairway. Some men in the doorway of the gaming room stopped to watch them, their sounds of approval reaching Rose's ears. She felt herself blush.

Rose purposely let Katy go first so Katy would make the first impression.

'Why, if it isn't Mr Flynn,' declared Katy halfway down the stairs. She extended her hand so he could assist her on the last few steps. 'Where is the marquess?'

Flynn's eyes followed Rose's slower progress as he answered, 'He will meet us at the theatre.' When Rose reached Katy's side, he said a curt, 'Good evening, Rose.'

'Flynn,' she answered, fearing matters would never be easy between them again.

'Well.' He looked at Katy, but only fleetingly glanced at Rose. 'You look very charming. I am indeed most fortunate to escort you.'

Katy took his arm, holding on to him much too close. 'Let us be off, then. We do not want to keep a marquess waiting.'

Flynn offered his other arm to Rose. Her fingers trembled as they lighted on his sleeve.

In the coach, Katy's lively chatter filled the air, so Rose could excuse it that Flynn did not speak to her. He said a word here and there to encourage Katy to rattle on, but his attention to her friend only made Rose feel worse.

Soon the coach pulled up to King's Theatre. As Flynn escorted them in, Rose forgot everything, even the admiring stares of gentlemen, as she took in the beauty of its grand hall, all marble and gold gilt. Flynn led them up carpeted stairs and past doors to what must be the boxes. They did not go far before he stopped at one and, after making a quick knock, turned the knob.

Katy nearly jumped up and down, but Rose held back, so it was Katy who first entered the darker interior of the box, where Rose could just make out the figure of a man.

He spoke. 'Good evening. You must be Miss Green.'

Katy replied, 'You are correct, sir. I presume you are Lord Tannerton?'

'I am indeed.'

When Rose's eyes adjusted to the dimmer light, she realised the marquess was the tall man she had seen standing near Flynn that first night at Vauxhall, the one with the casual air and affable expression.

'I've seen you at Vauxhall,' Katy said, as if speaking Rose's thoughts.

The marquess smiled. 'I have seen you too, Miss Green. Someone as lovely as yourself cannot be missed.'

Katy laughed, but softly this time. 'I thank you. But you must meet Miss O'Keefe.'

She stepped aside, exposing Rose, and the marquess turned his eyes on her. 'Miss O'Keefe, I am delighted you have come.'

Flynn stepped forward. 'Miss O'Keefe, may I present Lord Tannerton.'

Rose dropped into a curtsy. 'My lord.'

Tannerton extended his hand to her to help her rise. She had no choice but to accept it. 'It is my pleasure to meet you,' he said, holding her hand only a second longer than was comfortable.

He stepped back so that they could come farther into the opera box. Katy moved to the back, as did Flynn.

The Marquess spoke to Rose alone. 'We shall have some refreshments at the intermission, but I have arranged for wine now. Would you care for a glass?'

She needed something to calm her. 'Yes, thank you,' she said.

Flynn immediately poured the wine, but Lord Tannerton handed Rose's glass to her.

'It is French champagne. Bottled before the conflict, but I managed to acquire a case very recently.' He took his own glass. 'May I propose a toast?'

Rose inclined her head, wondering why a marquess would ask her permission.

'To new friends,' he said, turning to include Katy, but letting his gaze linger a bit longer on Rose.

'To new friends,' repeated Katy.

Rose did not speak, but she took a sip.

'Come now,' Tannerton gestured to two front chairs. 'Sit and be comfortable. The performance should start at any moment.'

Rose turned towards Katy. 'Perhaps Katy—Miss Green—would like to sit up front as well?'

Katy ignored Rose's silent plea. 'I'll sit behind you. Keep Mr Flynn company.' For emphasis she laced her arm through Flynn's.

'Come,' Tannerton repeated.

He settled Rose in an elegant brocade chair and sat beside her. For the first time she looked out into the opera house.

'Oh, my!' she exclaimed.

The theatre curtains were rich red with a gold fringe as long as she was tall, with the King's crest, also in gold. The curtains spanned nearly the whole distance from ceiling to floor, a space high enough for several tiers of boxes all around. Light blazed from huge chandeliers close to the stage and from candles all around the edges of the boxes. The orchestra floor was busy with people talking and laughing and moving around. Several of the boxes were empty, but in those that were not, elegant gentlemen were seated with ladies dressed in beautiful gowns. Some were looking straight into their box, pointing and whispering to their companions.

'It is rather thin of company.' Lord Tannerton smiled at her. 'But I hope you like it.'

'It is lovely,' she responded, trying not to think of what the other theatre-goers might be saying about her. 'Much larger than I even could have imagined.' She'd only read of theatres like this one. The closest she'd been to seeing one was when Miss Hart had taken them to Astley's Amphitheatre, but that was an entirely different sort of place. This was the best of theatres.

'I am pleased to be the first to show it to you. Flynn said you had a wish to see it.'

Flynn.

Flynn had made this happen for her. He alone knew how much she desired it. He must have forgiven her wanton behaviour, to give her such a gift. 'I did indeed.'

It had seemed natural to Rose to tell Flynn all about her mother singing in King's Theatre, about her mother's dashed dreams and shortened life. She had no such impulse to tell the marquess.

The musicians entered and took their seats, the violinists tuning their strings, horn players testing their instruments' sound. Though none played at full volume, the notes filled the huge room, and Rose found she was eager to hear the performance, especially the singing.

'Do you fancy yourself singing in this theatre some day?' Tannerton asked her.

Rose shot a glance at him. Had Flynn told him this as well? It seemed a betrayal of confidences. 'Why do you think so?'

He shrugged. 'King's Theatre is the pinnacle, is it not, for singers? At least others have told me so.'

Perhaps Flynn had not told him all her secrets, after all. She heard Flynn behind her talking quietly to Katy and wished he would speak loud enough so she could hear what he said.

Katy disappointed Rose, acting so subdued Tannerton would never notice her. In fact, Katy seemed more determined to have Flynn's company.

Tannerton handed her a paper. 'Here is the programme telling who sings tonight. I will get you a candle if you cannot read it.'

She took the paper and stared at it even though she could read but little in the dim light. It gave her an excuse not to talk to him.

'Thank you,' she said belatedly, briefly glancing at him.

Tanner smiled at her. He had a boyish handsomeness, she had to admit. An open countenance. He was tall and athletic and looked out of place in this elegant theatre, as if he would prefer hunting or whatever gentlemen did in the out of doors. By appearance, and so far by manner, he did not threaten, but Rose could not forget her father's warning. This was a man who possessed the power to ruin her ambitions. She turned back to staring at the programme.

'I think it is about to begin,' Tannerton said.

She glanced at the stage. The conductor of the orchestra took his place. The musicians quieted, but the audience seemed as noisy as ever. The music began. Rose could make out that the opera was one of Mozart's, but she had never heard the music before. Her school had not owned these sheets of music. She poised herself to listen and watch, not wishing to miss a bit of it.

When the curtain opened, she even forgot who sat beside her. The set was magical, looking so real she could barely believe she was not looking through some window. She heard singing voices like she'd never heard before, big voices, bigger than her own, big enough to fill this huge theatre. When the soprano sang, Rose held her breath. She wanted to open her mouth and mimic each note, to try to make her voice bigger, like this one.

She could understand none of the words. She was not even sure what language they were singing. It did not matter, however. The performers showed her the story, a shocking one, really. Don Giovanni was a seducer of women, a man who made conquests and who cared little of what havoc he wreaked in people's lives. When the character Elvira sang, Rose could hear her heartache and her rage. Elvira loved and hated Don Giovanni. Rose wanted to weep for her. How thrilling it would be to sing one's emotions like that.

When the intermission came, Rose felt bereft. She wanted to go on listening. She wanted to step on to the stage and be a part of it, to raise her voice with the others in the beautiful music they created.

Instead, a footman brought in some cakes and fruit and other delicacies.

'At intermission one often calls upon others in other boxes,' Tannerton told her. 'But I have asked the footman to stand outside and explain we do not wish to be disturbed.'

That was kind of him. The last thing she wanted was to have the magic of the performance interrupted by curious people come to see who sat next to the marquess. She was desperately trying to hold on to the music, replaying it in her head, silently singing, wishing she could sound like those wonderful performers.

They took refreshment around a small table. Flynn, sitting directly opposite Rose, poured more champagne.

'How do you like the performance, Miss Green?' Tannerton asked.

Katy grinned. 'It is fun, is it not? Don Giovanni is a clever rogue. I hope he escapes.'

'We shall see,' said Tanner, eyes crinkling into a smile.

Tanner turned to Rose. 'And you, Miss O'Keefe. What do you think of it?'

Rose looked up to see Flynn watching her. He quickly averted his eyes. She could barely speak. Words were not enough to convey what she felt. 'I have never heard such singing,' she said reverently. 'I like it very much.'

'Then I am happy.' Tannerton grinned boyishly. 'I have pleased you both.'

The second half of the opera was every bit as magical. Rose felt the music inside her. She was transported by its beauty, affected by its emotion, and invigorated by possibilities she had not known existed. To sing with such power and feeling. She could hardly wait to try to mimic their sound.

Too soon it was over, the music making its last crescendo. Rose felt as if her soul had been dropped from a great height back into her own body. She applauded with all the energy she possessed.

When the performers took their final bow, the only sounds that could be heard were the scuffling feet and muffled voices of people leaving the theatre.

Lord Tannerton put his hand on her arm. She had forgotten him, forgotten her purpose for being there.

'Time to go, Miss O'Keefe,' he said.

Chapter Seven

Flynn watched Tanner touch Rose's arm. His own hand tingled, as if it were he, not Tanner, who touched her. He stretched and flexed his fingers, trying to dispel the illusion, but it did no good, because Tanner touched her again, escorting her out of the box on his arm. He had known it would be difficult to see her with Tanner. He had just not anticipated how difficult.

There was no doubt in Flynn's mind that he'd chosen well when he'd picked King's Theatre as the place for Tanner to meet Rose. Tanner had grumbled—the man hated opera—but Flynn knew that this place would be more precious to Rose than a whole cask of emerald rings. She would never forget the man who gave her King's Theatre.

Flynn ought to be congratulating himself all round.

But every time Tanner had looked at Rose or leaned towards her or spoke to her it was like daggers were being thrust into Flynn's flesh. He was surprised that the champagne he'd consumed had not spurted out of him like from a water skin poked with holes.

They found Tanner's carriage among the line of vehicles

outside. Tanner lifted Rose into it, holding her by the waist. He assisted Katy in the same manner. Flynn was the last inside, taking his seat next to Katy. His gaze met Rose's, and she smiled, gratitude shining in her eyes.

He would not regret giving her this evening, no matter that it signified the loss of a brief, fanciful, mad dream.

The carriage made the short trip to Bennet Street in good time. As it pulled up in front of the gaming-house, Katy said, 'You must all come up for some supper. Madame Bisou has arranged a nice treat.'

'But—' Rose glared at Flynn.

He shook his head. He knew nothing of this.

Tanner gave the answer, agreeable as always. 'Of course we will. Very generous of the *madame.*'

So they all entered Madame Bisou's house and were escorted to a private parlour. The Madame was there to greet them.

'Good to see you, *chérie.*' She offered her cheek for Tanner to kiss. 'You have not favoured us with your presence in an age.'

'That is so.' He smiled apologetically. 'I must rectify that, mustn't I?'

Like two old friends, Tanner chatted with Madame Bisou while she ushered the others into chairs, joining them herself.

They were served cold meats and fruits and cakes and more wine. Tanner began to mellow from the drink.

'And what do you think of our Rose?' Madame Bisou asked him.

Rose stared at her plate, a blush staining her cheeks.

Tanner gazed at her. 'I think she is as lovely as her name.'

The words twisted in Flynn's gut.

Tanner continued to gaze at Rose in frank admiration. 'Do you sing at Vauxhall tomorrow night?' he asked. He gestured to the clock on the mantel. Dawn was not long away. 'Tonight, I mean.'

'I do, sir,' she responded in a quiet voice.

Tanner continued, 'Would you do me the honor of sharing a meal with me at the gardens tomorrow? We can arrange something, can we not, Flynn?'

Flynn nodded. He could arrange whatever Lord Tannerton wished. That was his job.

Rose glanced at Flynn with a silent panic he did not comprehend. She turned to Tanner. 'I hope you will not mind, sir, if we include the others present in that invitation? Miss Green, Mr Flynn and Madame Bisou?'

Flynn admired her skill in turning the invitation around, making it appear as if chiding Tanner for poor manners. Her reticence towards Tanner still bewildered him, however. Now that she'd met him, she could have no further objection to him.

Flynn noticed Katy flashing her eyes at Rose. Apparently Katy did not understand such behaviour any better than he did. Rose gave her a plaintive look in return.

Tanner's face showed dismay, but he answered in his typical affable tone. 'They shall be included if you wish it.'

Katy rolled her eyes.

Madame Bisou put a hand on Tanner's arm. 'Sweet of you to include me, *chérie,* but I have a business to attend to.' She stood. 'In fact, I must check on the gaming room now. I wish I could accept your invitation.' She smiled at Rose. 'I miss hearing our Rose sing.'

The connection between Rose and this mistress of a gaming hell was not lost on Flynn. Rose must not always have been under her father's thumb. The whole thing was a mystery, but the real mystery was why it disturbed Flynn so greatly.

Flynn and Tanner stood to bid Madame Bisou adieu,

thanking her for the meal. She tweaked Tanner's chin play-
fully and headed for the door, stopping to look back at him.
'Come play my tables, Lord Tannerton. Come join your friend
Pomroy. I believe he is here tonight.'

'Pomroy is here?' said Tanner with interest.

Before the gentlemen could sit again, Katy stood, stifling
a yawn that did not look quite real. 'I hope you will forgive
me,' she said in a ladylike voice. 'But I must bid you goodnight as well.' She curtsied to Tanner. 'It was a pleasure, sir.'

He gave her a charming smile. 'I will see you in a few
hours, Miss Green.'

Katy grinned back. 'You will, won't you?'

Rose also got up from her chair. 'I should retire as well.'

Tanner looked disappointed. 'Must you?'

She nodded. 'I must get some rest if I am to perform.'

'May I escort you to your room?' Tanner asked, somewhat
hopefully.

Flynn flinched, preparing for her to say yes.

Rose barely looked at Tanner. 'I do not live here, sir.'

'That is so.' Tanner responded. 'Flynn said you live with
your father. Do we return you to your father or do you stay
here this night?'

She glanced at Flynn, not Tanner. 'I should prefer to
return home.'

Tanner's face fell, but he recovered quickly. 'We will take
you home then, will we not, Flynn?' he said in a cheerful voice.

'Indeed,' Flynn responded, trying very hard to keep his
voice bland.

If Rose had allowed Tanner to come with her to a room
here, her acceptance of his interest would have been secured,
and only the financial arrangement would remain for Flynn
to manage. The matter would be at an end.

So how was it he was relieved she had not accompanied Tanner to a bedchamber abovestairs?

He followed Tanner as he walked with Rose out of the parlour. As they passed the game room, Tanner hesitated. 'I should like to greet my friend who is here.' He turned to Rose. 'Would you care to come in the game room a moment, Miss O'Keefe? Or would you prefer to have Flynn see you home directly?'

'I prefer to go home,' Rose replied. She extended her hand to Tanner. 'Goodnight, sir.'

He brought her hand to his mouth and kissed the air above it. 'I shall look forward to seeing you at Vauxhall.'

'At Vauxhall,' she said.

Flynn descended the stairway with Rose and collected their things from the footman. Neither of them spoke. Flynn ought to have manoeuvred Tanner to take Rose home. He could have done so with a judicious word. Dear God, why had he not?

He had done this to himself. He wanted to be alone with her in the dark confines of the carriage.

Rose felt a flare of excitement as Flynn assisted her into the carriage. She had been pining to speak with him, to thank him for this wonderful night. To share with him her reaction to the opera. She had so many questions.

He did not sit beside her, but rather took the back-facing seat. She could barely make out his features in the dim light that filtered in from the carriage lamps outside.

As soon as the carriage moved, she leaned toward him. 'Flynn, thank you for this night. I do not know how to express my gratitude.'

'My duty,' he responded curtly.

His stiffness took her aback.

He went on in a dry voice, 'I take it Lord Tannerton was pleasing to you.'

'Lord Tannerton?' She shook her head in confusion. 'I was not speaking of him, but of the opera! Of King's Theatre. I know that was your doing. You knew what it meant to me.'

He did not immediately respond. 'I thought only of what would best facilitate my employer's wishes.'

'That's foolishness you are talking,' Rose retorted. 'You gave me the opera. I know you did.' She hugged herself with remembering it. 'It was so grand! I've never heard such singing! The voices, Flynn. How did they make their voices so big?'

'Big?'

'You know, their voices seemed to come from deep inside them. The sound filled that huge theatre. How did they do that?' Even the mere memory of it excited her. 'I want to learn to do that. Do you think I can, Flynn?' She sang a note, experimenting. 'That is not it, is it? I long to understand how it is done.'

She wanted to practise right now.

'I am sure it can be learned.' His voice turned softer.

'I long to learn it,' She went on. 'I wish I could return to hear them again. I wish I could remember the music and the words. I could not understand the words. Was it Italian? I do not know languages. Just a little French and Latin, but very little.'

'It was Italian,' he said.

'Think how it must be to know what all the words meant.' Some day she would learn Italian, she vowed. 'I wish I had the music. I would memorise every part of it.'

'Lord Tannerton will be gratified that he pleased you.'

He'd not been listening to her. She'd been talking of the music, not Lord Tannerton. She closed her mouth and retreated to her side of the carriage, making herself remember the music.

He broke the silence. 'Did you find Lord Tannerton agreeable, Rose?'

'Everything agreeable,' she answered dutifully, trying to recall the melody Elvira sung.

But he'd broken the spell, and she remembered that she'd agreed to see Tannerton again that evening. 'At Vauxhall tonight. How shall I find you?' she asked.

'I will collect you from the gazebo when your performance is done.'

'Letty will be there. Come alone to fetch me, not with Lord Tannerton.' She did not need Letty speaking directly to Lord Tannerton.

'I will come alone, then,' he agreed. He talked as if they were discussing some manner of business, like paying Tannerton's bills. It was business, really. 'Will you see that Miss Green is also there?'

'I will.'

They rode in silence the rest of the way. When the coach came to a stop in front of her lodgings, Flynn helped her out and walked her to the door.

'I will walk you inside,' he said.

There was only one small oil lamp to light the hallway, and Rose heard mice skitter away as soon as their footsteps sounded on the stairs.

In front of her door they were wrapped in near-darkness, a darkness that somehow made him seem more remote and made the music in her mind fade.

'Goodnight, then.' She was unable to keep her voice from trembling.

'Goodnight,' he responded. He turned and walked to the head of the stairs.

She put her hand on the doorknob.

'Rose?'

She turned back to him.

'I am glad you enjoyed the opera.' Before she could reply, he descended the stairs.

That night Greythorne stood in the shadows of the Grove, watching and listening to Rose O'Keefe sing. If anything, her voice was richer this night, especially passionate. Such passion ought to be his, he thought. He'd be her conductor. She would sing only for him, notes only he could make her reach.

He spied Tannerton in the crowd. His adversary, a man who'd struck the initial claim. Greythorne would not let that impede him. It would only make the prize more precious to know he'd stolen it out from under the nose of the Marquess of Tannerton. The man was all Greythorne disdained, a Corinthian who cared more for horses than for the cut of his coat. Who would know they could share the same tailor? If it were not for Weston, the man would look like a ruffian on the street.

After Miss O'Keefe finished, Greythorne watched Tannerton say something to that secretary who always seemed to be about. The two men parted. Something was afoot. If not for a woman, neither he nor Tannerton would spend this much time in London with summer upon them, not when other pleasures beckoned at places like Brighton or even Paris.

Greythorne wondered what it would be like to take Miss O'Keefe to Paris, far away from familiar people or influences. Perhaps that was what he would do, but first he must discover what Tannerton planned for this night.

He followed Tannerton, but the man walked aimlessly, stopping to speak to the few persons of quality who were present at the gardens this night. He ought to have followed the secretary instead. That Flynn fellow ran the show. Greythorne hurried back to the gazebo in time to glimpse the secretary escorting two women, one wearing a hood. He tried to keep them in sight, but lost them in the crowd.

Cursing silently, he continued to search the line of supper boxes where Tannerton had dallied.

Finally he discovered them.

In one of the more private supper boxes, half-obscured by trees near the South Walk arch, sat Tannerton with the hooded lady. Greythorne wagered the woman was Miss O'Keefe. Greythorne waited for the moment he could make himself known.

His eyes narrowed as he watched Tannerton talking to the chit as if she were already his. The marquess had made progress, perhaps, but Greythorne was not ready to concede defeat. His little interlude of two nights before had quite fired his blood for more. He was more than ready to pluck another flower.

A Rose.

Greythorne left the shadows and sauntered across the walk up to the supper box. 'Good evening, Tannerton.' He tipped his hat.

'Evening,' Tannerton reluctantly responded, making no effort to change from his slouch in his chair.

'Forgive me for intruding.' Greythorne made certain to use his smoothest, most ingratiating voice. 'I could not resist the opportunity to tell this lovely creature how much I enjoyed her performance.'

Miss O'Keefe, who had been hiding behind her hood, gave a start. Though he could not see her clearly, he made out the tiniest nod of acknowledgement.

'Kind of you, I am sure,' Tannerton said in an unkind voice.

Greythorne tipped his hat again. 'Perhaps we will meet again, Miss O'Keefe.'

At that moment, the other woman in the box stepped

forward, bringing a glass of wine to the lovely Rose. It was Greythorne's turn to be surprised. She was the red-haired harlot whom he had seen with Sir Reginald, the one whose laughter had fired his blood. He widened his eyes in interest, an interest she caught.

She gave him an appraising look in return. 'Good evening, sir.'

He smiled most appealingly and doffed his hat to her. 'Good evening, miss.'

Tanner glanced up at the woman. 'Greythorne was just leaving.'

Greythorne did not miss a beat. 'Regretfully leaving,' he said in his smoothest voice. He tipped his hat again to Rose. 'Miss O'Keefe.' And to the redhead. 'My dear.'

He sauntered back to the South Walk, heading in the direction of the Grove. Not defeated. Exhilarated. Two flowers to pluck instead of one. He'd have them both and rub Tannerton's nose in it.

Rose shuddered. 'That was Lord Greythorne?'

'Who is Lord Greythorne?' Katy asked, still watching him walk away.

'He's a man who…who has asked my father about me,' Rose told her.

Tannerton's open countenance turned dark. 'Not a gentleman worth knowing.'

'Do you say so, Lord Tannerton?' Katy said lightly. 'He seems a fine gentleman to me.'

Tannerton grimaced. 'Something about the fellow. Can't remember it and neither can Flynn.' He turned to Flynn. 'Right, Flynn?'

'Indeed, sir,' Flynn replied.

Katy gave Tannerton's shoulder a playful punch. 'You are

just saying that because he wants our Rose.' She laughed. 'Do not tell me you fear a little competition?'

Tannerton sat up. 'I relish competition.'

Rose glanced in the direction where the man had disappeared. He had given her a shiver. She turned to Flynn to see his reaction, but his back was to her. He'd barely spoken to her again tonight, but he spoke easily enough to Katy.

Katy came back to him, grabbing his arm and squeezing it. Rose turned away.

Tannerton regarded Rose with a hopeful expression. 'The dancing has begun. Shall we?'

Rose glanced at Flynn, but he was still thoroughly occupied with Katy. 'Of course,' she said to Tannerton, taking his arm.

By the time they had entered the Grove, the lively country dance had ended, and the orchestra struck up a waltz. Tannerton took her by the hand, twirling her under his arm before placing his other hand at her waist. He led her into the steps with great energy, joining the other couples, who created patterns of wheels within wheels.

Tannerton held her with confidence and moved her skilfully. Rose had had little experience with dancing, less with the waltz, but she was aware of his grace and the allure of his physicality. This was a man who did not take a misstep, a man secure being a man.

Such virtues ought to persuade her to succumb to him. Unfortunately, she spied Flynn leading Katy into the dance, and all Rose could think of was how it would feel to be in Flynn's arms, to be staring into Flynn's eyes as they twirled under the magical lamps of Vauxhall.

When the dance was done, Tannerton did not release her hand. 'Come walk with me,' he urged.

She held back. 'Please, no. I...I have a thirst. From the dancing.'

He gave her a rueful smile that should have melted her heart, but did not. 'Then we must return to the supper box for more refreshment.'

Katy and Flynn entered the box behind them. 'Was that not fun!' Katy exclaimed, giving Flynn another affectionate squeeze.

Rose could barely look at her, she was so filled with envy. 'Next waltz you should dance with Lord Tannerton,' she blurted out.

The marquess paused only a moment before affably agreeing. 'A capital idea. We shall trade partners.'

Rose was mortified that she had spoken so impulsively. She tried to tell herself that she had done it because she wanted Tannerton to transfer his affection to Katy. But that would be a lie. She'd merely been jealous.

Mr Hook did not keep them waiting long for another waltz, understanding his audience's preference for the more intimate dance, where the man held the woman in his arms.

Flynn did not seem as eager this time to follow Tannerton to the dancing area. Rose felt another wave of guilt for pushing herself on him when he had placed her off limits to him, but Katy had so easily taken her place.

All such thoughts were forgotten when she faced him and stared up into his blue eyes. He swung her into the pattern of twirling couples, not nearly as skilfully as Tannerton, but it hardly mattered. Rose settled into his arms with the feeling she belonged there.

He did not speak, but neither did he take his eyes off hers. Rose's vision blurred everything but him, and for this small space of time, she pretended that there was no one in the world except the two of them. At first he held her lightly, as if not wishing to touch her at all, but with each turn he seemed to pull her closer to him. She wished they would turn and turn and turn until their bodies touched and they moved as one. She wished she could burst into a joyous song that would never end.

But the music did end. Flynn still held her.

'Thank you, Flynn,' she murmured, gazing into his eyes.

His eyes were dark and needful, and the blood raced through her veins in response. She felt herself pulled to him, closer and closer, just as the twirling of the dance had drawn them close.

He held up a hand and stepped back. 'Tannerton will be waiting.'

Chapter Eight

Two days later Flynn once more stood before the door of Rose O'Keefe's lodgings. Tanner had charged him with giving Rose something that would induce her to accept him. Something more precious to her than emerald rings. Something that was her heart's desire. Something that would ensure his winning over Greythorne.

Flynn had arranged it.

He listened to the voices of Mr O'Keefe and Miss Dawes inside, and hesitated a moment before rapping on the door.

'Answer the door,' Miss Dawes shouted from within.

Footsteps sounded across the floor. The door opened.

'Yes?' O'Keefe broke into a smile when he saw Flynn standing there. 'Why, it is Mr Flynn, is it not? Come in, sir. Come in.'

Flynn entered the room.

'Mr Flynn…' Miss Dawes's voice was syrupy '…it is a pleasure to see you.'

'I come to call upon Miss O'Keefe, if you please,' Flynn said.

O'Keefe looked hopeful.

Miss Dawes said, 'I hope you have come to make an offer. We cannot wait for ever.'

Flynn disliked such brashness. 'I would urge more patience. The marquess is taking the next step. That is why I have come.'

'Rose is at the market, shopping for dinner. She will be home shortly.' Miss Dawes gave a frustrated gesture, and Flynn spied the emerald ring on her finger.

Flynn frowned. 'I must take my leave. I shall return when Miss O'Keefe is home.'

Before they could object, he was out of the door, heading to the market in hopes of finding her. He passed stall after stall of fruits and vegetables, each owner loudly attesting that his wares were the finest. One stall even sold hedgehogs, an animal some Londoners fancied as a pet, mainly because of its appetite for beetles.

Covent Garden was also the 'den of iniquity,' the place where dolly-mops and lightskirts congregated, displaying themselves much like the colourful oranges, limes and lemons on the fruit stalls. Had Flynn wished for some female company, he had only to nod and show his coin, but he was intent on finding Rose.

He spied her at a stand where herbs were displayed, lifting a fragrant bundle of lavender to her nose. He navigated his way through the shoppers to reach her.

She saw him approach and put the lavender down. 'Flynn.' She gave him a cautious smile.

He tipped his hat. 'Good day, Rose.'

'What a lovely surprise.' Her smile fled as she glanced over to a group of doxies loudly hawking themselves. 'Are… are you here to shop?'

He saw the direction of her gaze and realised she thought he might be looking for female company. 'I came looking for you.'

'For me?' Her emerald eyes looked cautious.

'Come, let us walk together.' He reached for the basket she carried on her arm.

They strolled past the stalls in the direction of her lodgings, entering a quieter part of the street.

'Why did you look for me, Flynn?' She asked in a soft voice.

'Lord Tannerton has a gift for you.'

She blinked and looked away. 'I do not want a gift.'

'You will like this one,' he assured her.

She tossed him a sceptical glance.

'Lord Tanner has arranged for Signor Angrisani and Miss Hughes of King's Theatre to give you lessons in voice—'

She clutched his arm. 'You do not mean it!'

He tried to keep his face composed, but her excitement resonated inside him. 'Indeed. And if your voice is suitable, Lord Tanner has convinced Mr Ayrton to use you in the chorus, for at least one performance.'

'Mr Ayrton?'

'The musical director,' he explained.

Her eyes grew as large as saucers. 'I would perform on the stage of the King's Theatre?'

'Yes.'

'Oh, Flynn!' Her voice cracked and her face was flushed with colour. Every muscle and nerve in his body sprang to life.

'It is wonderful!' She twirled around, but stopped abruptly. 'Oh.'

'What?'

She stared into the distance as if unable to speak. Suddenly she turned back to him. 'Lord Tannerton arranged this?'

He opened his mouth to answer, but was silenced by another transformation of her features.

An ethereal smile slowly grew on her face, and she seemed

to glow from within. She lifted her jewel-like eyes to his. 'You arranged this, Flynn.'

Both gratification and guilt engulfed him. He'd pleased her, as he longed to do, but she must believe it was on Tannerton's behalf.

She touched his arm, the sensation of her fingers on his sleeve radiating through all parts of him.

'*You* arranged this for me.' Her voice was awed. 'Oh, Flynn!'

Rose took in Flynn's handsome, too-serious features, her heart swelling in her chest. He alone had known what this meant to her. Flynn was giving her what she'd dreamed of for as long as she could remember.

'You have arranged for my fondest wish to come true,' she whispered, gazing into the depths of his eyes.

Four young bucks staggered toward them, holding on to each other and swaying with too much drink. One of them grinned. 'You plucked a right rose,' he said to Flynn. 'M'hat's off to you.' The young man tried to reach his hat, but the lot of them nearly toppled over as a result. With his companions cursing him for nearly knocking them down, they stumbled away.

'They think I am your doxy,' she said to Flynn.

She'd received other frank remarks from men in the market that afternoon, remarks that made her cringe with discomfort and hurry on her way, but somehow she did not mind so much to be thought of as Flynn's doxy.

But he looked pained, so she changed the subject. 'Tell me where I am to go, what time, what I am to do.'

'If you are able, the *signor* and Miss Hughes will see you at King's Theatre tomorrow, at two o'clock.' He spoke stiffly, as if he were scheduling some appointment for the marquess. 'I shall come to escort you there.'

'You will?' That made her even happier. She wanted to share her dream with him.

They walked the rest of the way to her lodgings, she in happy silence. All she could think of was walking in to King's Theatre on Flynn's arm. Perhaps he would stay and listen to her sing. Perhaps he would escort her home and she could talk to him about each moment of the lesson.

Her building was in sight, and she was loathe to leave him, even though his expression was as hard as chiselled granite. This gift he would give her came with strings attached, she knew. The time was approaching when she must repay Lord Tannerton for what Flynn had done for her.

As they neared the door of her building, Flynn slowed his pace. 'I spoke with your father and Miss Dawes,' he said. 'They are pressing for Lord Tannerton to make his offer.'

She nodded.

'It is your move, Rose, but I urge you not to delay. Your father may accept another offer not to your liking.'

'With Greythorne?'

'Yes.'

Rose knew he spoke the truth.

'I must accept Tannerton,' she said in a resigned voice. 'I know this.'

His eyes seemed to reflect her pain. 'Soon,' he said.

The next day Rose and Flynn stood in the hall of King's Theatre with Mr Ayrton, the musical director of *Don Giovanni*.

'So pleased to meet you, Miss O'Keefe. Any friend of the marquess is certainly a friend to us. He is the most generous of men…'

He escorted them through the pit of the theatre to the

stage, where, standing next to a pianoforte, were two men and a woman.

'I am to go on the stage?' Rose asked in wonder.

'Indeed,' replied Mr Ayrton. 'What better place to examine the quality of your voice?'

Flynn held back, and Rose twisted around to give him one more glance before she followed Mr Ayrton to the stage entrance.

She was presented to Miss Hughes. 'Hello, my dear,' the woman said in her melodious Welsh accent.

'You played Elvira!' Rose exclaimed, stunned that this ordinary woman had transformed herself into that character, so much larger than life.

'That I did.' Miss Hughes smiled.

'I confess I am surprised you are not Italian. I could not tell, to be sure.'

The next person introduced to her was Signor Angrisani. 'And you were Don Giovanni,' Rose said, as he gave her a somewhat theatrical bow.

'That is so,' he said smoothly. 'And I am Italian, unlike Miss Hughes.'

The third man was the pianist, a Mr Fallon, who merely nodded.

'I shall leave you to these excellent teachers,' Mr Ayrton said. 'But I assure you, I shall listen with Mr Flynn.'

Rose's nerves fluttered, and she was grateful Flynn would be with her the whole time. She gazed out into the theatre, but it was too dark to see him.

She turned back to Miss Hughes and Signor Angrisani. 'Thank you both for taking your time to teach me.'

'Oh—' Miss Hughes laughed '—we have been amply rewarded, I assure you. Shall we warm your voice and discover your range?'

They began by having her sing what she could only describe as nonsense sounds, exercise for her voice.

'Some scales, if you please,' Angrisani said, nodding to the pianist, who played a scale pitched in middle C.

Rose sang the notes, concentrating on each one. They made her sing them again, and then went higher until Rose could feel the strain. They asked the same thing, going lower and lower.

Then Miss Hughes handed her a sheet of music. *In qulai eccessi* she read.

'I do not know these words,' Rose said.

'Do not distress yourself.' The *signor* patted her arm. 'Speak them any way you wish.'

She examined the sheet again, mentally playing the notes in her head as if plucking them out on her pianoforte.

She glanced at Miss Hughes. 'This is your song from the opera.'

'It is, my dear,' the lady responded. 'Now, let us hear you sing it.'

Rose tried, but stumbled over the foreign words and could not keep pace with the accompaniment.

'Try it again,' Miss Hughes told her.

The second time she did much better. When she finished she looked up to see Miss Hughes and Signor Angrisani frowning.

The *signor* walked up to her. 'You have a sweet voice, very on key and your…how do you say?…your diction is good.'

She felt great relief at his compliment.

'But your high notes are strained. You are breathing all wrong and you have poor volume,' Miss Hughes added. 'You must sing to the person in the farthest seat.'

Rose nodded.

'Sing louder,' Miss Hughes ordered.

She sang again, looking out into the house, thinking of Flynn sitting in the farthest seat. She sang to him.

But it did not please the *signor* and Miss Hughes. They fired instructions at her. 'Stand up straight.' 'Open your mouth.' 'Breathe.'

There was so much to remember.

'Breathe from here.' Miss Hughes put her hand against Rose's diaphragm. 'Not here.' She touched Rose's chest. 'Expand down with your muscles. You will get the volume.'

Rose attempted it, surprised when she sounded louder.

For the high notes, Signor Angrisani told Rose to lift the hard palate in the roof of her mouth. 'Inhale,' he said. 'As if you are about to sneeze. Drop your tongue. Now push out through your nose.'

She was dismayed at how many tries it took to co-ordinate all these instructions. When she succeeded, the notes came out crystal clear.

It seemed as if the lesson were over in the wink of an eye. Her mind raced with trying to remember everything they had told her. She must not have done too badly, because they invited her back in three days' time. As Signor Angrisani walked her back to the pit, Rose put her hand to her throat, wanting to protect it for the next lesson, hoping she would not strain it by singing at Vauxhall in a few short hours. She would fix herself some hot water flavoured with lemon juice to soothe it.

As the *signor* walked her through the theatre, she saw two men standing at the back. She could hardly wait to reach Flynn.

'I shall bid you good day.' Signor Angrisani stopped halfway through the theatre. He kissed her hand.

'Thank you, *signor,*' she said, trying to use the proper accent.

He smiled. 'Eh, you shall do well, did I not say?'

He had not said, but she was delighted to hear it now.

She felt like skipping the rest of the way to where Flynn waited.

As she got close, she saw that the gentleman standing next to Flynn was not Mr Ayrton, but Lord Tannerton.

She lost the spring in her step.

'Lord Tannerton,' she said as she neared him. She dropped into a graceful curtsy.

He smiled at her. 'How did you like your lesson?'

She darted a glance to Flynn, who stood a little behind him. 'I liked it very much, sir. I am indebted to you for your generosity.'

He waved a dismissive hand. 'Ah, it was nothing. Glad to do it if it gives you pleasure.'

'Great pleasure, my lord.'

Rose had no doubt the marquess could easily afford whatever sum it took to make Mr Ayrton, Miss Hughes and Signor Angrisani so agreeable, but she did not forget that it was Flynn who had made this happen.

'As much pleasure as I receive hearing your voice, I wonder?' His expression was all that was agreeable.

She cast her gaze down at the compliment.

'May I have the honor of escorting you home, Miss O'Keefe?'

She glanced up again. 'Oh, I would not trouble you. I am certain I might easily find a hack.'

'It is no trouble,' he reassured her. 'My carriage should be right outside. It shall give me the opportunity to hear your impression of your tutors.'

She'd been eager to tell Flynn everything, but now she could think of nothing to say about her lesson.

There was no refusing the marquess now, or, she feared, when he asked for more intimate favours. 'Very well, my lord.'

'I shall see you back at Audley Street, Flynn.' Tannerton said this affably, but it was still a dismissal.

Flynn nodded, but said nothing. He turned and walked out of the theatre.

Rose was alone with the marquess.

'Shall we go?' He offered his arm.

When they made their way to the hall, Rose saw Flynn just disappearing through the doors. By the time she and the marquess reached the street, she could not see Flynn at all.

'My carriage, Miss O'Keefe.' As he spoke, the carriage pulled up to the front of the theatre.

King's Theatre was located in Haymarket. She would have several minutes of riding alone with him to Covent Garden. He gave his coachman the name of her street and helped her into the carriage.

'And how did you find the lesson?' he asked after they were settled in and the coach began moving.

'There seems much to learn,' she replied.

'I suspect you will be a good student.'

He asked her other questions about the lesson, about what she thought she needed to learn, about singing in general. It was the sort of conversation intended to put a person at ease. She admired his skill at it. She had to admit his interest in her likes and dislikes seemed genuine, though she could not imagine him burning with ambition, as she and Flynn did. He could not possibly understand what it meant to her to sing, not like Flynn understood.

Rose glanced at him. He was a handsome man, more handsome, perhaps, than Flynn, whose features were sharper and his expression more intense. But Lord Tannerton did not make her heart race. When he gazed upon her, he did not seem to see into her soul.

'I have strict orders from Flynn not to walk you inside your lodgings,' Tannerton said as they passed Leicester Square. 'I gather he does not wish me to encounter your father.'

She almost smiled. More likely Flynn was protecting him from Letty.

'Mr Flynn is a careful man,' she said.

'Oh, he is exceptional, I'll grant you that,' Tannerton agreed.

'How long has Mr Flynn been your secretary?' She knew the answer, of course, but she would rather talk about Flynn than anything else.

He paused, thinking. 'Six years, I believe.' They walked on. 'Not that I expect him to remain,' he added.

This was new information. 'Oh?'

He gave her a sly glance. 'Can you keep a secret, Miss O'Keefe?'

'Of course I can.' She kept many secrets.

He leaned closer and whispered. 'Our Flynn burns with ambition, you know. He wants to rise higher than his present employ and deserves to, I believe. I have lately spoken to the Duke of Clarence about Flynn. His Royal Highness will come around, I think. God knows, he could use a man like Flynn.'

Flynn to work for royalty. For a Royal duke? All Rose knew about the Prince Regent's second brother was that his mistress had been Mrs. Jordan, a famous actress. But that poor lady had died not long ago. It was said the Duke would marry now. He would become more serious about his station in life.

Flynn would serve the Duke well, no doubt, Rose thought. Such employment meant the fulfilment of his dreams.

Both their dreams would come true. She ought to be happy. Only, at this moment, it merely made her sad.

'This is my street,' she said, looking out of the window. 'The coachman should stop here.'

He rapped on the roof of the carriage, and it slowed to a stop. He got out and helped her descend.

She pointed to a building two doors down. 'That is my building.'

He turned to see which one she meant and spoke suddenly. 'What the devil is that fellow doing here?'

She saw a man walk out of her building and turn in the opposite direction from where the carriage had stopped.

Greythorne.

Chapter Nine

Tanner asked his coachman to follow Greythorne. The man walked only a short distance before jumping into a hack, but luck was with Tanner—Greythorne left the vehicle at White's. He could not have picked a better place for an accidental meeting.

'I'll not need you,' Tanner told his driver. 'Take the horses back.' He glanced up at the threatening sky, wondering if he'd regret that decision if caught in a downpour.

He entered the gentleman's club and greeted the doorman by name, divesting himself of his hat and gloves. Sauntering into the dining room, he spied Greythorne alone at a table, placing his order with the footman. Tanner acknowledged the few other gentlemen in the room who gestured for him to sit down, but instead made his way to Greythorne.

'Well, look who is here,' said Greythorne, watching him approach.

Tanner grinned. 'I'll take that as an invitation to join you.' He signalled the servant for some ale and lounged in the chair opposite his rival.

'Ale?' Greythorne sniffed.

Tanner cocked his head. 'I like ale.'

Greythorne lifted his nose. 'To what do I owe this... honour?'

'Thought I would see how our game is going.' He leaned forward. 'Making any progress?'

Greythorne sneered. 'Do you think I would tell you?'

Tanner sat back again. 'Actually, I did. I mean, if you have won the girl, you would be more than happy to tell me.'

The servant brought Tanner his ale and brandy for Greythorne.

'So,' Tanner went on, 'you have not won the girl, but neither have you given up, I'd wager.'

Greythorne scowled at him. 'I am progressing nicely, if you must know.'

'Indeed?' Tanner said. 'So am I. What is your progress?'

Greythorne swirled the brandy in his glass and inhaled its bouquet before taking a gentlemanly sip. Only then did he answer, 'I believe I shall not tell you.'

Tanner lifted his tankard and gulped some ale, licking his lips of the remaining foam. 'Then I cannot very well report my progress either, can I? We are at a stand.'

Greythorne eyed him with disgust. 'I am sure it makes not a whit of difference to me.'

Tanner leaned forward again. 'Does not the competition fire your blood, man? The prize becomes more precious for knowing another covets it.'

'For you, perhaps,' Greythorne said with a casual air Tanner did not believe in the slightest.

'Where is your fighting spirit?' Tanner taunted. 'This is a manly challenge, is it not? Who will win the fair maid?'

Greythorne gave a sarcastic laugh. 'Shall we joust for our little songstress? Shall we don our chainmail and armour and wave our banners?'

Tanner pretended to seriously consider this. 'The Tannerton armour will not fit me. Too small.' He eyed Greythorne. 'Might fit you, though.'

The barb hit. Greythorne's eyes flashed with anger as he took another sip of his brandy.

Smiling inwardly, Tanner went on, 'No a joust would not do. How about fisticuffs?'

The man nearly spat out his drink. 'Do not be absurd!'

Tanner pretended to be offended. 'You proposed a physical contest, not I.'

'I am not going to engage in a physical contest to see who wins the girl,' Greythorne snapped.

Tanner lifted his tankard. 'I beg your pardon. I misunderstood you.' He took one very protracted gulp, knowing he kept Greythorne hostage during it. Finally he set the tankard back on the table and continued as if he'd never interrupted his conversation. 'So no physical contest for the girl. I do agree. That seems rather trite. How about a physical contest to learn this progress we each have made?'

Greythorne looked aghast.

Gratified, Tanner went on, 'If you win, I tell you what we have achieved in conquest of the girl. If I win, you tell me the progress you have made. Agreed?'

'No, I do not agree!' Greythorne looked at him as if he were insane. 'You would have us pound at each other with our fists over such a trifle? I assure you, I would do no such thing.'

Tanner did not miss a beat. 'Oh, not fisticuffs. That would not be a fair fight at all. I've no real desire to injure you—well, not much of a desire anyway—or to injure my hands.' He looked at his hands as if admiring them.

Greythorne's eyes shot daggers.

Tanner returned a sympathetic look. 'We could tame this

for your sake. Perhaps a game of cards, if a physical contest is too fearful—I mean, if it is not to your liking.'

The man straightened in his chair. 'I am well able to defend myself, if the sport is a gentlemanly one.'

'Oh?' Tanner lifted his brows. 'A race, perhaps? On horse-back or phaeton?'

Greythorne grimaced.

'No? Too dirty?' Tanner said. 'What then?'

He waited, enjoying the corner he'd put Greythorne in.

Finally Greythorne answered, 'Swords.'

Tanner grinned. 'Swords it is!'

When they walked out of White's, leaving a rustle of voices discussing what was overheard, it had started to rain. Grey-thorne opened an umbrella, not offering its shelter to Tanner as they walked from St. James's to Angelo's Fencing Academy next door to Gentleman Jackson's Boxing Club on Bond Street. To thoroughly annoy Greythorne, Tanner sustained his friendly conversation the whole way, as if they were fast friends instead of adversaries.

When they entered the Academy, Tanner received a warm greeting from the third-generation Angelo to run the establishment. Tanner and Greythorne both stripped to their shirtsleeves.

'Choose your weapon,' Tanner invited.

'Épée?' responded Greythorne. 'And shall we forgo masks?'

Tanner approved of that bit of bravado. He preferred clearly seeing the expression on his adversary's face. In Greythorne's case, he assumed it would be like reading a book.

'How many touches?' Tanner asked.

Greythorne thought a moment. 'Five.'

Tanner nodded.

With Angelo and a few others watching, they saluted and faced each other *en garde*. Tanner gave Greythorne invitation, carefully watching how the man moved. Greythorne engaged his sword, and the sound rang throughout the room. Parrying the thrust, Tanner executed his riposte with just enough speed and skill to keep Greythorne attacking.

Again and again, Greythorne lunged and engaged. The man was light on his feet and had a supple wrist. He also had confidence in his skill. Tanner had to concentrate to keep up his defence. Greythorne managed a clever glissade, sliding his blade along Tanner's, creating music not unlike a bow across a violin. The point of his sword hit Tanner's shoulder.

'Touché,' cried Greythorne.

'Bravo,' someone called from the sidelines. Gentlemen from White's, who had overheard the challenge, took their places to witness the fun.

Tanner acknowledged the touch, while a flurry of bet-making commenced among the onlookers. As near as he could tell, the odds were not in his favour.

He and Greythorne walked back to the middle of the room. Tanner glanced over and saw his friend Pomroy standing next to Angelo. Pomroy regarded Tanner with raised brows. Tanner lifted a shoulder and gave Pomroy a rueful smile.

He took position opposite Greythorne again.

'You will lose both this and our other little competition,' Greythorne boasted, as his épée clanged against Tanner's blade, driving Tanner backwards. Tanner allowed alarm to show on his face as Greythorne looked more and more self-assured. Greythorne whipped the blade upward, its edge catching Tanner's face before the point pressed into his neck.

'Touché,' Greythorne repeated.

Tanner felt a trickle of blood slide down his cheek. Greythorne's eyes shone with excitement, a change in demeanour Tanner did not miss. He swiped at his cheek with his sleeve, staining the cloth red.

The contest resumed, and the shouts of their onlookers grew louder. The épées touched in a flurry of thrusts and ripostes, clanging louder and louder. Salty sweat dripped down Tanner's face and stung the cut on his cheek. Greythorne sweated as well, his pace slowing, but his skilled work with the sword continued to keep Tanner on alert. When Greythorne earned one more touch, his laughter at the feat lacked force. Three *touchés* to Tanner's zero. The odds against Tanner winning went up.

Tanner breathed hard as they stood *en garde* again. Greythorne began the same pattern of thrusts and parries he'd executed before with great success. This time, however, they merely informed Tanner exactly what would happen next. At Greythorne's counter-riposte, Tanner parried and lunged, forcing Greythorne's blade aside. He quickly attacked again, the point of his épée pressing at Greythorne's heart.

The onlookers applauded, and the wagering recommenced. Greythorne's eyes widened in surprise.

They began again. This time Tanner went on the attack. He picked up the pace of his swordwork, then slowed it again, until Greythorne's brows knitted in confusion and he began making simple mistakes. Tanner drove Greythorne back again and again, each time striking a different part of his body, all potentially lethal had the épées not been affixed with buttons to prevent the sword from running straight through the flesh. He earned three more *touchés*.

With the score four *touchés* to Greythorne's three, Greythorne rallied, giving the contest more sport and increasing the frenzy of betting among the onlookers. The blades sang as they struck against each other, the sound much more pleasing to Tanner's ear than what he heard in King's Theatre or Lady Rawley's music salon. He relished it all. The strategy and cunning, the rumble of the onlookers, the danger, the sheer exertion.

He and Greythorne drove each other back and forth across the floor as the onlookers shouted louder and louder, odds changing with each footstep. Greythorne engaged more closely in an impressive display, the look of victory on his face. He lunged.

Tanner twisted around, parrying the attack from behind. He continued to spin, lifting Greythorne's blade into the air, forcing him off balance. Tanner made the circle complete as he swung his blade back to press against Greythorne's gut. The surprised man stumbled and fell backwards to the floor.

'That was five! Five *touchés!*' someone cried from the side.

Tanner continued the pressure of the dulled tip of his blade on the buff-coloured pantaloons Greythorne wore. The fabric ripped.

'You've damaged my clothes!' Greythorne seethed.

Tanner flicked the épée slightly and the tear grew larger. 'What say you?'

Greythorne moved the blade aside with his hand and sat up. He did not look at Tanner.

'What progress?' Tanner demanded.

Greythorne struggled to his feet. 'I am to dine with her tonight at Vauxhall.'

The onlookers had not attended to what must have seemed to them an epilogue to the drama. Wagers were settled and the onlookers dispersed, a few gentlemen first coming up to Tanner and clapping him on the shoulder. The winners of the betting, he surmised. Pomroy waited while he dressed. After thanking Angelo, he and Pomroy walked to the door. Greythorne was just ahead of them.

Outside rain was falling as if from buckets.

'My clothes will be ruined!' Greythorne snarled.

He held back, but Tanner and Pomroy did not hesitate to step out into the downpour, breaking into laughter as they left Greythorne in the doorway.

'Damned prig!' Pomroy said.

They ducked into the first tavern they came to, already crowded with others escaping the weather, including some of the gentlemen who had witnessed the swordfight. Tanner accepted their congratulations good naturedly. He and Pomroy pushed their way to a small table in the back.

When they were settled and some ale was on the way, Pomroy said, 'What the devil was that all about?'

Tanner grinned. 'I exerted myself to discover what Greythorne next planned in his conquest of Miss O'Keefe.'

'Such a trifle?' Pomroy pointed to the cut on his cheek. 'There was not an easier way to come upon that information?'

'And miss that sport?' Tanner felt his injury with his finger.

A harried tavern maid brought them their ale, and Tanner took a thirsty gulp.

'I discovered something about your fashionable adversary,' Pomroy said.

Tanner sat forward. 'Tell me, man.'

His friend took a sip of his ale instead. Tanner drummed the table with his fingers while he waited. Pomroy placed the tankard down and brushed the moisture from his coat sleeves, merely to delay and to annoy Tanner.

'I discovered…' he finally began, pausing to give Tanner a teasing smirk '…that your friend is not welcome at several of the brothels in town.'

'This is all?' Tanner took another drink.

His friend waved a finger in the air. 'Think of it. Why would a man be barred from a brothel?'

'Not paying?' Tanner ventured. 'Emitting too great a stench?'

Pomroy shook his head. 'He has been barred because of cruelty. He inflicts pain.'

Tanner recalled Greythorne's eyes when his sword drew blood. He frowned. 'I remember now. Morbery went to school with him. Told me once Greythorne passed around de Sade's books and boasted of engaging in his practices.' He halfway rose to his feet. 'Perverted muckworm. I must take my leave, Pomroy. The devil is set to dine with her this night.' He dug in his pocket for some coin, but sat back down. 'Dash it. I'm spoken for tonight. Clarence again.'

'Send the ever-faithful Flynn,' drawled Pomroy.

The rain settled into a misty drizzle that Flynn did his best to ignore as he stood under the scant shelter of a tree bordering the Grove at Vauxhall. There were a few other hearty souls who had braved the weather to listen to Rose sing, but Flynn had not seen Greythorne among them.

He'd listened with alarm to what Tanner had told him about Greythorne. A devotee of the Marquis de Sade, the man who said 'the only way to a woman's heart is along the path of torment.' Flynn knew the man's works. De Sade's books were more popular at Oxford than the texts they were meant to study. Flynn had read the forbidden volumes as assiduously as the other Oxford fellows. De Sade had a brilliant mind and a perverted soul; if Greythorne meant to practise his brand of pleasure on Rose, Flynn would stop him—no matter what he had to do to accomplish it.

As he listened to her, Flynn thought Rose's singing altered.

She sang with less emotion, less energy, perhaps due to the rain, or Greythorne, or strain from her voice lesson. He could tell she was attempting to put her newfound knowledge into practice, trying to breathe as they'd taught her, to sing the highest notes as they'd taught her, but she seemed self-conscious, as if fearing her knuckles would be rapped at any moment if she made an error.

He missed the undisguised pleasure that had come through in her voice before, but he well understood her determination to improve. His own ambition was as keen. They both burned with the need to rise high, as if achieving less than the highest meant total failure.

Flynn knew Tanner would let him open doors for Rose, like the one he'd opened for her at King's Theatre. The marquess had the power to fulfil her dreams.

When she finished singing her last note and curtsied to the audience, the applause was nearly drowned out by the sound of the rain rustling through the leaves and hissing on the hot metal of the lamps' reflectors. Flynn quickly made his way to the gazebo door. A few other admirers also gathered there.

He knocked on the door and gave his name and card to the servant who answered it. When he was admitted, he heard another not so fortunate fellow say, 'How did he get in?'

The servant left him alone in the gazebo's lower room, and a moment later Rose came rushing in, directly into his arms.

'Oh, Flynn! I hoped you would come!'

He could not help but hold her as she clung to him and buried her face in the damp fabric of his caped greatcoat. When she finally pulled away, tears glistened on her dark lashes.

'When does Greythorne come?' he asked.

She glanced up in surprise. 'You knew of it?'

He nodded.

A faint smile flitted across her face. 'He cancelled. Postponed, I mean.'

He gazed at her. 'Let us go somewhere we can talk.'

She went to take her cloak off a hook on the wall. When they walked out, the bedraggled men outside could be heard saying, 'That's her!' and 'Dash it! He's cut us out.'

He whisked her away, leading her down the Dark Path. It was dotted with small classical structures where couples could be private. Flynn tried the knob of the first one they came to, and, finding it unlocked, brought her inside. Rushlights lit the interior. A table was set with wine and two glasses.

'I am guessing this party has been cancelled,' Flynn said, gesturing to the table. 'Come.' He led her to the single *chaise-longue,* the only place to sit. 'If they do show up, we will make an apology and leave.'

He unfastened her cloak and laid it aside with his greatcoat, hat and gloves before coming to sit next to her. Taking her hand in his, he pulled off her gloves, one finger at a time.

She could barely breathe for the feel of his bare hand upon hers. 'Greythorne gave my father money for my company.'

He held both her hands in his.

She stared at them. 'But…but when the rain came he… begged off. He sent a message. So I do not know when I shall be required to meet him. I do not wish to meet him at all, Flynn!'

He nodded, squeezing her hands. 'Have no fear. I will think of some way to help.'

Rose gazed at him, feeling relief and something even more powerful. She could not believe he had come to her, rain and all. Now that his hands folded over hers, tethering her with his strength, she had not realised how keenly she needed him.

But he released her and stood, turning his back to her. 'Lord Tannerton is prepared to better any offer Greythorne makes.'

She bowed her head. Tannerton again. Standing between them. 'When?' She felt the gloom descend upon her.

He answered in a low voice. 'I must go to your father with Tannerton's offer. If he accepts right away and does not wait for Greythorne to make a counter-offer, then it would still take me a week to make arrangements.' He turned back to her. 'Two weeks, perhaps.'

'Two weeks,' she whispered.

He came to sit next to her again. 'There is no other choice, Rose.'

Her mind had accepted this. She wanted to sing. She wanted some day to sing Elvira's part in Don Giovanni, to be a name everyone knew, like Catalani, and she wanted nothing to stop her. She wanted to live the life her mother had lost.

Only her heart warred with that ambition. Her heart pined for love. For Flynn.

She pulled away from him and rose from the chaise. 'I do not want to stay here, Flynn. I…I feel as if I am trespassing.'

She bent down to pick up her cape. He came to her and took the cape from her hands, wrapping it around her. He fastened it under her chin and pulled the hood up to cover her head. She had difficulty breathing, he was so near. She dared not lift her chin to look into his eyes, because she wanted so dearly for his eyes to burn with the same desire raging inside her.

But she could not help herself. She tilted her head back. His eyes were dark with passion. The joy of it caused her knees to go weak. All she need do was close the distance between them and place her lips on his. What harm to taste his lips just once? Everyone expected her to be a wanton, why not behave like one now? She longed to be the wanton with Flynn.

'Flynn,' she whispered.

Rising on tiptoe, she touched her lips to his, lightly at first. When he did not move away, she slid her arms around his neck and increased the pressure. His lips parted, and she darted her tongue into his mouth where he tasted warm and wet and wonderful.

A low groan escaped him, and as she felt his breath cool her mouth, she grasped him tighter. His arms encircled her and he slammed his body against hers, his fingers pressing into her soft flesh. All sensation raced to where he ground himself against her, urging her on, thrilling her with the feel of his manhood hard beneath his clothes.

He wanted her, it meant. She was glad she'd learned about what was happening to him. And to her.

'Flynn,' she repeated, this time with urgency.

One of his hands slid around her body to her breast, rubbing and fondling until Rose thought she would cry out with the pleasure of it.

He unclasped her cloak and let it slide to the ground. Picking her up in his strong arms, he carried her to the chaise. She kissed his lips, his cheeks, his neck, anywhere she could reach.

'Make love to me, Flynn,' she begged.

He placed her gently on the *chaise* and positioned his body over hers. He bent towards her, closer and closer, and she thought she would burst from need of him.

Suddenly he broke away, so abruptly she looked to see if someone had pulled him off her, but there was no one there.

'You are bewitching me,' he rasped, grabbing her cloak from the floor. This time he merely tossed it to her and walked over to pick up his greatcoat and hat. 'I will take you back to the gazebo.'

Outside it rained harder than before. The Dark Walk was

darker and more deserted than ever now that the hour had advanced and clouds hid the moon. She could barely see where she was going, and she nearly slipped on the slick path trying to keep up with him.

She reached for him, grabbing his arm. 'Flynn! Stop.'

He stopped, but did not look at her. 'Rose, this attempt to seduce me was a mistake, do you understand? It must never happen again.'

'Seduce you?' she cried, 'You seemed willing enough, Flynn. Do not make the fault all mine.'

He turned to her. 'I will not betray Tanner.' Even in the darkness she could see his eyes flash at her. She took a step toward him, but he backed away. 'No, Rose.'

She lifted her trembling chin. 'You've already betrayed him, have you not, Flynn? By wanting me? You cannot be telling me you do not want me, because I know you do.'

'Wanting and taking are not the same thing,' he said through gritted teeth.

He started walking again. As she hurried to stay with him, he stopped again, so abruptly she nearly collided with him.

He whirled on her. 'What I do not understand is why you behave like a loose woman with me, but act as if bedding a marquess would be the worst torture in the world.'

'A loose woman!' she cried. 'Is that what you think of me?'

He did not appear to hear her. 'Do not tell me you merely want more money, because you do not behave as if you want any money at all. If you wanted another man, it would make sense, but why throw yourself at me—'

'I did not throw myself at you!' She swung her hand to slap his face.

He caught her by the wrist.

'You were the one who chose the Dark Walk, Flynn, who

brought me into that room. You chose that private place, and you dare accuse me of being the seductress?' She tried to twist away, the hood of her cape falling from her head.

He grabbed her other wrist and struggled with her, losing his hat and pulling her closer and closer until her body was flush against his and their faces were only a hair's breadth away, the need burning in his eyes.

'How do you explain this, Flynn?' Her voice shook. 'I am not throwing myself at you now, am I?'

He did not release her right away, but held her, his breath rapid, his flesh so hot it seared her senses. Then he released her and ran a ragged hand through his hair.

Rain battered their uncovered heads and streamed down their faces. Slowly, however, the flames of their anger and passion fizzled in the damp air, as if turning to ashes. To gloom.

Rose whispered to him, her words competing with the rain. 'What are we to do, Flynn?'

He did not answer, but his eyes shone an intense blue in the dim light, and the rain curled his usually neatly combed hair. He looked boyish. Vulnerable. He reached for her hand.

'We left our gloves back in that room,' he said, rubbing his bare thumb against her palm.

'Oh…' Rose closed her eyes at the exquisite feel of his touch '…I must retrieve mine. I have no other pair.'

He nodded and they started back, trudging through the puddles forming in the gravel of the walk. When they reached the small structure, he entered it alone and came out with both pairs of gloves.

They walked back in silence, Rose holding his arm.

''Tis odd the orchestra is not playing,' Rose said as they neared the gazebo. The paths were deserted. The supper boxes empty. 'Everyone has left.'

They hurried to the gazebo door. Inside the servant was sweeping the floor.

His broom stilled when he saw her. 'Miss O'Keefe, your father told me to tell you to ask the gentleman to escort you home, for Mr Hook told everyone to go home because of the rain and so your father did.'

Rose nodded. 'Thank you, Mr Skewes.'

The thin wiry man grinned. 'He said as long as it was the fellow that was here before—' he nodded to Flynn '—he'd not worry about you and neither was I to worry.'

'You are kind,' she said. 'We had better be off, then.'

She and Flynn walked back out into the rain.

There were a few other stragglers walking to where the hackney coaches waited beyond the gate. Rose's cloak felt heavy from the soaking rain, and she shivered.

'You are cold.' Flynn started to unbutton his greatcoat.

'No.' She put up a hand. 'Your coat is as soaked as mine. I will be fine once we are in the carriage.'

They waited in a queue until it was their turn. Flynn lifted Rose into the hack and called out her direction to the jarvey.

They sat closer together than was wise, given how easily passion had sprung up between them. Rose shivered again, more from frustration than the chilling damp, but he unfastened her cloak and bundled it out of the way. Then he shrugged out of his greatcoat and wrapped an arm around her to warm her.

She snuggled close to him and rested her head on his shoulder. The passion that had nearly driven them to a frenzied coupling had settled into something more intimate and infinitely more sorrowful. In silence they held each other all the way across the new Vauxhall Bridge, up the roads skirting the river to the Strand, and into Covent Garden.

When the vehicle stopped on Langley Street, Flynn wrapped Rose in her cloak again and helped her out. Asking the jarvey to wait, he walked her inside her building.

'Will you be all right?' He put his hand on her arm as they reached the top of the stairs. 'Your father will not be angry?'

Rose shook her head. 'Remember, he said he would not worry if I was with you.'

His fingers tightened around her arm.

He dropped his hand. 'I must go.'

She did not move.

He started to turn away, already grasping the banister, but he suddenly turned back to her. She ran to him, and he caught her face gently in both hands, kissing her, a slow, savouring kiss more steeped in sadness than in the fires of passion that had earlier burned them both.

Without speaking another word, he released her and hurried down the stairs.

Chapter Ten

$\infty\!\!\sim\!\!\sim\!\!\sim$

By the next morning, the rain had cleared and the day promised to dry up some of the damp. Still, Flynn was grateful Rose was not scheduled to sing that evening, and she had assured him no plans to dine with Greythorne would be made.

Flynn needed the respite from the turmoil raging inside him, but, more than that, he needed a very quiet place. He closeted himself in Tanner's library, busying himself with the most tedious of his many tasks.

Tanner breezed into the room, humming a tune, and causing Flynn to lose the tally of the long line of figures he was tabulating.

'I trust I am not interrupting something important,' Tanner said.

Flynn had done something uncharacteristic the night before. After leaving Rose, he availed himself of one of Tanner's bottles of brandy and downed the entire contents in the privacy of his own room. He now paid the price with a killing headache and a foul mood.

Head throbbing, he put down his pen and recapped the inkwell. 'Did you have need of me?'

Tanner picked up a ledger Flynn had left on the side table. 'No need, really.' He leafed through the ledger, slammed it closed, and dropped it with a thud that ricocheted in Flynn's brain. 'I did wonder how it went with Greythorne—and Miss O'Keefe, of course.'

Flynn's mood became blacker. 'He cancelled because of the rain.'

Tanner laughed, a loud guffaw that rattled painfully in Flynn's throbbing head. 'The fribble. He'd give her up to keep his coat dry.' He laughed again, then drummed his fingers on the wooden table. 'Did he set another date?'

Flynn gripped the edge of the desk, trying to remain composed. 'Not as yet.'

'Rain is good for something besides crops,' said Tanner cheerfully.

Flynn tried to look composed. 'It appears he is putting pressure on her father. He paid a sum for the opportunity to dine with her.'

'Ah ha!' Tanner cried.

Flynn pressed his fingers against his temple.

'We have more in our arsenal of weapons besides money, do we not, Flynn?' Tanner laughed again.

Flynn had not a clue what Tanner meant, but he would rather not ask and prolong this loud conversation.

But Tanner showed no inclination to be quiet. 'We have cunning, and we have friends in high places.'

'Indeed,' muttered Flynn, who did not care what the deuce Tanner meant, if he would only stop talking.

'Any fellow can throw money at a woman and win her, can he not?' Tanner went on, walking to and fro as he spoke, his footsteps pounding on the carpet. 'But we think of voice lessons and opera performances!'

'I am not getting your point, Tanner,' Flynn said tersely.

Tanner glanced at him quizzically, then peered at him more closely. 'You look ghastly, Flynn. What the devil is wrong with you? You look as though you are going to shoot the cat.'

Flynn's stomach did not react well to this reference to vomiting. 'I have a headache.'

'A headache from too much drink,' Tanner concluded. 'What did I miss last night?'

'Nothing. You missed nothing.' Merely a near-betrayal of all Tanner's trust in him.

Tanner continued stomping around the room. 'Good, because it was very fortunate that I was in the company of his Royal Highness, the Duke of Clarence, you know. Friends in high places!'

Flynn gave him a direct look. 'Am I supposed to understand you?'

Tanner laughed again, this time a loud, barking, brain-joggling laugh. Flynn pressed his temples.

'No need to heed me.' Tanner winked.

Did not Tanner need to meet someone at White's or bid on a horse at Tattersalls, or something? 'If you require my services, sir, I will endeavour to oblige you, but I was working on these sums…'

Tanner sidled up to the desk and leaned over Flynn to look at the numbers on the page. 'I trust nothing is amiss?'

Flynn could feel Tanner breathing down his neck. 'All is as it should be—but I have not tabulated the whole list.'

'I despise sums.' Tanner lumbered away, pulling books off the bookshelves, opening them, then slamming them shut again, and shoving them back into place.

Flynn closed his eyes and waited for the wave of hammering in his head to subside.

'So!' said Tanner, so loud Flynn thought his head would blow apart. 'What is next in this game of ours? I say, this is more like a chess game every day, except not so ghastly tedious.'

A chess game, indeed, thought Flynn. The Queen was the prize. And after his behaviour the previous night, Flynn was a rook. 'It is time to deal with the father. Make the offer.'

Tanner stood before him, hands on his hips, head cocked. 'I had surmised more pursuit was in order. The girl hardly seems willing.' He looked pensive. 'I knew she'd be a challenge. She should come around after Ayrton puts her in the opera. How long do you think that will be?'

'I believe he thought she could carry off a small part in the chorus in two weeks' time,' Flynn told him.

Ayrton had been impressed by Rose's natural talent, but he'd also confided to Flynn that she did not have the voice for the principal roles. For all her quick learning, Flynn was inclined to agree. In Flynn's opinion, she excelled at the sort of singing she did at Vauxhall, songs with words the common folk could understand. Flynn thought her voice belonged in English opera, in one of the smaller theatres where audiences could see her and hear every word.

'So, what say you?'

Flynn shook himself. 'I beg pardon, sir, I was not attending.'

Tanner walked over to the decanter and poured a bumper. He thrust the glass under Flynn's nose. 'Drink it. It is the only sure remedy.'

The mere smell made Flynn wish to cast up his accounts, but he did as his employer ordered. He took the glass in his hand and drank it down.

Tanner settled himself in a chair. 'I can see I shall have to exert myself even more. I shall have to make the plan.'

As far as Flynn could tell, Tanner had not exerted himself

at all, except to wangle the information about Greythorne's dinner plans, although Flynn did not know how he accomplished that feat. He'd jokingly said he'd fought a duel and won, but that was nonsense, even if he had come home with a cut on his cheek and no other explanation of how it got there.

Truth was, if Tanner would exert himself, he'd be happier. He had acted with dispatch in Brussels after the great battle. Had got his hands dirty there or, rather, bloodied, lifting the wounded off the wagons and carrying them into the makeshift hospitals he'd worked at setting up.

All of this made no difference, however. Flynn had already told him what needed to be done. The exertion would, no doubt, be Flynn's. The result, Tanner's conquest of Rose.

'Here is the plan.' Tanner poured himself half the amount of brandy he'd poured for Flynn. 'No more of this mucking around with voice lessons and such. We make a generous offer to the father, money for himself and that woman of his. An annuity, perhaps, and some sort of lodging—'

'For the father?' This seemed like an unnecessary extravagance.

Tanner looked at him. 'Well, you did say that Dawes woman was the greedy one. Give her money enough to keep her out of mischief and out of Miss O'Keefe's hair. It goes without saying that you will offer the lovely Rose her own money and lodgings. A pretty little house off St James's or something. The thing is, we bid high and leave Greythorne in the dust. The deal is done.'

Flynn's headache was already receding. 'You would do this without having won her favour?'

Tanner waved his words away. 'Gratitude is an effective aphrodisiac.'

Yes, Flynn agreed silently. Rose had been grateful to Flynn and look where it had almost led them.

'You would buy her lodgings, buy her father lodgings, and give both money for life with no guarantee?'

Tanner grinned. 'It does sound foolish.' He shrugged. 'It is a gamble. In any wager there are risks. We will just chance it. Cannot have Greythorne win, now, can we?'

On that point Flynn heartily agreed.

That evening Lord Greythorne prowled the paths of Vauxhall, stepping around the puddles that still threatened his boots. It was not his custom to trudge muddy paths, but Tannerton had raised his ire, and Greythorne needed a release.

Curse Tannerton. Ungentlemanly of him to force the swordfight in the first place, then to resort to trickery. Fencing was supposed to be elegant, like a dance of violence, with rhythm and grace. Not that back-and-forth business Tannerton engaged in. Ripping a perfectly good pair of pantaloons— Greythorne could never forgive that.

He scowled as he scanned the path. Tannerton had won a minor victory, but Greythorne would win the prize—Greythorne had plans for Miss Rose O'Keefe, and Tannerton did not figure in them.

He rubbed his hands and admired how the supple leather of his gloves moulded to his fingers. Gazing around at the women nearby, he imagined his fingers wrapping around a delicate cream-coloured neck, squeezing—

His excitement and his need grew. He began his search in earnest. Rose O'Keefe would wait for another day. This night Greythorne had hopes for another bloom to appear. She was present almost every night. He'd been watching. Tonight he was determined to get her alone.

He scanned the crowd, assured she would be easy to spot. He made a second circuit of the Gardens, running into some ladies and gentlemen of his acquaintance. He stopped to pass pleasantries with them. They could not know he had a mask in his pocket, no inkling that when he donned it he would engage in delights beyond which they could not imagine.

But at the moment, irritation battled with such delicious anticipation. If he failed to find the girl—

He heard the laughter behind him and paused by the Octagon temples to see who would pass by.

There she was, on the arm of that fool, Sir Reginald, again. Her auburn hair flaming loose over her shoulders, her gait bawdy and inviting. He stepped into the shadows and affixed the black cloth mask over his face. Then he followed her, biding his time. He knew it would come. It must come.

It did. Sir Reginald walked away from her to speak to another gentleman, and Greythorne made his approach.

'Are you left alone, miss?'

She turned, looking him up and down, too frank and bold for her own good. 'I am rarely alone for long, sir. Are you looking for company?'

He bowed. 'It would give me considerable pleasure to have your company, miss.'

She tossed her head. 'Call me Katy. Everyone does.'

'Katy,' he murmured, making sure he looked into her eyes. She returned a curious look, then smiled again.

He glanced toward Sir Reginald. 'Will your gentleman there object to my speaking with you?'

'Sir Reggie?' She looked amused. 'Do not worry over him.'

He took her arm and walked a few steps away from her former escort. 'I fear I desire more than conversation, my dear Katy.'

'Do you, sir?' She batted her eyelashes. 'I would desire more than conversation, too, but I'm holding out for a man of wealth.'

He took her hand and slipped it inside his coat to the pocket where he kept his coin purse. He let her feel the coins.

Her eyes crinkled in satisfaction. 'Shall we go, sir?'

He wrapped her arm through his and led her through the Colonnade. 'Let us not couple in some damp structure on the Dark Walk. I have a house, a wine cellar, a place where we might dally the night away. It will be as you have never before experienced. You reward will surpass your wildest dreams.'

She laughed, the laugh that had attracted her to him in the first place. He took her cheeks between his leather-sheathed fingers and squeezed, placing a wet kiss on her full, eager lips.

'My coach awaits.'

On Sunday morning Rose dressed for church, enduring Letty's taunts about pretending to be better than she ought. She needed to be outside, in some semblance of fresh air. She needed to do something to take her mind off of Flynn.

He'd consumed her thoughts all the previous day and night. She wanted him, needed him. This was what Miss Hart found with Sloane and what her other friends had found as well.

Love.

But like her mother's love, Rose's was doomed. For her love to flower would mean the ruin of Flynn's career and hers. If the marquess even knew Flynn had kissed her and almost bedded her, he would dash arrangements for Flynn's employment with the Royal Duke. Flynn's dream.

No matter if Rose were willing to choose love and risk her own career, she would not risk Flynn's.

Still, she wanted him, felt empty without him. She missed him with every fibre of her being, even to be deprived of his company for one short day. Her only consolation was knowing he would call on her tomorrow to take her to her singing lesson. It seemed an eternity to wait.

She walked to St Paul's nearby and sat in one of the back pews. The atmosphere was peaceful, and she enjoyed blending her voice with other voices in hymns so familiar she needn't use the hymnal. She recognised some women there. She'd seen them parading in Covent Garden. Their dresses were more modest and subdued this day, their faces scrubbed clean and nearly obscured by the brims of bonnets. This was their parish church, a place they ought to feel they belonged rather than looking so unsure of their welcome.

Were they praying for forgiveness, Rose wondered, for the Magdalene lives they led? Or were they praying for the chance to leave such lives behind, as Mary Magdalene had done? Rose was uncertain for what she should pray, so she merely sang the hymns and read the hymnal and listened to a sermon about love. God's love, but about love all the same.

After the service ended, she slipped out of the church, as did the other women sharing the back pews. She could not bear to return to Langley Street, so she walked the distance to call upon Katy, hoping the hour would not be too early.

Her knock at the door went unanswered for several minutes. The large footman finally appeared, looking as if his waistcoat had been hastily buttoned. He rubbed his eyes.

'I have come to call on Katy.'

He nodded and trudged up the stairs. The house seemed very quiet, and Rose regretted this impulsive visit. What if Katy were asleep? What if she were entertaining a gentleman?

But the footman appeared on the stairs with Katy behind him in a morning dress.

'Hello, Rose,' Katy said in a flat voice. 'Come on up.'

'I woke you,' Rose said apologetically.

Katy shook her head. 'I could not sleep.'

Katy led her into the dining room, where Madame Bisou stood talking to another girl. The girl left, and Madame Bisou walked over to them.

'Rose, how good of you to come.' She bussed both cheeks and turned to Katy. 'Should you not be in bed, dear?'

'In bed?' Rose asked.

Katy shook her head. 'I wanted to get up. Could not lie there, thinking all day.'

The *madame's* lips pursed.

'Are you ill, Katy?' Rose asked.

'Naw.' Katy lifted her hand to brush her hair away from her face.

Rose gently held her wrist. It was circled by reddish bruises and scrapes. 'What happened to you?'

Katy pulled her hand away and laughed. 'It is nothing.'

'Not nothing,' Madame Bisou said. 'And I could strangle that Sir Reginald—'

'Sir Reginald did this to her?' Rose said in alarm.

'Of course not,' Katy cried.

'But Sir Reginald was supposed to be looking out for you,' Madame Bisou scolded. 'You knew a man at Vauxhall hurt Iris! And you went with this one?'

Katy rolled her eyes. 'I know. You have said so repeatedly,' She put her hand on the back of a chair as if to steady herself.

'Come sit.' Rose put an arm around her.

Katy flinched.

She let go. 'I hurt you?'

'The man used a whip on her. Welts all over her,' Madame Bisou exclaimed. 'And those marks on her wrists are from leather straps.'

'Katy!' Rose eased her into a chair. 'Sit here. I will fix you a plate. What do you want?'

'I'm not hungry,' Katy said.

'I will bring you something none the less.'

Rose selected a dish of raspberries and some toasted bread and jam for Katy. She returned to the sideboard, selecting much the same for herself. Madame Bisou poured tea.

'What happened?' Rose asked as she sat down.

'I met this fellow at Vauxhall. He seemed respectable enough. Nice clothes and all,' Katy said. 'So I went with him.'

Madame Bisou crossed her arms over her chest, squeezing out even more décolletage than usual. 'It was like I said, he was one of those men—'

'Who enjoy hurting a girl.' Rose finished the sentence, remembering Madame Bisou's warning not so long ago. Rose placed her hand on Katy's. 'I cannot bear that this man hurt you. He whipped you?'

'Well, he did a little, until I got my hands free and grabbed him where it hurts.' Katy gave a brave smile, looking more like herself. 'He fell to the floor, he did, and I gathered my clothes and ran. Didn't care if I was naked. I found a place to put on my dress, though, so it wasn't so very bad.'

'Oh, Katy!' Rose squeezed her hand.

Katy pulled it away. 'I think the welts will heal. I don't think I'll have too many marks.'

'Where did he hurt you?' Rose asked.

Katy looked down at the table. 'He had rooms. Not a fancy house, I'm sure, but there was a cellar.'

'I meant where on your body?'

'Oh!' Katy shook her head at her misunderstanding. 'On my belly mostly. He was trying to hit my privates.'

Rose left her chair and hugged Katy, very gingerly. 'I am so sorry this happened to you.'

'I am sick over it.' The *madame* shook her head.

Katy pulled away from Rose, blinking rapidly. 'It is over and done. Not something to dwell on.' She cuffed Rose on the arm. 'But tell us. Have you accepted the marquess? Is that what you have come to tell us?'

Rose felt her cheeks flush. 'Not yet.'

Katy peered at her. 'You are not still acting like a wooden stick with him, are you?'

'She's just being coy,' the *madame* told Katy. 'Remember what I taught you, Katy. Act as if you care nothing for the man and he will give you the moon.' She turned to Rose. 'What has Tanner given you? Jewels? Has he offered a house yet? Tanner is an extremely generous lover. You are very fortunate.'

Rose could barely look at her. 'He has given me voice lessons at the King's Theatre. If I do well, I might perform there.'

'Voice lessons!' Katy gave a derisive snort.

'How odd,' agreed Madame Bisou.

'He gave me a ring, too, and I...I think more is forthcoming.' Rose paused. 'I am afraid my father will select this other man. Lord Greythorne.'

'Bah! Tell him not to,' said Madame Bisou. 'Greythorne is a bad one. He is one of those men like we have been discussing. I do not allow him in this place.'

Rose's eyes widened.

Madame Bisou rose. 'I must leave. Accept Tanner, *ma petite.* You cannot do better. He is generous. All the girls I have known have profited very well by the connection.' She stroked Katy's cheek. 'We must get you in front of some wealthy men, Katy. Vauxhall is not the place. You will not go back there unless it is with someone I trust. Not Sir Reginald. Bah! You must stay in the game room. I know the men who play there.'

Katy smiled. 'I'll keep an eye on who is winning, that is what I'll do.'

As soon as Madame Bisou left, Katy turned to Rose. 'The man wore a mask, Rose, but I knew who he was! He was that Lord Greythorne.'

Rose felt her face drain of blood. 'You are certain?'

Katy nodded vigorously. 'I never forget a body. Do not ever be alone with him, Rose.'

She did not wish to worry Katy. She would say nothing about her obligation to dine with Greythorne.

She said, 'I think he should be stopped, Katy. I should tell Flynn about him.'

Katy gave her a quizzical look. 'Flynn? What can he do?' She shook her head. 'Do not tell anyone about him, Rose. Promise me.'

'Why? We could stop him.'

'No,' she cried, rising from her chair. 'Nobody would believe me over an earl. But word would get out, and men would think I like that sort of thing. I could not stand it.'

'But—'

Katy's eyes pleaded. 'Promise me, Rose! You must promise me!'

Rose hugged her. 'Very well. But you have told Madame Bisou, surely?'

'No,' Katy said. 'You heard her. She knows enough about him. I'm only telling you to warn you.'

'If this is what you wish,' she murmured.

She changed the subject and cajoled Katy into eating. They talked about Miss Hart and the others and the fun they'd had together. Eventually Katy relaxed and laughed again and seemed more her vivacious self. When it came time for Rose to leave, she hugged her friend with great care and saved her tears of sympathy until she was back outside on her long walk home.

The streets were full of people now, and the hustle and bustle distracted her a little. She stopped by the market stalls and picked out some food for dinner. Her arms were laden with packages and she had to shift them all into one hand to get into the building, and then shift them again to enter their rooms.

'Here she is!' chirped Letty as Rose kicked the door closed behind her.

Lord Greythorne rose from a chair.

'Come in, Rose, dear,' continued Letty. 'We have a caller.'

Lord Greythorne crossed the room to her. 'Allow me to relieve you of your burdens.' He took the packages from her hands.

'I will take them, m'lord,' her father said, hurrying over.

Letty glared at Rose. 'For goodness' sake, take off your hat and gloves. Make yourself presentable.'

Rose left the room for her bedchamber, for once grateful to Letty for ordering her about. Her heart pounded with anger and fear. She had no desire to face this monster who had used whips and leather straps on her friend.

She took as much time as she dared taking off her gloves and hat and putting her hair in a cap. When she could delay no longer, she returned to the parlour.

Greythorne stood again. He now had a wine glass in hand.

Letty stomped over to her and snatched the cap off her hair. 'Go sit with our guest,' she hissed.

'Lord Greythorne has come himself to set a new date for dining with you,' her father said cheerfully.

'I am at your service.' Greythorne bowed to her. 'Name the day, the place, the time.'

Refusal was impossible. Her father had already accepted the money. She lifted her chin and glared at him. 'I will dine with you at Vauxhall on Tuesday, but I insist upon an open supper box.'

His smile stiffened. 'Of course. Vauxhall it shall be.'

She returned a smile equally stiff. 'If it does not rain, that is. I presume you will beg off if it rains.'

Some dangerous emotion flashed through his eyes. 'Indeed. We do not wish our clothing damaged by the rain.'

Rose thought of Flynn, hatless, heedless of the rain pouring down, soaking through his greatcoat.

'Sit down, my lord,' Letty said with exaggerated politeness, and more sharply to Rose, 'You, too, Rose. Entertain our guest.'

Greythorne waited until she sat in the chair near him.

'Our Rose has aspirations to sing in King's Theatre, my lord,' said her father in a proud tone.

'Do you, Miss O'Keefe?' Greythorne looked amused. 'You want bigger and better things than Vauxhall Gardens?'

'I am very grateful to be singing at Vauxhall, sir,' she replied. 'And I will be grateful for the chance to sing in King's Theatre as well.'

'What role do you hope to sing?' he went on.

His gaze was riveted on her, his expression conveying total interest, but the lack of feeling in his eyes frightened her.

She swallowed. 'Merely the chorus, sir.'

'A woman of your talents should desire more,' he said. This time when his eyes flicked over her, she felt as if he were seeing under her clothes.

It angered her more. 'Do you know so much of singing?'

'I know what I like.' His look was even bolder.

'Well, I think it is all foolishness,' Letty said. 'Singing in a chorus when she has been a soloist. One should never go backwards. I am sure you will agree, my lord.'

Greythorne glanced at Letty, than back at Rose. 'To enjoy the experience is the important thing.'

Rose had the feeling he was not referring to singing opera.

A knock sounded on the door.

'Now who could that be?' said Letty testily.

Rose's father walked over to the door, and Rose was glad for a reason to look away from Lord Greythorne. She twisted around as her father turned the knob and opened the door.

'Good afternoon, Mr O'Keefe.'

Flynn stood in the doorway.

Chapter Eleven

Greythorne's eyes narrowed as he spied Tannerton's man Flynn standing at the door. He was heartily sick of that cursed sycophant Irishman turning up everywhere.

'Oh, Mr Flynn…ah…do come in.' The simpleton O'Keefe shuffled aside.

At least O'Keefe acted as if this appearance was not expected. Greythorne detested anyone who withheld information from him. He knew the father would play him off against Tannerton, but he'd not be made the fool.

Flynn stepped into the room, stiffening when he saw Greythorne. Greythorne smiled inwardly in satisfaction. He'd knocked the oh-so-efficient secretary off kilter.

O'Keefe's woman laughed. She might be the commonest sort, but she had her eyes open. Greythorne made a mental note of the fact.

'Good day, Miss Dawes.' Flynn bowed, giving her more courtesy than such a base-born woman deserved. He turned to the daughter, the prize Greythorne coveted. 'Miss O'Keefe.' And finally to Greythorne. 'Sir.'

Insolent cur.

'Mr Flynn,' Rose responded in her melodious voice, no tension apparent.

Greythorne clenched his fingers around his glass. It appeared Tannerton had made headway. His Irish lackey had been treated to none of the reserve she'd shown him, to whom she'd acted as skittish as a colt. No matter. The way to win this woman was through her cowardly father and the money-grasping woman pushing him. Once won, he could make her sing a different tune.

Flynn turned back to O'Keefe. 'Forgive my interruption. I must speak with you, sir. If you name a time that would be convenient for you, I will be pleased to accommodate.'

Miss Dawes grabbed O'Keefe's arm, grinning. The man replied, 'Ah…ah…tomorrow, perhaps? Before I must leave for Vauxhall.'

'Excellent,' Flynn said.

Greythorne eased the pressure on the glass, though he'd much rather have shattered it. Tannerton was ready to make an offer, he surmised. Greythorne would discover some means of outsmarting the man. Perhaps he would devise the plan before supping with the girl two nights from now.

Flynn directed a worried glance in his direction. Good. The man ought to worry.

Rose stood up, bringing Greythorne to his feet as well. 'Would you like some tea, Mr Flynn?'

Flynn quickly glanced from him to Rose and back again. The man was rattled, Greythorne was gratified to realise.

But he frowned when Flynn's expression set with sudden decision. Flynn turned his eyes back on the girl. 'I fear there is no time. Lord Tannerton's carriage is waiting. He is most eager for your drive today. Are you quite ready?'

'Oh!' she exclaimed. 'How…how foolish of me. I shall get my hat and be with you directly.'

'You did not tell us of this, Rose!' Miss Dawes shrieked after her, but the lovely Rose had already disappeared through the doorway.

Flynn stood with a perfectly bland expression, which Greythorne would have liked to strike off his face with the slap of his leather gloves. Tannerton was moving in. Greythorne swore silently.

'Well…' Mr O'Keefe mumbled into the tension of the room.

Wheels seemed to be turning in Miss Dawes's head. She, no doubt, was trying to calculate how she might profit from this game's new hand.

Rose came rushing back into the parlour, still tying the ribbons of her hat. 'I am ready, Mr Flynn.'

Greythorne stepped forward, blocking her way. 'It has been my pleasure to pass these brief moments with you, Miss O'Keefe.' He took her hand and lifted it to his lips. 'Until we meet again.'

'Good day to you, sir.' She pulled her hand away and stepped around him.

'Where are you going, missy?' the shrill Miss Dawes cried. 'You had better behave yourself or you'll answer to your father!'

Flynn spoke up. 'A mere carriage ride, Miss Dawes. I assure you there is no reason to be concerned.'

Rose took his arm, and the two of them walked out of the door.

Greythorne swivelled to O'Keefe and his woman. 'You will receive an offer from that man. I will top it. But I warn you, do not cross me on this, if you value your lives. I mean to be the winner and I'll let no one stand in my way.'

* * *

Flynn almost carried Rose down the flight of stairs to the outside door, feeling as if the very devil was at their heels.

Greythorne.

When they reached the street, he paused.

She looked around. 'Where is the carriage?'

'There is no carriage,' he admitted. 'I invented the tale to get you away.'

'Lord Tannerton is not waiting?' she asked.

'No.'

She smiled and clutched his arm tighter.

'We had best move out of view, though. I would not put it past Greythorne to follow us.' He glanced around. 'Shall we walk to the river?'

They crossed through Covent Garden and continued to the Strand, where Flynn slowed the pace.

More private now, Flynn asked, 'What did Greythorne want? Did he make his offer for you?'

'I was not party to the whole of his conversation.' She stopped and looked at him worriedly. 'Oh, Flynn! I must take supper with him at Vauxhall on Tuesday night. I could not think how to avoid it.'

He frowned. 'You shan't be alone with him.'

'But I will,' she cried. 'I am to go alone with him!'

He touched her cheek, saying more softly, 'You shan't be alone with him. I will be nearby.'

Her eyes searched his. A breeze lifted her bonnet and played with a wayward curl. He tucked it under the brim and laced her arm through his again. They continued walking.

'I am thinking he is a bad man, Flynn.' He felt her shudder as she spoke.

When Greythorne had touched her hand, Flynn wanted to punch his face into a bloody pulp.

'I promise I will be there, Rose. You may not see me, but I will not leave you alone with him.'

She lay her cheek against his arm.

They walked down Savoy Street to the water's edge, standing below the new Waterloo Bridge that had just opened on the anniversary of the great battle. They stood side by side watching the wagons, carriages and riders cross. Flynn was only too aware of his desire to wrap his arm around her and to savour this closeness. They did not speak for a long time.

'Why did you call upon my father, Flynn?' she finally asked.

He could not look at her. 'To make Tannerton's offer.'

She moved away, ever so subtly, but suddenly a gap as wide as the Thames seemed to separate them. 'I see.'

'Lord Tannerton will make so generous an offer, Greythorne will not top it,' he said. 'We will not let him win you, Rose.'

She merely nodded.

He faced her, stroking her arms. 'Greythorne will not plague you again.'

She looked into his eyes. 'What do you know of him?'

He paused, unwilling to share the sordid details of Greythorne's perversions. 'As an eligible and wealthy earl,' Flynn said, 'he is welcome in the best houses. But he is essentially a cruel man.'

She seemed to weigh this scanty information. He thought she would speak, but she did not.

Her lids fluttered and she gazed up at him. The lock of her hair came loose again to play in the wind. The clatter of the vehicles crossing the bridge sounded in his ears almost as loud as the pounding of his blood.

He leaned down, knowing he should not, but unable to help

himself. With gentle fingers he lifted her chin, and she rose on tiptoe. He knew now how soft her lips were, how warm they felt, how she tasted. He placed his lips on hers and came home. He cupped her cheeks with his hands, fearing she would pull away before he'd taken his fill. There was nothing chaste about the kiss, although only their lips touched. It awakened his body and all his senses and sent him soaring into the heavens.

Finally, like a man waking reluctantly from a dream, he broke the contact.

'Flynn,' she whispered, sounding out of breath.

What was he to do with this passion he had neither the strength nor the desire to control? He might be betraying the man who employed him, who believed in him, and trusted him implicitly, but Rose brought him back to life, to home. With Rose, he felt like a boy again, running across emerald hills. He wished to raise his voice in song. He felt himself bursting to be free.

But he needed to bury himself again to play the dispassionate negotiator with her father, the faithful assistant with Tanner. What was painful now, merely watching Tanner talk with her, would soon become torturous when Tanner took her to his bed.

Flynn gritted his teeth. 'Tomorrow I must speak to your father. Make Tannerton's offer.'

The next day Rose waited for Flynn to call, knowing he would not escort her to King's Theatre for her lesson. Rather, he would closet himself with her father and determine her fate. When his knock sounded upon the door, she felt the familiar thrill at the prospect of seeing him, of feeling his gaze upon her like a soft caress. But she also felt despair.

Her father admitted him to the parlour. He looked so ashen, Rose feared for his health.

'Lord Tannerton is waiting below to take you to King's Theatre,' he told her. She hoped her father and Letty did not perceive the tone of doom in his words.

So, after an aching, shared, agonised glance, Rose left him standing with her father.

When she reached the outside, Tannerton walked up to her, smiling. 'Good day, Miss O'Keefe. Are you ready for your lesson? I thought you might enjoy a sporting ride to the theatre.' He gestured to the waiting vehicle, a high-perch phaeton drawn by two horses black as night and held in tow by a small man in livery.

She delayed. 'How am I to even get up there?'

He grinned. 'I will assist you.'

He climbed on to the seat and reached his hand down to her. She grasped it, and he pulled her into the seat as if she were made of feathers. As soon as she was settled, he took the ribbons in his hands, and the tiger, who had been holding the horses, ran to the back and hopped on.

He glanced at her. 'I hope you do not mind only two horses. I've raced the vehicle with four, but four on these busy streets make the journey tedious.'

'I am sure I do not know if I mind,' she responded. 'I've not been riding in a phaeton before.'

From the high, open seat Rose could see everything on the street. The novelty of it almost distracted her, but her mind was back with Flynn speaking to her father.

'Forgive me for not calling for you at your rooms. Flynn gave me strict orders to stay away.' Tannerton's expression was serious.

Perhaps his mind, too, had turned in the same direction.

'I see,' was all she could think of to say.

He gave her a wry smile. 'I suppose Flynn thought I would bollix the whole matter.'

'Bollix it?'

'I've no head for such things,' he explained. 'Flynn is the negotiator. I either say I'll pay the moon just to get the tedious business over with or wind up in fisticuffs.'

Somehow neither choice seemed to flatter her.

'Do not fear.' His voice turned kind and he placed a hand upon hers. 'Flynn will see everything turns out.'

He made a neat turn on to St Martin's Lane, tucking the phaeton between a hackney carriage and a curricle driven by a young man concentrating fiercely. Rose spun around to look at him. It was Robert Duprey, her friend Mary's husband! They must have returned from Bath. He did not notice her, however, being too intent on his driving.

'I have what I hope will be good news for you.' Tannerton looked as casual holding the ribbons as Duprey had been tense.

'Yes?' she said politely.

He cast her a quick glance. 'We have spoken with Ayrton…'

Rose could guess the *we* meant Flynn had spoken to Ayrton.

'Miss Hughes and Signor Angrisani will rehearse you for the chorus. You will perform with the opera.'

This was what she had dreamed about, but the expected elation did not come. 'Thank you.'

He stopped the phaeton in front of King's Theatre and helped her down from the high perch. Though his hands spanned her waist, she felt none of the thrill she experienced at Flynn's touch. He walked into the theatre with her and sat in the back while she made her way to the now-familiar stage.

Her lesson was gruelling, but, as before, so filled with

learning she did not mind it. She almost forgot about Flynn and her father. Miss Hughes and the *signor* taught her how a chorus must sing with one voice, how she must meld her voice with the others, like she had done in church. The girl whom Rose would be replacing came to sing the part with her.

During a break, Rose asked her, 'Do you mind if I take your place for one performance?'

The girl looked stunned at the question. 'Good heavens, no. I will make more money not performing.'

Flynn would pay the girl generously so Rose might have a dream come true. Rose corrected herself. Flynn might hand the money to the girl, but the money came from Tannerton. She wondered how much each of these people was being paid so she could sing at King's Theatre.

As the lesson came to its end, Signor Angrisani said, 'You must attend the performance tonight and as many times as you are able so you will see how you should move. Mr Ayrton has scheduled you to sing this next Saturday.'

Her life would thoroughly change.

When she walked back through the theatre to where Tannerton waited, her heart skipped a beat. Flynn was with him. She felt his eyes upon her as she made her way to him.

'Flynn?' she asked as soon as she came close.

He knew precisely what she asked. 'The offer is made,' he said. 'Your father has been compelled to wait for Greythorne before accepting.'

'Compelled?' she asked.

'Not a thing to be concerned about,' Tannerton interjected. 'Greythorne will be dealt with.'

The marquess was pacing the aisle, looking as if he were eager to leave the place. 'Shall we go?'

She nodded. He strode quickly to the entrance, leaving her to fall into step with Flynn.

'What does he mean, "Greythorne will be dealt with"?' she whispered.

Flynn shrugged. 'I presume he means we shall win. He dislikes losing.'

The phaeton was not out at the front of the building. She presumed the tiger was walking the horses around. Tannerton looked a bit more at ease out of doors.

He walked back to Flynn and Rose. 'Are you able to attend the opera tonight?' he asked her.

'Yes.' She thought she would attend even if she had to walk to the theatre and back.

'Good. Excellent.' The phaeton rounded the corner, and he walked back to the street. As it pulled up, he said, 'I believe I shall charge Flynn to take you.' He gave her a rueful smile. 'I cannot sit through the same opera twice. I hope you will forgive me.' He turned to Flynn. 'Are you able to do it? Are you able to escort Miss O'Keefe tonight?'

Flynn gave Rose a burning glance before answering, 'If you wish it.'

Greythorne had made certain he watched at the hour the secretary was to arrive at O'Keefe's lodgings. He watched the man arrive with Tannerton, watched the lovely Rose drive off with the marquess. Then he waited until the secretary left the lodgings again. Tannerton's offer was made, then.

Greythorne then had called upon O'Keefe and his avaricious woman. He'd put the devil's fear into them, telling them he would match Tannerton's offer.

The sums the marquess was prepared to settle on the beauteous Rose and her father were insane. Greythorne had no intention of paying so much. After the woman became a bore, he would cut off the money and seize the property. What could she or her father do? Go to the magistrate? Ha! Let her run to Tannerton then. He could pay for what was left of her.

Greythorne smiled inwardly, remembering the look of terror on O'Keefe's face at his parting words. A little menace always put a proper seal on a business transaction.

Chapter Twelve

That evening when Flynn helped Rose into Tanner's carriage for the trip to the theatre, her excitement was less for the performance than for being alone again with Flynn. She needed to talk to him. About the offer to her father. About singing in the opera. About kissing him.

She frowned when he did not sit next to her, taking the backward-facing seat. She looked at him questioningly.

'We must take care, Rose,' he said. 'It is madness to—to—'

'To kiss?' she said.

'Yes,' he agreed. 'To kiss.'

She stared at him, wanting to protest, but she saw the suffering in his eyes. She turned to the carriage window without attending to what she saw there. 'Tell me of your interview with my father.'

He explained the offer, and her jaw dropped in disbelief. Surely no man paid so much for the favours of a woman? Flynn explained that Tannerton wanted to ensure Greythorne bowed out.

By the time they sat in the opera box, Rose forced herself to attend to the performance. Flynn sat no closer to her there than in the carriage, but close enough that she could share with him all the impressions, all the questions, all the wonder she had kept inside the first time she had seen *Don Giovanni*. They paid particular attention to the chorus, to the role she would play, a role so small she suspected no one else in the audience gave it the slightest heed.

Rose contented herself with Flynn's company and his conversation. It might be all she had left of him.

On the ride home, he asked her, 'Do you prefer the opera, Rose? Would you rather perform there or at Vauxhall?'

She thought about it. 'The opera is so grand.' She thought of standing on the same stage as her mother had—only it was not the same stage, because that theatre where her mother performed had burned down. Still, she felt as if it were her destiny to stand in her mother's place, to sing as her mother had done, and perhaps realise the dreams her mother had harboured in her heart until childbirth had robbed her of her health.

'Which do you prefer?' she asked him, needing to stop thinking of this.

He did not hesitate. 'Vauxhall.'

Her brows rose in surprise.

'The opera is grand spectacle, I grant you,' he explained. 'But there is nothing more beautiful than you singing at Vauxhall.'

Her insides melted.

The warm feeling remained with her the rest of the carriage ride, to the door of her lodgings, to the door of her father's rooms.

She turned to him, extending her hand, keeping within the boundaries he had set for them. 'Thank you, Flynn.'

He took her hand in the dim hallway, but used it to pull her to him, to where she truly belonged. In Flynn's arms.

He kissed her, long and hard, like a man returning home from a long journey.

Tannerton sat in one of the comfortable chairs near the bay window at White's, nursing a brandy and mentally tabulating his winnings at whist. It was hopeless. He could not remember how much he started with, how many vouchers he'd written, then torn up, how much his last hand had netted him. Suffice to say he'd come out ahead. Let Flynn do the sums.

The door opened and he heard an angry voice call, 'Where is Tannerton?'

Tanner grinned. He'd wondered how long it would take. He sat tight until the man rushed towards the card room. He imagined him searching the coffee room, the game room, the privy. He started to hum, swinging his leg, watching in the direction from which the man would return.

He caught himself humming that ghastly tune those opera people had Miss O'Keefe sing over and over until Tanner thought he'd go mad if he heard it one more time. Now it was still plaguing him. He was not putting up with another voice lesson. Let Flynn take her. Flynn actually liked that ghastly music. Why could they not sing the kind of music found in dark taverns smelling of ale and the sweat of men who actually toiled for a living? Give him a bawdy song any day. At least a bawdy song had some wit.

A few moments later the man came rushing back. He grabbed one of the servants walking by. 'Where is Lord Tannerton?' he demanded.

The servant merely turned his head about five degrees and said, 'There, m'lord.'

Tanner lifted his glass in salute.

Greythorne glared at him and pushed the servant out of the way.

'Come here for some sport?' Tanner said affably. 'Or is today not your lucky day?'

'I came here looking for you and well you know it.' Greythorne's face was an alarming shade of red.

'Oh, I doubt I could guess the workings of your mind.' He pointed to one of the chairs. 'But now you've found me, have a seat and tell me what I can do for you.'

Greythorne hesitated, obviously thinking to sit would be too cordial in his advanced state of rage. But he did finally lower himself into a chair.

'We can get you some brandy, I am sure, if you have a little patience.' Tanner looked around, but the servant had left the room. 'Or some ale.'

'Never mind that,' Greythorne growled.

'Not thirsty?' Tanner acted surprised.

Greythorne looked daggers at him. 'You play an unfair game, Tannerton.'

Tanner feigned shock. 'Do you accuse me of cheating at cards? Please do not, or I shall have to call you out. I have no wish to kill you.' He reconsidered. 'Well, perhaps, not a very big wish to kill you.'

'Cut line, sir,' Greythorne cried. 'You know very well what I am talking about. You have overstepped the bounds of what is gentleman-like behaviour in contests such as this.'

'There you go again.' Tanner shook his head. 'Accusing me of not being a gentleman would also force me into a duel. With my luck I'd kill you, but be hanged for it. That seems like a terrible waste to me. The hanging part. Of course, I

could have Flynn attend to it. Then I suspect it would come
out satisfactorily—'

'Enough!' Greythorne's eyes bulged. 'You have used an
unfair advantage to win this contest, and I will not hear of it!'

Tanner leaned forward and gave him a level stare. 'Yes,
enough, sir. I have used all the cards at my disposal, and it is
not my problem if you lack a full deck.'

Greythorne shot to his feet. 'I will win her, Tannerton.
That is something you may depend upon. You forget I have
her all to myself tomorrow night.'

But Tanner could trust Flynn to make certain Greythorne
had company. 'I am shaking in my boots,' said Tanner.

'You are a disgrace.' Greythorne trembled with indignation.
'Wearing boots in the evening.'

With one last scathing look at Tanner, he stormed out of
the club.

Tanner stared down at the black boots on his feet, a bit
scuffed after wearing them all day. He looked over to the
door through which Greythorne had fled and started to lift his
glass to his lips, stopping halfway. He glanced down at his
boots again and burst into laughter, a loud boisterous laugh
that rang throughout the gentleman's club.

When Rose stood on the balcony to sing the next evening,
she tried to find Flynn among the onlookers, but she could not
see him. She found Greythorne easily enough, looking at her
as if she were the meal he would be eating that night. Her eyes
did not linger long on him.

She had warmed up her voice as Miss Hughes and Signor
Angrisani had taught her, and she rehearsed how to breathe.
There were so many new things to think about when she sang,
she almost forgot the words. She sang her usual tunes, but con-

centrated on her breathing and the volume of her voice. She was not happy with the result.

Still, her audience applauded when she finished, and she curtsied to them.

As she was walking to the stairs, Mr Hook stopped her. 'What is it, Rose? You are not singing as usual.'

She bowed her head. 'I know. I did not do well, did I?'

The music director gave her a stern look. 'No, you did not. You sing the words without the meaning behind them as if they were just notes on a page.'

'I have been taking lessons, Mr Hook,' she explained. 'Learning to breathe and to make my voice carry better. I was thinking of those things.'

He put a fatherly hand on her arm. 'Sing the words, Rose. Make them mean something. That is what they want.' He gestured in the direction of the audience.

'I shall try, Mr Hook,' she said. 'I shall do better tomorrow.'

He patted her arm. 'I am sure you will, child.'

He returned to the orchestra, and she started down the stairs, pausing halfway. She did not wish to disappoint Mr Hook, who had believed in her and had given her this important job. She began to question if she could sing at all. Would she make a fool of herself at the opera? Could one chorus member ruin a performance?

She took two more steps and stopped again, remembering that Greythorne would be waiting for her. Flynn said he would be here to protect her, that Tannerton would send two of his footmen as well. She wished she had seen Flynn. Something very easily could have prevented him from coming. Like a carriage mishap. Or an errand for Tannerton. Or a sudden fever.

She leaned against the wall for support. If he ever were hurt or sick, she could not bear it! She must not think of such things. She must handle Greythorne by herself. Madame Bisou had taught her how to fend off unwanted advances, not quite as effectively as Katy had used on Greythorne, but Rose would not allow matters to advance that far.

She entered the downstairs room, and Greythorne stood waiting there for her.

Letty rushed up to her, carrying her cloak. 'What kept you so long, Rose? It is not polite to make a gentleman wait.'

She took the cloak from Letty. 'Mr Hook stopped me.'

Letty turned to Greythorne. 'See, m'lord. 'Twas nothing at all. Mr Hook is the director, you see. It is he who employs her.'

Greythorne bowed and directed his gaze at Rose. 'I was not worried in the least.' He held out his hand. 'Shall we go, my dear?'

Rose avoided his hand by busying herself with donning her cloak. As she walked to the door, Letty hurried behind her and pulled up the hood to cover Rose's head.

'Wait,' Letty said. 'Let me see who is outside.' She slipped out of the door, only to return a minute later. 'If you leave right now, no one will see you.'

'Then shall we?' Greythorne offered his arm and Rose could think of no way to refuse it.

As they reached the outside, she shook her head so that her hood fell away and Flynn would be able to see her better. She glanced around, but could see no one watching.

'I hope you have honoured my wishes to remain in the open, sir,' she said.

He reached across and covered her hand with his own. 'I assure you, my dear, I am determined to please you.' He rubbed her hand with his thumb, a slow seductive touch.

She wanted to pull away and run from him, but he let go and acted as if nothing had happened.

'I have engaged a supper box,' he said in a smooth voice. 'And we shall have all the delicacies Vauxhall can offer.'

As they crossed the Grove, a voice called out, 'There she is!' and she heard footsteps hurrying behind her.

Her heart beat faster in the hopes that she would see Flynn behind her, but it was a younger man who caught up with them.

He doffed his hat. 'I enjoyed your performance, Miss O'Keefe,' he said, walking sideways to keep pace.

'Thank you, sir.' Unlike other nights, she was glad to be accosted by an admirer, especially since there was no sign of Flynn.

'Would—would you accept my card?' He extended it to her.

'Yes…' She reached for it.

Greythorne pulled her away. 'Leave her,' he snapped.

He hurried her to a supper box as private as one could get in the Gardens, the last one on the Grand Walk. Fewer people would pass by and those who did would be interested only in their own company, not what occurred in a nearby box. The three supper boxes next to this one were also empty, and Rose suspected he had rented those as well.

'I asked for a public place and you have made this one private.' She had no reason to speak politely to him.

He had the gall to give her a wounded look. 'I assure you, it was not my intention. This is what was offered to me.'

She did not believe him.

The thin slices of ham and tiny chickens were waiting on the table, as was a bottle of wine. There was not even a servant in sight. Several lamps lit the walk in front of them, but only one inside the supper box. She suspected it would be difficult to see into its recesses. The table had only two chairs, side by side.

He must have seen her looking at them. He said, 'I instructed the servant to place the chairs so we might watch the passers-by, and so you will feel more…chaperoned.'

So he might be close enough to take liberties, she feared. He escorted her inside the box and pulled out the chair for her to sit. When he sat in his chair he moved it even closer to hers. With a show of solicitude he poured her wine and placed some ham on her plate. She ate and drank because it saved her from speaking to him.

'Is the food to your liking?' He leaned a bit closer.

'It is satisfactory,' she replied in a flat voice.

He leaned forward even more. 'You sound unhappy, Miss O'Keefe. Tell me how I might please you?'

She faced him directly. 'It was not my choice to be here, but my father's. You paid him money for my presence. I had no choice but to comply.'

The smile on his face stiffened. 'You are not yet twenty-one. You must do your father's bidding.'

'Yes, I must,' she retorted. 'But I do not enjoy your company.'

His eyes flashed. 'Perhaps you will learn to enjoy it.'

She swept her arm over the area. 'It does not help that you choose a secluded spot when I requested a public one. Or that you arrange the chairs so I cannot move away from you. That there is not even a servant here. How am I to enjoy myself when you do everything in your power to see I do not?'

He averted his gaze for a moment, then with a sudden resolve moved his chair farther away, glancing at her in a silent question.

'That is better,' she said.

'How else might I please you?' he asked. 'Would you like to walk through the park?'

She feared Flynn would never find her if she did not stay in one place. 'No, I would not.'

'Your pleasure,' he said with some irony in his voice.

Just then the young man who had stopped her earlier came into view, dragging a friend with him. 'See? She is here. I told you she was.'

The friend came over to the box, leaning on the wall. 'Miss O'Keefe! It is you! I have come every night to Vauxhall in the hopes of meeting you.'

Rose would have been embarrassed at the admiration, except she was so relieved to see other people. 'You are too good, sir.'

He stuck out his hand into the box. 'I have this for you.' In his hand was a pretty pink rose.

She left her chair to accept it. 'Thank you, sir. I shall keep it.'

The young man put his hand over his heart in a dramatic gesture. 'It is I who should thank you!'

Greythorne also stood up. 'Run along now and leave the lady in peace.'

It was their presence that gave her peace.

The two young men backed away, throwing her kisses as they went.

'Come, sit.' Greythorne's tone was unfriendly.

She remained where she was. Where was Flynn?

Greythorne walked back to his chair and waited for her. 'I dislike them annoying you,' he explained.

She returned to her chair and he refilled her wine glass. She sipped it, her eyes on the walk. A man crossed in front of her, walking alone. She hoped that was one of Tannerton's footmen, but it could have been anyone.

Charles Dignum finished singing, and the dance music began. She listened to the first set, a country dance, and watched the walk. Once in a while a couple strolled by, but no one else.

He poured her more wine.

The ham and her nerves had made her thirsty. She sipped this third glass, but felt the wine's effects and decided she should drink no more.

'You like to dance, I think,' he said, smoothly. 'You made a pretty figure with Tannerton last week.'

'Were you watching me?' The idea made her shiver.

He widened his smile, showing his white, even teeth. 'I am not so different from your two young admirers. As smitten as they. Perhaps more.'

'Somehow I do not think those two young men would have paid my father to spend time with me.' She lifted her glass to her lips.

He gave a soft laugh, but one with no cheer in it. 'I suspect they would not have thought of it, nor had the funds.' He leaned towards her again. 'I did what would achieve my aims, Miss O'Keefe. I desire your company above all things and will do what I must to have it.'

She finished her wine after all.

He stood and extended his hand to her. 'We shall dance.'

She glanced out at the walk again, but there was no one in sight. Nothing but trees, dark and shadowy where the lamplight did not reach. At least the Grove would be filled with people.

She took his hand, feeling dizzy from the wine as she stood. Her limbs felt like malleable clay as they walked to where the dancing took place under the gazebo. She glanced up and could see her father holding his oboe, waiting for the signal to start, but he was oblivious to her distress.

The waltz began, and she had to endure Greythorne's hands upon her. As he twirled her into the dance, she felt nauseous and unsteady. He swung her around, and she had difficulty remaining upright. The lights blurred and blackness filled her vision.

Suddenly he was walking with her down a path. She must have fainted, she thought, assuming he was taking her back to the supper box.

'I would rather go back to the gazebo,' she mumbled, but he paid her no heed.

The path got darker and darker, and she realised this was not the way to the supper box.

'Let me go.' She fought to stay alert.

He pulled her into the trees where no one could see. 'I have won you, Rose. Tannerton thinks he has foiled me, but he has not.' He gripped her so tightly she could barely move.

In the vice of his arms, he put his lips on hers. Her stomach swam with nausea, and she hoped she would vomit all over him. As she struggled he rubbed against her and she felt his arousal. 'It is time to claim you—'

He started to lift her skirt. She tried to kick upwards with her knee or free her hand to hurt him as Katy had done, but to no avail. Her muscles would not obey, and he held her too tight.

'I will have you now, right here, and then I will take you with me. Tannerton may be slow to act, but I am not—'

She wrested one hand free and grabbed for his throat, squeezing as hard as she could. His grip loosened.

Just as she was about to push away, she glimpsed someone behind him, a man in a mask. The man grabbed him by the collar and pulled him off her, sending him rolling on to the still-damp ground.

Rose propelled herself into the masked man's arms. She knew it was Flynn. Greythorne slipped as he tried to pick himself up, swearing about the damage to his clothes.

'Come.' Flynn half-carried her, while Greythorne shouted obscenities behind them. Waiting on the path were her two young admirers. Tannerton's footmen, she realised.

They did not slow their pace until reaching the supper boxes along the South Walk. They paused under the last arch.

'You came,' she murmured to Flynn, blinking hard to keep herself awake.

'Do you think he knows who you were, Mr Flynn?' one of the men asked.

'I hope not.' Flynn pulled off his mask. 'But what can he do? No one would show him sympathy for forcing himself on her.'

Flynn, arm still around Rose, shook hands with the two footmen, who said they would stay in the Gardens and keep an eye on Greythorne.

'Thank you,' Rose mumbled. After they left, she put a hand to her head. 'I feel dizzy.'

'He must have drugged you, Rose.' Flynn's arms around her kept her from sinking to the ground. 'I am taking you out of here now.'

Chapter Thirteen

Flynn refused to take her to her father's rooms, to the man who had taken money and compelled her to accept Greythorne's company. He told the jarvey of the hackney carriage to drop them off at the only other place he could think of, Madame Bisou's.

In the coach she snuggled against him, her head resting over his heart. She fell asleep even before they'd pulled on to the road. Occasionally she mumbled something incomprehensible, assuring him she was asleep and not unconscious.

Even through his worry, he savoured the feel of her so trustingly nestled in his arms. He relished the warmth of her body, the sound of her even breathing, the chance to hold her without apology.

When the hackney stopped on Bennet Street, Flynn did not rouse her from her sleep, but carried her to the door. The footman answered his knock right away, recognising them both.

'What is wrong with the miss?' he asked.

Flynn did not wish to explain the whole. 'She's ill. Drugged, I suspect. Is there a bed for her?'

'Drugged!' exclaimed the large footman. He seemed to be cogitating on that. Very slowly.

'I need a room for her,' Flynn repeated. 'Tell the *madame*. Quickly!'

The man nodded. 'Follow me. There's a room up the stairs.'

Flynn followed him up three flights of stairs to a room with a bed, card table and chairs. His arms straining at this point, he placed her on the bed, while the footman lit two candles from the lamp in the hallway.

'I'll alert Madame.' The man left.

Flynn unfastened Rose's cloak and unwrapped it from her body. He pulled off her elbow-length gloves and removed her shoes. Lastly he took the pins from her hair, combing out the tangles with his fingers.

There was a brief knock on the door, and Madame Bisou entered. 'What has happened?'

'She was in the company of a man who must have drugged her wine. I found her in time,' he told her.

'*Mon Dieu,*' she cried. 'I thought we taught her of such dangers! Was she not listening?'

Flynn did not understand, but this was no time to ask what she meant. 'May she stay here?' he asked. 'It was her father who arranged this meeting with the man, you see. I cannot take her back to him.'

'That ruddy bastard,' she mumbled, French accent gone. 'Of course she may stay here.'

The door opened, and Katy burst in the room. 'Cummings said Rose was sick!'

Madame Bisou put her finger to her lips. 'Shh! She is not sick. She's been drugged.'

'Drugged!' cried Katy, so loud Rose stirred on the bed. 'What happened?'

'I think we should give her water,' Flynn said. 'To dilute what she has ingested.'

'I'll fetch some.' Madame Bisou rushed out.

Katy knelt at the bedside. 'What happened, Mr Flynn?' she asked more quietly.

'Her father arranged for her to take supper with Lord Greythorne. I—the marquess, I mean—was suspicious of him, so we put a guard on her. Greythorne paid her father for her company. He put something in her wine and tried to take advantage of her.'

Katy looked directly at him. 'Greythorne,' she repeated in a low flat voice. 'To the devil with him.'

'Indeed,' Flynn agreed. 'We—Lord Tannerton, that is—must protect her from him.'

Katy glanced away. 'Well, it is about time the marquess did something. Where is his lordship? I did not see him here.'

'I am here on his behalf,' Flynn answered her.

She turned her attention back to Rose. 'Let's get her clothes off so she can rest comfortable.'

He did not move. Undress her?

She smiled. 'Do not fear, Flynn. I'll do the undressing. You do the lifting.'

Katy removed Rose's stockings and they rolled her over on her stomach. Katy wore elbow-length gloves on her hands, so it was difficult for her to unfasten the tiny pearl buttons along the back of Rose's dress, the same dark red dress she'd worn when Flynn first set eyes on her. Flynn undid the buttons.

'This is a Paris dress,' Katy said in admiring tones.

Where had Rose purchased a Paris dress?

'Now lift her a little.' Katy bunched the skirt in her hand. 'I'll pull it over her head.'

Rose murmured when Flynn lifted her and Katy pulled the dress off. Katy unfastened her corset next. Flynn could not help but watch. Katy caught him looking, but merely grinned.

'She's a beauty, our Rose.' She sounded proprietary. 'The prettiest one.'

Flynn lifted her again, her curves soft underneath her thin muslin shift. Katy turned down the bedcovers. They soon had her tucked into the bed.

Madame Bisou returned. 'I've brought some water.'

Flynn sat on the bed, propping Rose up with one arm and putting the glass to her lips, giving her a little at a time.

Madame Bisou regarded her with pursed lips. 'We shall watch over her well, Mr Flynn. No need for you to stay.'

He felt stricken. How could he leave her without knowing for certain she would wake in the morning and be recovered?

'Oh, let him stay, if he has a mind to,' Katy said.

Flynn hastily added, 'I think Lord Tannerton would insist upon my staying.'

Katy winked at him.

'Very well.' Madame Bisou looked around the room. 'If you need anything, Katy can get it for you. I had better return to the card room.'

'Thank you, Madame,' he said.

After she left, Katy stood. 'Something tells me you would fancy a tall tankard of ale, am I correct? And maybe some bread and cheese?'

He gave her an appreciative smile. 'You are indeed correct.'

When she brought back the food, they sat at the table, eating and watching Rose.

'I did not realise I was hungry and thirsty,' Flynn said. 'Thank you, Katy.'

She gave him a pleased expression. 'Figured you had not eaten, if you were watching out for Rose.'

'I had not even thought of eating.' He'd thought of nothing but of keeping Rose safe from Greythorne.

Rose stirred, and they both waited until she settled herself again.

Katy spoke. 'You are worried about her?'

He did not quite meet her eyes. 'Well, yes. I mean, Lord Tannerton has charged me with her care. I would be remiss in my duties—'

She grinned over the rim of her tankard. 'Duties my mother's uncle. You look at her as if your breathing is about to stop, Flynn. You don't do that because your marquess told you to.'

His gaze returned to Rose, but he did not speak.

Katy persisted. 'My guess is that you've fallen head over noggin for her, haven't you?'

He tried to keep his expression impassive.

Her eyes softened. 'Must not be a treat to fall in love with the woman your employer wants you to procure for him.'

She made it sound so sordid. He was not procuring Rose for Tanner. If anything, he was trying to ensure her future. To protect her through Tanner.

He stared at her friend.

'Very well, don't admit it, but I know it's so.' She glanced back to Rose. 'She's lucky, she is. Our Rose. Lucky you were there to save her from that blighter.' Still watching her, she went on, 'You know, of all of us, Rose seemed the most— what's the word? When you don't listen but look like you are thinking about something else?'

'Distracted?' he suggested.

'Yes! That's it! Distracted.'

Flynn took a sip of his ale, trying to make some sense out of this. 'What do you mean by "of all of us"?'

She reddened. 'Lawd, I meant nothing. Nothing at all.'

He peered at her. 'Come clean, Katy. How do you and Madame Bisou and Rose know each other?'

She merely stared at him.

He persisted. 'You told me before that you went to school with Rose, but it doesn't fit. Rose has not been in England for very many months, and I would wager a pony you have never been to Ireland.'

Her eyes widened. 'I'm not supposed to tell.'

'Tell *me,* Katy. If I am to help her, I must know about her.'

She tapped on the table, still staring at him.

He glanced away and back again. 'If you believe what you do about me, you must know I would do nothing to hurt her or anyone she cares about.'

She took a long time thinking, squirming in her chair, eyes darting about the room. Suddenly she leaned forward. 'Well, it is a secret, and you must swear on your mother's grave that you won't tell anyone.'

'My mother isn't in her grave. She's alive and well in Ballynahinch.' At least he hoped she was. She was when her last letter arrived three weeks ago. Flynn promised he would reply to the letter this very day.

Katy puzzled over his words. 'Well, then, swear on your mother's grave for when she's in it. Some day.'

He was Irish enough to think that would bring bad luck. 'How about I swear on my grandfather's grave? He's the sort who would rise out of it if I broke my word.' Flynn had a flash of the old man giving him a tongue lashing that stung worse than a switch to his buttocks.

'Very well.' She screwed up her face as if it would be hard to force the words out. 'Me and Rose did go to school together. It was not that Irish school of hers. It was a…' she paused and took a deep breath '…a courtesan school.'

'A what?'

'A courtesan school. A school to teach us to be courtesans

and not merely girls in a bawdy house. This lady—and I'll never give her name, I don't care how many graves you swear on—she started the school, so as we would wind up better than we was—I mean, than we were.'

Flynn was not certain he heard correctly. 'A *lady* ran this school?'

Katy nodded. 'Right in her home on—never mind what street. See, her maid was wanting to run away to a bawdy house, but the lady did not want her to. She said girls were better off to be courtesans, like Harriette Wilson. We met Harriette Wilson, too. She came to the lady's house.'

Flynn gave her a sceptical look. The famous courtesan received in a lady's home? It was not to be believed.

'Anyway,' Katy said. 'Mary and me—Mary and I—ran away from the house where we were working because we heard the lady talking about it to Mrs Rice and we found our way to the lady's house where she had the school.'

'Mrs Rice?'

Katy narrowed her eyes. 'The abbess who ran the bawdy house. She was a bad lot.'

'Rose was in a bawdy house?' He did not want to believe this.

'Not in our bawdy house,' Katy replied. 'Truth to tell, I'm not sure where she came from. Ran away from her father, I think. She heard Mary and me talking on the street, and she came with us to Miss H—' She clamped her mouth shut.

'So the three of you went to this lady's house because she had a courtesan school?' He was still trying to comprehend this.

She gave him a patient look. 'Well, there was her maid and that made four of us. The school was started for us, and Madame Bisou was hired as our tutor.'

'But…why?'

'I told you why.' She sounded exasperated. 'Because the

lady thought a courtesan had the best kind of life. A courtesan could pick and choose what men to bed, and make lots of money, too, and no man could take her money away from her, like a husband can do.'

There was some logic to this. It was, after all, the excuse he made to himself when he'd negotiated with Tanner's mistresses in the past.

Flynn took a long sip of his ale, trying to digest this still incomprehensible information. He'd only fleetingly harboured the illusion that Rose was an innocent—she'd too often alluded to a past, after all—but if she had so single-mindedly pursued the life of a courtesan, why did she hesitate to accept Tanner's interest? Tanner was a courtesan's dream.

He looked at Katy. 'How is it that Rose did not come here with you? Why was she with her father?'

Katy threw up her arms. 'You ask me that? I cannot know. You might as well ask me why the others chose to get married. Especially Mary, running off with that numskull, Du— I mean, getting married was one of those things we were taught not to do. Why shackle yourself to some man who takes your money and then goes off and gives it to a mistress? Better to be on the other side.'

Another all-too-true statement, Flynn thought.

They fell silent until Katy said, 'Come to think of it, Rose met up with her father that night we all went to Vauxhall. That's when Mr Hook let her sing. I think the old man talked her into coming back to live with him. If she'd asked me, I'd have told her she was daft.'

They finished eating, and Flynn moved his chair closer to Rose's bedside. He gave her more water, propping her up again with his arm. Her eyes opened and she smiled.

'Flynn,' she whispered.

She drank a few sips, licking droplets from her lips. He returned the glass to the bedside table and helped her settle under the covers again. Her eyelids soon grew heavy again, fluttering closed finally in sleep.

He glanced up to see Katy watching him, sympathy in her eyes.

Rose struggled awake, eager to escape disturbing dreams of dark shadows and sinister creatures.

She forced her eyes to open, though the light from the window hurt them. She blinked. The room was strange. She sat up in alarm.

Flynn was there, rising from a chair next to the bed. 'It is all right, Rose. You are safe.'

'Flynn!' She reached for him and he enfolded her in his arms. In his embrace, she indeed felt safe.

He released her and gestured to the table in the centre of the room. Katy, head resting on her arms, was fast asleep.

'I brought you to Madame Bisou's,' he told her. 'I could think of no other place.'

'Greythorne?' she rasped.

'I am certain he cannot know where you are.' He brushed her hair away from her forehead.

There was so much she could not remember. She recalled the supper box and Greythorne asking her to dance. She recalled feeling dizzy, then all was dark and she struggled to free herself.

'You rescued me.' She remembered the masked face that had been Flynn's.

His expression acknowledged this. 'Greythorne does not know who rescued you, although he may suspect. We must decide what to do about him, but that can be attended to later. How do you feel?'

She grabbed his hand and held on to it. 'My head aches.'
She took in his face, the stubble of beard shadowing his jaw.
He was dressed only in his shirtsleeves, neckcloth untied,
waistcoat unbuttoned.

He sat in the chair next to the bed, still holding her hand.
She glanced down at herself and realised that she was dressed
only in her shift. She ought to be embarrassed at her disha-
bille—and his—but she was not. It seemed natural they should
be together this way.

She glanced over at Katy. 'Katy stayed all night, too?'

He nodded.

'Is she feeling well enough?'

He looked puzzled. 'Yes, she seemed well.'

Rose tried to clear the muddle from her mind. 'Did Greythorne put something in my wine?'

He nodded. 'Laudanum, most likely.'

'I'm thirsty.'

He took his hand from hers and poured her some water.
She drank eagerly.

When she handed the glass back to him, she reached up to
run her finger along the scratchy beard on his jaw. 'Thank you,
Flynn. For everything.'

She slid her hand around the back of his neck and urged
him toward her, her heart racing at the anticipation of his lips
upon hers.

There was a rustling behind him. 'Aw, I fell asleep!'
Katy cried.

Rose let go and Flynn sat back in the chair.

Katy stretched. 'Are you awake, Rose?'

'Yes,' she said. 'But I only just woke. Flynn said you
stayed with me the whole night. I hope that was not too
much for you, Katy.'

'Naw.' Katy grinned. 'I figured you needed a chaperon.' She stood and stretched again. 'Anybody hungry? I'm hungry as a duck.'

'Would you like some breakfast, Rose?' Flynn asked.

She nodded. 'Some tea would be lovely.'

'Can we bring her some?' Flynn asked Katy.

'No,' Rose said, putting her hand on his arm. 'I would rather get up.'

Katy walked over and leaned her elbows on Flynn's shoulders. Rose narrowed her eyes at this intimate gesture.

'Tell you what,' Katy said. 'I'll find you a nice dress to wear, and we'll get you fixed up to come to the supper room. Mr Flynn can join us there.'

Katy breezed out of the room.

Flynn stood. 'Forgive my appearance.'

Rose thought he had never looked so handsome.

He turned his back and hurriedly buttoned his waistcoat. As he reached for his coat, he caught her gaze again. It was just as if he'd touched her, the sensation was so intense. She wished he would cross the room to her. She wished he would share her bed in the way men share with women, the way he wanted her to share with Tanner.

Instead he put his coat on and sauntered over to the window.

Katy returned, carrying a pale pink day dress. 'Now off with you, Flynn. Ask Cummings to give you a razor. You look a fright.'

Rose wanted to protest, but he gave a wry smile. 'I must indeed.' He glanced at Rose again, a look that seared her senses. 'I will see you in the supper room.'

Before she could form a reply, he left.

Katy started to help her out of bed. 'Are your legs wobbly?'

'My knees feel a bit weak,' she responded.

Katy laughed. 'My knees would be weak too, with a man like that looking at me.'

Rose peered at her. 'What man?' she asked.

Katy looked at her as if she were a lunatic. 'Flynn, of course. He looks at you like a cat looks at a dish of cream.'

'Oh, Katy!' Rose leaned against her friend. 'Do not say it. He merely acts for Lord Tannerton.'

Katy hugged her. 'Do not try to flummox me, Rose. The two of you look like April and May. The thing is, what are you going to do about it?'

Rose sighed, pulling away and walking over to the pitcher of water and washing bowl. 'There is nothing to do about it. Flynn is employed by Tannerton, and Tannerton wishes to offer for me.' So long as Tannerton held the key to Flynn's future success, she could not risk turning him against Flynn.

Rose dampened a towel and wiped her face.

Katy went on. 'Tannerton's no fool, you know. He's bound to catch on.' Katy tapped her forehead. 'I know! What you do is take Tannerton up on his offer, get a house out of him and who knows what else, and then when he tires of you, you'll have the all-clear with Flynn, plus a tidy sum to live on, too.'

Katy's practicality sounded sordid.

Rose washed herself off, while Katy fetched her corset, saying, 'I tell you, if that Flynn took a fancy to me, I might give him a jolly run for his money.'

Rose felt as if she could not breathe, although it had nothing to do with Katy tightening the corset's laces. It was probable Flynn would turn to some other woman. Why not Katy, so lively and bright and sympathetic?

'Are you interested in Flynn, Katy?' Rose tried to sound calm, but her voice wobbled.

Katy laughed and gave her a quick hug. 'I'm interested in any man, long as he has money.'

It was not a particularly reassuring answer.

Katy helped her on with the dress and brushed her hair, tying it back in a ribbon. They were soon entering the supper room. Flynn, clean-shaven again, was seated with Madame Bisou.

The *madame* sprang from her chair and hurried over to Rose. 'How are you feeling, Rose, *ma petite?* What a fright you gave us.'

'Just a little shaky, Madame,' she said.

Flynn stood and pulled out a chair for her. 'I will fix you a plate. What would you like?'

'Some toast and jam, perhaps?'

Flynn brought her the food, and Madame Bisou poured the tea. They said little while she nibbled on her piece of toast. She ate slowly, feeling a touch of nausea.

Flynn finally spoke. "We must consider what to do next. I confess, I do not want you to go back to your father's house.'

'Of course she must not go back there!' cried Madame Bisou.

'My father will be worrying about me,' Rose said.

'Mr Flynn can send word to him that you are in a safe place.' The *madame* grasped her hand and squeezed. 'You must stay here, Rose, dear, for as long as you like.'

Flynn nodded in approval.

'I...I thank you, Madame,' Rose said, moved by the woman's generosity. She glanced at Flynn.

Flynn gave her a steady look. 'You must let me deal with your father. He will want to follow Lord Tannerton's wishes. Trust me, Rose. We will keep you safe.'

With Tannerton's name and Flynn's energies, Rose had no doubt anything could be done.

Chapter Fourteen

When Flynn walked into the Audley Street town house, Tanner was just descending the stairs.

'Where the devil have you been?' Tanner's typical affable tone was notably absent.

Flynn glanced at the footman in the hallway who was making an ill-disguised effort to appear as if he were not listening to every word. 'I'll tell you the whole, if you have a moment. In the library?'

Tanner led him directly to the library. He turned to face Flynn as soon as Flynn closed the door. 'My men said you left them in Vauxhall and that you had Miss O'Keefe with you.'

Flynn answered, 'That is so. Wiggins and Smythe told you about the rescue, no doubt. Greythorne drugged her wine. I brought her to Madame Bisou's and stayed to make certain she was recovered. I thought that a better plan than taking her to her father's residence.' Flynn felt a pang of conscience. His actions had been more complicated by emotion than this dispassionate explanation implied.

Tanner gave him a level gaze. 'You could not have sent word to me of this last night?'

Flynn felt his face grow hot. 'I confess, I never thought of doing so.' His mind had all been on Rose.

Tanner waved his hand. 'It is of little consequence. She is well, I hope.'

'Yes. She's unharmed.'

Tanner sank into a chair. 'I was up half the night imagining Greythorne had done you an injury. Finally sent one of the men to his residence, but all was as I had intended.'

'Greythorne seemed more worried about his soiled clothing than about chasing us.'

Tanner grinned. 'That is what Wiggins said. He said, "the man was cursing something awful, m'lord."' Tanner mimicked his footman's accent perfectly.

Flynn peered at Tanner, the earlier comment just registering in his brain. 'You sent someone to Greythorne's residence?'

Tanner crossed his legs and leaned back in the chair. 'I do occasionally rouse myself to have a thought or two. If Greythorne had done a mischief, I wanted to be prepared to deal with it.'

Or to send someone else to deal with it, Flynn thought.

Tanner absently swung one leg up and down, certainly not exerting himself at this moment to think through what they must do next. Flynn felt out of patience with him, although Tanner was truly not behaving at all out of the ordinary.

Flynn spoke more sharply than he intended. 'We must make plans, my lord. There is Greythorne to consider. He is certain to try again. And we cannot return Miss O'Keefe to her father. He is not strong enough to protect her.'

Tanner grinned. 'Oh, we need not fear Greythorne.'

Easy for Tanner to make light of this. He had not seen Greythorne's hands all over Rose.

Flynn frowned. 'He is an unpredictable enemy, Tanner. He cannot be expected to behave like a gentleman.'

Tanner laughed. 'Indeed!'

'Some gravity, if you please, sir.' Flynn started to pace. 'Miss O'Keefe's well being is at stake.'

Tanner's leg swung up and down, up and down. 'It is not as bad as all that. You might be shocked to discover, my dear Flynn, I have actually exerted myself to deal with Greythorne.' He looked heavenward. 'An inspired solution, I might add.'

Flynn stopped pacing. 'What did you do?'

Tanner uncrossed his legs and leaned forward, mischief in his eyes. 'I asked his Royal Highness, the Duke of Clarence, to *require* Greythorne's company.' He pulled his timepiece from his pocket and opened it. 'In fact, they ought to be on the road to Brighton this very hour.'

Flynn gaped at him. 'You asked the Duke what?' He laughed. 'Greythorne must accompany the Duke to Brighton?'

Tanner grinned. 'His Royal Highness is somewhat of a romantic, you know, so he was quite willing to foil Greythorne's ungentlemanly interference in my interests. Greythorne was mad as a hornet about it. Saw him at White's.'

Flynn gaped at his employer. 'I am all admiration. That was well done, indeed.'

Tanner's expression turned pensive. 'Not quite so well done. I fear my machinations precipitated that rash act of his. I had not thought he would sink so low.'

Flynn frowned. Luckily they'd known enough to keep watch over her.

'I need to speak to her father.' Flynn started pacing again, half-frustrated, half still annoyed at Tanner. 'It is that Dawes woman who is the real problem there, however.'

Tanner shrugged. 'Give them money.'

Flynn turned around.

Tanner gave him a patient look. 'Regard me, Flynn. Miss Dawes is motivated by greed, and the father is weak. If we cut them out, the woman will remain a thorn in our sides, plaguing us, Miss O'Keefe and her father from now until the girl reaches her majority. I say give the father an outrageous sum of money, send them off to Bath, and be done with them.'

Tanner's approach would be effective. It was a rare problem that could not be solved by throwing great sums of money at it. It was typically Flynn's job to find some more economical solution.

Flynn would be happier to see Greythorne—and Miss Dawes—transported to Botany Bay, although the law would likely not consider their offences as warranting such a punishment. The rights of one minor girl were practically non-existent, after all.

'You are certain you wish me to spend your money in this way?' Flynn asked.

Tanner shrugged. 'Send them to Bath. Unless you think you can pack them off to Scotland.'

Scotland? There's an idea, thought Flynn.

'I'll attend to it right away.'

After donning clean linen, Flynn set off for Langley Street to confront Rose's father. He entered the building and climbed the stairs with determination. As he neared the door, he heard voices and sounds of movement inside.

He knocked and all sounds ceased. 'Mr O'Keefe?' he called through the door. 'It is Flynn.' More silence. 'Please open, sir. You will want to see me.'

He put his ear to the door and could hear footsteps approaching.

'Are you alone?' O'Keefe asked through the closed door.

'I am alone,' Flynn replied.

Flynn stepped back from the door and watched a shadow darken the keyhole. O'Keefe was peeking through it. The door opened a crack, and Mr O'Keefe peered out before opening it wider.

'So sorry. I must be careful, Mr Flynn.' O'Keefe said.

'Careful of what?' Flynn asked.

O'Keefe stepped aside to let the younger man enter. 'Do you know where my daughter is?' he asked. 'She went off with some fellows last night.'

'She's safe,' Flynn assured him.

Her father patted his arm, his eyes moist.

Flynn walked in. The room was in disarray. Clothes strewn about. A trunk half-filled. Papers piled on tables. Letty Dawes, looking haggard, walked out from the bedchamber carrying a portmanteau.

'You are leaving.' Flynn surmised.

'Indeed we are.' Miss Dawes gave a dramatic huff. 'No thanks to that girl of his.' She gestured angrily towards O'Keefe. 'Ran off last night, she did. Left that rich Lord Greythorne, mud all over him, spitting mad, I'll tell you. He said he'd make good his threat and I've a mind he means it.'

'His threat?' Flynn asked.

Mr O'Keefe spoke up. 'Threatened our lives if Mary Rose did not return and accept his money—'

'He was going to give us money, as well. More than that marquess,' added Miss Dawes. 'Just like her to go off with some no-good fellows. Common blokes, his lordship told us. Flirting with her while she was supposed to be cosying up to him. I tell you, she did it on purpose, just to cut her poor father out.'

O'Keefe looked away, shamefaced.

'I am beginning to understand.' Flynn frowned. 'But I cannot yet comprehend why you are leaving.'

O'Keefe glanced at him. 'He said he would kill us if we don't give him my Mary Rose.' His voice broke.

'As if we knew where to find the girl.' The wattles on Miss Dawes's neck shook with emotion. 'In some common man's bed, giving it away just to spite us! If that marquess of yours had only made his offer sooner. I do not care if he is rich and has a lofty title, he is a slow-top and a fool!'

'Letty,' O'Keefe said in a low voice. 'Mr Flynn says Mary Rose is safe.'

'Hmmph!' She put her fists on her hips. 'Well, that does not help us, does it?'

Flynn barely maintained his bland, negotiating demeanour in the face of this outrageous woman. 'You feel Greythorne will make good his threat?'

Miss Dawes wailed, 'Of course he will! That girl has all but destroyed us, and what do we have to show for it? The paltry sum his lordship gave us for her to be nice to him last night. And trinkets!' She thrust her hand in his face, the emerald ring still on her finger. 'I've half a mind to take her dresses with us and sell them. If we had a bigger trunk that is exactly what I would do, but that trunk she had in her room is much too small.'

Flynn spoke quickly, thinking even faster. 'I am certain the marquess would lament this turn of events. He is a sympathetic man.' This was a deal Flynn never guessed he'd be making.

'We will die of starvation!' Miss Dawes cried. She flung herself into a chair.

'Now I can still work, Letty, dear.' O'Keefe patted her shoulder.

'I concur that you must get away,' Flynn broke in. 'The marquess with help you. Where would you like to go?'

'Where can we be safe?' wailed Miss Dawes.

'Glasgow,' said Mr O'Keefe in a quiet voice. 'It is a big city.'

'Glasgow?' Miss Dawes huffed.

'I could find work there,' said O'Keefe.

Flynn dipped his hand into his coat pocket. 'The marquess will help you.' Flynn withdrew the money he'd been carrying. 'Five hundred pounds.' He handed it to Mr O'Keefe. They could survive on the interest of five hundred pounds.

Miss Dawes snatched the notes from O'Keefe's hand and counted.

'Glasgow,' Flynn repeated. There was opportunity in the Scottish city. Many a merchant there became rich from the city's easy access to shipping, and would want a rich man's entertainment. A musician like O'Keefe might well find work.

'Glasgow.' Miss Dawes smiled, clutching the bank notes to her ample breast.

Later that afternoon, Rose gazed out of the bedchamber window where she'd spent the night. Flynn had assured her she need not miss her voice lesson if she felt well enough to attend. Her head ached just a little, but not enough to keep her away.

She caught sight of Flynn crossing the street at the end of the road. Leaning against the window frame, she watched his progress. He moved with such purpose, tension in his stride, as if he were so intent upon where he was going, he never stopped to think if that was where he wanted to be.

As he approached the door, Rose could no longer see him without hanging out of the window. She stepped away and smoothed her skirt. She hurried to the mirror, checked her hair, and pinched her cheeks to add some colour to her face. After one more quick look in the mirror, she left the room. As she descended the stairway, she heard laughter. When she reached the hall, Katy had her arm through Flynn's.

Katy glanced up and saw Rose. 'Look who is here, Rose! I'm trying to steal him away, but he'll have none of it.'

Rose found no humour in Katy's jest. 'Mr Flynn goes where he pleases, I am sure.' She bit her tart tongue.

Katy laughed some more. 'He ought to go where he pleases.'

Katy released Flynn. Rose felt her insides melt as his gaze followed her progress down the stairs.

'I am ready,' Rose said in a quiet voice.

'Are you certain you feel well enough?' His expression was full of concern.

She nodded. 'I want to attend the lesson.'

'Let us go then.' He offered her the arm that Katy relinquished.

'Enjoy yourself, Rose!' Katy exclaimed.

Feeling guilty for her jealous thoughts, Rose stepped away from Flynn and hugged Katy.

When they were outside, Flynn said, 'We should find a hack.'

'Can we walk?' she asked.

The day was warm, but it felt good to be free of the confines of the four walls. Besides, it would give her more time with him.

'As you wish,' he said.

They started on their way and, while they walked, he told her about his visit to her father.

'Is my father in danger?' she asked, her brow furrowing.

'I doubt it.' He pulled her arm tighter through his. 'Greythorne is no fool. Murder would be a foolish risk.'

Rose thought Greythorne very capable of murder. Anyone who could do what he did to Katy…

'I am glad my father is leaving,' she said. 'I am wanting

him to be safe. But Greythorne will come after me, will he not? He will be coming to Vauxhall.'

Flynn placed his hand upon hers where she clutched his arm. 'No need to fear. He is gone for the moment.' He explained the trip Lord Tanner had arranged for Greythorne.

She widened her eyes. 'Lord Tanner knows the Prince so well to ask such a favour?'

'I suppose he does,' Flynn said.

Then surely Tannerton would be successful in convincing the Prince to employ Flynn.

Flynn went on, 'All that remains is to find you lodgings and hire servants to attend you.' His voice was matter of fact, but Rose felt like a door was slamming.

'I have sent one of Tannerton's maids and a footman to your father's building to pack up your clothes and your pianoforte and have them sent to Madame Bisou's.'

He had remembered her most precious possession—her pianoforte. 'Thank you, Flynn.'

It was bittersweet to have Flynn walking next to her, the man she wanted to love her, when she was more and more destined to be in the bed of another. She delighted in Flynn's touch, his scent, and how the sun lit his face. The memory of how he'd looked that morning, rumpled and unshaven, made her tremble.

At King's Theatre Miss Quinn and Signor Angrisani were all smiles at her progress. They rehearsed her in the chorus part, walking her through it, showing her where she would stand, how she should move. She would perform on Saturday. She would perform in King's Theatre, as her mother had done.

When the lesson was over, Mr Ayrton escorted her through the theatre, but instead of finding Flynn waiting for her, Lord Tannerton stood there. Flynn was nowhere in sight.

'My lord.' Rose curtsied.

'Miss O'Keefe.' Tannerton smiled at her.

Mr Ayrton spoke to him. 'She must practise each day this week, but she is welcome to join the chorus on Saturday.'

'So I heard you say.' Tannerton offered his hand to the man. 'Thank you.'

When Ayrton left them, the marquess said, 'My carriage is waiting. I came to escort you to Madame Bisou's.'

She could not refuse. It was time for her to accept what he offered.

Inside the carriage, she said, 'I have much to thank you for, my lord.'

He waved a hand. 'I assure you, all was easily done.'

Easily done by Flynn. She caught herself in the unfair thought, remembering what Tannerton had done. 'Greythorne is far away, because of you,' she said. 'Flynn said you asked the Duke of Clarence.'

He laughed. 'Flynn told you of that, eh? It was an inspired idea, I'll agree.'

She could not contain her curiosity. 'And did you convince his Royal Highness to employ Mr Flynn?'

'I did,' he said proudly. 'Have not told Flynn yet, however.' He gave her an impish look. 'You must keep the secret a little longer.'

'Yes, my lord.'

She could not help but be disappointed that he'd been successful so soon. As long as Flynn remained in Tannerton's employ, she'd at least be able to see him, even if it was as Tannerton's mistress. When Flynn went to a Royal palace to work, she would never see him again.

Tanner smiled at her. 'Would you allow me to escort you to Vauxhall this evening? Perhaps afterwards we could eat supper there.'

Of course she must accept this invitation. It would be churlish not to. Would he think she was accepting more?

'My lord,' she began, 'so much has happened. I...I am not certain I am...'

He seemed to take no offence at her discomfort. 'If you like, Flynn and your friend Katy can come as well.'

She released a relieved breath. 'Then I would most graciously accept.'

Chapter Fifteen

⟨⟨⟨⟩⟩⟩

The next two days followed the same routine. Flynn arrived to take her to her lesson, and Lord Tannerton escorted her back. They all four went to Vauxhall and supped afterwards. Rose consoled herself with the pleasure of having at least one dance with Flynn each night.

She forced herself to think only of performing in the opera in her tiny chorus part.

On the Saturday of her performance, Flynn brought her to King's Theatre early where the rest of the company rehearsed with her. One of the girls let it slip that they had been paid well for their time.

Flynn had been very quiet on the walk to the theatre, and she'd sensed the pent-up emotion inside him. Was he suffering as much as she? She was afraid to ask. Once in the theatre, he wished her luck, giving her a kiss on the forehead she could feel still, though hours had passed and the performance was about to begin.

Then she was onstage performing her minor part in *Don Giovanni*. Rose imagined her mother walking a stage much like this one, looking out into the same vastness of the theatre audience, wearing the same heavy paint on her face and the same sort of costume. Though Rose's nerves jangled throughout the performance, she did not miss a cue and she remembered all the lyrics.

Lord Tannerton, Flynn and Katy were in Tannerton's box, Rose knew. Tannerton—through Flynn, of course—had even included Madame Bisou. Rose could imagine them in their seats watching her. She knew Flynn's eyes would be upon her the whole time. She knew he wished her well.

She managed to get through the entire performance without a mistake. When the final curtain call brought shouts of 'Bravo!' for Miss Quinn, Signor Angrisani and the other principals, Rose felt a rush of relief. She had done it. She had performed in King's Theatre.

Afterwards, dressed again in her own gown, the other girls took her with them to the theatre's green room, the room where gentlemen came to meet the female performers. She endured many frankly admiring glances from the waiting gentlemen before she saw Lord Tannerton standing with Mr Ayrton.

'Ah, here she is.' Tannerton stepped forward to take her hand.

She dropped into a curtsy.

'You did very well, Miss O'Keefe.' Tannerton smiled at her. 'At least as much as I know of it. Flynn said so, in any event, and he knows of such things. I can only say I enjoyed it.'

Mr Ayrton bowed to her. 'I have been speaking to the marquess, as you can see. We have made a nice arrangement. If you should like to remain in the chorus, it will be my pleasure!'

Rose surmised the 'arrangement' meant some sort of monetary compensation for having her perform with the company, employment based on the fact that she had a wealthy and generous patron.

She managed an appreciative expression. 'How kind of you, sir.'

Tannerton offered his arm. 'Shall we be going? Our party awaits.'

She walked out on Tannerton's arm, eager to see Flynn, wanting to explain to him how she'd expected her spirits to soar with joy at having her dream come true. She was happy to have performed at King's Theatre, but it had not compared to the first time she sang at Vauxhall, that magical evening when Mr Hook let her sing one song. Flynn would understand.

As they walked down a hallway, the marquess leaned down to her, his eyes twinkling. 'I have a surprise for you.'

She was not sure she wanted more surprises.

They turned a corner and there waiting with Flynn and Katy were Mary and Lucy, the girls she knew at Miss Hart's, and their husbands. Rose was speechless in disbelief.

Tannerton whispered in her ear, 'Surprise.' He gave her a little nudge.

She ran towards them, Mary, Lucy, and Katy meeting her halfway with hugs and tears.

'Madame Bisou sent us messages that you were performing,' Mary said. 'What a lovely surprise!'

'It was grand!' Lucy said. 'I've never seen the like, and to think you were there on that big stage!'

'Oh, never mind that!' Rose cried. 'How are you both faring? Is there any news from Miss Hart—I mean, Mrs Sloane?'

Lucy gave a shy smile. 'I call her "Miss Hart," too. Can't help it.'

'Lucy has a letter. Tell her, Lucy!' Mary said.

'Later,' Lucy said. 'I have it with me. But say hello to Elliot!'

Mr Elliot, Lucy's husband, stepped forward and Rose

could not help but give him a hug, and Mr Duprey, Mary's husband, as well.

'So good,' Duprey said. 'Nice performance. First-rate.'

'Thank you.' Rose wiped tears from her eyes. 'I'm thinking it is good to see you, too. I have missed you so. I did not know you had returned to town.' The Dupreys were to have spent the summer in Bath, and the Elliots at Mr Sloane's country estate.

'Come, let us depart.' Lord Tannerton shooed them on. 'They are to dine with us, Miss O'Keefe. You shall have plenty of time for conversation.'

At Madame Bisou's, Tannerton and Flynn talked with Elliot and Duprey while Rose read Miss Hart's letter, all the way from Venice. Her friends looked on.

'Oh, she is increasing!' Rose exclaimed, the news oddly making her feel like weeping.

Mary leaned over to her and grasped her hand. 'I am, too.'

'As am I!' Lucy added.

Tears did spring to her eyes then. Her three friends, all to have babies. She hugged them again.

The meal was a lively affair, with much conversation and many toasts, most led by Tannerton, who seemed bent on making the ladies laugh. Rose noticed that Mr Elliot and Flynn were often conversing together. After the meal she found herself near Elliot.

'Do you know Mr Flynn, then?' she asked Elliot, who was Mr Sloane's secretary.

He answered her, still sipping a glass of wine, and more tipsy than she'd ever seen him. 'We've met a time or two. He's a good man.'

That made Rose feel proud, though she had no right to pride about Flynn.

Elliot went on, 'They say he's destined to great things. An

MP or something. It is known that Tannerton is grooming him for more.'

For a prince, thought Rose.

She glanced over at Flynn, at the moment talking with Duprey. Flynn looked up at the same time. Their eyes met.

After Elliot moved away, Katy sidled up to Rose. 'What will you do?'

Rose blinked. 'About what?'

'About him.' Katy cocked her head in Flynn's direction.

Rose looked at Katy, unable to disguise her emotions. 'I do not know, Katy. I do not know.'

When the first light of dawn appeared in the city sky, the party broke up. A very sleepy Mary and Lucy left in the arms of their husbands. Rose watched them. They both had chosen not to become courtesans. Instead they had fallen in love.

Now they were both so happy.

Tannerton walked up to Rose. 'I'll bid you goodnight, Miss O'Keefe.' He swayed from too much drink.

She dropped into a formal curtsy. 'Thank you again, my lord.'

He took her arm to make her rise and spoke with good humour. 'None of that. I'd rather a kiss.'

Rose panicked. He wanted her to kiss him? She glanced wildly around the room for Flynn, but he was busy assisting Katy to stand. Katy laughed shrilly and wrapped her arms around Flynn's neck.

Rose glanced up at Tannerton, still smiling down at her. She lifted her face to him.

He gave her a kiss on her lips. His lips were as soft as Flynn's. They were as moist and as warm. They even tasted of the brandy he'd been drinking. But that was all.

He broke contact and gave a crooked grin. 'Flynn will make the next arrangements.'

She knew what he meant, and her heart depressed to a cavernous state. She glanced over at Flynn again. Katy was no longer wrapped around him, but could be seen staggering out of the room. Flynn gazed back at her, eyes burning into her, his anguish unguarded and as clear to her as her own.

In the next few days, Flynn walked around like an automaton, winding himself up in the morning and wearing down by nightfall, falling into bed with eyes open, unable to sleep.

His task had been to find a house for Rose. A place convenient for Tanner, who preferred his mistresses to be in easy walking distance. There were plenty of such residences close by St James's Street and the gentlemen's clubs. The difficulty was finding one for sale or lease, one that would provide the comfort Flynn wished Rose to have.

Even more difficult was examining bedchamber after bedchamber and having to imagine Rose and Tanner sharing the bed. The images were too vivid, as vivid as the memory of Tanner kissing her, a now nightly occurrence Flynn was forced to witness when they escorted Rose to Vauxhall, then back to Madame Bisou's.

To his dismay, Flynn discovered a small set of rooms on Great Ryder Street, tucked away and private, but not too far from White's or Madame Bisou's, which should please Rose. Two parlours on the main floor, a bedchamber and sitting room on the first floor. Maids' rooms above that. The kitchen was in the basement, as well as more servants' rooms. The place was furnished so tastefully not a thing need be changed—except to find a corner for Rose's pianoforte.

He made the deal, even managing to get the price lowered significantly, a last-ditch effort to sabotage himself that failed. His success made him inexplicably furious.

She could move in within days. It had been equally as easy to line up servants, a housekeeper, a cook, a housemaid, a lady's maid, and a footman. She had one more week to sing at Vauxhall. She could move in before that week was over, and then she would be Tanner's.

But as long as she performed at Vauxhall, he could see and listen to her as he had that first night. Perhaps if she accepted the offer at King's Theatre, he could watch her there, where her beautiful voice would be lost in the meld of other voices. The thought did not cheer him.

Still, on stage she could be a dream, but everywhere else she must be Tanner's mistress. The very idea seemed to unleash some deep Celtic rage, heretofore lying dormant in Flynn's Irish soul. Perhaps Tanner would even send him on errands for her, purchasing and delivering gifts, arranging and cancelling meetings.

His fury burned hotter.

Flynn thought of the letter he'd posted that morning, addressed to his mother, informing her he was coming home. He had been ready to do battle if Tanner protested, but Tanner approved the request without question. Flynn planned to be gone no more than two months. Surely he could recover from this madness in two months.

Feeling as if he would combust from the inside, he walked back to Audley Street to inform Tanner the residence was acquired.

He entered the game room where the Marquess, in his shirtsleeves, played at billiards.

Upon seeing him, Tanner threw him a cue stick. 'Join me in a game.' He set up the red ball and aimed his cue ball for it. It hit, the red ball missing the pocket by a hair.

Flynn was determined Tanner would not win the game. He

placed his cue ball on the table and made the shot, nicking the red ball just enough to put it in.

'Lucky shot.' Tanner grinned.

As Tanner lined up his next shot, Flynn said through gritted teeth, 'I have found a residence for Miss O'Keefe.'

Tanner looked up. 'Oh? Where?'

'Great Ryder Street. Complete with furnishings and at a good price.' Flynn tried to keep the anger from his voice.

He tried to remind himself that Rose was better off with Tanner, the Englishman who could make her dreams come true, than with the likes of Greythorne, who merely wanted to hurt her. What could the Irish Flynn offer her? Nothing.

Besides, he tried to console himself, he still had his ambition. Where he wanted to go, a courtesan songstress would not be welcome. An Irishman especially must be above reproach if he was to achieve high goals, and that would be true of his wife, as well. Rose would be shunned, a fate she did not deserve.

This was all useless pondering. Nothing had changed, Tanner had won Rose. Not Flynn.

Flynn frowned as Tanner replaced the red ball on to the table. "I must alert the servants I hired. All will be ready within a week."

'Ah.' Tanner sounded as if he were barely listening. Flynn had lately seen him more excited by the purchase of a new hunter at Tattersalls. Somehow this merely made Flynn angrier.

Flynn took his next shot, hitting both the red ball and Tanner's cue ball, but did not pocket either one.

'By the way…' Tanner took his turn '…I am dining with Liverpool tonight, so I must beg you to escort Miss O'Keefe alone.' He knocked both balls into the pocket, flashing Flynn a grin. 'The man is bent on keeping me busy for a few days. I do hope he does not prose on about Blanketeers and habeus corpus.'

Habeus corpus—the right of a detainee to appear before a court—had been suspended by Parliament that year, because of protests such as the Blanketeers and the mobbing of the Prince Regent's carriage.

'These are important matters,' Flynn responded, but now the blood had begun to race through his veins.

'I know. I know.' Tanner gestured for him to take his turn. 'It is just that Liverpool is so damned repressive and he proses on for hours. It becomes tedious after a while.'

Flynn had stopped listening. All he could think was he would be escorting Rose without Tanner.

That evening, when he knocked on the door to Madame Bisou's gaming-house, he vowed to do nothing to spark the tinder of his passion for Rose. He would simply enjoy her company.

The footman Cummings admitted him, and soon Katy came into the hall. Katy would act as chaperon, Flynn reminded himself. Her presence would assist him in maintaining his proper place.

'Is the marquess waiting in the carriage?' she asked.

'He shall not attend tonight.' Flynn did not explain. Katy would have less wish to hear of Blanketeers than Tanner did.

Her brows rose. 'So you are alone?'

'I am.'

She stared at him, her hands on her hips. Finally, she blurted out, 'I cannot go to Vauxhall either. I have a…a gentleman who is meeting me here. I am expecting Sir Reginald. You met Sir Reginald before, didn't you, Flynn?'

'Katy…' he began, but Rose appeared on the stairway, lovely in her deep red gown. She held her cloak over her arm.

'I can't go with you, Rose,' Katy called to her. 'So sorry.' Katy did not sound sorry in the least.

Rose was putting on her gloves. 'But, Katy—'

Katy interrupted her. 'The marquess isn't going either, so Flynn is going to escort you. You do not mind, do you?'

Rose turned her eyes on Flynn, and the desire he was so intent on dampening flared into life.

'I am thinking I do not mind.' Her voice was low and sultry.

Flynn took the cloak from Rose and wrapped it around her shoulders. Without a word, they hurried out of the door to Tanner's carriage.

He lifted her inside, his hands spanning her waist. Her eyes were dark, her lips tantalisingly parted. He climbed in and signalled the coachman to start. As soon as the carriage moved off, Rose launched herself on to his lap, into his arms.

'Flynn,' she cried as her lips rained kisses on his neck and cheek. 'I never thought to be alone with you again.'

He was a lost man. He sought her lips with all the hunger that had built up over the days he'd barely dared to look at her. He tasted her and pressed her hard against his groin. Nothing existed for him but Rose, her scent, her softness, the urgent sounds she made in the back of her throat.

Flynn wanted them both free of clothing, no barriers to impede them, but the confined space of the coach made this difficult. He freed her breasts from her low-cut dress and let his tongue play on the pebbled skin of her nipples. She moaned with pleasure. He no longer cared if the space was confined. He began to pull up her skirts.

The coach hit a rut and tipped suddenly, throwing her off him. It righted itself immediately, but the jolt was enough to return him to his senses.

'We must stop this,' he said. 'It is madness.'

In the dim light of the coach's interior, he could see her eyes still wide with passion, her breath still rapid. Slowly, like a sleeping child awaking, she nodded.

She fussed with the bodice of her dress.

'Did I damage it?' he asked, knowing he'd been close to tearing it off.

'No.' She looked up at him and smiled. 'I'm just needing to put myself back in it.'

After setting herself to rights, she straightened his neck-cloth and waistcoat, and then laid her head on his shoulder. 'And don't you be saying you regretted that, Flynn. Because you know you did not.'

No, he did not regret it. His only regret had been stopping.

Chapter Sixteen

Rose whispered to Flynn to secure one of the rooms on the Dark Walk for them, while she prepared herself to perform, and to watch her sing from the place where she first saw him. While she warmed her voice like Miss Hughes and the *signor* had taught her, Mr Hook walked by, looking displeased at her. She could not care. This was her night with Flynn. Her only night with Flynn. Nothing would make her unhappy.

When she stood in her place on the balcony facing the audience below, she immediately looked to the spot where Flynn would stand. He was there, face lifted towards her, as he had been on that first night. She smiled down at him.

The music began, and, like that first time, she sang 'Eileen Aroon.' Though she swept her gaze around the crowd, she returned to Flynn, and sang:

> Changeless through joy and woe
> Only the constant know…

She would be constant to him in her heart, even though she must release him into the world where he would achieve great things. She would take whatever brief time they had together and make it enough to last a lifetime. This was not a night for grief, but a time for joy and for love, and she poured these emotions into her song, forgetting how to breathe, forgetting how to project her voice.

Her song filled the night air, and the one after that, and the one after that. She listened to her voice as she sang. The sound was richer, fuller, louder. It was the sound of joy.

She would strive for this always, in each performance. For Flynn. It would be her own secret way to celebrate the love she had for him, her own way to hold on to him.

She finished with a sad song, 'The Turtle Dove Coos Round My Cot,' a widow's song. She would be like a widow, she thought, after this night, but for now she intended to live and love.

The audience burst into applause with shouts of 'Bravo!' for her. She glanced at Flynn, who stood as still as a statue, as rapt as he'd been throughout. She blew him a kiss, then blew other kisses to cover what she had done.

Finally, filled with happiness and anticipation, she turned and moved towards the balcony stairs.

Mr Hook stopped her. 'Much better, my dear.'

She grinned and impulsively kissed him on the cheek before hurrying away, knowing she would soon be with Flynn.

'There's more fellows out there tonight,' said the servant, Skewes. 'And yer father is not here to deal with ''em.'

She peeked through the curtain. 'I will deal with them myself.'

She opened the door and stepped out. The men were so surprised they gasped and fell back.

'How kind of you all to come,' she said. 'I am engaged for the evening, but if you wish, I will accept your cards and flowers, but, please, no gifts.'

The men came forward, but with such politeness and

reserve, she wondered why she had ever been frightened of them. As she accepted cards and bouquets of flowers, she spied Flynn watching her at the fringe of the group. She felt giddy at seeing him, as if she could flutter above these men like a butterfly.

'Thank you,' she said to each of them.

Some of the young ones—her age, she supposed—were more frightened of speaking to her than she could ever have been of them. She laughed as her arms were piled with flowers. Some slipping to the ground. The throng thinned, and Flynn stepped closer, picking up the fallen blossoms.

Finally, they drifted away, and Rose turned to go back into the gazebo's waiting room.

'One moment, miss!' a voice cried. A young fellow humbly dressed hurried up to her. He bowed. 'A gift for you.' He handed her a box, about the size of a glove box, only deeper. Its red ribbon had come loose, the ends dangling over the edge.

'I do not accept gifts,' Rose told him.

The man looked stricken. 'I've orders to give this to you and I dare not say I failed.'

'Who gives you the orders?' Flynn asked.

The man glanced around anxiously. 'He…he was here-abouts a minute ago. I don't know his name and he paid very well, but he said I must give this to you.'

'Oh, very well,' Rose said, reaching for the box and placing it on top of her mountain of flowers. 'You have done your job.'

The man bowed again and hurried off.

Flynn opened the gazebo door and followed her inside. 'You needn't have gone out there. I would have played your father's part, you know.'

She grinned impishly at him. 'I do not wish you to be

fatherly with me. Besides, it was not so terrifying as it once seemed. I do not know why I feared it so.'

The orchestra was playing a very loud piece, the drum making the walls shake. Rose was eager to leave with Flynn. She walked over to a table and dropped the flowers and box on to its surface. She let the cards slide out of her hand, and reached for her cloak on a peg on the wall.

When she swung the cloak around her shoulders, it knocked some of the flowers and the box to the floor. Flynn stooped down next to her to help pick them up. The box had fallen on its side, its top off. When Rose reached for it, a foul smell made her blink, and something wrapped in a scrap of thin muslin rolled out of the box. Rose picked it up and lifted a corner of the cloth.

She screamed and flung it away.

'What? What is it?' Flynn was right there, holding her.

She shook her head, unable to speak. Skewes bent down to look.

'Eucch!' he said, standing up again.

'What is it?' Flynn still held Rose.

'It is a ring,' said the servant. 'With the finger still in it.' He kicked it toward Flynn.

It was not just any ring. It was the ring Tannerton gave to her, the one Letty had snatched away and placed upon her own finger.

'It is Letty's finger, I think,' Rose managed.

The servant picked up something else. 'This looks like a reed.'

Rose glanced at it and turned to bury her face into Flynn's chest. 'My father's. For his oboe.'

Flynn released her long enough to retrieve the finger and the oboe's mouthpiece, wrap them in the cloth, and return them to the box.

'He is out there, isn't he, Flynn?' she rasped.

Flynn stood. 'I fear so. I am taking you home immediately.' He scooped up all the cards the men had given her and stuffed them into his coat pocket.

'I'd as leave you keep me out of this!' cried Skewes.

'If you speak of it to no one,' responded Flynn. 'Can we depend upon it?'

'Well…' the man prevaricated '…times is fairly tough…'

Flynn reached into another pocket and pulled out some coins. 'Will that do?'

The man snatched them from his hand and nodded, apparently satisfied.

'We leave now, Rose.' He picked up her cloak and put it around her.

She did not argue, but clung closely to him as they hurried through the gardens, heading to where the carriage would be waiting.

From the shelter of nearby trees, Lord Greythorne watched the door of the gazebo open again, the cloaked figure walking out on Tannerton's secretary's arm. Disappointing. The gift had been intended for Tannerton as well as for the chit. Greythorne had counted on shocking Tannerton with the return of his own gift in a most dramatic manner.

Greythorne frowned, touching the mask that hid his identity. Once again Tannerton had spoiled his carefully made plans. Surreptitiously following the hurrying pair, Greythorne consoled himself. They rushed as if the devil himself were chasing them.

He chuckled, enjoying himself in the role of the devil. If the lovely Rose thought his little gift frightening, she could anticipate so much more. He would show her fear. She would not escape like that strumpet friend of hers. She would experience the fullness of his wrath. The thought made him tremble with excitement.

As he anticipated, they were leaving the gardens, to return to that gaming hell where she'd gone to live, he suspected. He disliked her selling her favours to other men, but he was reasonably certain that Tannerton had not yet bedded her. Not if his spies reported accurately.

When they headed to where the carriages waited, Greythorne decided not to follow. The time was not yet right to escalate the tension. Let her live in fear of him for a while. The secretary would inform Tannerton, Tannerton would know who was the craftier. He'd know Greythorne would win.

Tannerton surely did not think he would stay in Brighton with the Prince, did he? The Royal Duke was easily fooled. All Greythorne had to do was come down with a disease of the contagious sort, and the Duke wanted him nowhere near. Greythorne paid his footman to impersonate him, to stay in his rooms at Brighton, having meals sent up and his valet to attend him. Good that both men were as loyal as money could buy. They would be well compensated for this little charade.

The only distasteful part had been dressing in his footman's clothes and returning to London in a common post chaise. He knew better than to return to his town house, so he went to the other place, to where he was not known as Greythorne, but merely as Mr Black, a man with plenty of coin and a willingness to pay for whatever needed doing.

He had easily discovered Miss O'Keefe's whereabouts after the…departure…of her father and his odious woman. Greythorne smiled again at that memory. Even he had not anticipated the heady exhilaration of wielding power over life and death. Even now he was hungry to experience the feeling again.

He'd had a watch kept on Rose, had seen her perform at King's Theatre, had been present at Vauxhall. He wanted the coveted Rose, the one men pined for as she sang into the cool Vauxhall nights. She had looked exceptionally desirable this night. He wanted her because the Marquess of Tannerton had dared to compete with him. He would show the marquess that Greythorne never lost.

Except once. He'd lost the Diamond once, but he would not repine over that, a mere trifle compared to the delights now ahead of him.

Greythorne turned back to the Grand Walk, filling himself with need again. He could prowl through the gardens looking for some willing girl who could be lured by a few coins, or he could stoke the fires within him, letting them build into white-hot fervour, striking when the time was perfect.

He decided to scour the gardens. Maybe that pretty little red-haired harlot would be in the gardens again. He needed to settle a score with her, did he not? And if he could not find her, he would simply feed his fantasies of all he might do in a few days' time, when his revenge on Tannerton would be complete.

He laughed aloud, and people turned to stare at him. He stared back until they hurried away. When the devil sought revenge, there would be nothing Tannerton could do to stop him.

Flynn reluctantly left Rose at Madame Bisou's, in the care of the *madame* and her burly footmen. He did not trust anyone but himself with her care at such a time, but there was much to do to ensure her safety. He was only sorry the hour was too late to go directly to the magistrate.

Not that the magistrate could do much until Greythorne's whereabouts were established and more of a connection between the severed finger and the earl could be ascertained.

He shuddered to think what treachery Greythorne had committed, but the fate of Mr O'Keefe and Miss Dawes was fairly clear. Rose had said so as well.

Flynn had underestimated the danger from Greythorne, and his guilt over Rose's father and Miss Dawes scraped him raw. He should have seen they needed more safeguarding.

Flynn entered Tanner's town house carrying the box containing the gruesome gift. Wiggins attended the door.

'Has Lord Tannerton returned?' Flynn asked.

'Not as yet, Mr Flynn,' the footman replied.

Flynn gave Wiggins his hat and gloves. 'When he comes in, tell him to come to the library. I need him.'

Wiggins nodded, following Flynn into the library, lighting the candles for him. Flynn set the box on the desk and thanked the footman, who left the room.

Flynn poured himself a glass of brandy from the decanter on the side table. His mind was busy, planning what they must do to find Greythorne and to keep Rose safe.

After an hour, Tanner walked in. 'Flynn? Wiggins said you wanted me.'

'Rose—Miss O'Keefe received a gift tonight after her performance.' Flynn did not know how to convey the horror to Tanner other than to show it. 'The box is on your desk.'

Tanner's brows rose in curiosity. He walked over to the box and opened it, unfolding the muslin to see what was inside.

He stared at it a long time. 'This, I assume, is the ring you purchased for Miss O'Keefe?'

'It is.' Flynn poured Tanner some brandy and placed the glass on the desk for him. 'We must surmise that the finger belonged to her father's companion. The other object is the mouthpiece to an oboe, presumably Mr O'Keefe's.'

Tanner closed up the box. 'Revolting. And loathsome.' He

pulled out his handkerchief and rubbed his hands with it, even though his fingers had not touched the objects. 'Are we to assume Greythorne is behind this?'

'Who else?' Flynn responded.

'Indeed.' Tanner picked up the glass of brandy and backed away from the desk. 'I had not imagined he was so dangerous.' He crossed the room to the chairs, but did not sit. 'Why did his Royal Highness not send word Greythorne was not in Brighton?'

Flynn shrugged, knowing Tanner did not expect an answer. 'The man obviously made good his threat to O'Keefe and Miss Dawes.'

Tanner curled one hand into a fist. 'I dislike underestimating an adversary.'

'Madame Bisou's footmen will be guarding Miss O'Keefe.'

Tanner stopped. 'Yes, very good. She is in danger, certainly. How does she fare?'

Flynn thought of her frightened eyes and her stoical insistence she would be all right. 'More frightened than she chooses to reveal.'

Tanner nodded. 'I will send Wiggins and Smythe to help guard her. We must show the magistrate this appalling gift.'

'I agree. We can inform him of Greythorne's threat.' Flynn disliked the idea of identifying Rose. The newspapers thrived on stories such as this one. 'I say we go to the magistrate with this evidence. We cannot keep Rose's name out of it, so we say she has many admirers, Greythorne included.' Flynn reached into his pocket and pulled out the cards Rose had been given. 'I can make a list of these men and add Greythorne's name to it.'

Tanner rubbed his chin. 'Perhaps it would be best to keep my name out of it, Flynn. God knows, having a marquess mixed up in this business will bring on the gossip-mongers.' He frowned as he thought. 'I have it. We tell the magistrate you are Miss O'Keefe's admirer, not I. You have been seen with her more often than I, so that should be no difficulty.'

Flynn could not argue that fact, though it was closer to the truth than he dared to admit.

Tanner went on, 'I will go to the Bow Street Runners and engage them to find Greythorne. They will have the skills to prove Greythorne is behind this dastardly plot.' Tanner gained energy with each step of his plan. 'Explain to Miss O'Keefe that I will not be much in her company for a few days.'

Flynn would have more time alone with her? He dared not think about that. 'What of her new residence? In three days' time, she is expected to move in.'

Tanner shrugged. 'Let her move in, if she wishes it. I see no reason to deny her that comfort. Besides, I can visit her in her own lodgings more discreetly than at Madame Bisou's. Might be easier to guard her there, as well.'

He can visit her. Flynn knew what that meant. He poured himself another brandy.

Tanner watched him drink it. 'I endangered her,' he said in solemn tones. 'And got her father and his woman friend killed.' He shook his head. 'Ghastly.'

The next morning, as early as he deemed practical, Flynn made his way to the magistrate. At the same time, Tanner headed for Bow Street.

The magistrate listened to Flynn's story, peered at the dismembered finger, and began to shuffle papers on his desk.

'Ah.' He held one paper to his nose, peering at it through his spectacles. 'This is the one.' He handed it to Flynn.

It was a report of the bodies of a man and a woman found

in an alley two days ago. One finger was missing on the woman's hand. Evidence of torture was gruesomely detailed.

'They've not been buried yet.' The magistrate restacked his papers and folded his hands on the desk. 'We thought to wait a few days to see if someone would claim them, and here you are. Would you be so good as to take a look?'

Flynn had no choice but to agree. He followed the magistrate's man to the cellar of a building nearby.

'They were stripped naked, they were,' the man said conversationally. 'Most are, you know. Especially anywhere near a rookery. I'd say these two were meant to be discovered, just left in an alley, easy enough to see.'

The bodies lay on a large wooden table and were wrapped in roughly woven cloth stained with God-knew-what. The man waved to Flynn to lift the cloth. Holding his breath from the overpowering stench, Flynn lifted one, then the other.

They were, indeed, Mr O'Keefe and Miss Dawes. Or what death had done to them. He glanced to the man and nodded, and they quickly vacated the room.

Flynn returned to the magistrate and finished the business, such as it was. When the magistrate learned Rose lived at Madame Bisou's and sang at Vauxhall, he gave Flynn a knowing look and accepted the list of men Flynn had compiled from Rose's Vauxhall admirers.

'You say the Earl of Greythorne threatened to kill these two if the father did not sell the girl to him?'

It was bluntly stated, but accurate. 'I do, sir.'

'Seems a great deal of fuss over one fancy piece.' His gaze was frankly sceptical. 'They told this to you, eh?'

Flynn flinched when the magistrate called Rose a fancy piece. 'That is the gist of it, sir.'

'Bring the girl to me,' he told Flynn. 'I must question her.'

Flynn agreed to do so.

Before he left, Flynn made arrangements for proper shrouds for the bodies, wooden coffins and a Christian burial. They would be buried that very day, the magistrate's man assured him.

With the scent of death still lingering in his nostrils, Flynn made his way to Madame Bisou's.

Rose received him alone in a small parlour. When the door closed, Rose came into his arms, not in passion like the night before, but in need of comfort, which he was glad to provide.

'How do you fare, Rose?' he asked when they finally broke apart. He held her hands and searched her face.

'I did not sleep well.' She gave a wan smile. 'But, I suppose that should be expected. Katy was a dear and stayed with me all night.'

He stroked her cheek with the back of his hand. 'I am glad you were not alone.'

They stared into each other's eyes for a long moment, before she turned away. 'There is tea. Shall I pour for you?'

'If you like,' he said.

'I remember how you take it.' She sat in the nearby chair, putting in the cream and sugar.

He sat near her, waiting for her to finish pouring.

'I have news,' he said in a tight voice.

She nodded and met his eyes.

'Your father and Miss Dawes have been found. They are dead, Rose.'

She nodded again.

'I...I saw them.' He could not think of words to speak, unwilling to tell her the horror of what he'd seen.

'Were they whipped?' she asked.

'Whipped?' Her question was odd, but the bodies had indeed been riddled with whip marks.

She blinked. 'I mean, do you know how they died?'

Yes, he did know. The magistrate's report listed every cut on their bodies, including on their genitals. A physican had concluded they bled to death.

'Stabbing,' he abridged.

She turned away and moaned.

He took her hand in his. 'I've arranged for a proper burial, Rose.'

'Must I attend it?' she asked in a shaking voice.

'No, you do not have to attend it.'

'My poor father!' Her face crumbled, and he took her in his arms again, holding her until her sobbing slowed, holding her still. 'I know he did not seem like much of a father, Flynn, but he paid for my schooling. He wanted me to have a good life.'

He stroked her hair. 'When I last spoke to him, Rose, his concern was all for you.'

She nestled against his chest. 'I'm thinking I killed him. And Letty, too. They would be alive, if not for me. They wouldn't have suffered—'

He felt her shudder in his arms. 'You are not responsible for this, Rose. Greythorne did this, and it is he who should hang for it.'

'Oh, Flynn.' She pulled away and looked at him with eyes of pain. 'I'm thinking I could have stopped him. I…I knew about him, you see, but I promised not to tell.'

His gaze flew to hers. 'You knew about him? What did you know?'

She inhaled a ragged breath. 'I knew he liked to hurt women.'

Flynn glanced away. 'We knew it as well, Rose. Tanner and I. We did not stop him.' He did not know if he could forgive himself that lapse. All he knew was, Greythorne would be stopped now, before he hurt Rose. He looked at her again. 'How did you discover this about him?'

'I…I cannot tell you. All I can say is, I knew someone hurt by him. Whipped by him. I'm thinking if I had not promised to be quiet about it, maybe he would have been put in prison.'

He stood, drawing her to her feet and enfolding her in his arms again. 'We are all thinking we might have stopped him. We will stop him now, though. I have to take you to the magistrate, Rose. He will ask you questions…'

He explained to her all that he and Tanner had discussed, how Tanner would set the Bow Street Runners on Greythorne, how she would be guarded at all times, how they would pretend it was he, Flynn, who was her protector, not Tannerton.

'You are my protector, Flynn,' she murmured. 'I'll not forget.'

Chapter Seventeen

Rose walked with Flynn through St James Park after her interview with the magistrate. The trees and grass and lake were calming, and she could almost forget everything but being on his arm.

The magistrate had questioned her about admirers. Rose left out Tannerton's name, but was required to speak of Lord Greythorne's interest in her. The magistrate produced the list Flynn had compiled from the cards she had received. He then asked her how many of these men she had 'been with.' His implication had been clear.

This was the life she had chosen, she could almost hear her father say. Her eyes pricked with tears again. Her poor, poor father. Her father had loved her in his way, but now he was gone, lost for ever.

And soon Flynn would be lost to her, too.

Flynn's eyes darted to and fro, alert, she knew, for any danger. The park was blessedly peaceful, however, and she was convinced she would be safe in daylight as long as she was not alone. She was safe with Flynn. Rose always felt safe with Flynn.

'I neglected to tell you something,' Flynn said in an ominous tone, a sombre contrast to the colourful riot of flowers they strolled by.

Not more bad news. Could she beg him to withhold it? She had been trying to forget everything but walking with him, like the other couples who strolled in the park as if without a care.

She sighed. 'What is it?'

'I have found rooms for you.' He seemed to force some cheer into his voice. 'A nice little place on Great Ryder Street, not too far from Madame Bisou's.'

'When must I move in?'

'A few days.' There was tension in his tone.

They walked in silence along the lake where swans and geese glided past.

Her throat grew tight. 'What is to happen, then?'

'Happen?' He paused. 'What is to happen is Lord Tannerton will have fulfilled the terms agreed upon.' He spoke like a stranger, like she imagined a man of business might sound. 'The contract will be complete—'

'Yes, I know that,' she broke in. 'I was thinking, what will happen to us?'

They stopped at the water's edge. The swans swam to them in the hopes they carried crumbs in their pockets.

He stared out at the water. 'We have been through this, Rose. It will be over.'

It had been foolish of her to ask when she knew the answer, like rubbing salt into a wound. She watched the swans swimming in pairs. At school she'd learned that swans mated for life. How did they select each other? she wondered. Did they know so quickly, as she'd known with Flynn?

As if in silent agreement, she and Flynn turned and started walking on the path leading out of the park.

Rose took a last look at the swans and turned to face him.
'I'll miss you, Flynn.'

They entered a part of the path where the trees formed a
canopy, blanketing them with shade and sheltering them mo-
mentarily from view.

Flynn stopped suddenly and pulled her into the shrubbery.
'Rose,' he murmured, folding her in his arms.

She hungered to taste his lips, and he obliged her, kissing
her with desperation and need. She forgot where they were,
or did not care. Knocking his hat off, she buried her fingers
in his thick dark hair. He leaned her against the tree,
pressing himself against her, lifting her a bit so she fitted
against the hard shaft she felt under his clothes. He kissed
her face, her neck, the bare expanse of skin exposed by her
gown's neckline.

How could she bear this with any other man?

Laughter and voices sounded, coming closer. He released
her. The moment had passed. She straightened her clothing
while he retrieved his hat. The people on the path walked by
and their voices faded into the distance.

Rose forced Flynn to look at her. 'There's no denying this
between us, Flynn.' All her desire was reflected in his eyes.
'I'm thinking we must do this. Just once, perhaps, but we must
do it. I'm not Lord Tannerton's yet. I'm still a free woman.
I'll honour my obligation to him, but first—' she broke off,
her voice cracking '—first I want to be with you.'

He wrenched away from her and stood, his gaze averted
from her, arms crossed over his chest. Finally his arms
dropped to his sides and he turned back to her. He nodded and
the ache inside her eased.

'Tomorrow.' His voice was deep and resonant. 'Tomorrow
I will show you your new residence. The servants do not

come until the following day, and you may move in the day after that—'

The day Lord Tannerton would visit her, no doubt.

'But tomorrow we will be alone.'

She stepped towards him, putting her arms around his neck. He held her again, and they clung together for a long time.

The next day, no one at Madame Bisou's questioned it when Flynn arrived to take Rose out. Although it was an earlier hour than usual, his escort of her was too commonplace to remark upon. Katy, too, was silent, but Katy had been silent and preoccupied since Greythorne had killed and was supposed to be lurking about.

Flynn had hired a hackney carriage, even though her new rooms were an easy walk. He instructed the jarvey to drive around the streets, a precaution against Greythorne discovering her new address.

But Rose did not wish to think of Greythorne. She was in such a fever of excitement she could hardly sit still. Only knowing they had the whole day together kept her hands off him.

They switched vehicles at Westminster Abbey, its grey towers rising majestic above them. Some day she'd like to look inside the Abbey. It was said there was much to see there—old tombs and altars and things—the sort of experience she'd like to share with Flynn.

But she had no desire to dwell on the fact that this would be her one precious day with Flynn. She would merely savour it.

The hackney let them off near the Mason's Yard on Duke Street. All they had to do was turn a corner and they were there, on a private little street one could almost miss unless looking for it. No one would see her enter with Flynn, she was certain, and just as certain no one could take heed of their leaving. She did not sing at Vauxhall this night, so they might stay as late as they wished.

Inside, however, she felt suddenly sheepish. As she untied her bonnet, she glanced around the small hall, noticing the narrow stairway in front of her, the one that undoubtedly led to the bedchamber.

Flynn, as well, seemed to take his time removing his hat and gloves. He rubbed his hands together. 'Shall I show you the rooms?'

'Very well,' she responded, leaving her things on the table next to his. Rose cared little about the rooms, but perhaps by the time the tour was done the shaking inside her would stop.

'Let us start at the bottom.' He showed her to an even smaller staircase that led to the basement rooms. In the small kitchen was a basket of food. Fresh bread, cheeses, wine.

Flynn said, 'I thought we might get hungry.'

She smiled at him. He thought of everything.

She peeked into the servants' rooms and followed him back to the main floor. In the front was a pretty little drawing room, behind it, a smaller parlour set up for dining.

Flynn stared at her. 'Shall we go abovestairs?'

A thrill rushed through her. She nodded.

His eyes darkened and he took her hand, leading her up the stairs. He first brought her into a cosy sitting room, its main piece of furniture an elegant *chaise-longue*, large enough for two.

'The bedchamber is next,' Flynn told her. He lifted her hand to his lips, and she felt the kiss echo in every part of her. He backed toward the doorway, pulling her along. When his hand rested on the doorknob, he paused. 'Are you sure of this, Rose?'

Her nerves had fled with his kiss. 'I am sure.'

He opened the door.

Prominent in the room was the loveliest bed she had ever

seen. Its wood was dark and it had four posts and beautiful ivory brocade bed curtains and bed cover. It was every bit as pretty as the bed in Miss Hart's room in Mayfair, but Rose had never thought to sleep in one like it.

The thought that she must share this bed with Tannerton flitted through her mind, but she ruthlessly chased it away. Today there was no one but Flynn.

He looked at her questioningly.

She laughed and pulled him into the room. 'I'll not be changing my mind, Flynn.'

She kicked off her shoes and tugged him over to the bed.

He lifted her hand to his lips. 'I'll not change my mind either, Rose, but I want this to be right for you. We have all day for lovemaking…'

She unbuttoned his waistcoat and spread her hands on his shirt. 'I was thinking the same.'

His eyes were fixed on hers as he shrugged out of his coat, letting it fall to the ground. Rose slipped off his waistcoat and turned around so he could undo the laces of her dress. It seemed right for him to touch her, to remove her clothes. She marvelled that it could feel so right.

In the courtesan school, all the talk of undressing had seemed silly to her, but now she understood its power. Every layer removed brought them closer, and she wanted to be close to Flynn. Katy had always insisted that lovemaking brought pleasure. Rose could now agree and they'd barely begun.

Her dress slipped to the floor, and he worked next on the laces of her corset. When that too was tossed to the floor, he stood behind her and removed the pins from her hair. As her hair cascaded down her back, he combed it with his fingers. Nothing could feel so glorious, she thought—until he reached around her and cupped her breasts. Glorious was too tame a word for the sensations he created. Suddenly even the thin muslin of her shift seemed too thick.

She turned. 'Sit on the bed and I'll remove your boots,'

This task was harder than she'd imagined, and she had to tug hard to free his feet, almost falling backward when the second boot came loose.

She laughed, hurrying back to him. She'd suddenly remembered more of what she'd been taught at the courtesan school.

'Watch me!' She slowly pulled off her shift. Standing before him naked, she was exhilarated by the appreciation in his eyes. She lifted her arms and did a joyous pirouette. 'Your turn,' she cried playfully.

He gave her a wry look. 'I cannot compete.'

She climbed on the bed and sat cross-legged, pretending to appraise him. He made a show of removing his stockings, his shirt, his pantaloons, and finally his drawers. Her lively mood fled for a moment as she ran her eyes over him. He was lean and muscular—and, she noted, a smile growing across her face, very aroused.

'Do I disappoint?' he asked, his voice rumbling and low.

She slowly shook her head and lay back against the bed's pillows. 'Never.'

He climbed upon the bed, but did not touch her, taking time to simply gaze at her. Rose realised what happiness could be. Happiness was being alone with Flynn, knowing he was hers, all hers for the moment.

He smiled and very slowly brought his lips to hers in a slow lanquid kiss that made her feel as pliant as grass on the hills of Killyleagh. She savoured the warmth of his lips, the stroking of his tongue, the scent and taste of him, as she might relish a whole day to wander the countryside, no hurry to rush home.

His hand skimmed her bare skin, easing any remnants of tension. Time seemed to stand still, and she had the notion her precious day would never end.

He broke off the kiss, letting his lips slide downward, to the sensitive skin of her neck and to the now-aching flesh of her breasts. His mouth closed over one nipple and sensation shot deep inside her, making her arch her back and knead her fingers into his buttocks. It surprised and delighted her that his muscles were firm.

The delicious things he did to her breasts made her writhe beneath him. Need grew, and suddenly the slow pace seemed torturous.

'Flynn,' she rasped, her tone urgent.

'Soon,' he murmured as his kisses trailed farther down her body.

The pleasure was excruciating. She flung her arms over her head, unable to bear another moment.

'Why not now, Flynn? Now, please?' she begged.

He lifted himself above her in all his glorious manhood. She was breathless with anticipation, every nerve in her body throbbing with need of Flynn, to unite with him, be one with him, to bind herself to him for ever, even though she would lose him again in a day's time.

No, she would not think of losing him now, not when he sought that private part of her, not when he sought to join her as completely as she could imagine.

Her legs spread and his pace slowed again. He entered her with a gentleness that she knew was borne of his love for her. She urged him on, wanting him inside her totally, unable to be still when it seemed ecstasy was so near.

With one final thrust, he plunged into her. She cried out with the pain of it and felt the moisture of her blood.

He froze, still inside her. 'Rose? What the devil?'

'Do not stop, Flynn,' she said, moving beneath him, the need returning as quickly as the pain fled.

But he pulled out of her and sat up. 'You are a virgin!'

Rose sat up as well. 'Was a virgin,' she corrected, misery invading. 'But I'm not understanding why that means anything.'

'It means a great deal!' His voice rose in pitch.

Flynn rang a ragged hand through his hair. He felt a pang of guilt for shouting at her, but nothing to compare with the guilt of taking her innocence. His emotions were scattered helter-skelter, but the raw physical need of her still pulsed within him.

She was a virgin. Not a courtesan. Not an experienced girl.

He got off the bed and padded over to a small bureau in the corner. From the pitcher that rested on top of it, he moistened a towel. He had prepared the water and the towels, but not for this purpose. Not to wipe away blood.

He handed the towel to her and moistened another one for himself.

She looked as if she might weep. 'You must explain to me, Flynn, why it means anything at all, because I'm not understanding still.'

He could not even heed her question. 'You deceived me, Rose.'

'Deceived you?' She blinked rapidly. 'How? You never asked me, Flynn. I would have told you.'

'The devil with that. You were trained to be a courtesan. What else was I to think?'

She gaped at him. 'You knew about the courtesan school?'

He glared back at her. 'Katy told me. She told me you were trained by Harriette Wilson, for God's sake. What *virgin* is trained by the most notorious courtesan in London?'

She looked away. 'She only called upon us the one time.'

'Katy met you on the street, she said.' He was still trying to make sense of this. It changed everything for him. Everything.

She pulled off the bed linens and wrapped them around herself. 'I'm thinking there are many virgins who walk to the shops. That is where I met Katy and Mary.'

He shook his head. 'You told me yourself you had been with other men.'

She blinked. 'I never did.'

He took a step closer, suddenly realising he was still naked. He snatched up his shirt and wrapped it around his waist. As he was tying it, he gave her an accusing glance. 'You told me you had gone driving in the park.'

'And you thought that meant I was bedding a man? It was an outing for us. Robert Duprey took us in turns.'

He stared blankly. He'd assumed she was a seductress from the moment he'd first seen her upon the balcony at Vauxhall.

God help him. He had almost delivered a virgin to his employer. Worse, he'd deflowered her himself.

She lifted her chin. 'I went to the courtesan school because I had nowhere else to go. Letty had a terrible row with my father about me and I needed to be somewhere. And, besides, I was thinking I needed the polish Katy and Mary were talking of when I overheard them. I was thinking it would help me on the stage, and so it did, because Mr Hook thought I was worth hiring.'

He refused to bear the total responsibility for what happened between them. He gave her a level stare. 'You pushed yourself on me, Rose. Almost from the beginning. Were you trying to practise with me, so you would be ready for a marquess? Or did they not teach you in your courtesan school that virgins command a higher price?'

She rose to her knees, eyes flashing. 'I was not so foolish, Flynn, to be thinking I could sing on stage and not lose my virtue some time. Lord knows, at school—at Killyleagh—they drummed into us what girls like that were. Trouble was, I wanted to be one of those girls. My mother was one of those girls. All I was hoping was the man I bedded would be—would be someone I could have regard for. Like in the story-books, you know. Romantic. Do you see?'

'So I was to be your hero in some blasted Minerva Press novel?' He gave a dry laugh.

She lifted her chin. 'I thought you a man I could have regard for.'

He bowed his head. Not only had he taken her virtue, he'd stolen her affection as well.

With great dignity, she climbed off the bed and reached for her shift. Turning away from him, she let the bed linens slip from her body, revealing her creamy skin and a figure that was sheer perfection. The image of her dancing playfully for him just a few moments before returned. He'd felt joyous at seeing her. Had rejoiced at holding her in his arms, at making love to her. He'd held at bay the shattering knowledge that it would be Tanner making love to her in two days' time. How could he pass her off to Tanner now?

He whirled on her. 'If you have such regard for me, how can you go from my bed into Tanner's in the space of a few days?'

She looked as if she were glass about to shatter. 'What choice do I have?'

He was forced to avert his eyes.

Her voice was quiet. 'What they did not teach me in courtesan school was that your feelings for a man was what made you want to have intimacies with him.' She gave a choking sound. 'I want this with you, Flynn. Maybe I will never truly want it with another man, but I want it with you.' She swallowed. 'I only had this one chance.'

He felt as if he'd been pushed into a dark pit and was still falling, deeper and deeper into blackness. Everything she said made painful sense. It was he who had transgressed, the smart, ever-efficient Flynn who never missed an opportunity to be with her. He even used her dreams as a reason to tie her closer to him. Had he wished, he could have done his employer's bidding without making himself so indispensable.

'I am sorry, Rose,' he said in a soft voice. 'I've wronged you and I am sorry. I did not mean the words I've said to you. I am merely angry at myself for not knowing…'

The air seemed to go out of her, and he wanted to wrap his arms around her and never release her. Like a shaft of light, it came to him what he must do. What he most desired to do.

It took all his effort to keep from shouting it out loud to her. He must not be heedless. He must not tell her now. He must show her first.

'Rose?'

As her shift slipped down over her body, she turned her head.

'Are you still wanting me, Rose O'Keefe?' he asked, using the brogue he'd so carefully erased from his speech.

Her eyes widened in surprise. She answered him in a serious voice. 'I'm still wanting you, Jameson Flynn.'

Chapter Eighteen

Flynn crossed the room to her, lifting her chin with his fingers. He leaned down and kissed her, hoping she could feel his apology, his promise.

Their gaiety had fled, but had turned into something far more precious to him. He was no hero in a Minerva Press novel, but his heart had finally been opened. He'd been telling himself it was mere base desire, borne of hearing her sing a song.

'Cupid oft in ambush lies…' She'd sung those words that first night, and the cherub had certainly struck Flynn with his arrow, but he'd not known until now that the arrow carried love.

He would give his love back to her, show her with all the passion exploding inside him. Passion for her and for life. It had been so long since he'd wanted merely to celebrate life.

He tore his shirt away and lifted her on to the bed. Lying next to her, he slipped his hands under the skirt of her shift, lifting it higher and higher until he pulled it over her head. This time he explored her reverently, gently. She was subdued and wary, and he mentally kicked himself for making her so.

She accepted his touch, but passively, and he could not

blame her. He would not rush her, though, because they would have plenty of time to retrieve the joy he'd chased away.

Slowly she came alive beneath his touch, her back arching, her lips returning his kisses, but he still waited, allowing her to show him when she was ready.

She made an urgent sound and grasped at him, and he knew the time was right. He positioned himself over her again, but gazed into her eyes.

'I love you, Rose,' he murmured, kissing her again.

When he broke off the kiss, tears had pooled in the corners of her eyes, but she reached for him, and nothing in the world would keep him from giving her a woman's pleasure.

He entered her, mindful now that this part of lovemaking she'd never experienced before. She was moist and more than ready for him, but he moved with easy strokes, slowly, until she met his rhythm, the eternal rhythm between man and woman.

Suddenly his own need took over and his pace quickened. She met him stroke for stroke until he felt her climax quiver against him and he exploded inside her.

She cried out, as did he, in a blast of pleasure that sent him to heights he'd never imagined. While he crashed back to his senses, she still grasped him to her, still in the throes of her own ecstasy.

When her body went limp, he collapsed on top of her, feeling triumphantly male for having pleased her so well. He slid off, gazing upon her face, flushed and glistening and beautiful.

Her eyelids fluttered and she opened them to gaze back at him.

'I'll not be forgetting that, Rose,' he murmured.

'Nor I,' she responded breathlessly.

She nestled against him, her graceful hand resting on his chest. 'Did I please you, Flynn?'

He gave a rumbling laugh. 'You pleased me very well.' He kissed the top of her head.

She gave a satisfied sigh. 'I was expecting something good, but I'm thinking that this was even better.'

'Are you feeling any pain?' He was mindful that he'd not gone easy on her at the end.

'No pain,' she said.

They lay there and Flynn thought he had never been more comfortable, more satisfied than at that moment. It reminded him of home, a place so familiar it inhabited the very pores of your skin, a place you knew you belonged. He felt as if his bones had left his body, his limbs were so relaxed, and he smiled, because he knew this time would not be the last.

As if she read his mind, she stirred beside him, moving on top of him, straddling him. She leaned down to kiss him as he had kissed her before. He grew hard again.

She noticed.

Regarding him shyly, she said, 'Harriette Wilson talked about the woman sitting on top.'

He was half-embarrassed by her frankness, half-tantalized. 'Did she now?'

'She did.' Her silken hair tickled his chest.

He gave her a twisted smile. 'And I suppose you'd be wanting to practise such a thing?'

She grinned at the return of his brogue. 'I would, if you'd not be minding too much.'

He kissed her, a hungry, demanding kiss. 'I'd not be minding.'

Rose lay in the bed, stretching luxuriously as she thought of what had transpired between her and Flynn. She'd imagined it would feel wonderful making love to him, but she'd never guessed it could be so magnificent, nor how it could change her. She rolled over, thinking of his touch, feeling her body come alive with the mere memory.

'Here we are.' Flynn appeared in the doorway, carrying a tray with the bread and cheese on it. The wine bottle was tucked under his arm and the stemmed glasses were between his fingers.

She sat up. 'I'm hungry.'

He set the tray on the bed and kissed her. 'I am hungry, too.'

She grinned against his lips. 'Perhaps there will be dessert.'

He moved back, smiling ruefully. 'Too much will leave you sore.'

Rose was not certain she cared. She wished to feast the day through and worry later about whatever was to come after. She placed her palm on her belly, daring to hope a baby might come from this coupling with him.

Tannerton would think the child his, she supposed. That thought disturbed her. If she bore Flynn's baby she would want to shout it from the rooftops, not pretend it to be another man's.

She could use the skills Madame Bisou taught to prevent a child from Flynn, but she could not bear the thought of preventing something so wonderful. Prevent another man's child, yes, but not Flynn's.

He poured the wine, and she glanced at him through her lashes. He might not realise it at the moment, but there would be more lovemaking before the day was done. She was hungry for him again, hungry for more memories to treasure in the desolation of future days. She loved what their lovemaking had done to him, making him relaxed and easy with her, even loosening his tongue into its brogue.

They supped like lovers and talked as if the day would never end. At times Rose glanced at the window, seeing the changing sunlight, the reminder that time was passing, but she quickly turned away.

She begged him for one more time of lovemaking, but he resisted her, insisting it would make her sore, vowing he would not give her pain. It occurred to her that he might be worried about Tannerton. Perhaps if she were sore, Tannerton would wonder why. Flynn would not want the marquess to guess at the events of this day, would he?

She chastised herself. Flynn's concern was for her, not worry over what the marquess would discover.

They spent the afternoon in each other's arms, and fell asleep in the warmth of each other's bodies.

Rose woke, noticing the light in the window had changed some more. She looked into his face and saw he was watching her with a contented expression.

'How long did I sleep?' she murmured.

'An hour or more,' he responded.

She hated losing that much time with him.

He toyed with a strand of her hair. 'We must leave soon.'

Her insides twisted. 'Not yet.'

He ran a finger down her cheek. 'The hour is late.'

'I do not care.' She rolled over and began to stroke his chest with her fingers. She kissed his neck and let her fingers trail down his body.

'Rose,' he warned.

'I do not care,' she repeated.

He made no effort to stop her.

She was now glad of the lessons that had taught her how to please a man, because they had instructed her how to touch him, how to convince him that one more time of lovemaking would not, indeed, hurt.

She let herself become very bold, touching the most male part of him, glorying in her power to arouse him.

He gave no further argument, allowing her to explore him as wantonly as she wished, until suddenly he grabbed her and turned her on her back. He kissed her fiercely this time, as if their hunger for each other had not been slaked earlier that day—twice. This hunger came from it being their last time. She felt it, too, ached with the knowledge.

She did not choose to hurry, but their urgency was borne of despair. She felt the need to grab all of him at once, to hold on to him and never let go.

His touches were equally as driven, but so filled with passion that her senses were quickly roused to a fever pitch. This was frenzied lovemaking, ungovernable, unstoppable. She heard her own panting mingled with his, felt the dampness of his sweat against her own, smelled the musky scent they created. Even so he tried for restraint as he entered her. Even in this maelstrom, he sought not to hurt her.

He need not worry. Her body was more than prepared for him, moist and slick with her need of him. Their coupling was as blazing as her feelings for him. It was fast and hard and rough.

She'd thought he'd already shown her what passion could be, but she'd been wrong. This was different, something wild but freeing.

He drove her higher and higher, until she called out his name, and her pleasure broke free, sparkling like the illuminations at Vauxhall, lighting the dark spaces of her loneliness, searing the memory on her soul.

He spilled his seed inside her at the same moment, holding her even tighter as his pleasure rocked him, carrying her along as well.

But, as it must, the ecstasy ceased, plummeting them back

to reality. When they collapsed beside each other, Rose felt bereft. This was goodbye. This was the end. This was final.

He gazed at her with an aching expression of love, one she tried to etch on her memory for ever.

'We ought to get dressed,' he said.

She nodded.

He got off the bed and walked over to the pitcher, wetting a cloth for her. She cleansed herself and stood, surveying the rumpled bed linens, stained with her blood and with other signs of what they had shared together.

'What shall we do about the bed linens?' she asked.

He was donning his trousers and shirt. 'I will take care of it, never fear.'

She found her shift and slipped it on. He came to assist her with her corset. She blinked away tears as he helped her fasten it. He picked up her dress and held it so she could put it on.

As he was tying the laces of her dress, she murmured, 'I do not want this to end.'

He turned her around and kissed her with exquisite gentleness. 'It will not end.'

'Oh, do not tease me.' She stifled a sob, determined to be strong.

'I do not tease you, Rose.' He wiped a tear from her cheek with his thumb. 'I, too, do not wish this to end. You must marry me so that we will have the rest of our lives for this.'

She went still as a stone statue, unsure of what she heard. 'Marry you?'

He smiled. 'I do not know why I did not think of it before. It is the only way—'

She pulled away from him. 'But you cannot mean it!'

'Of course, I mean it,' he said, reaching for her. 'I love you, Rose.'

She took a step back, shaking her head. 'Is it because I was a virgin, Flynn? That is foolish.'

'Not that.' He watched her with wary eyes, his voice less certain.

'But what of Tannerton?' she asked.

He shrugged. 'He will fire me, I am certain, but that is of no consequence.'

She wrinkled her brow and turned away from him, her mind whirling. She did not for once believe her virginity was not the cause. He was just the sort of man who would feel some foolish obligation for that reason. She ought to have realised he would experience some misguided sense of duty, but she'd thought the virtue of a woman on the stage meant little to any man. All she'd wanted was for him to be the first.

She could not allow him to throw away everything for which he'd toiled. Not for her sake. She could not allow him to give up a prince for her. He did not yet know what he would give up, but she did.

She girded her resolve. 'I was not meaning what Tannerton would do to you, Flynn. I was meaning what the consequence would be for me.'

He grew silent.

Finally he spoke, his words as Irish as his birth. 'I'm not understanding.'

She set the expression on her face before turning to him and speaking in the same hardened tone used by Harriette Wilson. 'Well, I would lose this house, would I not? And all the money Tannerton's going to give me? I can live well on that, even when he tires of me, can I not? He would even pay so I can work at King's Theatre, perhaps even something better.'

A muscle flexed in his cheek. 'Is that your worry, then?'

She made herself laugh. 'But of course, Flynn. Marriage

to you—to any man—would be madness, would it not? We were taught that a courtesan has the best life. Her property is her own and no man can tell her what to do.'

'A courtesan…' His voice trailed off.

She walked over to him, taking the risk of touching him, running her hand through his hair. She'd never precisely told him she loved him, as he had done while they made love. She'd held back, thinking it would protect her own heart when she was forced to say goodbye to him. Now she was glad she'd not told him she loved him, because it would make it better for him. She must convince him that it was not love she shared with him, but something more carnal.

'I'm not saying I do not fancy you, Flynn. I do not care that you have no money, if you've a mind to visit me now and then. Lord Tannerton need never know.'

He twisted away. 'I'll finish getting dressed and take you back to Madame Bisou's.'

Her heart was breaking into a thousand pieces. She pressed on, giving a loud sigh. 'If you must. Though I would not mind it at all if we undressed again and returned to the bed.'

She made herself want to cry, but her goal now was to convince him he must not give up his dreams for her.

He turned to her with anger in his eyes, the anger of a lover scorned. She almost wished he would unleash that rage at her. She deserved to be punished for hurting him. He would never strike back at her. Never. And she loved him for that, even while she hated herself.

When the prince returned from Brighton and called for his employment, he would be grateful she'd refused his guilty proposal of marriage.

While he dressed silently, she twisted her hair into a hasty knot, fastening it with the pins he'd removed earlier. Without seeming to take notice if she was ready, he left the room and descended the stairs to the hall. By the time she joined him, he was already in hat and gloves, waiting by the door for her. She hurried into her bonnet and gloves and he opened the door.

'We can walk, I believe.' He spoke stiffly. 'Greythorne will not know from where we came.'

She had forgotten about Greythorne. After he closed and locked the door, she glanced back at it, the place she'd felt such joy, such desolation. Outside its door nothing remained but the horror of Greythorne, the loss of her father, and the sordid prospect of becoming Tannerton's kept woman. Even worse, she would have to face all, knowing she'd lost Flynn totally.

She soon was out of breath trying to keep up with Flynn's stride. In too short a time they were at Madame Bisou's door.

'I leave you here, Rose,' he said. 'I suggest you remain indoors tomorrow. Tannerton will send word to you.' He turned to leave.

She grabbed his arm. 'Flynn!' she cried, forgetting everything but loving him. 'Will I see you again?'

The eyes that regarded her were like ice. 'If the marquess requires it, I shall comply.'

He turned away as Cummings opened the door, but she did not enter until he rounded the corner and she could no longer see him walking away from her.

Chapter Nineteen

Flynn walked immediately back to the rooms, dreading a return to the bedchamber, the place of loving her.

Inside, he took the steps two at a time, figuring it best to discharge the task quickly. He entered the room and strode directly to the rumpled bed, tearing off the linens and cramming them into a bundle he intended to throw away. Then he set about erasing all evidence of what they had shared in the room. It ought to have felt cathartic to do so. Instead it felt wretched.

How big a fool could he have been? She had completely misguided him. Even now he could not tell the exact nature of her character. Was she the virgin who schemed to be a courtesan, as she'd insisted? Or an innocent caught up in her own desires, and he the man who had awakened them?

No more than an hour later Flynn left the house as if he had never entered it with Rose. He walked back to Audley Street, telling himself he had no need to understand Rose. She would go to Tanner, and that would be the end of it.

As he walked, Flynn laboured to rebuild the wall that hardened his heart. But then he'd catch a memory of her scent, the flash of her smile, or her face flushed with passion, and the wall would crumble, leaving him with no shelter at all.

He was startled by a man who emerged from the shadows, a man who turned and walked in the other direction. Flynn's heart went cold.

He'd almost forgotten there was a man out there who had killed over her, who might be stalking her at this very moment. No matter his tattered emotions, she still needed to be protected.

He entered Tannerton's town house at the same moment Tanner strolled out of the library and saw him.

'Where the devil have you been all day?' The question was a typical one for Tanner to ask when Flynn had been busy performing one task after another on his behalf. Today, however, his employer's voice grated on Flynn's shredded nerves.

'Errands,' Flynn replied, keen to get away.

It was no use. 'Come here a moment,' Tanner said. 'I have news.'

Resigned, Flynn turned and followed Tanner into the library.

'What news?' He tried to sound interested.

Tanner leaned casually against the desk, crossing his legs at the ankles. 'I heard from the Bow Street Runner I sent to Brighton yesterday. He returned not an hour ago.'

Flynn came alert. 'And?'

'No one has seen Greythorne for several days.'

Flynn's fingers curled into a fist. 'This is no surprise.'

'Indeed.' Tanner lifted his finger in the air. 'But it foxed me that the Duke did not send a message alerting me to that fact. It seems Greythorne arrived with his Royal Highness, but quickly shut himself in his rooms with reports he was suffering from some sort of contagious blight. Only his own servants attended him.'

'Clever of him. He appears to be in Brighton, but is not.

And when he has finished his treachery towards…Miss O'Keefe…' Flynn's voice faltered. He had difficulty even speaking her name.

Tanner did not seem to notice. Rather, he finished Flynn's sentence. 'He will return to Brighton and show himself miraculously recovered.' Tanner pushed away from the desk. 'The Runner who went to Greythorne's town house is convinced he did not return there; however, in the part of town where the bodies were discovered, there had been talk that a gentleman had paid someone to dump them in place where they would be easily found.'

Tanner had spared no expense with these Bow Street Runners. How many had he hired?

'Thing is,' Tanner continued, his expression stricken, 'I didn't outwit Greythorne, Flynn. I merely made him more dangerous. Some game I engaged in.' He gave a frustrated sound and rubbed his brow. 'Where the devil is he?'

Greythorne disdained the plain black coat pulling across his shoulders. Its cut was common, as was its fit. But if he were going to pretend to be a merchant, he had better dress like one.

He looked down his nose at the creature standing before him, common to the core, but useful. 'Like I said, the gent and the girl left in a coach. I was able to follow it a ways. Heading into Westminster, it was, I'd wager on it.' The man wiped his nose on his sleeve.

Greythorne cringed.

The man continued, 'Couldn't keep up, I couldn't. So I waited for 'em to return and, let me tell you, they took their time. Took all day, it did.'

Greythorne stifled a yawn. 'If you have information of value, I beg you would get on with it.'

The man grinned, showing the gap of a missing tooth. 'Most sure it is of value, sir. Worth a pound or two, I expect, but I'll let you decide, sir.'

'Get on with it,' Greythorne repeated. Paying well was the best guarantee of loyalty, he could agree, but this man was trying his patience.

'Well.' The man took a breath. 'Finally, after I waited all day—and let me tell you how hard it is to wait all day—'

'Do not.' Greythorne glared at the man.

'Anyways, when they finally arrive back at Madame Bisou's gaming-house, they are walkin', y'see. And seeing as how the gent left and didn't take a coach, I followed him.'

This account was tedious in the extreme. Greythorne amused himself by imagining what this creature's face would look like if a leather strap were twisted around his neck, cutting off the air—

'Interestingly enough,' the man went on, 'the gent didn't go in the direction of that fancy town house. He went the other way into a building on Great Ryder Street.'

Greythorne sat up. 'Is that so?'

'Stayed a few minutes, then come out with a bundle. Tossed the bundle and then walked all the way back to Audley Street.'

This was curious. 'What was in the bundle?'

The man rubbed his neck. 'Don't know, sir, some rascally boys grabbed it afore I could get to it, so I hurried off to see where the gent was going.'

Greythorne grimaced. If this business meant Tannerton got to the O'Keefe chit before he did, he would be very unhappy. 'Tell me, what did the gentleman look like?'

'Dark-haired fellow. Looked Irish, if you ask me.'

Greythorne gave a silent laugh. The secretary, Flynn. Excellent. Greythorne had already discovered that Flynn had procured a set of rooms and hired servants. This must have been the girl's inspection of her new home.

Greythorne stood. 'Show me this place, and the two pounds will be yours.'

Rose sat at the window, watching gentlemen walk in and out of Madame Bisou's house, but none was Flynn. There was no use to hope for him to return. She had ensured he would not.

A knock sounded at the door, and Katy came in. 'Why don't you come downstairs, Rose? You could sit in the supper room. Those footmen Lord Tannerton sent over could sit nearby.'

Rose shook her head. 'I'll stay here. I'm thinking I'm in need of an evening to myself.' She didn't sing at Vauxhall this night.

Katy plopped on the bed. 'Don't sit here alone all that time. You'll think of your father or something.'

Her father. The grief of losing her father only made losing Flynn worse.

'I'll not think of my father, I promise,' she told her friend.

Katy swung her legs as she sat, looking like a little girl eager to play. 'Where were you all day, by the way? Cummings said you went out early, when I was still sleeping.'

'It was not that early.' She and Flynn had picked a time anyone might go out.

Katy's eyes lit up with understanding. 'You were with *Flynnnnn.*' She emphasised Flynn's name, drawing it out. 'Where did you go? I hope not to the magistrate again.'

'Not the magistrate,' Rose replied.

Katy waited for more.

Rose took a breath. 'Flynn showed me the rooms he found for me.'

Katy leaned forward. 'The ones Tannerton purchased?'

She sighed. 'It is just like Harriette Wilson told us! You get property of your own. Tell me. Are they grand?'

Rose tried to sound as excited as Katy. 'They are pretty rooms, really. There is a kitchen and a drawing room, a dining room, and abovestairs, a sitting room, and…a bedchamber.'

Katy looked rapturous. But Rose turned away.

'There is something you are not telling me,' Katy said.

Rose felt tears spring to her eyes. 'There is nothing.'

Katy got off the bed and stepped in front of her. 'What is it, Rose?'

Rose turned away again.

Katy turned her back. 'Rose?'

Rose clamped her mouth shut.

'Oh, Rose! You were with Flynn!' Katy held her shoulders. 'Ack! I do not know whether to congratulate you or to shake you!'

'I am not saying I was with Flynn,' Rose retorted. 'I am not.'

Katy gave her a hug. 'Foolish, Rose. What are you going to do?'

'I am doing nothing,' Rose insisted. 'Nothing at all.'

'Tell me what happened,' Katy said.

Rose backed away. 'Katy, there is nothing I can tell you.'

'Well, did you take care of yourself?' Katy asked. 'You know, like Madame Bisou taught us.'

Rose did not answer her.

There was another knock on the door, and Katy hurried over to answer it.

The footman Wiggins stood there. 'Beg pardon, miss,' he said to Rose, 'Mr Flynn sent word we were to stay right outside your door.'

Her stomach did a flip-flop at hearing Flynn's name. 'Why, Mr Wiggins?'

'He said Lord Greythorne was about, and it would be best to guard you close. Me and Smythe will take turns.'

Katy turned pale.

'Thank you, Mr Wiggins,' Rose replied, walking over to the door. 'I shall feel very safe with you there.' She closed it behind him.

Katy trembled. 'He is near?'

It was Rose's turn to comfort. 'We are very safe, Katy. You are safe. He does not know you reside here, does he?'

She shook her head. 'I never told him.' She gave Rose a very intent look. 'Wait here.'

Katy returned a few minutes later. She lifted Rose's hand and placed a small sheathed knife in her palm. 'Take this, just in case. Wear it on you somewhere.'

Rose looked at the small weapon. 'I should not know what to do with it.'

Katy's eyes turned fierce. 'Jab it into his throat.'

The next afternoon, Cummings sent word that Rose had a visitor waiting in the parlor. The hope that it was Flynn swelled inside her. Wiggins and Smythe accompanied her, telling her to stay back while they entered the parlor first. They immediately emerged with grins on their faces. 'You can go in, miss.'

Nearly giddy with anticipation, Rose stepped into the room.

Tannerton stood there, smiling in greeting.

Her spirits plunged. 'Good day, sir,' she managed.

'And to you, Miss O'Keefe.' He crossed the room and blew a kiss over her hand. 'I thought to call on you to see how you were faring.'

'I am well, sir.' As always, she did not know what to say to this man. 'And you?'

He waved his hand dismissively. 'I am always well.' He gestured for her to sit on the room's sofa.

She hesitated, thinking he would sit beside her, fearing he would touch her. She was not ready for that. But she must become accustomed to doing what he wanted. She would be his mistress in one day's time.

She sat on the sofa.

To her surprise he flung himself in the adjacent chair. 'Flynn is over at your rooms, seeing all is in order. He told me he showed them to you. Are they to your liking?'

Hearing Flynn's name was painful, and it was painful to think of him in those rooms where she had been so briefly happy. 'They were very pretty. I'm thinking anyone would say so.'

'Excellent!' He seemed genuinely pleased. 'Tell me, are Wiggins and Smythe keeping watch over you?'

She nodded. 'They follow me everywhere.'

'Like spaniels!' He grinned. 'They are good fellows.'

She had no response and the awkward silence made her face grow hot with shame. Why could she not converse with him? He always behaved very well toward her. Even his kisses did not ask more of her than she could give.

'By the way—' he gave no indication that he had noticed the lapse in their conversation '—I can release you from your promise.'

Her heart pounded. 'My promise?'

He winked. 'To keep the secret I told you about. Flynn's new employment.'

She gaped at him. 'Flynn will work for the prince?'

'As soon as his Highness has returned from Brighton, assuming this Greythorne business does not change matters. I told Flynn yesterday.'

Her throat felt suddenly raw. She was happy for Flynn, she

told herself. He would get his greatest desire. 'He must have been very pleased.'

He tilted his head. 'Well, not as much as I thought he would be, but you can never tell with Flynn. Let me warn you. Never play cards with the man. He gives away nothing of what he feels.'

She could disagree. He'd shown her all too well. Briefly.

'Flynn will go to the Prince after he returns from Ireland.'

'Ireland?' She sat up straighter. 'He is going to Ireland?'

'Wants to visit his family, I believe,' he said. 'Cannot fathom why he did not ask to do so before. Deuced long time to be away. I was beginning to surmise he had no family.'

Rose was suddenly homesick for Ireland herself, for its green hills and fresh air. For the lilting speech she'd sought to rid herself of, the kind of speech she and Flynn so gaily shared.

Tanner tapped his lips, looking thoughtful. 'I wonder what the prince will think when he finds out Greythorne deceived him.' He regarded her. 'The Bow Street Runner discovered that Greythorne gave his Royal Highness the slip. But, then, we knew he was back in London.'

Not knowing how else to respond, she merely nodded.

His mouth fell open. 'I do beg your pardon. I never offered my sympathy for the death of your father and his lady friend. Such a shock for you.'

'Yes,' was all she could say.

He took her hand, and it was all she could do to keep from pulling away. 'I promise you, we shall find Greythorne and bring him to justice for this. You have my solemn word on it.' He squeezed her hand in reassurance, nothing more.

'Thank you, my lord,' she said.

He stood and gazed down at her. 'I underestimated Greythorne, Miss O'Keefe.' He looked genuinely regretful. 'I am profoundly sorry for it.'

She rose, touched by his sincerity. 'I am not blaming you, sir,' she told him. 'It was Greythorne who…who killed them.'

His eyes did not lose their hint of pain, and she realised that this was indeed a good man. She wished she could rejoice in his interest in her and return the affection he deserved.

He averted his gaze and made to look at his timepiece. 'I had best be on my way.' He started for the door, but turned back to her. 'Flynn made all the arrangements for you to occupy the rooms tomorrow. I shall send my carriage in the afternoon, if that is to your liking.'

No, it was not to her liking, but what else could she do?

'I shall be ready.'

He smiled. 'Good! About three o'clock, perhaps? You will have time to get settled, then I will escort you to Vauxhall, if you like.'

She merely nodded.

He started off again, but again turned back, walking over to her. He gave her a quick kiss on the lips. 'Until then, Miss O'Keefe.'

The servants lined up in the small hallway for Flynn's final inspection of the preparations for Rose's arrival. Wiggins and Smythe would also join the household as Rose's constant guards, with Bow Street Runners to relieve them.

Flynn questioned the house servants in turn, and each declared that they were ready to serve Miss O'Keefe. And ready to serve Lord Tannerton, as well.

Before turning to leave, Flynn glanced one last time up the stairway towards the bedchamber.

It was doubtful he would ever return to these rooms, now that Lord Tannerton had arranged his employment with the Duke of Clarence. Flynn could not have expected a better

situation. The Prince was third in line for the throne, though
the Princess Charlotte might knock her uncle down a peg
when her baby was born. Still, the Duke of Clarence was
much higher than Flynn had dared hope.

He ought to have whooped with excitement and clasped
Tanner's hand in a vigorous handshake when he'd heard the
news. Instead, he had coolly clarified his intention to travel
to Ireland first.

If the joy of this advancement had been leached from his
emotions, Flynn was at least satisfied with the honour of it.

He left Rose's new apartments and walked towards St
James's Street. Crossing Piccadilly into Mayfair, Flynn told
himself not to think of Rose or of Tanner, who would accompany her back to Great Ryder Street from Vauxhall.

Flynn returned to Tanner's house and almost feared encountering his employer on the stairway again. He entered the
library and pulled out papers from the drawers, determined
to work. Tanner's affairs would be in order before he left for
Ireland, he vowed.

He began making a list from the papers he'd taken out of
the drawer. They were bills he'd not yet paid, correspondence
he'd not yet returned. Proceeding methodically through the
stack, Flynn began to feel more settled. The mundane task
kept his mind occupied, and he so much wished to keep his
mind occupied.

He came across the bill of the Bow Street Runner who had
travelled to Brighton, tallying his charges and expenses. Flynn
placed the pen back into its holder and dropped his head into
his hands. He could not leave Tanner's employ until he knew
Rose was safe from Greythorne.

He tried to tell himself he could trust Tanner to see to her
safety. It was the sort of challenge Tanner might skilfully

meet, but Flynn would not rest while Greythorne still lurked about, waiting for his chance to capture Rose.

An image of her tied up and at Greythorne's mercy came to his mind. It would never happen.

Never.

Flynn rose from his seat, too restless to work. He stacked the papers again and returned them to the drawer.

Rose would be most vulnerable at Vauxhall, Flynn surmised, no matter how many men Tanner had hired to guard her. Flynn must go to Vauxhall, no matter how painful it would be to see her and know she would never be his. He must watch for danger. She would not have to know he was there, but he would ensure she made it to her new bed in safety.

Greythorne reviewed the plan one more time. It was a masterpiece of logistics, if he did say so himself, an elegant means of wreaking vengeance on Tannerton for presuming Greythorne could be disposed of so easily.

He looked at the men standing before him, an unkempt, unsavoury lot, but the sort you could pay to do whatever you wanted of them.

'You know your tasks?' he asked.

'That we do, sir,' one said.

The others nodded or mumbled agreement.

'You shall capture them, not harm them,' Greythorne reminded them.

The pleasure of harming them would be his alone.

Chapter Twenty

Flynn came to Vauxhall in a mask, ordinary garb in the place where nothing was as it seemed. What he'd once disdained he had grown to fancy over these summer weeks, now finding delight in the magic of the pleasure gardens. This, after all, had been the place he'd heard her sing, danced with her in his arms, and stolen kisses under the flickering lamps.

He stood in the Grove, off to the side where he could peruse the crowd, but still easily view the balcony. He fancied every unaccompanied man to be a danger to Rose, every masked one to be Greythorne. He spied Wiggins and Smythe easily enough and two of the Bow Street Runners who earlier had reported to Tanner their failure to find Greythorne. Flynn spied Tanner, too, also scanning for danger.

The orchestra sounded her introduction, and Rose appeared on the balcony. Flynn forgot everything else but the elegant tilt of her head, the graceful poise of her posture.

She began with 'Eileen Aroon,' and he was transported to the time he'd first set eyes on her. She was more beautiful now, if such a thing were possible. Her voice was richer, stronger, more suffused with sensuality. He let her voice envelop him as once her arms had done.

Her eyes searched the crowd as she sang. He longed to have her eyes find him, as they'd done before. He'd seen the awareness in her face that night, an awareness he shared. The magic connection they made that night was one his grandfather would have blamed on the fairies, the ancients, on Cupid.

She sang song after song of love, its joys, its loss. Never had her voice so plucked the strings of emotion, enough to crack the hardest heart. Flynn heard sniffles in the crowd, saw more than one person dab their eyes with a handkerchief. It was he who ought to weep, he thought. It was he who had lost her.

Ironically, though, her voice consoled him. Healed him. By the time she began her last song, he felt whole again, instead of a man torn into pieces.

She sang:

> Young I am and yet unskilled,
> How to make a lover yield…

He recognised the words, although he'd not heard her perform this song before. Its lyrics were from a Dryden poem about a girl who knew no love would be as pure or as true as her first love. Any men who came after would receive only a pretense of love.

'He that has me first, is blest,' she sang with undisguised honesty. It was as if a lightning bolt came from the dark night sky, striking him, filling him with its light.

She'd lied to him when she'd refused his proposal, Flynn realised. For some unfathomable reason, she'd lied about wanting Tanner's money, about wanting to be a mistress instead of a wife.

He was filled with energy, with excitement. He could hardly wait to find her, to tell her he knew the truth.

The truth was in her song.

It no longer mattered that he would make an enemy of a marquess and dash his dreams of serving royalty. The truth was, he coveted Rose more than that dream. He would marry her. Take her to Ireland with him. Show her off to his family and receive their blessing. Somewhere they would find a new life, a fine life, a life worth singing about.

> Take me, take me, some of you,
> While I yet am young and true.

Yes, Rose, he vowed. *I will.*

Her song ended, and the applause thundered like never before. Shouts of 'hurrah' and 'bravo' filled the air, over and over. She looked stunned, but dropped into a graceful curtsy before turning away and fleeing. The crowd surged forward, shouting, 'Encore!'

Flynn tried to push his way through the still-cheering audience to reach the gazebo door. When he finally got near, more admirers than ever crowded the area. Through the throng of men, he glimpsed Tanner, arm protectively around Rose, leading her away, flanked by Wiggins and Smythe. Flynn struggled to reach them, but the crowd forced him farther and farther behind.

He finally broke free on to the Grand Walk, but lost sight of them. Hurrying to the gate where Tanner's carriage would be waiting, he reached it in time to see Tanner help Rose inside the coach and Wiggins and Smythe climb on top. As the carriage sped away, Flynn caught a glimpse of a man crouched down and hanging on the back.

The hairs rose on the back of his neck.

Greythorne was making his move.

Flynn ran to the nearest hackney coach and shouted, 'Follow that carriage, and I'll triple your fare.' He climbed up next to the jarvey, who looked stunned.

It took some time for the hackney coach to manoeuvre on to the road, but Flynn could still see Tanner's carriage in the distance. The hackney coach's old nag was no match for Tanner's team, and soon all that was visible of Tanner's vehicle was the faint glow of the carriage's lamp.

'Sorry, guv'nor,' the jarvey said.

Flynn pulled the mask off and rubbed his face. 'Try to keep the lamplight in view.'

But that, too, quickly faded from sight.

Rose shivered, even though she wore her cape and the inside of the carriage was warm.

'That crowd was quite unexpected,' said Tannerton. 'But you are safe now.'

'Safe,' she repeated.

She had not been thinking of her safety from the crowds nor even from Greythorne. She'd been thinking about Flynn. Somehow, singing made her feel closer to him, as if he were with her still and would always be with her. As she'd sung the words of the love songs, the emotion behind them filled her soul, and it was as if a bright light illuminated their meaning. The songs, the music, the emotion, all were entwined with Flynn. She still shook inside from the power of it, the power of her love for him.

She glanced at Tannerton, who had leaned his head against the fine upholstery of the carriage seat and closed his eyes.

It would be wrong to pretend at loving with this man, she suddenly realised. Had she never met Flynn, never fallen in love with him, never made love with him, she might have formed some true affection for Tannerton, but, as it was, she would always resent him for not being Flynn.

She felt bereft, but at the same time liberated. It no longer mattered to her that she sing at King's Theatre or Vauxhall or any other place. Nothing would replace what she'd so briefly had with Flynn. Nothing mattered as much.

She blinked away tears. She wanted to go home. To Ireland, even though she had no home there, no family left anywhere. Perhaps she would return to the school at Killyleagh and beg for work there, any work.

She pressed her palm to her belly, hoping that she might be with child. Bearing Flynn's child would be a joy. She would find some way to rear the babe, to bestow on Flynn's child the lessons of love.

She remembered suddenly that her mother had never spoken of leaving the London stage with regret. She never lamented the choice she had made, the choice of being with the man she loved and bearing his child.

Rose stared at Tannerton again. His face was softer than Flynn's, unlined, untroubled. He was a handsome man, the sort Katy would say made a girl's head turn, and a kind man. Whether he knew it or not, he deserved more than a pretence of love.

'Lord Tannerton?' She spoke quietly, not certain if he slept.

His eyes opened. 'Yes?'

'I have something to ask you. To tell you, really.'

'Then tell, Miss O'Keefe.' He smiled. 'Or shall I call you Rose, since we are about to begin our association?'

Their association. 'If you wish.'

'What is it, then, Rose?' His expression conveyed only mild curiosity, as if whatever she said would be easily forgotten. He did not realise how important her decision would be for him.

She drew in a long breath. 'About tonight, sir—'

Before she could speak another word, shouts sounded from the outside and the carriage came to a lurching halt.

Tannerton was instantly on the alert. 'Stay in here.'

He was halfway out of the carriage when a shadowy figure on the outside brought a club down hard upon his head.

Rose screamed.

Tannerton was shoved back into the carriage and fell into a crumpled heap beside her. She grabbed his coat and tried to set him upright to see if he were still alive.

A man climbed in. 'Good evening, Rose.'

Greythorne.

She lunged towards the door, but he shoved her back in her seat and was quickly on top of her. Rose tried to push him off, but he was too heavy. He pulled her cloak off her and tossed it upon Tannerton's body. Rose clawed at Greythorne's face and nearly succeeded in opening the carriage door so she could jump out. No matter it was now moving fast, she preferred jumping into the darkness to being Greythorne's captive.

But he seized the back of her dress and hauled her back in the seat. His hand closed around her neck like a vice as he straddled her again. His lips crushed against hers as his fingers cut off all air. Feeling herself blacking out, she prayed not to die with that man's lips on her.

Laughing, he suddenly released her. She gulped in as much air as her lungs could hold.

'I am stronger, Rose. Remember that.'

While she could do nothing but gasp and cough, he pulled

out a cord from his pocket and tied her hands and her feet. She tried to scream for help, but only a rasping sound came out. He produced a piece of cloth and tied it around her mouth so even that pitiful sound was muffled.

'You are at my mercy,' he went on in a menacing voice. 'And I intend to show you precisely who your master is. You will do my bidding, if you want to live.'

He pulled more cord from his pockets and bound Tannerton's hands behind his back and tied his ankles. The marquess remained senseless. Rose prayed he was alive.

As if in answer to her prayer, Tannerton moaned.

'This man thought he could thwart me, fool that he is. Your father and that cow of a woman also thought they could thwart me.' He lifted Rose's chin, forcing her to look at him. 'I assume you know what happened to them.'

Perhaps she ought to have prayed instead that Tannerton had escaped the fate that awaited them.

Greythorne rubbed his hand on her neck, pretending he was going to squeeze it again, and laughed when she recoiled. He slid his hand down to her chest, pushing his fingers under her dress to roughly fondle her breast.

Bile rose in her throat, and she swallowed it, fearful she'd choke.

'Has he touched you like this?' he asked, his eyes boring into her.

For a moment she thought the 'he' Greythorne referred to was Flynn, but his glance slid to Tannerton.

She shook her head.

'Then I am not too late.' He squeezed her, watching her face as she tried to cry out in pain, the sound impeded by the gag in her mouth. He laughed again.

His eyes glittered in the scant light from the carriage's

outside lanterns. He looked like an engraving she'd once seen of the devil.

She had the distinct feeling she was about to descend into hell.

Flynn peered into the night, hoping to catch sight of the carriage again. He was tempted to urge for more speed, but the hack's horses were already pushed to the limit and travelling faster on the dark road was too risky. There was only one way the carriage might go, at least for several miles, across the Vauxhall Bridge and on the road along the river. Flynn tried to remain calm.

Suddenly two men appeared at the side of the road, waving frantically for the hackney to stop. The jarvey did not rein in his horses.

'Wait!' cried Flynn. 'Stop the coach.'

'Could be thieves,' the man said.

'No, stop the coach.'

They had gone past the men by this time, but, as the coachman pulled the horse to a stop, one of the men ran toward them.

'Your assistance, sir!' the man cried. 'We have an injured man here.'

Flynn recognised him. 'Wiggins!' He jumped down.

'Mr Flynn, sir!' Wiggins said with some emotion. 'Wait for us. Smythe is hurt.'

He ran back to where another man he recognised as Tanner's coachman John stood next to Smythe, seated on the ground. The two men hoisted Smythe to his feet and carried him to the hack.

'Put him inside,' Flynn said. 'John, climb above and watch for Tannerton's coach.'

He helped Wiggins get Smythe into the carriage.

'It's my leg,' groaned Smythe. 'Broke it, I think.'

Flynn spared no time for sympathy. 'Tell me what happened.'

Wiggins's hand was bloody and limp. 'Two men on horseback stopped the carriage. They grabbed the horses, and one of them came alongside and pulled John Coachman off—'

'We tried to stop him,' Smythe broke in.

Wiggins nodded. 'Then, while we were pulling on him one way and the blackguard the other way, some fellow comes from behind and pushes us off.' He winced. 'I saw his lordship get hit on the head. With a club. It was that Lord Greythorne, I'd wager a year's pay on it. He got into the carriage and it drove off with the lot of them, before we could even get to our feet.'

Flynn frowned. Where were they headed? The Bow Street Runners had discovered nothing about where Greythorne had gone after sneaking out of Brighton. Was he even in London? 'We'll take you both to Audley Street and send for the physician.'

Never had the trip back from Vauxhall seemed so slow. It gave Flynn too much time to think. Too much time to remember the marks of torture on O'Keefe's and Miss Dean's bodies. Too much time to fear finding a shrouded Rose carelessly laid out on a wooden table.

He forced himself not to turn his mind in that direction, but something kept drawing him back. Something nagging.

By the time the hackney coach pulled up to the Audley Street town house, Flynn had the answer. He helped the injured men out of the coach and dug in his pocket for the promised triple fare. The jarvey stuck his whip in its holder and Flynn froze.

He turned to Wiggins. 'Get the physician and send a message to Bow Street. I need some men to help. Tell them to go to Madame Bisou's. I will leave the direction there.' He put the money in the jarvey's hand. 'I require more of you. To Bennet Street.' He climbed inside the hack.

When he reached Bennet Street, he hurried to the door. When Cummings answered it, Flynn said, 'Where is Madame Bisou? I need her.'

'Game room,' Cummings replied.

Several men and one or two women looked up from their play when he rushed in. He went directly to Madame Bisou.

'I would speak with you a moment,' he said, taking her arm.

Katy was standing nearby at the hazard table. 'What is it, Flynn?' She followed them out.

He took them aside in the hallway. 'Greythorne has captured Rose and Tannerton. I need to know who told Rose he used whips.'

Madame Bisou glanced towards Katy. Flynn swung around. Katy's face was white and she backed away.

He stopped her. 'Was it you, Katy?'

She shook her head and tried to get away. 'It was Iris. Ask Iris.'

'Iris is not here tonight,' Madame Bisou said in an alarmed voice.

Flynn grabbed Katy's arms. 'I must know, Katy. Tell me what you know.'

She trembled all over, and he thought she might sink to the floor. He put his arms around her. 'Katy.' He spoke kindly but firmly. 'I need you to help me find Rose. I am afraid he will kill her, and Tanner, too.'

'Tell him, Katy,' the *madame* cried, but Katy merely buried her face in Flynn's chest. 'He whipped her skin raw,' Madame Bisou said. 'But she escaped from him.'

Flynn made Katy look at him. 'Then you know the place. You must show me where it is.'

Her eyes were panicked, but she finally pursed her lips and nodded.

'Make haste!' Flynn pulled her towards the door.

'Take Cummings with you!' called Madame Bisou.

Rose pulled against the leather bindings on her wrists, but they held her securely to iron rings imbedded in the wall. Similar bindings held her feet. Katy had loosened her bindings when she'd been his captive, and Rose was determined to do the same.

Greythorne had carried her inside a town house, down a narrow set of stone steps, deep into a basement, to this room with its thick wooden door and long table with metal rings attached to it. The table frightened her. Would he bind her to it next? Another man had hauled Tannerton, dumping him on the floor like a sack of potatoes. Tannerton still lay on the stone floor. He moaned every so often, so at least he was alive, but for how long? Greythorne certainly intended to kill him.

Rose made her hand as narrow as she could and tried to slip the binding off, but it cut into her skin. She tried again, until her wrist bled.

Greythorne had warned he would be back when Tannerton regained his senses. Greythorne wanted the marquess to watch whatever he planned to do to her. She shuddered, knowing from Katy that he would strip off her soiled and ripped clothing and strike her with one of several whips that hung on one wall as orderly as teacups in a cupboard.

Tannerton moaned again, but this time he jerked against his restraints. 'Deuce!' he mumbled. 'Where the devil?'

'You are in a house in London. He didn't take us very far.'

He glanced over at her and struggled more, then shut his eyes and moaned. 'Greythorne.'

'He hit you on the head,' she told him.

He rocked himself into a sitting position. 'I feel it. Where is he?'

'Abovestairs.' She tried to speak calmly, but her voice shook. 'He said he wanted you to be awake. While he waited, he said he would change his clothes and have some supper.'

'Damned inhospitable of him not to offer us supper.' He leaned his head against the stone of the wall and closed his eyes again. 'I am sorry, Rose. Ought to have left the whole matter to Flynn. He'd not have made a muddle of it.'

She had been trying not to think of Flynn. Her dear Flynn, who would undoubtedly be called upon to view their bodies and tell the magistrate who they were.

'Did the bastard hurt you, Rose?' he asked.

She decided not to tell him about Greythorne strangling her. 'Not as yet. I'm thinking that comes later.'

'Deuce.'

She had been a prisoner once before. Miss Hart had freed her with cunning and bravery. She must be brave this time. And cunning. When dressing for Vauxhall, she'd stuck Katy's knife under her corset. She had no hope of reaching it, but Tannerton was less fettered than she.

'Lord Tannerton, can you get over here and stand?' she asked.

He opened his eyes in narrow slits. 'I have no idea. Why?'

'I have a small knife under my corset.'

He laughed, then winced in pain. 'Damned good place for it.'

'I didn't know where else to put it.' she said. 'If you can move over here, I think you will be able to get it out.'

He used his legs to push himself over to her. His head lolled back and forth as he moved, showing how dizzy he must be.

When he got to her, he said, 'I must grab on to you to pull myself up. It will put a strain on your arms.'

'No matter,' she said firmly. 'Just do it.'

It was difficult for him to pull himself up with his hands behind his back. It took him several tries before he stood. She thought her arms would come out of their sockets with his weight.

She tried to ignore the pain. 'Pull up my skirts. It is right at my waist under my right arm.'

He swayed as he lifted her skirt, and she knew he would not be able to keep his balance for long. She finally felt his fingers on her bare skin. She stretched her torso as best she could to give his fingers room to pull out the knife.

'Got it!' He tugged on it and it clattered to the floor. He swayed, and his eyes rolled back.

'Hold on to me,' she ordered. 'Lower yourself slowly.'

Somehow he did as she asked, finding the little knife and hiding it between his hands.

He sat very still. 'Dizzy.'

She feared Greythorne would find him next to her and become suspicious, but after a minute or two, he moved back to his place by the wall.

'Katy told me to carry the knife,' she said, still trying to battle panic.

'Good girl, Katy,' he mumbled.

She watched him awkwardly work the knife against the cord tying his hands. 'You were about to tell me something in the carriage.' He spoke as if they were sitting in some elegant drawing room.

'It does not matter now.'

'No, tell me,' he insisted. 'We must talk of something.'

'I will tell you if we escape.' She could not tell him she did not love him, not when he might die this night.

He did not persist. After a pause he said, 'De Sade. Wrote these books. Forbidden books. Passed around everywhere, naturally. Read them at Oxford. In French. *Les Prospérités du Vice. Justine.*'

She tried twisting her hands in their bindings. 'I am not understanding you, my lord.'

He opened his eyes and gave her an urgent stare. 'Listen, Rose. When he starts in on you, grovel, cower, beg for his mercy. Promise him you will do whatever he wants.'

She glared back. 'I never will.'

'Do it,' he ordered. 'He will enjoy your fear. It is the only way to outwit him.' He swallowed. 'Give him your fear, and he might release you from your bonds.'

If she could get free like Katy had done, she could fight him off. They would have a chance.

There was the scraping of a key in a lock. They both swivelled their heads to the door.

Greythorne entered, dressed in a brown banyan of figured silk, slippers and night cap.

He turned to Tannerton. 'You are awake. How splendid.'

'You have hurt him badly.' Rose turned her voice into a whine. 'He doesn't stay awake.'

Tannerton let his head droop. Had he caught her cue, or was he really passing out again? Greythorne marched over and pulled his head up by the hair. 'Stay awake if you know what is good for you.'

Tannerton's eyes rolled.

Greythorne approached Rose more slowly. She had never seen a snake, but she thought a snake must move the same.

'Don't hurt me, sir.' She tried to sound weak and frightened. It was surprisingly easy because it was so close to the truth. 'Don't hurt me. I'll do anything you ask, just don't hurt me!'

His eyes glittered with pleasure. He slithered up to her and took the pins from her hair. Flynn had done the same, she remembered, but out of love. Her hair tumbled down on her shoulders. He examined one of the pins, grinned, and made as if to poke her with it.

She shrank back.

He laughed. 'You think this pain?' He put his face an inch from hers and pushed the point of the hairpin into the flesh of her arm. 'You do not know what real pain can be.'

'I will do anything. Anything.' She looked around wildly. 'Do...do you want me to undress for you? I will undress for you, my lord.'

His eyes widened with interest.

'You will like it, my lord,' she said.

He glared at her. 'Have you ever undressed for Tannerton?'

She shook her head. 'I've never been with him, sir. Tonight was the night. I...I think I can please you, if you give me a chance.'

He walked over to the wall and selected one of the whips and cracked it next to her ear, so that she felt the wind it produced against her cheek. 'You have to be punished, you know.'

She nodded.

He undid her bindings and she fell to the floor, pretending to be afraid. When he stepped closer, his banyan fell open and she saw her chance.

She grabbed where he was most sensitive and squeezed with all her might, like Katy had done. He cried out, dropping the whip and doubling over. Tannerton had freed himself and was struggling to get to his feet. He dropped the knife, which clattered to the floor. He tried to reach for it, but she grabbed his arm.

'Come!' She pulled him out of the door, slamming it behind her.

He stumbled towards the stairs, but could only crawl up.

Rose followed behind, pushing him. 'Make haste.'

Suddenly Greythorne caught her and dragged her back to his room of torture. He threw her with such force she rolled on the floor and hit the wall with a painful thud.

He hauled her upright again, but she twisted away from him.

'Stay away!' she cried, grabbing one of the whips and driving him back with it, until he wrested it out of her hand.

'Bitch!' With eyes red and bulging, he slapped her across the face so that she fell to the ground. This time her fingers closed around Katy's knife. She silently swore she would use it.

When he pulled her to her feet, she came at his throat with the knife, jabbing it into his skin until he bled.

He staggered backwards and she ran out of the room once again.

Tannerton was trying to come down the stairs.

'Hurry.' She pushed him ahead of her. 'I've stabbed him.'

They stumbled out into a hallway, just as the door of the town house crashed open, and Flynn and Cummings rushed in.

'Flynn!' Rose fell into his arms. 'I think I've killed him.'

He held her. 'Rose.'

Tannerton leaned against the wall. 'Get her out, Flynn.' He slumped to the floor, and Cummings ran to assist him.

Flynn released Rose. 'I'll see to Greythorne. Then we'll summon the watch.' She did not want to leave his side.

As she led Flynn to the basement stairs, Greythorne burst through the doorway. He lunged at Rose, but Flynn knocked him aside. The two men grappled, pounding each other with fists.

'Flynn!' Rose cried in alarm, more fearful for Flynn than she'd been for herself.

Greythorne was wild with rage, swinging recklessly as Flynn hit him again and again. Greythorne crashed into a table and it shattered beneath him, but he jumped to his feet, brandishing the jagged end of one of the table's broken legs.

'Stay back, Rose.' Flynn pushed her behind him and backed away from the newly made weapon.

Suddenly Katy appeared behind Greythorne.

She hit him on the head with a bottle, shattering it, sending wine and glass flying.

'See how you like it,' she shrieked. 'See how you like pain!'

Greythorne stumbled towards the stairs to the basement, his foot slipping on a piece of wood from the broken table, then let out a cry as he tumbled down the hard stone steps, hitting the floor below with a sickening thud.

Rose followed Flynn to peek down at the crumpled, contorted form. 'Is he—?'

Flynn descended the stairs slowly, lest Greythorne rise up once more. When he reached the body, he pressed his fingers to Greythorne's neck.

'He's dead.'

Chapter Twenty-One

❦

Flynn dispatched Cummings to summon the watch, and by the time Cummings returned to this Fleet Street residence where Greythorne was known as Mr Black, the Bow Street Runners had also arrived. Any servants who might have been in the house had run off, and Flynn suspected none would dare return. He also doubted the other ruffians who had assisted Greythorne would ever be found.

The Bow Street Runners and the watchman took charge of the situation, saying there was no need for anyone else to remain. Flynn was glad to get Rose away from there, but before leaving, he penned a letter for one of the Runners to carry to the magistrate asking him to call upon the marquess the next day.

Flynn decided they all must go to Audley Street, where Tanner could be tended to in his own bed. He sent Katy, Cummings and Tanner in one hackney carriage. He and Rose rode in another.

Alone with Rose at last, Flynn put his arm around her and held her close. 'How are you faring, Rose?'

She snuggled against him. 'I am faring very well now, Flynn.'

They did not speak. After the horror and danger she'd been through, he wanted only to give her peace. In their silence the closeness between them returned, as if their thoughts were one and there was no need to speak aloud. Flynn was content to have her in his arms. He had come so close to losing her, he doubted he would ever take a moment like this for granted.

He'd thought her asleep, but she murmured, 'I have something to tell you, Flynn.'

Flynn kissed the top of her head. 'I have many things to tell you, Rose.'

'Will you give me time to talk with you after we arrive at Lord Tannerton's?'

He gave a soft laugh. 'Indeed, I will.' Brushing her hair from her forehead, he asked, 'You do not mind I'm taking you there?'

She sighed. 'I'll mind nothing if it means being with you.'

They reached the town house right behind the other hack, and Flynn left her side to help with Tanner, who was only half in his wits. He could not walk without assistance, so Cummings and Flynn assisted him to the door and other servants took over once inside. The physician had not left from tending to Smythe's leg and Wiggin's hand, so he was present to take charge of Tanner's care. Flynn told the housekeeper and butler to give their guests, Rose, Katy and Cummings, some food and whatever else they needed.

'Wait for me in the dining parlour,' he whispered to Rose.

When Flynn finally reached the parlour, Rose was there alone.

She poured him some wine and fixed a plate of food for him. 'Cummings went off to share sleeping quarters with one of your footmen, and your housekeeper set up one of the bedchambers for me and Katy. Katy should be sleeping now.'

When she set the plate down in front of him, he grasped

her hand and pressed her palm against his lips. He sat her on his lap while he ate.

'Will Lord Tannerton recover?' she asked him.

Flynn nodded, swallowing some wine. 'The physician believes so, after a rest.'

'You ought to rest, too, Flynn,' she said.

He smiled at her. 'I intend to go to bed directly.'

Rose leaned down and kissed his lips. 'As do I.'

She knew without asking him that she would be sharing a bed with him, not with Katy. With fingers entwined, he led her to his bedchamber, a room so neat and plain, she wanted to weep for its starkness.

Once the door was closed, Rose helped him off with his coat and boots. She unbuttoned his waistcoat.

He touched her neck and pain filled his eyes. 'You are bruised.'

She did not wish to bring the memory of Greythorne into this room. 'Do not talk of that. It is over.'

He stroked the skin of her neck and she fancied his touch erased the marks of Greythorne's cruelty.

He shrugged out of his waistcoat and reached around her to untie the laces of the dress that had been found for her. It was an easy matter for him to pull the dress over her head and to undo her corset. That done, she unbuttoned his trousers.

Their undressing felt like a dance to her, she taking one step, he taking another until all the barriers fell away. He lifted her on to the bed, not as grand as the one they had shared before, but tinged with his scent.

Their dance continued, though his hand faltered with each mark he found on her. He kissed the bruises on her neck, the scrapes and cuts on her wrists, the mark of Greythorne's hand on her cheek. Nothing could have felt more healing.

She traced the contours of his muscles, the roughness of his stubble. She let her fingers play in his dark, silken locks. Reverently they traded touch for touch, until soon he was above her and it was time to dance in unison.

When he entered her, she almost wept with joy. Only the day before she'd believed she would never feel the glory of him moving inside her again. Her back arched and she pressed her fingers into his skin as he set the pace.

As if following his lead in a waltz, she joined her movements to his. They had become one person, moving together, thinking as one person, feeling as one. She gazed into his eyes, and even their souls became one.

Together the excitement grew, the pleasure intensified, and their fevered panting melded like the voices of the King's Theatre chorus. She would savour this unexpected moment for the rest of her days.

Suddenly they reached the peak together, their pleasure intensified by its being shared by the other. Together they cried out as the waves of ecstasy washed over them.

Together they collapsed when the ecstasy waned, but as Flynn slid off her their connection held fast.

He kissed her. 'Now, what was it you were wanting to tell me, Rose?' Still holding her against him, he stroked her arm with his thumb.

She took a deep breath and released it slowly. 'I made a decision tonight to refuse Tannerton. To not go to bed with him, Flynn. I started to tell him when…when everything happened.' She pushed away that memory. 'I can never repay the money he spent on me—or repay you for doing so much for me in his name—but I cannot be his mistress.'

She expected him to be surprised by this pronouncement, but even the rhythm of his thumb against her skin was unchanged.

'Why, Rose?' he asked as if the question were expected of him.

She knew she must tell him what she had not said to him before. 'I love you, Flynn. I do not wish to bed another man.'

'You do not wish to be a courtesan?' His tone was almost teasing.

'I was not truthful when I said that.' She quickly added, 'I'm not expecting this to change anything for you, Flynn. You must take your employment with the Duke of Clarence. It is what you dreamed of.'

He leaned on one elbow to look at her. 'You knew of that?'

She nodded. 'Lord Tannerton told me a long time ago.'

The hard planes of his face seemed to soften. 'Working for a prince is no longer my dream, Rose. My dream is you.'

She was afraid to believe him. 'You don't need to be worrying about me.' She took another breath. 'I was thinking I could sell my pianoforte. It would give me a little money, enough to go home. To Ireland. I'm thinking my old school might still want me to teach music.' Or scrub the floors or work in the scullery, it did not matter.

He leaned down and kissed her so tenderly she ached with longing again. 'Come to Ireland with me.'

She wrinkled her brow.

He smiled. 'I want to marry you, Rose.'

She opened her mouth to speak, but he put his fingertips on her lips.

'Do not pretend you do not wish to marry me, Rose. I was at Vauxhall. I heard the truth in your song.'

Her heart beat faster. He'd learned the truth in the songs, just as she had.

His eyes filled with pain. 'I almost lost you, Rose. I'll not chance losing you again.'

She flung her arms around him. 'You'll not be losing me, Jameson Flynn.'

Tanner's head still hurt like the devil, but he'd risen early, dressed—or rather his valet dressed him—and had been reasonably coherent when the magistrate had come with his interminable questions.

To Tanner's surprise, everyone who had been involved in the previous night's fracas were gathered in his drawing room for the magistrate's visit. Rose, Katy, the Bow Street Runners—even Cummings was there. Flynn explained that Rose, Katy and Cummings had stayed the night, which certainly must have given the servants plenty to gossip about. Tanner wondered how long it would be until the whole of Audley Street knew he'd housed not one, but two ladies of questionable virtue.

When the magistrate came, Flynn and the others had done most of the talking. Fortunate, because Tanner could barely string two words together, let alone remember the events as anything more than a jumble.

Now they had all left and the drawing room was blessedly quiet. Tanner lifted a cup of tea to his lips, tea being the only beverage he could tolerate with his headache, which was a pity.

He put the cup down and rested his eyes, flashes of memory still coming to him. He'd thwarted Greythorne in the end, all right, but at what cost?

He forced his eyes open. It was not in his nature to dwell on such unpleasantness, especially his role in it. Besides, his head pained him more when he tried to think.

There was a knock on the door, and Flynn poked his head in. 'May I speak with you?'

Deuce. More talking. 'Of course.'

Flynn entered, followed by Rose, who held on to his arm. Tanner tried to rise.

'Do not stand, Lord Tannerton,' she said solicitously.

He gratefully sank back into his chair. 'Then please sit, both of you. Have some tea.'

They declined the tea and sat down next to each other on the settee.

'There's something I must be telling you, my lord,' she began, her expression serious.

Lord, he was not in the mood to hear more unpleasantness. Then a memory returned. She'd started to tell him something in the carriage. 'Oh, yes.' He took another sip.

Flynn turned to her, placing his hand on hers. 'You should allow me to say it.'

She looked back at Flynn, setting her chin firmly. 'No. I must do it, Flynn.'

Tanner would be delighted if one of them said it so they could go on their way.

Rose turned her gaze to him. 'It is only that I…I wish to back out of our arrangement.'

'What arrangement?' he asked, then it dawned on him. 'Oh, our *arrangement*. I'd quite forgotten about that.'

She continued, 'I know you spent a lot of money on me—'

He was having difficulty following the thread of her words. What had money to do with it? He'd been engaged in a contest, had he not? He always spent money to win a contest. 'What the devil are you talking about?'

Flynn broke in. 'It is my doing, Tanner. Mine alone. I have a confession of my own—'

Tanner groaned. Now he must listen to Flynn bare his soul? Could they not get to the point?

He released an exasperated breath. 'One of you. Explain.' His head hurt too much to make sense of their nonsense. He lifted his teacup to his lips.

Flynn leaned forward. 'Rose does not wish to become your mistress, Tanner, because she is to become my wife.'

Tanner almost dropped his cup. 'What?'

'It is something that happened between us from the first. And then we were in each other's company so often, it just grew stronger,' Rose explained. 'But I was most at fault. I wanted Flynn, you see. He resisted. He was always loyal to you.' She glanced away as if considering. 'Well, loyal except the one time, but I had insisted on being with him. Twice if you count last night.'

Tanner just stared at her.

Flynn spoke up. 'I wanted her just as much as she wanted me. Rose cannot take all the blame on to herself.'

Tanner held up his hand, comprehension reluctantly dawning. 'You mean to tell me you two were in bed together behind my back?'

They glanced at each other, but said nothing.

Tanner stared back at them. 'You carried on this affair the whole time?' He shook his head.

And burst out laughing.

'Lord Tannerton?' Flynn looked at him as if he were crazy.

He tried to sober himself. Laughing created havoc with his headache. 'I'll be damned. I had no idea. No suspicion whatsoever. Right under my nose.' He pressed his hand on his chest.

Rose and Flynn began speaking all at once about falling in love at first sight at Vauxhall. About Flynn asking her to marry him and her refusing at first. About how he would write to the Duke of Clarence, refusing the position. Rose apologized for taking his money for the voice lessons and for the ghastly King's Theatre opera, and Flynn said he would repay Tanner for everything, which was quite illogical. Flynn did not have that kind of money.

Rose looked at him with sympathy. 'It is for the best for you, too, Lord Tannerton. Like the song said, lovemaking should be be "full of love and full of truth." Otherwise it is not love.'

He congratulated himself at asserting some self-control. He refrained from rolling his eyes.

'We have no desire to embarrass you in this, Tanner,' Flynn went on after a tender look at Rose. 'We will go to Ireland—'

'Wait a moment!' Tanner broke in. 'You mean you are not coming back?'

They both looked stunned.

'You would want me back?' Flynn asked.

Tanner pressed his fingers to his temple. 'Well, I do not know. A married secretary would not entirely suit, but surely you will return to London.'

'I had assumed my presence in London would not be desired.' Flynn said.

'What of Miss O'Keefe's singing? There is no theatre to speak of in Ireland, is there?' Tanner had never known Flynn to speak such drivel.

'Surely you will tell everyone not to hire me,' Rose said.

'Why the devil would I do that?'

These two must be in love, Tanner thought. Their brains were more addled than his was.

'I cannot think with this headache.' He pressed his hands to the top of his head. 'Go off and get a special licence or something, but leave me now. We can determine your future at a…a future time.'

Flynn gaped at him. 'You are not angry?'

Flynn's words stopped him. He considered this. No, he was not angry, Tanner realised, although he ought to be.

'I am persuaded you deserve each other.' He made a shooing gesture. 'Go.'

Rose and Flynn stood up, regarding him with so fond a look he felt like a favoured uncle or something as ghastly. Then Rose walked up to him and placed a warm kiss on his cheek.

'Thank you, my lord,' she whispered.

He glanced into her eyes, so filled with happiness and love that a sharp pang of envy shot through him.

His head hurt worse. 'Go,' he said again, more gently. 'We'll sort the rest out later.'

Flynn stepped forward and clasped Tanner's hand. The expression of gratitude on Flynn's face actually stirred Tanner's emotions.

Flynn put an arm around the coveted Rose and the two walked toward the door, Rose turned back, and Tanner smiled at her.

When the door shut behind them, Tanner lowered his head into his hands, his eyes stinging.

It was not that he'd wanted her, because he knew now that it had been winning that had mattered, not winning Rose. It was just that he...envied them.

He glanced at the brandy decanter, but lifted the teacup to his lips instead. He supposed he'd have to tell Pomroy. He imagined relating all this to his friend. The dramatic confession. The tender love scene. He could just see Pomroy's amused face. Tanner would never hear the end of it. A secretary cuckolding a marquess.

Tanner blinked away the stinging in his eyes and began to laugh.

Wait until he told Pomroy.

Epilogue

Flynn stood backstage, his heart still racing, as it had done unceasingly from the moment Rose stepped out on stage. The Dublin theatre was packed, although he suspected half the seats were taken up by Flynns and relatives of Flynns.

Ever since he and Rose had stepped off the ship at Belfast, husband and wife, they had been enveloped by a swarm of Flynns. His brother Aidan and sister Siobhan had met the ship that day, although Flynn had written that they would be travelling straight to Donnanew House, the home where he'd spent his boyhood, the home where his parents, Aidan and oldest brother Colman lived. Siobhan and her husband, with Aidan and his wife, escorted them to Donnanew House, to the welcoming arms of his mother and father, grey haired now and frailer than he'd like to admit.

Still, his mother and father made the trip to Dublin this day, to this new theatre for its opening night.

There were even a few O'Keefes in the audience. After they had arrived in Ireland, Flynn had searched out Rose's family to inform them of her father's death. It turned out Rose was not as bereft of family as she'd thought. Mr O'Keefe's brother was still living. Miraculously, he and a number of cousins had welcomed her like a prodigal child.

It had been a year of miracles—this theatre itself one of them. Flynn still pinched himself to see if he really did own it, was really manager of its first production. Until he'd viewed the theatre, abandoned but needing little repair, he'd not realised this was the challenge for which his soul had yearned. He and Rose had brought it back to glorious life.

For the opening night, they'd staged a Sheridan classic, *The Rivals,* knowing its Mrs Malaprop would guarantee laughter and delight. Rose played Lydia and a more beautiful Lydia there never could be. They had just made it through the play, but still Flynn's heart would not rest. Rose had stepped out on stage to sing a selection of songs.

The musicians began playing and Rose stole one glance to her husband before raising her voice:

> *When, like the dawning day*
> *Eileen Aroon*
> *Love sends his early ray...*

Flynn laughed softly, remembering the night at Vauxhall when he'd first heard her sing this very song. How much had changed since that night.

Rose had transformed his life. She'd given him what he had not even known he'd lost. Happiness.

At the end of 'Eileen Aroon,' there was silence and Flynn's stomach wrenched for Rose. The next moment, however, brought a shout of 'Bravo!' and waves and waves of applause.

Rose went on to sing other Irish songs, and he could feel

the theatre-goers embrace her, more lovingly with each verse. At the final song, she needed to beg her audience to quieten down so they could hear her.

'This is the last,' she told them, and they groaned in disappointment. 'You must sing along with me!'

Flynn's brow furrowed. They had not planned such a thing. Rose gave him another glance, then hurried to where he stood in the wings. She pulled him back with her to the centre of the stage, hanging on to his arm as if fearing he'd run off. She was flushed with excitement.

Extending her free hand to the audience, she began to sing:

> *His hair was black, his eye was blue*
> *His arm was stout, his word was true…*

It seemed as if the whole body of the theatre gave a collective sigh. By the refrain, their voices—including Flynn's own—were thundering:

> *Shule, shule, shule agra…*

When the song came to the end, the audience rose to their feet. Flynn thought they might never cease their clapping, their 'Bravos' and 'Well dones.' Flowers cascaded on to the stage.

The other performers came out for final bows, but Rose did not release Flynn. It seemed an eternity before the audience settled down and rumbled their way to the exit doors.

Rose and Flynn had no more left the stage when Flynn's parents and brothers and sisters met them and showered them with hugs and kisses. Flynn was grateful his family had accepted his new ambition, a somewhat unusual one for a landowner's son. He doubted any English lord would have understood his choosing a poor Irish theatre over service to a Royal Duke. But none of that mattered any more.

Rose was being embraced by her uncle when she said, 'I must hurry to the dressing room.'

Flynn began herding the relatives away. 'Yes, we will see you all for supper at the hotel. It is all arranged.' He found his father for another hug. 'Thank you for it, Dad.'

He rescued Rose and put his arm around her as they walked to her dressing room.

'I'm thinking it was wonderful, Flynn. I sang with my heart.'

He kissed her on the cheek. 'You were wonderful, Rose.'

She laughed. 'Mr Hook would be proud of me.'

Flynn squeezed her tighter. 'He would indeed.'

Her voice softened. 'And my father, too.'

Flynn stopped to caress her cheek and look into her eyes. 'I fancy your mother and your father are looking down at you this very moment and are feeling proud.'

She smiled and gave him a quick peck on his lips. 'What would I be doing without you, Jameson Flynn.'

He did not answer, but he knew her life would have been quite different if the Marquess of Tannerton's secretary had not been an overly ambitious Irishman who'd fallen deeply for her from first sight.

They hurried through the labyrinth of backstage until they reached her dressing room.

A young maid stood as they entered, an infant in her arms. 'The babe just started her wailing,' she said.

Rose reached for their daughter. 'Oh, she's hungry, poor dear.' She held the baby for a moment, trying to quieten her, but the scent of her mother only escalated her cries. Rose handed her to Flynn. 'Hold her for a moment. Dierdre, help me out of these clothes.'

Flynn gazed at the biggest miracle in his life, his daughter, only three months old, still needing her mother's breast. 'Now, hush, little rosebud,' he murmured.

Soon Rose changed into a white gauze dinner dress, and her face was scrubbed clean of stage make-up. She looked more beautiful than ever. Her maid carried the costume out to be brushed and readied for tomorrow's performance, and Rose settled in a chair to nurse the baby, whose suckling sounds were the only noise in the suddenly peaceful room.

Flynn gazed down at them. 'Do you know how much I'm loving you, Rose, and my little rosebud, as well?'

Her beautiful green eyes glittered up at him. 'I know,' she whispered.

A knock sounded at the door and Flynn opened it a crack to see who it was. His assistant manager peeked in.

'A gentleman to see you, Mr Flynn.' He lowered his voice significantly. 'A real gentleman.'

Flynn glanced over to Rose, who grabbed a shawl to cover herself and the baby, and he opened the door.

Lord Tannerton ambled in. 'Thought I'd offer my congratulations,' he said as if he'd just wandered away from his billiard table.

'Tanner!' Flynn exclaimed. 'My lord.' He was too dumbstruck to say more. Never had he anticipated that the Marquess of Tannerton would make the trip to Dublin.

'Lord Tannerton!' Rose cried happily. 'We never expected you! How lovely of you.'

He gave Flynn a wink and crossed the room to Rose. 'Are you hiding something?'

She moved the shawl away so he could see.

He gazed at the baby for a long moment. 'She is just as

Flynn described.' He gave Rose a wistful smile. 'As beautiful as her mother.'

Rose reached for his hand and squeezed it.

Flynn finally roused himself to walk over and shake Tanner's hand. 'I am speechless. Delighted you have come.'

Tanner found a chair and dropped himself into it. 'Well, I had to see to my investment, did I not? There's all manner of things I must attend to myself since I lost my secretary—my efficient secretary, I should say. This new one requires significant effort on my part.'

Flynn searched the room, finding the bottle of Irish whiskey he kept there. He poured Tanner a glass and handed it to him. 'Investment is hardly an accurate word.'

When Flynn had written to Tanner to ask if the marquess would vouch for him for a loan, Tanner instead sent enough money to buy the theatre and to renovate it. He'd written it was a wedding gift, adding that Flynn could repay the amount if he wished, but there was no obligation.

'I consider it an investment,' Tanner said. 'An investment in your future.'

Rose interrupted, perhaps sensing Flynn had again been rendered speechless. 'Lord Tannerton, you must come to supper with us and meet the relatives.'

Rolling his eyes, he responded, 'I have already encountered more Flynns and O'Keefes than I could have imagined in existence.' He grinned. 'They are a jolly lot. I would be happy to join you.'

The marquess left a few minutes later, after finishing his whiskey and again promising to come to the hotel for supper.

When Flynn closed the door behind him, he turned to Rose. 'I am astounded.'

The baby had finished nursing and Rose lay her over her

shoulder, patting her back. 'You always told me he was the best of men.'

'Indeed. The very best of men.'

She stood, still holding their daughter against her shoulder. She walked over to her husband and he very gently put his arms around her, embracing them both. He leaned his forehead against hers and they stood there together like that, swaying slightly.

'I always disagreed with you, you know,' she murmured.

'You did?' He was lulled by the feel of her, the warmth of their infant, the scent of mother's milk.

'You are the very best of men, Jameson Flynn.' Her voice cracked with emotion. '*You*, my husband.'

* * * * *

Turn the page for a sneak preview of
IF I'D NEVER KNOWN YOUR LOVE
by
Georgia Bockoven

From the brand-new series
Harlequin Everlasting Love
Every great love has a story to tell. ™

One year, five months and four days missing

There's no way for you to know this, Evan, but I haven't written to you for a few months. Actually, it's been almost a year. I had a hard time picking up a pen once more after we paid the second ransom and then received a letter saying it wasn't enough. I was so sure you were coming home that I took the kids along to Bogotá so they could fly home with you and me, something I swore I'd never do. I've fallen in love with Colombia and the people who've opened their hearts to me. But fear is a constant companion when I'm there. I won't ever expose our children to that kind of danger again.

I'm at a loss over what to do anymore, Evan. I've begged and pleaded and thrown temper tantrums with every official I can corner both here and at home. They've been incredibly tolerant and understanding, but in the end as ineffectual as the rest of us.

I try to imagine what your life is like now, what you do every day, what you're wearing, what you eat. I want to believe that the people who have you are misguided yet kind, that they treat you well. It's how I survive day to day. To think of you being mistreated hurts too much. If I picture you locked away somewhere and suffering, a weight descends on me that makes it almost impossible to get out of bed in the morning.

Your captors surely know you by now. They have to recognize what a good man you are. I imagine you working with their children, telling them that you have children, too, showing them the pictures you carry in your wallet. Can't the men who have you understand how much your children miss you? How can it not matter to them?

How can they keep you away from us all this time? Over and over, we've done what they asked. Are they oblivious to the depth of their cruelty? What kind of people are they that they don't care?

I used to keep a calendar beside our bed next to the peach rose you picked for me before you left. Every night I marked another day, counting how many you'd been gone. I don't do that any longer. I don't want to be reminded of all the days we'll never get back.

When I can't sleep at night, I tell you about my day. I imagine you hearing me and smiling over the details that make up my life now. I never tell you how defeated I feel at moments or how hard I work to hide it from everyone for fear they will see it as a reason to stop believing you are coming home to us.

And I couldn't tell you about the lump I found in my breast and how difficult it was going through all the tests without you here to lean on. The lump was benign—the process reaching that diagnosis utterly terrifying. I couldn't stop thinking about what would happen to Shelly and Jason if something happened to me.

We need you to come home.

I'm worn down with missing you.

I'm going to read this tomorrow and will probably tear it up or burn it in the fireplace. I don't want you to get the idea I ever doubted what I was doing to free you or thought the work a burden. I would gladly spend the rest of my life at it, even if, in the end, we only had one day together.

You are my life, Evan.

I will love you forever.

* * * * *

Don't miss this deeply moving Harlequin Everlasting Love story about a woman's struggle to bring back her kidnapped husband from Colombia and her turmoil over whether to let go, finally, and welcome another man into her life.

IF I'D NEVER KNOWN YOUR LOVE
by Georgia Bockoven
is available March 27, 2007.

And also look for
THE NIGHT WE MET
by Tara Taylor Quinn,
a story about finding love
when you least expect it.

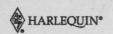

HARLEQUIN® *Romance.*

presents a brand-new trilogy by

PATRICIA THAYER

Rocky Mountain
B R I D E S

Three sisters come home to wed.

In April don't miss
Raising the Rancher's Family,

followed by

The Sheriff's Pregnant Wife,
on sale May 2007,

and

A Mother for the Tycoon's Child,
on sale June 2007.

REQUEST YOUR FREE BOOKS!

Harlequin® Historical
Historical Romantic Adventure!

2 FREE NOVELS PLUS 2 FREE GIFTS!